THE GODDESS QUEEN

Also by Nicole Vidal

EMMANUEL

SCHEHERAZADE

THE GODDESS QUEEN

A Novel Based on

THE LIFE OF NEFERTITI

NICOLE VIDAL

Translated from the French by
JOHANNA HARWOOD

DAVID McKAY COMPANY, INC.

New York

THE GODDESS QUEEN

ORIGINALLY PUBLISHED IN FRENCH UNDER THE TITLE

NEFERTITI

COPYRIGHT © 1961 EDITIONS GALLIMARD

ENGLISH TRANSLATION COPYRIGHT © 1965
ANDRE DEUTSCH, LTD.

FIRST AMERICAN EDITION 1965

LIBRARY OF CONGRESS CATALOG CARD NUMBER: 65-16906

MANUFACTURED IN THE UNITED STATES OF AMERICA

PROBABLE GENEALOGY

End of the XVIIIth Dynasty (1580–1350 B.C.)

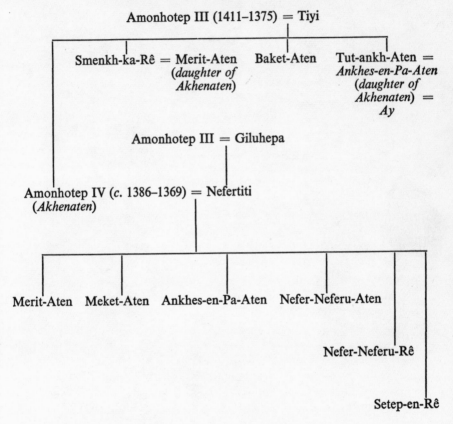

Amonhotep III (1411–1375) = Tiyi

Smenkh-ka-Rê = Merit-Aten (*daughter of Akhenaten*) Baket-Aten Tut-ankh-Aten = Ankhes-en-Pa-Aten (*daughter of Akhenaten*) = Ay

Amonhotep III = Giluhepa

Amonhotep IV (*c.* 1386–1369) = Nefertiti (*Akhenaten*)

Merit-Aten Meket-Aten Ankhes-en-Pa-Aten Nefer-Neferu-Aten

Nefer-Neferu-Rê

Setep-en-Rê

PART ONE

THE GODDESS QUEEN

CHAPTER ONE

THE young girl had fallen asleep with her
back against the big sycamore in the south-east corner which
shaded the terrace outside Houia's apartments. Houia was the
man in charge of the royal harem. Because it was peaceful, and
because the chatter from the women's quarters was drowned by
the soft rustling of the leaves, this was the girl's favourite place
for a siesta. The flies ran over her golden skin with tiny padded
steps as friendly and caressing as the breeze from the north when
the dog days came, while the full force of the summer sun remained outside the mosaic of light and shade which surrounded
the base of the tree.

Suddenly the sound of laughter broke through her dream,
dragging her back to reality. Her heart beating wildly, she sprang
to her feet like a frightened animal whose hiding place has been
discovered, and only then did she recognize the voice of her
nurse, Ti. The girl shrugged and picked up her rush fan which had
fallen to the yellow sand. She was annoyed that she, the daughter
of Pharaoh, had shown fear like a common Nubian negress, and
not unnaturally she directed this anger against her good, her dear
Ti. What was she doing with Houia at a time when she should
have been resting on her mat, or at least fanning her husband
while he slept?

Houia wasn't a eunuch like Mose, for her nurse to permit
herself to joke with him at a time when men were busy in bed!
It was she who had said one day: 'My gazelle, if you want to
discuss anything but love or licentiousness with a man, visit him
before noon at his work-place, or in the evening as he starts to
eat: a man at work thinks of the business on hand, and a man in

front of a roast goose thinks of the good meal to come, but go to his room to talk, and while he's listening he'll suddenly see his bed. So he thinks "bed", and then "woman in bed", and then "woman": his thoughts turn to you, his eyes grow moist, his arms insistent, his ears deaf to what you are saying, and may Isis who gave birth in the marshes come to your aid!'

At the idea of old Houia thinking 'bed' and of Ti agreeing to it, the young girl frowned, and decided that her outraged sense of propriety was as good an excuse as any for indiscretion. She tucked up her long white tunic, revealing the vigorous thighs of a child just reaching adolescence, and climbed easily up the sycamore as far as a branch which brushed against the white roughcast wall on a level with the window. From there she could only see the top of the fresco painted on the inside wall, and the papyrus-shaped cornices of two thin wooden columns covered with green stucco, but she could hear the conversation as clearly as if she were in the room, and was unpleasantly surprised by what she heard. True, Houia and Ti were talking neither of love nor licentiousness; much worse, they were talking about her. She hated being talked about behind her back: it seemed a kind of betrayal, especially by Ti, who knew all her little faults and was well placed to criticize.

'Nefertiti* is of age,' Houia said.

'You needn't tell me that! She's of age all right . . . for a good two months now she's been looking at men below the waist!' answered Ti in a disagreeable voice which must certainly have curdled her milk more than once when she was the 'royal wet-nurse'.

You're an evil-minded old woman and I hate you, thought the young girl, her face reddening with anger.

'She's fourteen years old,' went on Houia with a laugh, 'and at fourteen one has the right to wonder about life and death, the gods, and what men's loincloths hide . . . for in the house of the

* Nefertiti means 'The beautiful one cometh', or 'Here is the beautiful one'.

10

royal children she ran naked with her naked brothers and surely cannot understand the necessity of clothing round the waist.'

'All men are naïve or stupid, and you are the stupidest of the lot. At eight a girl knows everything, at ten she dreams, at twelve she is ripe for marriage.'

You're dirty, dirty, dirty! the young girl wanted to shout, as she clung for dear life to the sycamore branch.

'Good! Then everything's perfect,' said Houia, still laughing, 'since Pharaoh wants a co-regency, the young Gazelle need wait no longer to marry Amonhotep, our new rising sun . . . to whom all health and prosperity. . . .'

'To whom. . . .' murmured Ti devoutly, and then continued more shrilly: 'I'll have given suck to a Queen of Egypt . . . I, the humble Ti, will have given my breast to the Mistress of the Two Kingdoms! Just think, Houia, what joy a mortal feels at the idea that her own flesh has fed a Goddess . . . My White Lamb! My Lotus Flower! My Green Frog! I held her in my arms, I rocked her when she cried, I cured her ophthalmia, poor Graceful Ibis! Ah, Houia! How I watched over her when she was ill! You have no idea how devotedly I tended my child: for she was like a child born of my own body; if she laughed, I laughed with her: when she was sad, my heart was torn in pieces. She knows it too, the dear little thing: it won't be easy to remind her I'm only her nurse. She would deprive herself of everything for my sake. Why, only the other day she gave me a pair of ear-rings which I was foolish enough to admire. "They're yours," she said, "how could I wear something for which your ears yearn?" Ah! She's got a kind heart, my Gazelle. So quiet! So good! The Two Kingdoms will be lucky to have her for a queen, and Amonhotep won't have cause to complain either. Except for the great Queen Hatshepsut, there'll never be another so worthy to wear the crown of Uraeus.'

Ti's voice had taken on a mournful note and Nefertiti could imagine her ostentatiously wiping a tear from the corner of her eye: Ti was inclined to consider herself exceptionally sensitive, and liked everyone else to think the same.

Nefertiti was coldly furious: she shut her mouth tightly and her big eyes flashed.

11

Don't worry, I'll remember you're only my nurse, she thought: you're evil and I hate you. As for the pair of ear-rings I gave you, I'll throw them into the Nile and the crocodile's wife can wear them to please her husband. She could well be mistaken for you . . . she cries just as easily when she wants to trap the cranes.

'Ah well,' continued Ti more calmly, 'it's getting late, and my Spring Moon will be worried if she doesn't find me when she wakes. "Where is my good Ti?" she will ask. "I hope nothing has happened to the dear woman." What shall I say? "I have spoken with Houia longer than was seemly and he told me you are to mount the throne of the co-regency?" '

'The secrets of the great may be discussed but not divulged,' replied Houia, 'for tongues which are too long can be cut out, and ears which hear too much can be cut off. If my ears hear too much, and my tongue is too long, let these little peculiarities remain our secret. You grew up with me, Ti, and when I was a child I fetched you marsh-bird eggs from the heart of the papyrus islands, at the risk of being devoured by crocodiles . . . so now, at the risk of being devoured by impatience, pretend you know nothing, and I will consider it an act of real affection. Let your husband Ay fall asleep each evening in ignorance, until the day when Pharaoh . . . to whom life, health, prosperity. . . .'

'To whom. . . .' echoed Ti piously.

'Until the day when Pharaoh speaks of his decision. Then let your eyes open with happy surprise, and let your hands clap many times together! That too will I consider an act of real affection.'

Judging the conversation at an end. the young girl slid down the sycamore, to lessen the risk of being found the embarrassed possessor of 'ears which hear too much'. And, though she wanted to laugh, she was still annoyed and decided to sulk until the evening meal, unmoved by the Lotus Flowers, White Lambkins and Green Frogs which Ti was certainly going to shout at the top of her voice in all the rooms and gardens of the palace. Nefertiti knew a tiny island in the Nile, a little further downstream, where as a child she had often hidden with Maï, the son of the Lord

High Chancellor. Maï was her best friend. He had grown up 'naked' with all the other court children, and he had always been her special favourite. Perhaps because they were the same age: perhaps also because they had the same tastes. He had been honest and gay, quick of action and of thought, ingenious, proud and loyal: he didn't know the meaning of fear, and though Ipy the scribe said he was lazy, Nefertiti didn't think this fault was likely to hold back a boy of his intelligence. Amonhotep was a hard working student, but in her opinion that one quality was not enough for someone who was going to govern Egypt.

Suddenly the young girl realized the full importance of the conversation she had overheard between her nurse and Houia, the harem overseer. At the time she had been so angry with Ti she had hardly realized they were going to marry her to her half-brother Amonhotep. Now that walking had calmed her down a bit Houia's words came back to her.

'Since Pharaoh wants a co-regency, the young Gazelle can marry Amonhotep.' Amonhotep! They were going to give her to that tall, thin, ugly fellow who always stood with his stomach thrust forward, as if he were exhausted because he hadn't been born with a wall to lean against. He was much older than she was, too – eighteen at least – and he spent all his time hanging round the petticoats of priests, and cavilling over the attributes of the gods. As if theology were something difficult which required complicated brain work! He'd do better to be about his father's business and inspect the Syrian frontier. She couldn't imagine herself married to her 'holier-than-thou' half-brother. If only he were fun to be with! But he passed by, remote and silent, never even condescending to smile. The other evening was the first time Nefertiti could remember him speaking to her, and then he had only been disagreeable. Pointing with annoyance to his sister's youthful chest, he had remarked shortly: 'Cover your breasts now you're growing up.' Maï, when he came up from Tanis with a letter from his father to Pharaoh, had been much more gallant. He hadn't seen his friend for over a year, and when he visited her he had paid her a very pretty compliment. 'You're becoming a woman, Nefertiti,' he had said. 'See, already your breasts are like two water-lily buds bursting through the smooth spring waters.' After all, now she thought about it, Maï was of noble family, and the crown of Egypt was inherited through the female line, so she really didn't see why it should not be up to herself, as Pharaoh's eldest daughter, to name her husband and co-regent. She would go to her father and talk to him about it. She would say: 'I love Maï, I think he'd be a good son to you and even a good co-regent for the Two Kingdoms. He is handsome, noble, and his sidelock of youth doesn't spoil his looks, while your eldest son Amonhotep is ugly, graceless, cares nothing about winning glory for you, and his sidelock seems to have been plaited with three hemp fibres.'

Nefertiti started to laugh.

'Three hemp fibres. . . .' When she saw Amonhotep she would say to him: 'I don't want you, because you are so old you have only three hairs on your head to plait together, and you won't give me a child.' Her brother would certainly be furious at hearing himself spoken to like that. He would hurry off and take orders in the religious college of Thebes or of On*, so as to be able to cut as quickly as possible the appendix which had brought him nothing but shame and rebuff.

At this thought Nefertiti grew calmer.

Now she was nearing the steps which led to the Nile. It was there that, early in the morning, the palace laundrymen went down to the river banks with their wooden beaters and their bundles of dirty linen, followed by the head laundryman, the 'furious Hori'. Hidden in her nest of rushes, Nefertiti had often watched them, and consequently she had learnt the whole of a chief laundryman's vocabulary: 'Son of a miscarriage—Fruit of a drunken night—How right your father was to call you misbegotten—No mother ever brought you normally into the world—Your arm is as strong as a ripe banana and your hand as useless as a mouldy leaf—You'd better get castrated and tend the royal sows: then they needn't fear your excess energy—If I made you eat all the filth you leave on the washing you'd be as fat as the son of Mut.' And many other and even funnier expressions which

* On: Old Heliopolis.

14

Nefertiti allowed herself to use from time to time when she wanted to shock the noble ears of Ti. She didn't much like 'furious Hori', because he had a sharp voice and treated his inferiors badly, but she had never denounced him as her obscene language teacher because he didn't beat the laundrymen, and in any case it would have upset her to think that his tongue might be pulled out as a punishment for using bad language in the hearing of a royal princess. But she had no respect for him, and whenever she saw his mouth pursed up primly as he flattered someone more noble and highly placed than himself, she couldn't help laughing. Her nurse had noticed this and remonstrated with her about it, saying, in that pompous voice she used for announcing rules of good behaviour: 'My child, Hori is a person of quality; he keeps his place and bows his head before his betters; he knows when to speak and what to say. Why make fun of someone with such good qualities?'

And Nefertiti had answered, biting her lips to stop herself laughing: 'You're right, he's like the perfect man in King Asosi's book of good manners: he's "an artist in speech, for speech is more difficult than any other undertaking".'

What hypocrites men are! the young girl thought bitterly. Ti likes Hori because when he speaks to her his words are sugared as figs split open in the sun; she never wonders if his heart is filled with filth! As for herself, she's always hugging me to her myrrh-perfumed bosom and then behind my back she lies to Houia about me . . . perhaps all men are the same; everyone has a stick to beat with and a golden tongue in order not to be beaten. But I won't be like that. I'll tell Amonhotep he's ugly, and I'll tell his mother Tiyi she can find him a she-monkey for a wife.

At these thoughts Nefertiti grew angry again. The great sky cow could fall on her head before she'd hesitate to speak her mind! Even if it meant giving up Maï in order to mount her father's throne, she would give him up, she would mount the throne, and her reign would be a reign of truth as naked as an innocent babe, not yet clothed in the hypocritical loincloth of men.

So! For two months now she had been looking below men's waists? What an evil mind Ti must have. She no longer hated Ti, she despised her. And Hori, the others, all her father's posturing women, even her own mother Giluhepa, the beautiful Mitanni princess in whose honour her father had ordered a hundred big scarabs carved to commemorate their marriage. But what good were scarabs, now Giluhepa was nothing more than a harem woman? Amonhotep's mother, Tiyi, was the Great Royal Wife, and in her presence Giluhepa was as respectful as all the others . . . yet Nefertiti had heard her mother say, 'Tiyi is a common woman; there is more nobility in my little finger than in all her deformed body!'

'Who knows, perhaps Maï is a hypocrite too?' murmured the young girl, with a savage desire to reach the lowest depths of bitterness.

All right then! She would never get married: she would be like the great Queen Hatshepsut after her husband Thutmose died, and reign on her own, alone against them all. Her reward would come later, when the children of the Two Kingdoms would be told: 'Nefertiti the First loved a truthful heart and despised falsehoods. She rewarded those who said her neck was too long, if they really thought so, and she had ignoble, obsequious flatterers smeared with pig dung, so the world could see what their inner souls were like. In her day head launderers were only promoted when their consciences were whiter than their bleached linen, women only became royal wet-nurses when they had proved that their minds were as pure as their milk, and the people were happy, for they lived naked in innocence and purity.'

By this time Nefertiti had boarded her little boat, made of lashed papyrus reeds. It was a flimsy craft and could only just support her weight and Maï's, but she knew how to steer like a real sailor through the clumps of rushes and lotus which obstructed the smooth waters of the river. She feared neither crocodiles nor hippopotami; the hippopotami had moved from the vicinity of Thebes long ago, and the crocodiles preferred the northern marshes where priests and nobles pastured their flocks during the hot season.

Soon she neared her island . . . a small tongue of mud, grown over with papyrus, where the ruins of a hut built by unskilled hands still stood, hidden among the reeds: the palace of Nefertiti and of Maï, king and queen of the country of the sacred ibis and the butterflies.

Nefertiti hadn't been back since her friend had left for his father's *nome*.* Sadly she eyed the magnificent kingdom of her childhood, a childhood which had died on a sycamore branch that afternoon, because an evil-minded nurse had said a princess looked below men's waists.

She would be forced to marry Amonhotep and live for ever afterwards in a palace of stone and stucco among courtiers whose only interest was the acquisition of titles and women whose principal preoccupations were the painting of their faces and the anointing of their bodies with sweet-smelling oils. She would sit on the throne like a living mummy, and the only birds she would see would be plucked, roasted and served up on meat dishes.

There was a bitter taste of tears in Nefertiti's mouth. She was alone; terribly alone; no one was with her to weep for the dead queen of the sacred ibis country; no one could give her a magic spell to protect her from sadness and despair in the hard world of men: her mother cared only for the green malachite she painted on her eyes, and the red dyed ostrich feathers which adorned her fans. Her nurse was delighted with herself and with the noble lineage of her foster-daughter. Her father was concerned only with the choice between an African greyhound from the land of Punt which he wanted to train for gazelle hunting, or a cheetah from the Miserable land of Kush† which he could feed from his throne. Maï was far away (and perhaps even now he was making fun of all he had loved in order to amuse the daughters of his father's wives!). Tiyi adored her eldest son to the extent of thinking him handsome and worthy of any amount of amorous success, and as for Amonhotep himself, he only felt kindly towards the temples of the gods.

He would get married without even looking at his wife and

* *Nome:* Territorial division in ancient Egypt.
† 'Miserable land of Kush': Expression of scorn at the time of the Pharaohs, referring to Nubia.

never speak to her except to tell her to hide her growing breasts. She was terribly alone.

Thinking this, she started to weep beside the young gingerbread tree she had once planted with her own hands, knowing with quiet certainty that one day she would see it sheltering her wonderful palace of mud and reeds.

None of her subjects drew near to try and comfort her distress. Hidden in the thick bushes they wondered what this intruder from across the frontier was doing on their island . . . this queen from the Black-Land-of-Kemet which some call Egypt.

CHAPTER TWO

TI was annoyed to hear the sudden burst
of laughter from the harem buildings. It was getting late, and she
was beginning to be seriously worried by Nefertiti's absence. To
think that soon the dear child would be sitting on the throne of
the co-regency! At this thought Ti's eyes grew moist with affection, for then she herself would bear the title of Great Royal
Nurse; she would have a signet ring made, she would be known
officially as 'Friend of the King and Queen', and all the noble
princes would envy her intimacy with the royal couple.

A self-satisfied smile hovered round Ti's lips, and for a good
ten minutes she dreamt of wealth and glory, before she remembered her present anxiety. Where could Nefertiti have got to? On
entering the young girl's bedroom, Ti had only found Mischere,
the little Syrian slave, asleep against the wall. Ti had shaken her
awake roughly; she considered it inadmissible that a servant
should rest while she herself was obliged to be busy. Mischere,
panic-stricken at being caught asleep, had muttered something
about searching for her mistress, and had disappeared.

But Ti hadn't really begun to worry until dusk. She had already
noticed that her foster-daughter seemed to avoid company (even
such pleasant company as Ti's), and though this hurt her feelings
she put Nefertiti's sudden unsociability down to her 'awkward'
age; it was a well known fact that a child of fourteen will over-
estimate its own intelligence and under-estimate other people's to
such an extent that it enjoys no company but its own. Once this
difficult time had passed, Ti was sure her Gazelle would return
to the ample bosom which had consoled so many childish ills.
Once again a tender, cajoling, grateful Nefertiti would ask Ti's

advice in respectful tones; then, jokingly, would remind Ti of her little adolescent pranks. At this point Ti would confess that she knew of the hiding place in the rushes near the wash house, and that she had seen her one day climbing down from the sycamore beside the artificial lake. Then Ti would say to her: 'I never told you I knew about these hiding places for fear you would feel compelled to find other and more dangerous ones, which I mightn't have discovered for ages.'

However, at sunset, urged on by her anxiety, Ti had gone down to the hiding place in the reeds, and had even called under the sycamore beside the artificial lake. . . . But her Lambkin wasn't hiding in the rushes, hadn't answered from among the leaves. She wasn't with her mother, or with Pharaoh, or with Tiyi; the gardeners hadn't noticed her in the gardens and Nefer-Kheperou hadn't seen her in the house of the royal children. She must have another hiding place, Ti told herself, in an effort to calm her fears, but this time I shall scold her. It's nearly time to eat and she hasn't come yet for her bath. If a queen of Egypt doesn't mind being smelly and dirty the peasant will never learn to use perfume and the slave will be contented in his sweat.

Another burst of laughter from the harem buildings infuriated Ti.

'The beauties are very gay this evening,' she grumbled, 'but one can't expect born idiots to react like sensible human beings; one can't expect foreign concubines to know how to behave. There's still so much sand on them from their native deserts they'd be capable of singing and dancing on the ill-omened fourteenth day of the month of Tybi! As if no one had ever told them that the great sky cow could fall on their heads!'

Nefertiti's nurse disliked foreigners; they were all negroes and bedouins, she thought, not really human at all. This deep dislike was caused by the memory of the Hyksos, the shepherd kings who had oppressed Egypt for almost a hundred years. True, the gods had spared Ti from being born during those dark days of tyranny and mourning but, ever since one of their distant ancestors hadn't been so lucky, the women of Ti's family had suckled their babies on this hate, and in her heart of hearts, Ti hoped she had passed it on to her foster-child, because Nefertiti herself was, alas! the fruit of a Hurrian womb and it would never do if the Queen of Egypt's origins led her to be indulgent towards such 'mongrel swine'.

While Ti was still grumbling about the cursed Asian girls who cared nothing for the troubled world outside their own apartments, Nefertiti arrived, with poor Mischere trotting after her like a frightened mouse.

The princess's face was pale and her mouth tightly closed. Seeing her foster-child's expression, and the attitude of her slave, the Lady Ti jumped at once to the conclusion that Mischere had committed some punishable fault, and for a moment she forgot her annoyance with the queen, her Gazelle, her Marsh Bird, believing it her duty to miss no opportunity of criticizing the defects of Syrian servants, of whom Mischere was a sad example. Turning towards her she said harshly:

'I see you've displeased your good mistress again! All you Hittites are ungrateful wretches! Go quickly and fetch food for your mistress and her nurse, and, if you fear my anger, take care not to spill any, for I have neither the patience nor the sweetness of the divine Nefertiti. If a hand doesn't serve me, I cut it off! If a tongue chatters, I tear it out! Hurry, and pray Isis I don't cast a spell on you!'

Mischere scuttled off without trying to find a reason for the noble Ti's anger, for she feared Ti more than she feared Pharaoh himself. As soon as she saw her, Mischere's little heart would start beating as wildly as if she had been caught doing something wrong, and from the moment she was given to the young princess as a New Year's gift, she had never been sure of making a complete mummy one day (if she ever obtained enough royal favour to hope for a dignified burial). If she went to sleep once more beside her mistress' empty bed, Ti would certainly have the eyes which hadn't known how to watch, put out.

Inwardly furious, Nefertiti watched the scene without a word. What right had Ti to give orders to *her* servants? If Ti thought the title of Great Royal Nurse allowed her to behave like this, she was mistaken! Even though her husband was the powerful Ay, the 'Divine Father', that didn't make Ti any less foolish, vain or hypocritical, and Nefertiti despised her.

'What are you doing here at this late hour? Isn't it the time for wives to carry out their duties to their husbands? Or is he tired of you too?' asked the young girl scornfully.

Poor Ti blinked at her. Certainly she knew her foster-daughter was at an awkward age, but her Lotus Flower had never shown quite such hostility towards her before. Worn out by the day's successive emotions and unable to control her feelings, Ti took refuge in weeping. A tear rolled from her eye, gathered some *mesdemet** from her lower eyelid, and traced a thin black line down her flabby cheek, to symbolize her soul in mourning.

'You weren't hiding in the reeds and you didn't come when I called near the sycamore beside the artificial lake. . . .' she said, in a shaking voice, and then fell silent, sure that if she didn't stop talking quickly she would sob aloud.

Nefertiti shrugged her shoulders with annoyance. She hated Ti crying; even if they were crocodile tears, Nefertiti still felt badly about them. She knew only too well that Ti's silent distress would be followed by lamenting declarations of affection which she could never resist for long; she herself was afflicted with a hatefully soft heart, and she knew that in the end she would throw herself repentantly onto the soft, dried-up bosom which had once suckled her. But this time she was determined to fight against such deplorable tendencies. Ti was becoming a nuisance; despite what she had told Houia she too often treated Nefertiti like a little girl, and now that she had chased her from the kingdom of her childhood, now that with one phrase she had made her understand she was old enough to be married, Ti was going to be punished. Then perhaps she would regret the days when she ordered Mischere around and took all the decisions in the house of her foster-daughter.

'I wasn't hiding in the reeds and I wasn't sitting on a branch of *that* sycamore either,' replied Nefertiti crossly, 'though perhaps

* *Mesdemet:* a kind of khol; black-coloured cosmetic.

22

I wish I had been! But what does it matter to you where I am? Don't you think the time has come for you to stop watching where I go and what I do, and for me to stop having to tell you everything? I'm fourteen years old, Ti, fourteen, old enough to go where I like and do what I want.'

A really awkward age, reflected poor Ti again, clinging to this thought desperately.

'You have served me well, loved me well, and I'd be worse than the rabbit which eats its children if I wasn't grateful to you. But you must understand that I can't grow old sitting on your knees nor wait for my hair to turn white beneath your wig. Since Mischere is mine, let her cease to take orders from others. Since this room is my room, let me not be obliged to get scratched by reeds and cut by sycamore branches if I want to be alone for a while. From now on this room will be my only hiding place. You will no longer need to cover me with shame in the eyes of my father's women and his slaves by calling my name to the four winds until I answer you. You won't need to ask the gardeners whether they've seen me, or to inquire of the serfs if I ordered them not to tell you which direction I took. Because I'm not going to hide any longer; I'll be here or elsewhere, and if you want to talk with me you can knock on the door of my room, or wait till you see me somewhere. One day you said a wise thing to me: "The true friend is not a dog, following his master's footsteps and worrying him by licking him, but is present when one needs affection and leaves again before becoming a nuisance." You also said to me, "A man of breeding who is invited to share the morning meal takes care not to put his host to bed that night." So don't follow in my footsteps and don't put me to bed! Let me not hesitate to tell you of my joys and sorrows for fear you will think yourself indispensable night and day. If your affection isn't forced upon me I'll come looking for it: if you are not always present I'll regret your absence and my pleasure at seeing you again will be sincere. "If one hugs too tightly, affection dies, but who can resist throwing themselves into open arms"; thus you taught me and you spoke wisely. So now I say to you: don't worry about me any more, but have the rest you deserve. You have done your duty and watched over my helplessness, but I am no longer a child, and will never be one again. Now you know this, you will have time to dream in the gardens and sleep under the sycamores, to talk with Houia or to laugh with your husband. I'm sure he has often regretted the rising of your milk. He took a wife to grace his house, and she went to live elsewhere. But now your work as nurse is finished. I can lift food to my mouth myself. So don't deny your husband your presence at his meals; don't wait till I am sleeping before you join him in his bed; waste no more time watching over every step I make, for my bare foot is as sure as an ibex hoof; it knows the difference between soft sand and a nest of scorpions, and your husband, for whom you were born, is still wondering when you will have time to mend his sandals. Don't cry, Ti, I speak thus because the time has come for it. Perhaps I regret my lost childhood more than you do, but it has happened and we must get used to it; it is only natural that one day the child is weaned and the nurse's breast grows dry. There . . . I have said all that is needful, and if you wish to share the meal for *two* people which Mischere has brought, I *invite* you willingly. I will send Mischere to find a scented cone to place upon your head-dress, so as to honour you as a princess honours a dear friend; and because I won't often have the pleasure of sharing my meals with you, I will offer you fine wine from Syria and beer from the land of Kede . . . not that which is brewed by our foreign slaves in the Kedian way, but beer imported by my father, in the holds of his merchant ships. Instead of ordinary bread, would you like bread made from the flour of Zeret corn? Shall we have roast goose instead of this scraggy quail? Don't be frightened to ask, for in my apartments your wish is my command.'

Nefertiti's young voice, which had been hard when she started talking, had gradually softened, and ended on a note both light and affectionate. She hadn't meant to say so much, nor to use such fine phrases, but the various expressions which she had seen passing over the flabby features of her dear, good Ti during the course of this surprising monologue, had made Nefertiti wickedly determined to state her point of view. The pleasure of getting it off her chest had stimulated her brain, the knowledge that she was speaking intelligently had cooled her anger. She no longer felt either scorn or dislike for Ti, only the pity of an adult before the naïve helplessness of a child. She had passed her first test as a woman brilliantly, and the death of the queen of the sacred ibis country no longer seemed so tragic.

As for poor Ti, she was eyeing her Lambkin with alarm. Any inclination to weep had vanished; her mind searched for some explanation of the magic which had changed her foster-child, who that very morning had been all grace and careless unconcern, into this mature and eloquent young woman. All at once her frightened Gazelle had become poised and assured, her head held proudly upon the long neck which up to then Ti had considered an unfortunate blemish and which now turned out to be both graceful and impressive. Suddenly Nefertiti looked like a queen of Egypt, and this idea struck Ti so forcibly it took her breath away. Into her superstitious mind came the thought that the royal line was certainly divine, because on the very day that plans for Nefertiti's accession to the throne were in the air, the little princess had shaken off her childhood and clothed herself in sovereign majesty. That was how it had been for the great Queen Hatshepsut and for Nefertiti's own father, the powerful Pharaoh Amonhotep III, to whom life, health, prosperity! Thoth, the ibis-headed god of wisdom, had murmured her mother's name, Amon-Rê had put on a likeness of the king to quicken the seed, Khnum of the ram's head had used his potter's wheel to form the body of the child and also its Protective Spirit, the Ka. Frog-headed Hekt had blown life into this sacred clay and the goddess Hathor had lent her cow to give it milk. . . .

At this last thought Ti felt her breasts swell with pride. Perhaps she herself had received grace from Hathor when she was chosen to be the wet-nurse; perhaps she herself contained part of the sacred cow! Who knows, later on, the bas-reliefs which would cover the walls of the queen's tomb might show an effigy of Ti herself, giving her udder to the princess, in agreeable bovine form.

At the prospect of this future joy Ti forgave the impossible behaviour of her child. But, not feeling able to pull herself together right away, she preferred to refuse the invitation to the sumptuous meal.

'To you life, health, prosperity,' she stammered respectfully. 'Allow me to retire; I have a thousand things to do in your service and that of Pharaoh your father, to whom health, prosperity, life.'

With these words she hurried off to repeat to Houia all that she had, with her own eyes, seen, and with her own ears, heard. He was the only person to whom she could speak and she had an urgent need to unburden her mind before nightfall, in case the excitement prevented her from sleeping.

As soon as Nefertiti was sure her nurse was out of ear-shot she started to laugh, much to the astonishment of Mischere, who still clutched an alabaster tray on which two roast quails and two slices of beef were growing cold. The young slave had understood nothing of the scene save her mistress' victory and the defeat of the person who frightened her; her timid soul was lost in admiration for this princess, hardly older than herself, who had held her own against the tyranny of the powerful Ti.

As for Nefertiti, she couldn't stop laughing. 'To you life, health, prosperity' her good nurse had said . . . as if her foster-child were already sitting on the throne of the co-regency, with all the insignia of supreme authority. So that was that! One spoke a bit loudly, a bit rudely, and Ti's vanity shrunk like a swollen stomach doctored with *degem** fruit mixed with beer.

Mischere eyed her mistress' hilarity respectfully, and couldn't help wondering if, on this special occasion, she shouldn't show a little initiative by running to the kitchens to fetch some more hot food before anyone told her to. But in the end she didn't have to make this difficult decision; Nefertiti finally noticed her and said, in a voice still shaking with laughter: 'Come here, Mischere; my heart is warm enough for my stomach to eat cold meat, and I feel so happy I'll let you put your hand to the plate at the same

* *Degem:* Probably castor oil plant.

26

time as I do. So take Ti's place and make sure she hears about it: thus she will know that in the palace of my father I have the power to give or take away as I please.'

Mischere blushed, and protested in a frightened voice: 'I'm not fit to eat with you, my mistress, and if the Lady Ti should hear about it she would have me beaten for my insolence.'

Nefertiti no longer felt like laughing. She said, almost crossly: 'Ti has no authority over my servants; for each blow you got on her account, she would receive ten.'

Mischere wondered anxiously whether she would be able to appreciate the sight of the Lady Ti covered with bruises, if her own bones had already been broken, but she was afraid of annoying her mistress by not seeming grateful for her kindness, so she forced herself to smile as happily as possible.

However, the princess seemed to have changed her mind: she lay down on her bed and her face was thoughtful: 'Leave the tray and go,' she said calmly, 'I don't need you any more this evening.'

Mischere didn't wait to be told twice. She put the tray on the carpet and left with little mouse-like steps. She was glad she didn't have to put her hand to the food at the same time as her mistress, because her hand was graceless and uneducated: it was a stumpy hand, and her skin was thick and yellow, full of hard places and only meant to be stretched upon the ground before the Great One's feet, or to carry out the thankless jobs of the most humble slaves. But she would remember until her dying day that a royal princess had invited her to share her meal. She would remember it with gratitude and use the memory to keep her pride alive. One day she might even throw it in the face of someone who wanted to insult her.

Nefertiti wasn't to know that in her over-anxiety to minister to Ti's distended vanity she had gained the devotion and affection of a little Syrian slave, whose timid heart was too small to love more than one master at a time.

CHAPTER THREE

NEFERTITI decided to clarify her position once and for all, and she knew that if she wanted to talk about it, or any other affair of State, she should see, not her father, but the noble Tiyi. Tiyi was the Great Royal Wife and a woman of character. It was she who took all the decisions and nothing was done without consulting her. Nefertiti didn't like her much, but she respected her, and had felt like laughing when her mother Giluhepa had said to her one day: 'Tiyi is only a common woman, jealous of the nobility and proud when they bow their heads before her. It's a scandal that my husband didn't banish her to the harem and put me by his side, the day he took me from my father, King Sutarna, son of Artatama. It's a scandal my father didn't insist that I, a royal princess, should have the throne of Egypt. But it's the greatest scandal of all to see how blind Pharaoh is to the intrigues of that woman, who makes as much noise as a swarm of wasps and is no more use than one of them. If only she could die! Then I would reign, and we'd soon see which of us wore the Uraeus crown with the most dignity.'

Nefertiti knew her mother well enough to be sure she would make a wretched Great Royal Wife. She was a flighty woman, who would do nothing but give feasts and demand from the vassal countries tributes of gold, precious stones, feathers, incense and ebony, to satisfy her love of luxury and elegance. She would believe everything the courtiers told her, and would favour flatterers: the one who complimented her most gracefully would become Vizier, the best-looking young man would command the army, the most elegantly dressed be put in charge of the royal granaries.

28

There was nothing like that about Tiyi. She was far-seeing, energetic, a good judge of character and never gave a man a job he wasn't capable of doing properly. She had a cold manner which froze the unworthy compliment on the flatterer's lips, and the languid young men got nowhere with her. She always dressed simply, scorning to wear the sumptuous jewels which were hers by right; she seemed to consider too much elegance a sign of weakness and stupidity. It was from his mother that young Amon-hotep had inherited the austere manner which made his half-sister so dislike him.

Nefertiti crossed the women's garden and opened the door in the eastern corner which led to the courtyard of the king's palace. The door was never guarded because all the serfs who worked near by were castrated, like Meri-rê, the harem steward. It was early and the young girl was sure of finding the queen taking her bath or being rubbed with perfumed oil; that was Tiyi's only luxury and Giluhepa always commented: 'It's a sure sign she was born on a muck-heap! She perfumes herself all the time so the dung-flies don't pester her right into the throne room!'

Under the veranda, bathed in the early eastern sun, two laughing, chatting servants fell silent as they saw the princess.

'Is your mistress here?' Nefertiti asked shortly. She didn't like any of Tiyi's slaves, suspecting them of being paid to spy, and relate to Tiyi what they had seen and heard.

'She's in her apartments with the noble ladies Nacha and Kheti, who have the honour of handing her her mirror and her wig,' replied the younger of the two girls.

Nefertiti went down the corridor and knocked on the door.

'Enter—Her Majesty says you may enter,' said a sharp voice which the young girl recognized as Nacha's.

Nefertiti pushed open the door and went in, bowing slightly, her arms stretched out in front of her in a sign of respect. When she reached the queen she remained motionless and waited for her to speak.

The Great Royal Wife was sitting on a mohair carpet, supported by sleek cushions of material from the Miserable land of Kush.

29

Beside her the Lady Kheti, over-dressed as usual, held out the big mirror of polished metal with an ivory handle in which Tiyi examined her reflection without appearing to notice the presence of the young princess. She adjusted her large wig, an old-fashioned one, with long heavy plaits covering her shoulders. Giluhepa had started a rumour that Tiyi was bald as an ostrich's egg, and that no ointments could cure her, even those made of donkey's hoofs cooked in oil, together with date stones and dog's paws, because Tiyi wasn't naturally bald but was the victim of a magic spell. Hadn't Giluhepa found, among the possessions of one of the other harem women, a cone of perfume in which the sweet-smelling oils had been replaced by a paste of an'art worms? And for whom had this mixture been intended if not for the much-feared Tiyi? As everyone knew, an'art worms were the most dangerous things of all for a healthy head of hair.

Only the Ladies Kheti and Nacha could have said what lay beneath the wig of the Great Royal Wife, because only they were admitted to her rising in the morning and her retiring at night . . . but they were silent, and didn't that in itself prove they were ashamed for their queen?

At last Tiyi looked inquiringly towards her step-daughter. She was very fond of her, in her severe, cold way, and she was glad her eldest son was going to marry someone worthy of him; for, though she had never seemed to take much interest in Nefertiti, she had in fact watched closely to see what kind of woman she would grow up to be, and Nefertiti's character pleased her: proud, independent, insolent too, but that was good in a future queen. She was also intelligent, observant, generous, and though at present she was still over-sensitive and changed her mind too often, those faults were due to her youth. Such was Nefertiti, the wife Tiyi had chosen for her eldest son.

'How kind of you to come and wish me good health so early,' she said with a touch of irony, 'for I suppose that was your intention, child?'

Nefertiti lowered her arms and stood up straight before her step-mother, annoyed at having been left in a humiliating position for so long.

30

has neither helped nor hindered me. She is a stranger, and if you hope I will speak badly of her to you, as she hopes I will speak badly of you to her, you misjudge me. I don't follow affairs of State closely enough to know if you handle them better than she could, but if you handle them worse, I wouldn't blame your origins, only your brains. I have come before you on my own account, and I say this to you: I don't want to marry your son, not because you are his mother, but because I don't love him and never can love him. But I'll fight for my throne, with any means which come to hand, so take care, Tiyi, for things may go against you.'

Tiyi laughed good-humouredly. She was glad she hadn't underestimated the spirit of this girl who would be co-queen of Egypt and wife to her eldest son. The child was not fifteen, yet she had spoken with the skill of a mature woman.

'What do you think of the lamb which enters the lion's den to warn it of traps set across the entrance to the sheep fold?' she asked: 'for you are the lamb and I am the lion. Your supporters are a garrison of women, dancing girls and concubines who bark more than they bite. One glance from me and they are on the ground, one gesture and they kiss my naked foot. Those are the soldiers you would put against my army generals, all chosen for their worth and loyalty. Which of us do you think would win? I am glad you are going to mount the throne, Nefertiti; it is I who wish it thus, for I think you will make a good queen. But on the day of your coronation there must be no innocent blood shed . . . only your own in the nuptial chamber. Don't make the women get their throats cut for a lost cause. For nothing. And don't refuse to marry your brother, for, in truth, I know no other wife for him but you. You think of me as a stranger, but I know you well. I have watched from a distance to see what kind of person you would become. Go back to your apartments, and reflect that the destiny of a great Empire is worth some personal sacrifice. You are a child still, your heart is like a fledgling. Let it grow in the warmth and goodness of my son, for you are made for him as I was made for your father.'

Nefertiti knew despairingly that she would never be able to

stand up to Tiyi's strength of character. Feeling a sob rise in her throat, she turned and fled, shouting through her tears: 'I hate him and I hate you!'

Tiyi closed her eyes and smiled to herself.

CHAPTER FOUR

NEFERTITI had thrown herself on her bed, and much to Mischere's distress, was weeping with despair and rage. The young princess had unkindly suggested that her slave should go and feed crocodiles in the Northern marshes, but Mischere had stayed where she was, silent and miserable, her arms hanging helplessly by her sides, while ten different and equally important thoughts chased each other through her troubled mind. Why must she go and feed crocodiles? Especially in the terrifying Northern marshes? What had she done to merit such a fate? Yesterday she had been invited to share a meal with her divine mistress . . . today she was being sent to certain death: for Mischere knew quite well she would never live to a ripe old age among the crocodiles. Perhaps her mistress was already weeping for her. Ti must have decided to get rid of a slave who went to sleep when she was supposed to be on duty, and the princess had had to agree . . . who knows, maybe the great queen Tiyi herself had given the order? Mischere had never seen her young mistress cry before. Nefertiti either laughed or grew angry, chatted or day-dreamed; she had seemed a stranger to grief. Now she was so upset it must be for something really serious. A question of life or death . . . the death of her little servant! for even a princess can feel sorrow at the sad fate of a slave.

At the thought that the daughter of Pharaoh was weeping over her sad destiny, Mischere also burst into tears. She sank to the ground, put her head between her knees, and gave way to despair.

When Nefertiti heard the strange sobbing sounds, curiosity made her forget her own grief for long enough to glance around the room. When she saw the miserable, hiccoughing little heap which was Mischere she frowned, annoyed that someone had been watching her.

'What are you doing here?' she asked harshly. 'Didn't I tell you to leave? Are you spying on me? And anyhow, why are you crying like an idiot?'

Mischere raised a swollen face and stared at her with red, astonished eyes.

'I wasn't spying,' she answered shakily, 'and since you wish it I will go and feed crocodiles in the Northern marshes. But you mustn't cry for me, my well-beloved princess, for a Syrian slave is nothing, nothing at all . . . her place is with the crocodiles, and not with Pharaoh's daughter.'

With which words the heartbroken Mischere got to her feet and walked away towards her destiny.

For a moment Nefertiti was so astonished she didn't understand what Mischere was talking about. Then suddenly she remembered how she had dismissed her servant when she had entered the room, and she couldn't help laughing a little, despite her own distress.

'Wait,' she said, and from her voice no one who hadn't witnessed it would have suspected her recent grief.

Mischere felt hope flooding back. She went towards her princess' bed and waited respectfully for her to speak.

Nefertiti looked into her sad little face and smiled.

'You were going to the Northern swamps, just like that?' she asked. 'Do you even know where to find the herd of crocodiles in your charge? Near Tanis? Near Saïs? Do you think the north is the name of a place in Egypt? That all you have to do is ask the way and get the reply: "Turn left, then right!" In any case, have you any idea how crocodiles are fed? Do they eat cattle cake, like oxen? Don't you think if they open their jaws wide enough they'll be more likely to swallow you?'

At this terrible picture Mischere started shaking, and her eyes overflowed like the Nile at flood time.

Nefertiti laughed in a way her servant considered heartless.

'You've no sense, no sense, Mischere,' she said. 'If I'd said to you, "go and pull Pharaoh's beard, I wish to know if it is false or if it has grown old with him," you wouldn't have hesitated

38

before his anger, you'd have gone up to the throne, put out a sacrilegious hand and tugged the lock of plaited hair with which my father decorates his chin! My father's ears would have been half-pulled off, and you'd soon have found yourself without eyes, without a nose, without hands, without feet, without a head perhaps! Without a head! That wouldn't be easy, because it seems to me you've not got one to cut off. My poor Mischere, stop sniffling. It annoys me. Of course no one's going to send you to be eaten in the Northern swamps. Not even I, who must nevertheless put up with your stupidity. What I said meant: go away, leave me alone . . . that's all.'

Mischere blushed and hung her head in shame. She had no sense. She had displeased her mistress, who would never again give her the least little crumb of affection, because her mistress was too intelligent to like a stupid slave. One day perhaps, in order to be rid of her, she would give her to a friend as a New Year's gift and, in a strange household, Mischere would surely die of a broken heart. Anticipating the worst, the little servant cried louder than ever, much to her mistress' astonishment.

'Haven't I just told you no one's going to give you to the crocodiles!' exclaimed Nefertiti crossly. 'Didn't you understand?'

Mischere could bear it no longer; forgetting etiquette, which forbade a slave to disclose her innermost feelings to her masters, she tried to explain what was wrong: 'I'm crying because I've displeased you,' she sobbed, 'that's why I'm crying . . . I wouldn't mind being eaten by a crocodile, or by a hippopotamus even, if you still liked me . . . but now you're displeased and you'll never like me again . . . and when the New Year comes you'll give me away to one of your friends and I'll die if I have to leave you because I love you . . . and I'd rather have my nose, my hands, and the head I haven't got, cut off, than displease you . . . but I have displeased you. I've displeased . . . you. . . .' Her sobs prevented her from saying more.

Nefertiti stared at her servant as though she'd never seen her before, and was so moved she felt like crying herself. Here, in her father's cold palace, among all the heartless people who surrounded her, there was a little girl who loved her, who preferred

39

death to the possibility of not serving her any longer. Nefertiti almost felt happy again at the idea she was no longer alone in the hard world of men. From now on she knew she mattered to someone, even if that someone was only a slave, and the child of a slave. Mischere was not very clever, certainly, but she was still very young.

'How old are you?' Nefertiti asked gently.

Mischere sniffed loudly.

'I . . . I don't know,' she replied hesitantly. Then, frightened of looking stupid and displeasing her mistress again. 'I'm twenty-five!'

She chose that number because she had often heard the people round her saying that Pharaoh's reign was in its twenty-fifth year, and then adding, 'Yet he is still like the early rising sun'. Mischere was young, but she wasn't a child any longer . . . consequently she thought that if she wasn't quite twenty-five yet she couldn't be far off. She didn't know how to count and had no notion of time. All she was sure of was that she had seen the Nile in flood only once. Before that she had lived in a little village on the Syrian coast, with people who beat her. She had slept with the pigs ever since she was born, it seemed, and a handful of flour and a red onion had been her only food. One day she and some other women had been sold to a slave trader and had gone on a long and difficult journey. She had been surprised to learn that her virginity gave her a certain market value. Her new master had fed her better, and had often felt her all over to see if flesh was growing on her bones. When she remembered his big hands moving over her skin, grasping her buttocks and pinching her narrow hips, she still felt a kind of anguished shame. One day she had been respectably dressed in a short waist-cloth and had been made to chew a mouthful of honey and *kyphi* to sweeten her breath, after which she and some other slaves had been put up for auction in a Theban market place. Standing there, terrified, she had heard that she was too skinny for the price, that her head was badly set on her shoulders, her ankles too thick, her flanks too bony, her stomach flabby, her feet turned out, her chest hollow, her buttocks flat, her navel too prominent, her breasts non-existent . . . and one man, pulling aside her waist-cloth, had sworn that a sow would be more use.

'She's a virgin, and who can say the same about your own daughter?' her master had shouted, while the crowd jeered and cracked dirty jokes. The man had lost his temper and struck her master, and a fight had started. The police had arrived with cudgels to restore order, and the spectators bore witness to what had happened. Which was how Mischere, her master and the other man, came to be taken before the Vizier in Pharaoh's palace. The great Queen Tiyi had passed judgement on them: she had ordered a beating for the man who had disturbed the public peace, and a beating for Mischere's master, to teach him not to insult the daughter of one of Pharaoh's subjects. Then she had looked at Mischere, trembling with fear and shame, and had commanded that her nakedness be clothed. She had added: 'Let her be the New Year gift which, for the twenty-fifth year of his reign, Pharaoh offers to his eldest daughter Nefertiti. She seems timid as a mongrel kitten which has escaped before the others of its litter were drowned. We will call her Little Kitten—Mischere. Go, Mischere, and serve your mistress well, so that the blows your last master receives in payment for you are not in vain.'

Mischere hadn't understood all Tiyi said, but she had remembered the words because they had marked the beginning of her new life. From that day on she had never been beaten without good reason, she had slept in peace without fearing to wake and feel hairy hands all over her, and she had discovered the wonder of loving with all her heart. Yes, though she had lived through many long days of misery and suffering, in truth she had been born on the first day of the twenty-fifth year of the reign of Pharaoh, 'to whom life, health, prosperity'. Because of this, her number was certainly twenty-five.

Nefertiti smiled.

'You are still small and your breasts are like pyramids three-quarters buried in the sand . . . mine are only half-buried so I must be older than you. Two whole years perhaps, unless Syrians of twenty-five are very slow developers. No, I don't think you can be more than eleven. Come now, don't cry any more. I have no

41

friend to give you to, and in any case, I wouldn't, because you haven't displeased me.'

Mischere gazed at Nefertiti and her eyes filled with gratitude and love. If a crocodile had come through the door at that moment she would have offered herself to it willingly in order to distract the monster's attention from the tender flesh of her gentle princess. The only fear life now held for her was to displease the princess whose devoted slave she would always remain. And in her heart of hearts she hoped that one day she would get an opportunity for such a 'trial by crocodile', so as to prove to her mistress the extent of her devotion.

'Go now. I need to be alone and think. Don't come back till it's time to eat. Oh! and find Ti, tell her I'm sleeping and don't want to be disturbed.'

Mischere knelt and ceremoniously kissed Nefertiti's feet. Because she loved her she would go and face the Great Royal Nurse . . . but it was rather like hurrying to meet a hungry crocodile! One day, in a moment of anger, Ti could easily take hold of some sharp instrument placed by Mischere's unlucky destiny ready to hand, and finally carry out her varied cutting threats.

Nefertiti watched her servant leave. She felt much better now she knew she could count on the real devotion and affection of one person at least. Mischere was sincere and guileless, her simplicity was genuine. As for her affection, it showed in her eyes like that of a faithful dog; the only reason Nefertiti hadn't noticed it before was because it hadn't occurred to her to look. But then she was used to slaves being either servile or obsequious. In the whole world, the young princess had only two friends: Maï and Mischere . . . Maï . . . if only Maï were with her! He would certainly have helped her to find a solution. Perhaps he would even have given her a child. Amonhotep would naturally refuse to marry a fallen woman. Except that then he would marry a younger sister and still keep the throne. But did Nefertiti really want to be a queen? She didn't see much reason to envy a Great Royal Wife: having to put up with the continuous chattering presence of the court ladies who, if they were not kept busy by the innocent occupations of lady-in-waiting, willingly used their leisure hours to plot against the crown. Having to spy on the people round one to save oneself from early death . . . having to follow all the rules of etiquette to the letter, in order to set others a good example . . . being bored to death during religious ceremonies and Ambassador's parades . . . never being able to make a mistake, for fear of starting the harem tongues wagging . . . never being able to have any fun except in the presence of the courtiers, whose gratified vanity guaranteed their fidelity. And in the evening, having to reveal your baldness to two court ladies, the custodian of the royal wig and the mirror bearer, knowing all the time that despite their respectful airs they made fun of you behind your back. In short, never to have a moment's peace and quiet. That was the fate of the Great Royal Wife. Truly Nefertiti didn't feel any aptitude for such a task. Let Egypt go its own way, and she would go hers like a simple commoner. She would have a house, slaves, a husband, children, she would climb sycamore trees whenever she felt like it, and dream on islands of mud and papyrus. Her days would be full of the peaceful joys of a free woman, and no ridiculous etiquette would cramp her style. But how could she gain the right to such a life unless Maï gave her a child? And as quickly as possible; there were only twenty days to the end of the year and Pharaoh would surely proclaim his son co-regent on New Year's morning.

No sooner had Nefertiti renounced the throne than a kind of relief swept over her, for, though she had never been very certain of beating Amonhotep in the race for the crown, she did think she might have a chance of winning her fight against Tiyi's matrimonial plans. Tiyi could persuade her son to marry a half-sister he didn't love, but she couldn't make him accept a 'spoiled wife', whose easy virtue was a guarantee of future bastards. In this case the prudish Amonhotep would certainly find sufficient energy to refuse to carry out his mother's plans.

Coolly and swiftly Nefertiti decided what to do. She had twenty days in which to act. She didn't want to send Maï a message: first because there was a good chance her messenger would be intercepted by the prudent Tiyi: then, even if Maï received her call for help and came as fast as possible, he couldn't arrive in time. The

43

New Year would have come, the co-regency would have been proclaimed and Nefertiti married to her half-brother Amonhotep. Anyhow, once in Thebes, Maï would be hard put to it to find the time and place in which to give his childhood sweetheart a baby. He was considered an adult now and kept well away from the women.

There was only one other solution; she must go to him.

For a month now the Nile had been rising steadily. Already the current was stronger and soon it would be rushing past. The *nome* which Maï's father governed was in the eastern part of the delta, so it would be quite easy to take a boat and allow the current to carry one downstream. Certainly it was a long way, and not without dangers, when one thought of the wild animals which lived in the stretches of marshland near the river, but Nefertiti told herself she would choose a big boat, solidly built of several sheaves of papyrus lashed end to end. She would take plenty of provisions, a thick mat to protect her from the night humidity, her clay egg, engraved with a spell for use against crocodiles . . . and perhaps also Mischere. She hesitated at the idea of involving the girl in an adventure bristling with difficulties, but the idea of finding herself alone in the middle of a hostile river frightened her, so she convinced herself she must take her slave for the good reason that if she stayed behind there was a strong chance of her being severely punished either for complicity or negligence.

At the same time it would give Mischere a splendid opportunity of proving her affection and devotion to her mistress; after all, it was easy to boast about these things when the moment to prove them was distant, and hadn't she spoken that very morning of going to the Northern swamps to feed the crocodiles?

Nefertiti smiled. Poor Mischere. What a baby she was! She couldn't be eleven; at eleven Nefertiti hadn't been so naïve.

Having thus recovered her good temper, Nefertiti put out of her mind the reasons why she shouldn't run away, and thought only of the heady pleasure of being free for a while, far from the court and the turpitude of men. She imagined eating in the open air, discovering nests in the rushes, the joy of hearing nothing but bird song and the murmur of water against the boat's hull . . . she could

44

see all this in her imagination already and excitement spread through her body until she could no longer lie quietly, resting and thinking; she had to do something, to tell Mischere her plans and pack what she was going to take.

Nefertiti found her little slave crouched outside the door, and, putting a finger to her lips to indicate silence, she gestured to her to enter.

Astonished, Mischere followed her into the room.

'Did you see Ti?' Nefertiti asked quietly.

'I saw her and told her what you said to tell her,' answered Mischere.

'Not so loud!' whispered the princess, frowning. 'Can we be overheard by anyone?'

The young slave shook her head, frightened to open the mouth which had so nearly displeased her mistress.

'Listen then, did you mean it when you said you'd die rather than leave me?'

Mischere nodded energetically.

'It wasn't just the flattery of a slave?'

Mischere looked hurt and shook her head. She didn't know why her mistress was whispering, nor why her eyes shone so excitedly, but she felt the moment had come to prove her affection and she had a strong suspicion that the proof concerned, if not crocodiles, at least imminent danger.

'Would you rather come with me or stay here and face Pharaoh's anger?'

Mischere opened wide, scared eyes. Pharaoh's anger didn't frighten her nearly so much as Ti's 'cutting' remarks. As she could see no way of answering Nefertiti's question by a movement of the head, she opened her mouth and stared stupidly.

'Well?' said the princess impatiently, 'Say something!'

Mischere swallowed and managed to get out, in a voice sufficiently low not to incur her mistress' anger:

'I'll go where you go . . .'

Nefertiti smiled.

'This evening we'll take the big papyrus boat moored to the washermen's wharf, and load food and mats aboard . . . go now to the kitchens and ask for fruit, bread, beer, roast geese, vegetables, as much as you can take without attracting attention. You can say that Ti sent you . . . or I did . . . anyhow, you think of something. We won't eat all our food at mid-day, that'll add to our provisions. Above all, keep it a secret. I'm trusting you, Mischere! So be careful, for if you breathe a word of what I've said, you'll be sorry you ever served me. Now go!'

Mischere trotted off towards the kitchens. Embarking on a light papyrus boat didn't worry her too much, despite the fact that she couldn't swim and had a horror of deep water. For the time being the thing which paralysed her with fright was the extreme difficulty of her present mission, which consisted of extracting from a chief cook who was suspicious by nature, provisions which, while seeming to constitute a meal for one person, would be sufficient to feed two for several days. There was only one solution: to fetch her mistress' mid-day meal at once, announcing vaguely that the princess was very hungry, to wait two hours and then go back in search of bread and dates, proclaiming loudly that the divine Nefertiti had never had such an appetite . . . and so on, every two hours until the evening meal.

'So long as I don't have to steal fruit from the hot-houses!' thought the agonized Mischere.

She was so worried she didn't ask herself a single question regarding the reason for this journey, or where their wanderings would finally lead them. In any case, what did it matter to her? Not for all the jewels in the royal treasure houses would she want to stay in the palace if her princess had decided to leave it.

CHAPTER FIVE

NEFERTITI and Mischere had put the mats and the provisions on board before the moon rose. Then, hidden in the rushes, they had heard the closing of the heavy door which, every evening, isolated the gardens from the road: after that they crept furtively down to the river, pushed the boat out onto the dark surface of the water and began their journey, to the soft accompaniment of muffled night noises.

Lying full length in the prow, Mischere's task was to push aside the reeds and water lilies which hindered their progress; but she carried out this work half-heartedly, reluctant to put her hand into the water. She believed that hands were considered particularly tasty morsels by the monsters of the deep.

After a while Nefertiti noticed her lack of enthusiasm and told her curtly to go to sleep, adding that she must have been crazy to bring with her a goose not even fit to roast. Mischere made a feeble effort to blame her lack of energy on indigestion, brought on by the two sticky lumps of barley flour on which she had dined that evening, but faced by her mistress' scornful silence she resigned herself to curling up sadly under her mat, acutely conscious of being both useless and cowardly. Soon, in the thick darkness of her shelter, the little girl's imagination began to work feverishly, suggesting to her a series of hardly encouraging tableaux depicting the varied and imminent deaths which could precipitate her soul onto the last judgement scales. She was unpleasantly surprised to find her sins coming one after the other to mind: once she had put out her tongue behind Ti's back . . . several times she had lied to avoid a beating . . . and one evening she had stolen fruit from the bowl in her mistress's bedroom. Yes, she had even done that!

'It was a very small fruit . . . and there was a worm in it. And anyway, the princess didn't really want it,' she was astonished to hear herself murmur, as if it were urgent that she defend herself. For a moment the whispered sound of her voice relieved her anxiety: she just had time to smile and think, bah! The Egyptian gods won't punish me for sins I committed in Syria! before her imagination got the upper hand again with a vengeance, reminding her how strict the Egyptian gods were over the least little peccadillo, and recalling to her attention the things Noubkhas had said: Noubkhas, the woman who plucked the royal geese, and who had one day told her about the horrible things which happened to people who didn't help companions in distress. For instance, if a lazy child saw a poor woman tiring herself out plucking game and didn't squat down to help her, Gebga. the demon servant of the gods, was ordered to make her swallow a crocodile egg. The egg soon hatched . . . and the ferocious animal lost no time in devouring the tender flesh inside the stomach, while the wicked child suffered colics as painful as if she had eaten a whole harvest of green dates. If such rigorous punishments were inflicted on the living, one must expect an extremely unpleasant future for one's Ka in the kingdom of the dead.

This conclusion led Mischere's inflamed imagination to start working on the highly-coloured subject of the posthumous wanderings of her Ka once it was separated from its mummy, floating pale and terror-stricken in the haunted realms of the invisible: a universe seething with 'Blood Eaters', 'Shadow Swallowers', 'Flame Breathers', 'Bone Breakers', 'White Teeth', 'Back-to-Front Faces' and other dreadful monsters all eager to eat the poor Ka if it cannot discourage their appetites by incantations, magic spells and a solid background of virtue while on earth.

The sound of Nefertiti's calm voice made the little girl jump. Her mind still full of her horrific visions, she shot out from under her mat with the speed of a frightened hare, lost and bewildered, her neck muscles taut, her eyes staring, her heart beating wildly.

When she recovered her wits sufficiently she heard her mistress say: 'You have slept since the star 'Arje rose from the horizon . . . now it's five feet above and it's my turn to sleep. Take my place

48

and paddle gently, keeping the boat always the same distance from the bank. Above all don't do anything stupid and don't wake me because of imaginary dangers. Fear creates shapes out of nothing. . . . In any case, here is my clay egg; if you see a crocodile, hold it towards it and speak the spell out loud. I did it each time I saw one and we're still alive.'

Mischere, who hadn't been asleep, didn't dream of suspecting her mistress of lying. She simply thought she had spoken the charm so quietly her servant hadn't heard her. But at the idea she had escaped death several times without knowing it, she couldn't stop her teeth from chattering. And now she was going to have to watch over their safety on her own! Her princess would go trustingly to sleep and never doubt the watchfulness of her slave.

The little girl was so worried that even the moonlight didn't reassure her; on the contrary, she positively hated the pale star obstinately pointing its finger of light towards the river, and even right onto their boat, as if trying to indicate the fugitives to the monsters of the deep.

Despite this, however, Mischere bravely took her turn on watch. She strained her eyes to make out the enemy in the papyrus thickets, and her ears to catch the champing of eager jaws above the thin croaking of frogs; she sniffed the air carefully to distinguish the foetid breath of Gebga from among the smells of vegetation and humidity—Gebga, the demon with snarling jaws, clever enough to take on an innocent disguise. And all the time she clutched the clay egg convulsively and waited tensely for the moment when she would have to wave it to save their lives. She had already done so several times, without any other reason except to discourage the crocodiles from their gluttonous desires before the appetizing aroma of young girls reached their nostrils. Had she dared, she would have kept her arm in the air till Nefertiti woke, but she refrained for fear that between two naps her mistress would surprise her in this inglorious position and reproach her sharply for her cowardice.

Suddenly, in the deep shadows of a clump of papyrus which rose, hostile and mysterious, from the centre of the river, Mischere thought she saw a secret, slithering movement and a beam of moonlight caught a ripple as it came to rest against the hull, exactly as if something living had shivered a few feet downstream.

The papyrus clump was coming quickly nearer, and Mischere was seized with panic. She opened her mouth to shout, but no sound came from her paralysed throat and in her confusion she forgot she held within her hand the power to save them both.

A dreadful, evil-smelling monster appeared between the papyrus stems, swaying from side to side as a cat gathers itself before springing on its prey.

The closeness of the danger gave back to Mischere her sense of self-preservation. All at once she screamed, waved the clay egg and gave the paddle a thrust which swung the boat round at right angles. It plunged vigorously into the reeds and stuck fast almost under the nose of the fearful animal.

Nefertiti woke and jumped to her feet, her heart beating wildly. In the moonlight she saw Mischere clearly, screaming with terror, and waving one arm so frantically above her head that at any moment she might capsize their little craft. Quickly Nefertiti turned towards the danger. She shivered, for she had never yet met a crocodile face to face in such black solitude, and though she knew all the spells considered most effective to frighten their cruel hearts, she wasn't too certain of their worth; many fishermen were eaten every year, and surely they never ventured into the marshes without a protective egg and magic spells?

Her hand reached for the two-pronged harpoon which she had taken the precaution of bringing, as well as a boomerang, so she could fish and hunt if provisions ran short. It wasn't the heavy harpoon reserved for hippopotami and other large animals, with a detachable shaft which fell off as soon as the head reached its target; it was more like a light javelin, sufficient for impaling fish but certainly useless against the tough hide of a Nile carnivore. Nevertheless she felt safer with the weapon in her hand. She was responsible for Mischere and was prepared to defend her to the death. Already her mind was at work: she would throw the harpoon at the monster's nose, and take advantage of its recoil to free the boat from the rushes and push it back into the current . . . then, if the animal got over its surprise and followed she would throw to it, as far away as possible, the few roast geese which Mischere had been able to get from the kitchens.

The terrible monster was still swaying from side to side among the papyrus. It wasn't a crocodile, and it was paler in colour than the nose of a hippopotamus. . . . Suppose it were a watery relation of the fabulous animals which haunted the deserts? A kind of falcon-headed Sag whose lioness' body was replaced by that of a marshland pachyderm? Nefertiti thought she could just make out the black beak . . . and a terrible anxiety gripped her . . . perhaps the Nile Sags didn't like roast geese! Perhaps they were implacable in their ferocity!

Just then a floating object knocked against the watching 'thing' and in a swirl of water it moved out of its papyrus refuge, its enormous jaws drifting with the current. As soon as the dark mass emerged into the moonlight Nefertiti saw that it was a dead donkey; she had mistaken its swollen stomach for a monstrous head, its sexual organs for the Sag's beak. It drifted quietly away, indifferent to everything, even the fact that for a brief moment it had been vested with the terrible powers of a swamp monster; now it was nothing more than a poor little donkey whose braying had never frightened anyone but birds.

Nefertiti began to laugh hysterically. As for Mischere, she remained petrified, her arm in the air, her mouth open, ridiculous and incapable of speech. Her terror mingled with shame, and she would have liked to drown herself on the spot, before her princess' eyes, but she didn't know how to swim, and, strange though it may seem, it was this thought which prevented her from throwing herself into the water then and there.

She turned away like a dog expecting to be beaten, its tail between its legs, and Nefertiti felt sorry for her. She said, more derisively than angrily: 'Fool! don't look like that! Pull yourself together and help me free the boat. Then you can lie down and I'll take over. I'm not sleepy any longer and you're too frightened to be any good.'

Mischere had guessed rightly: she had made so much fuss over a dead donkey, that she had lost her mistress' confidence for ever!

With an aching heart she helped to free the small boat from the

51

tangle of rushes; then, without a word, she gave back to Nefertiti the insignia of her charge, the unlucky clay egg whose engraved spells had begun to rub off in her perspiring hand, and like a dismissed general going shamefully to exile she went back to the prow of the boat, hid herself under her mat and wept.

Sleep came while she was still trying to think of a heroic action which could bring her back to favour, and she dreamed that the dead donkey really was Gebga, disguised in order to deceive them. The frightful demon was now waiting for them in a thicket further downstream, chuckling joyfully at the idea that his ruse had succeeded, and the beautiful princess was no longer suspicious . . . but, seeing him from a distance, Mischere cried out: 'I see you, Gebga! Come out from your dead donkey skin!' Then Nefertiti laughed unconcernedly and said to her, 'How stupid you are, my poor Mischere, it's nothing but a very dead donkey.' 'Don't believe it!' warned Mischere. 'It's Gebga, I recognize him because he sways from side to side like a cat about to pounce.' At this, Nefertiti laughed louder than ever, and just as the fearful demon was going to jump on her, Mischere threw herself into its gaping jaws. . . . Then, as the jaws closed on her slave, Nefertiti exclaimed: 'My poor Mischere, you'll always be stupid! This monster really is nothing but a dead ass!' And in the dank, cold stomach of Gebga, Mischere wept because she wasn't understood.

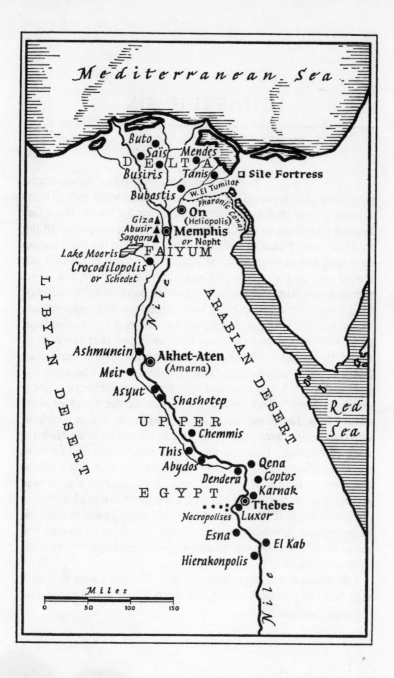

CHAPTER SIX

For eight days the boat drifted downstream, sometimes accompanied by bunches of water-weed pulled from the river bed or clumps of papyrus torn from the banks. These last floating fragments were often large enough to be dangerous to the frail craft, and Nefertiti preferred to keep close to the bank during the night, but as soon as the sky began to whiten in the east she moved out to the safety of the middle of the river, for when morning came the people who lived on the banks left the shelter of their houses to spend the day out in the sun. She was sure her father was combing the country for her and that orders had been given to stop the two fugitives, but she hoped that the current would be swifter than the royal messengers. Several times they had met heavy sailing ships, helped on their way to Thebes by the light north wind, and now and then long transport vessels going down to Noph*, had passed them with all the speed of their twenty oars. These were the most dangerous; as well as merchandise they could carry men whose mission it was to bring Nefertiti back to Pharaoh. That was why, when their prows first came in sight, she disappeared hurriedly under the reed mat, first warning Mischere to keep well in to the bank. Mischere had a plain face and a big nose; her coarse skin and her narrow forehead indicated her lowly birth. If she were seen drifting downstream in a simple papyrus boat it would be easy for the searchers to assume she came from some nearby village and was consequently of little interest to them.

Life was now well organized on board. The two young girls took it in turns to paddle. Practice had given Mischere assurance, and

* Noph: Memphis.

with assurance came a peace of mind which was almost courage. When her mistress lay down to sleep and Mischere watched, alone, in the stern, she eyed the waters carefully but without undue nervousness, and the hand which steered was firm. When she watched at night, if her heart beat faster than usual because of the loneliness, the rustlings in the reeds and the closeness of the ragged banks where a crocodile might be asleep, she had learnt to laugh at her own foolishness and had no difficulty in recalling the adventure of the dead donkey to calm her over-active imagination.

But above all it was the gentleness of her princess which helped Mischere to be brave. Nefertiti treated her with kindness and affection; she never raised her voice, but from time to time gave her a smile of complicity as, with her beautiful, delicate hands, she passed her some fruit, a dry fish, or a slice of salted goose. Neither did she keep the best or biggest pieces for herself, but divided everything as fairly as if Mischere had grown up with her, naked in the house of the royal children, and had been her playmate instead of her slave. And when, the first time, Mischere, overcome by so much honour, had hesitated to eat at the same moment as Pharaoh's daughter, Nefertiti had said, shrugging, but without any other sign of anger: 'Get it into that black-granite head of yours that this river which flows from the southern horizon and swells the sea at the northern horizon is not vassal to my father, for it passes his capital without entering it to carry tribute to his throne room. On it, we are two strangers in exile, far from the place of our birth. I don't wear the royal insignia, nor you your master's seal. Hold up your head with pride and eat in my company with a steady hand, for in truth, this boat is our kingdom and since we govern it for twelve hours each, it is only just that we share equally the honours due to heads of state.'

Despite the elating feeling of freedom this life gave her, away from the worry of etiquette and the noisy presence of her nurse, Nefertiti grew more and more uneasy as they approached Noph. That morning, their ninth day, she had seen bright points on the western horizon and knew they were the pyramids, whose polished alabaster sides reflected the rays of light from the early sun. In her childhood the whole court had once visited Noph and she remembered well the frieze of monuments which ran along the edge of the desert, starting at least twenty miles above the old capital and continuing on past it for a distance of twelve miles downstream. All the pyramids were old, so old that many of their temples no longer had priests to serve them, but the most beautiful were still the three large ones guarded by Horm-akhet*, that 'old crouching beast' whose colossal body was sanding up again, now her grandfather Thutmose was no longer alive to protect it from the invading dunes.

From Noph onwards, Nefertiti would be travelling through low-lying land and then the difficulties would begin, for in the delta the river spread its fingers like an open hand. Once Maï had explained to her how one got to Tanis: he had said: 'The current which leads there turns above Horm-akhet in the direction from which the dawn arrives. After two days you see blue smoke from the herdsmen's camps floating above the bushy banks like incense to the marsh gods. Another day of sail and Tanis rises beautiful above the water, lying along its dykes as if on a sacrificial altar to Seth, the divine warrior and vanquisher of Osiris.'

Up till now Nefertiti had considered these directions sufficient, because the Nile hadn't a thousand tributaries to offer her . . . but in the delta it was only necessary for the night to be extra dark or for her or Mischere to be inattentive, and they would miss the place where the river divided, and would go on down to the sea.

Nefertiti felt discouraged, and suddenly the whole adventure seemed ridiculous madness, not worthy of her intelligence. She should have considered the situation calmly, firmly refused to marry her half-brother, and proudly stated that she preferred to renounce the honours of the throne. The nobles, who rated riches and respect so highly, would have disapproved; the harem women would have considered her an idiot, Pharaoh would have looked bored, Tiyi would have gone white with anger at this affront to her beloved son . . . and perhaps rage and vexation would have heated the blood of her good Ti until she fell down dead, as

* Horm-akhet: The Great Sphinx.

parched as land which is not irrigated. But in any case nothing and nobody could have forced Nefertiti to marry Amonhotep. There was no law about it. None. What evil spirit had clouded her wits and prevented her from reasoning thus before starting out on this mad expedition? It was too late to go back now, the flood water was getting stronger every day . . . she often felt like crying with exhaustion and despair.

She looked without amity at the sleeping form of her slave who rested while her mistress watched, and shouted at Mischere rudely: 'Get up, you lazy thing! I've been steering now for over six hours. Do you think you can get out of working? Unpack our food, I'm hungry. I believe I've given you bad habits, my girl.'

Mischere opened her big, frightened eyes. In one moment she lost all the assurance she had gained during the last nine days, and once again was scared and miserable. Feverishly she searched in the big basket of provisions, brought out a dry and shrivelled fish and offered it to her princess.

'It's the last of the string,' she said in a voice strangled by anxiety at having to give her mistress such bad news.

Nefertiti frowned.

'Well then, cut it in two,' she said sharply, 'can't you see I'm busy?'

Mischere had just reminded her that a new worry was in store: that of finding food for herself and her slave. Why hadn't she been able to steal more salted quails and geese from the store rooms, and how stupid of Mischere to get so little fruit and poultry from the kitchens! Because of Mischere's stupidity Nefertiti was going to have to hunt with a boomerang and fish with a harpoon. . . . In the excitement of leaving she had thought it would be fun to provide for their needs; she had pictured herself throwing her weapon at a duck and hitting it on the head at the very moment it rose up from the rushes. She had also seen herself plunging her harpoon skilfully into a shoal of fish and pulling it up to find its two barbs adorned with succulent carp. She was skilful at aiming, quick at striking and often, with Maï, she had practised all kinds of hunting skills, but she had forgotten that the speed of the current would affect the harpoon; she hadn't remembered that the unknown swamps she must enter to find the game might be alive with dangerous animals. She should have thought to bring with her one of the cats specially trained to hunt in papyrus forests; her father had some magnificent specimens and prized them highly. They were clever at penetrating the thickest clumps to retrieve the wounded birds, and they never got eaten by crocodiles. Sure-footed and supple, they could climb easily up the papyrus stalks to reach the birds which clung there desperately rather than fall and die in the mud.

'Never mind,' she thought, 'I'll wait till after Noph. There will be plenty of swamps in the delta. I'll use the fishing spear to get the dead birds from the reeds. After all, we'll only be three days from Tanis then — if we're not on our way out to sea.'

She looked without interest at the countryside she had formerly found so beautiful, and she envied the flock of ibis which flew over the malachite-coloured stretches of the delta: they at least knew the position of the current which turned towards the rising sun and washed the banks of Tanis.

Nefertiti wasn't religious, but after Noph she found the necessary words and asked Isis to protect her.

'I'm going to pass the "old crouching beast" in the middle of the night,' she said, 'so look down on me with kindness or I'll miss the current to the east. As you love Osiris, I love Maï, and I go to the marshes where you gave birth to Horus, so a child may live in me. Are we not equals? And because of this, will you not guide my boat to the threshold of my loved one's palace?'

She decided to watch until dawn rather than entrust the paddle to Mischere. She steered close to the eastern bank, ready to run into the reeds if she suddenly saw several different channels in the moonlight, for then she would need time to decide what to do.

For a long while the prow pointed steadily northwards. Around the sixth hour, just as the star 'Arje was moving into the central vault of the sky, the boat glided past an imposing group of three big pyramids facing the long desert dunes and gleaming gently in the moonlight, while at their feet lay the monstrous Horm-akhet, breast-high in sand, its eyes fixed on a secret dream begun thousands of years before. Hardly three miles further downstream, the river separated like two friends taking leave of each other. Nefertiti sighed with relief: Maï hadn't been wrong, she didn't have to choose between ten channels, but only two. Not bothering to run into the reeds, she continued along the eastern bank, certain now that the sun would rise from below the horizon towards which the Nile now flowed.

She began to laugh, thinking how stupid she had been to worry, and to have regretted her adventure. After all, these nine days had been amusing, and the idea of having a baby wasn't bad at all. Tomorrow she would go into a swamp, and it would be the fault of evil spirits if she couldn't kill enough game for the three days which separated them from Tanis.

'Isis is good,' she murmured, 'to have watched over me. On the morning of the New Year, when your soul, which lives in the heart of Sothis* rises blue in the first dawn, I will remember your goodness and bring you offerings of perfume and food.'

Then, considering she had promised enough to gladden the heart of Isis, she called Mischere to take her place at the paddle.

When Nefertiti woke, the sun was high. She smiled at Mischere and asked contentedly: 'Mischere, since it was you who saw the coming of Rê, tell me if the god rose out of the Nile?'

Because of her mistress's cheerful tone, Mischere thought she was amusing herself by using another phrase like, 'Go and feed crocodiles in the Northern marshes', an expression which didn't mean what it said. Not wanting to appear stupid, she replied, already blushing at the thought of her clever answer: 'He rose from the Nile and his golden rays dripped like lotus stems when one picks them.'

Nefertiti laughed with pleasure and the little slave felt herself swelling with pride at having shown how quick-witted she was.

The princess hugged her knees. The time had come to tell the

* Sothis: The star Sirius.

little girl the reason for their journey. Mischere had asked no questions and she had the right to be told . . . anyway, Nefertiti was too happy not to speak.

'Do you know where we're going? Do you think we're on our way to the marshes where the crocodiles feed? Or the palace of Rê?' she asked good-humouredly.

Mischere shook her head. She had followed her mistress in order to be with her and nothing that had happened had surprised her.

'We're going to the palace of Tanis,' continued Nefertiti, 'we're going to see my husband.'

The little girl opened her eyes wide at this, and a shadow of fear clouded the happiness she had felt at being with her mistress and having shown intelligence.

'Perhaps your husband won't like me,' she said in a changed voice. 'Perhaps he'll tell you to get a different servant and will even give you a great number of them!'

Nefertiti started to laugh: 'Don't be so foolish, Mischere! My husband will be grateful to you for not having abandoned me when I needed your help. Perhaps you'll even become my children's nurse. You'll certainly be given the "Presentation of Gold". Meanwhile, before you sleep we're going into a swamp to hunt for food, because we have only onions left, and that's not enough for me.'

Some time later they were pushing their boat through the abundant lotus flowers which choked a backwater. The further they went up this stream, whose green opaqueness certainly hid dangerous appetites from view, the more nervous they became. Silently they studied the ripples on the surface of the water. Nefertiti held her clay egg in one hand and her harpoon in the other, ready to brandish them in case of need, and in her head she repeated over and over the spell against crocodiles:

> *I am the Chosen of millions, from the infernal regions*
> *But my name must not be known.*
> *Speak his name beside a river, it runs dry*
> *Speak his name on land, it catches fire*

I am Shu, the image of Rê, seated in his father's eye
If he in the water opens his jaws
If he in the water strikes with his claws
I will make the earth fall into the seas so the south
Becomes north and the world turns over.

The swamp swarmed with hidden life. The big papyrus plants were shaking, and an attentive ear could make out the slitherings, the crawlings and the rustlings of a thousand animals who cowered in the thickest clumps of vegetation when they sensed the approach of man. A frog jumped into the water near the hull, a big thunder-fish whipped across the surface of the river, a cloud of mosquitoes hummed . . . and Nefertiti saw her first crocodile. It was sleeping on a narrow bank of sand, its back greenish in the sun, its head towards the water's edge, as motionless as a dead tree trunk. Instinctively the young girl raised the two hands which held her only means of defence, but she didn't dare to speak the spell aloud for fear of waking the creature and thus reminding him that it was time to hunt. She contented herself with whispering the necessary words, hoping their magic influence would be enough. Mischere was seated in the stern, trembling like a papyrus flower-head with a mongoose climbing up its stalk. Noubkhas, the goose plucker, had taught her a prayer to Khnum, the god with seventy-seven eyes and seventy-seven ears, but the words got muddled in her head and nothing understandable came out.

Luckily Khnum had such sharp ears that he heard the mumblings of his servant, and was broadminded enough to consider Mischere's fanciful invocations orthodox. He took pity on these miserable children of men and sent help in the form of a big, muscular man, entirely naked, his body burnt black by the sun. He came out of a thicket as silently as a wild animal, holding in his hands a strong lasso which it seemed he was just about to use. He didn't once glance at the two girls, who were too frightened to move, but advanced towards the dreaming crocodile, stepped unconcernedly across it and, one foot on either side, lowered the loop of the lasso nearer and nearer to the monster's jaws.

Then, quick as lightning, the man shouted loudly and slipped the running noose round the crocodile's head as it lifted in surprise; at the same time he dropped down to sit astride its rough back and pulled on the thick ropes with all his strength, his two heels solidly jammed into the sand. The animal lashed its tail wildly and clawed at the ground ... then suddenly there was a dry snapping sound, and it was dead.

The man got to his feet and the two girls let out the shout of terror which had been frozen on their lips.

The man turned with a laugh.

'It's only a small one,' he said, 'I've killed much larger ones than this ... at least eight to ten cubits long.'

He was exaggerating in the hope of gaining the two travellers' admiration: one of them, the girl holding the harpoon, was very pleasing to his eyes.

'What's your name?' he asked her, 'and what village are you from? I haven't seen you on my master's lands, nor among Lord Peser's slaves when we went there to collect his oxen. Were you hidden in your mother's house for fear a man would steal away your beauty? Or are you new and only just been bought?'

He laughed as he spoke and his white teeth flashed in a face burned dark as a Nubian's.

Such insolent words terrified Mischere. Was it possible this slave didn't realize he was speaking to a Goddess? Certainly her mistress was simply dressed and her robe wasn't clean ... she wore no jewellery and her skin was sunburned: but any imbecile, the first country bumpkin they met, could recognize her nobility and majesty.

But Nefertiti knew that her incognito was more important than an oxdrover's respect; in addition, she felt much safer in this swamp now the crocodile lay dead upon the sand. She took time to pick up the fishing spear and stick it into the muddy river bed; like that the boat, already held fast in the lotus plants five feet from the bank, was securely anchored. Then she said calmly: 'Herdsman, I am neither your master's nor Lord Peser's slave, and this girl with me is my servant. I am boating to Tanis, three days from here, where my husband is a scribe, beloved by his prince. I pray you, treat me according to my rank or run the risk of a good beating; but if you make yourself useful you will be rewarded for your services. From Tanis I will send you perfumed oils and the Prince will know you saved me from a dangerous animal. Now fetch me some fish and birds, for I don't dare to use my boomerang without a trained cat to retrieve the game, and I am not very skilful at harpooning.'

The man was puzzled. Certainly this young girl seemed to possess the self-assurance which came from education and rank: she spoke in an educated way and her companion did, in truth, seem to be a slave.

'Tanis isn't three days away,' he replied cautiously, 'Tanis is to the east; if you follow this current you'll only reach Saïs in the north. Is it in Saïs that your husband is a scribe?'

This news was such an unpleasant surprise to Nefertiti that at first she refused to understand.

'Are you deaf? I told you my husband is waiting for me in Tanis!' she remarked irritably.

The man shook his head.

'In that case, you won't be there in three days: the Nile has started rising; it will take you some time to go back upstream to the place where you turn off, and then start down again.'

Nefertiti paled, glanced at poor Mischere who was trying to make herself as small as possible in a corner, and asked sharply: 'Didn't you say this morning the sun rose out of the water?'

'That's what you said, my mistress! I told you it was wet . . .' stammered Mischere in a voice hoarse with fright.

'But didn't it rise from the end of the river?' cried Nefertiti, in a tone of voice which convinced the man once and for all that she was a young girl of high rank accompanied by a humble slave.

'It came like it always does, on the right!' replied Mischere, who could feel tears springing to her eyes.

'Imbecile! Idiot! Stupid ass! I'll have you thrown to the crocodiles in the lake of Moeris! When I woke you last night I'd passed the place where the river divided and was on the branch which flows to Tanis . . . what did you do? Which way did you go? Didn't I tell you: "Follow the eastern bank"?'

Nefertiti was almost hysterical with anger. If she hadn't held herself back she would have hit Mischere. Suddenly her anger gave way to an immense despair. She was lost among the northern herdsmen, wild men who lived like swamp animals, uncivilized, naked, dirty, stinking . . . she would never have the strength to go back upstream to where the river divided, and if she didn't want to end up at sea she would have to stop at Saïs, where the prince of the town would recognize her. Everything was finished . . . finished.

She sank to the deck of papyrus stems, and wept.

CHAPTER SEVEN

SEATED on the sand beside the dead crocodile, the man waited patiently until the young girl and her slave stopped crying. He had a wife in his village, and knew from experience that a flood of feminine tears was like the rising of the Nile: one could do nothing about it except wait till the season was over. When utter exhaustion put an end to the sobbing he said: 'Lady who goes to Tanis, you can't turn back and fight against the stream in your present state. Come and rest at the camp of the herdsmen who work for my masters the Lord Khen and the Lord Peser. We will build a papyrus hut for you and your servant to sleep in, and if the head drover allows it (and how can he refuse the wife of a scribe beloved-by-his-prince) I will take your boat part of the way for you . . . at least until you reach a village where you may find a donkey and a guide to show you the way to Tanis.'

Nefertiti only half listened to what he was saying, but she didn't object when he took her silence to mean acceptance, and threw his lasso round the stern of the boat. Then he pulled it towards the bank and went aboard, leaving the crocodile where it was. He took the paddle from Mischere's nerveless hands and paddled as far as the boat-hook still stuck fast in the middle of the lotus plants. Then he moved to the stern and used the boat-hook to punt them through the forest of papyrus.

The head drover was a man conscious of his responsibilities. When he heard from the herdsman what had happened he immediately decided to help the young girl, who was certainly well-born, despite the fact that her dirty clothes showed clearly how far she must have travelled before she reached the swamp. He knew what troubles and difficulties she must have had, and understood her impatience to rejoin her husband. The more he looked at her pretty, worried face, the more sorry he felt for her. He was a good man, was Pibes, head of the drovers in the house of Khen. His master appreciated him, and Pibes' knowledge of the marshes and the fords brought Khen five calves and ten cows a season, for he hired him to his neighbour the Lord Peser, who had no herdsman capable of being in control. Pride at being hired for such a price made Pibes careful not to displease the great. He thought, albeit modestly, that the young wife of the scribe-beloved-by-his-prince would be grateful for his help, and would speak well of him, and that this praise might come to his master's ears. She would probably give him a present too, but that wasn't so important. As long as the Lord Khen was pleased with his servant, he would be satisfied.

Pibes knew what was fitting, and insisted that his men dress in their plaited reed loincloths, so their nudity would not offend the eyes of his noble guest. Then he mobilized a gang to construct a papyrus hut, gave orders for some fat poultry to be plucked and didn't neglect to engrave on the tablets where he kept an account of the herdsmen's activities: 'Pikamen rescued a traveller of noble birth, who had got lost in the swamp.'

When Mischere came to wake her next day, Nefertiti didn't say a word to her, didn't ask where she had slept nor what she had done before sleep. She rose and went out, followed by her slave, whose heart was a bottomless pit of sadness and despair. Dawn was just breaking. A haze lay so thickly over the meadows and marshes that the high heads of papyrus only just showed above it.

In the grassy stretches the oxen, with their lyre-shaped horns, had begun to graze through the mist. The herdsmen were sitting round a fire, still wrapped in their mats, waiting while one of their number finished roasting a goose which he held above the flames on a stick stuck down its neck as far as the gizzard.

When he saw his guest, Pibes rose to pay his respects. Bowing deeply he said: 'A fire has been prepared for you and your servant, and some pigeons await your pleasure. I have had a basket filled with food to see you to the village. The herdsman Pikamen, whom you already know, will go with you, not naked of course. That will save you tiring yourselves out by having to row. I'd like to have seen you to safety myself, but my master relies on me and I must consider his interests, and also Lord Peser's, for the Lord Peser pays my master a high price for my services. But fear nothing, for Pikamen is skilful, and don't speak badly of me, for I have given you what I could.'

'You needn't fear either,' said Nefertiti bitterly, 'I'll send you a reward.'

Men were all the same, everywhere under the sun, from the highest to the lowest . . . they never acted with disinterest. The hand they opened to give stayed open to receive, and didn't close till it was filled.

Pikamen was standing beside the boat, waiting for them. He leant nonchalantly on the long boat-hook, his wistful eyes turned towards the eastern horizon where, beyond the meadows, the swamps and the innumerable river channels, stood Tanis. He knew Tanis; he had been there in his youth, when his master had thought him too young to make a good herdsman, but old enough to row a transport ship. He remembered its magnificence and reflected that if he had been better born he would have liked to be a scribe in one of its palace rooms. Alas! his fate had been to remain naked in the marshes, to drive oxen to the fords and to chase crocodiles, a pastime, incidentally, at which he was past master. He hadn't been back to fetch the reptile from the tongue of sand; there couldn't be much of it left by now, the powerful jaws of its brothers had probably torn the corpse to pieces, delighted at finding food so easily.

When he saw his passengers he bowed deeply. Pibes had told him a dozen times to be respectful towards the wife of the scribe, who, if she had power over her husband's heart, could reward him with perfumed salves. Pikamen rated such a present higher than ornaments or jars of beer, for, in the rotting swamps, sweet smelling oils were pleasant and effective against the bites of furious mosquitoes.

Nefertiti took her place, reclining in the stern; Mischere crouched down near the basket of food, and the long journey began, in a silence broken only by the soft splash of sluggish water as air bubbles rose and broke on the surface between the large water lily leaves.

Nefertiti hadn't inquired where Pibes was sending her, she hadn't even been curious enough to ask Mischere if she knew. She just allowed herself to be taken, tired and sulky, so depressed she didn't even worry about the presence of the crocodiles which slept on the tongues of mud or slithered into the green water, half-submerged like rotting tree-trunks.

At the hour when the sun was half-way to its zenith, the boat reached the far side of the wide swamp. Then Pikamen said: 'You and your servant must get out now, and I will carry the boat on my back, like a papyrus bundle. We'll walk across the meadows to the swamps on the land of the Lord Zaroy and this evening we will reach his house, which stands on the western bank of a channel of the Nile.'

Nefertiti didn't answer.

For a long time they walked across fields of green grass, water-logged from underground infiltration. The man went first, walking fast, seemingly unimpeded by the size of the boat held on his back by a simple band of plaited reeds which came round and knotted on his forehead. The stern was at least ten feet above his head, the prow didn't quite reach his buttocks, in order not to hamper his stride.

Nefertiti came next, followed by Mischere, who laboured under the weight of the provision basket and the goatskin bottle of fresh drinking water.

When the sun reached the zenith, Pikamen lowered his burden to the spongy meadow and invited the girls to sit and eat. He himself preferred to squat down some distance away, so the wife of the scribe would not consider the strong smell of his dry fish a boorish incivility. He let them rest a while and then the silent journey began again, under the warmth of Rê.

They crossed yet another marsh, then a meadow where fat-tailed sheep grazed, and big oxen with short horns and oryxes with horns like sabres, who, because of their fierceness, were tethered to stakes. Dogs barked at their heels and enormous naked herdsmen called to Pikamen in the patois of the Northern marshes, which the two girls couldn't understand. He replied without slackening his pace and the herdsmen laughed. Nefertiti was sure he had made a vulgar joke. She straightened her shoulders, assumed a haughty expression and promised herself she'd have him beaten for his insolence.

At last they reached fields of green *sekhet* which women, naked to the waist, were busy harvesting. As the travellers approached they stopped working, despite the presence of the harvest over-seer, who was squatting beneath a sickly-looking fig tree. He raised his head and shouted that the donkeys were waiting on the threshing-floor to separate the straw from the grain, that backs were made for blows and that a stick never refused to work nor did its job half-heartedly. Then he noticed Pikamen, followed by the two young girls, and stopped shouting to examine them curiously. After a moment he decided it wasn't necessary to make the effort of getting up to greet people so unimportant they travelled on foot like common slaves, and he resumed his sleepy overseeing.

The house of the Lord Zaroy stood on a dyke of mud, in the midst of a garden of acacias and sycamores whose shadows stretched towards the east at that evening hour when the sun goes to rest.

The Lord Zaroy must certainly be very rich; his buildings were many and his big grain silos, in the form of the 'white crown of the south'*, covered a lot of ground . . . twelve of them could be seen clearly rising above the rough-cast western wall.

Nefertiti's brain suddenly started to work again. She told herself that the Lord Zaroy was sufficiently wealthy to hold some important position in the administration of Lower Egypt, and in consequence he had certainly been told of the flight of Pharaoh's

* The head-dress of the Pharaohs of Upper Egypt before the reign of Menes, the 'Uniter of the Two Kingdoms'.

eldest daughter. She caught up with Pikamen and said: 'Listen, my servant and I will sit down here and wait. Leave the boat with us and go to see the master of this house. Tell him you are the servant of a scribe's wife who is travelling to Tanis and ask for lodging for the night. Be sure to say your mistress is tired and wants to sleep, but doesn't wish to intrude in any other way, for she is modest before his splendour and her husband's humble rank does not permit her to disturb such an important lord. Tomorrow at dawn we'll go on to Tanis, cutting across meadows and swamps as we have done today, and I promise on my honour you will be rewarded beyond your wildest dreams; in addition I will pay a large sum to your master for the days you pass in my service.'

Pikamen hesitated. He hadn't much confidence in the fortune of scribes, even scribes-beloved-of-their-princes . . . perhaps this young woman was making idle promises and once she arrived at her destination she would forget to send his master Khen the price of a herdsman's hire. If that happened Pikamen would be beaten for having wasted his time.

Nodding his head, he put down his burden and went off towards the house of the Lord Zaroy determined to see how the land lay. The lord of this place might even have a merchant ship bound for Tanis and about to be hauled up to the river confluence. That would save Pikamen a lot of trouble.

Nefertiti sat on the boat and watched him until he disappeared through the gate to the enclosure. She wondered why she had made this last effort, when only that very morning she had given up and resigned herself to returning to her father. Perhaps it was just a young girl's obstinacy . . . or perhaps she had confidence in this herdsman, who seemed to know the way well. Perhaps also she was refusing to admit the failure of her long adventure. In any case, one thing was certain: Tanis didn't seem as far away now as it had the night before. She glanced sideways at Mischere and shrugged her shoulders irritably at the sight of her poor little face, drawn with exhaustion, the eyes filled with such distress.

'Don't look like that, Mischere,' she murmured, and her voice

70

was not as harsh as she intended. 'Who knows! Your stupidity may die with the old year. Surely your brains can't delay their coming much longer.'

Mischere didn't reply for fear of bursting into tears.

A flight of cranes crossed the western sky. In the distance, near the *sekhet* fields, the women workers had tied the harvest into sheaves and were carrying them towards the threshing ground where three donkeys trampled endlessly, urged on by the wild shouts of a little boy. It was that hour among all hours peaceful, the hour 'when the sun goes to its rest'.

Pikamen came back out through the enclosure gate.

The Lord Zaroy had good servants to watch over his comfort. His first scribe counted the harvests and could induce the farmers to part with their riches without feeling impelled to tell his master what methods he used to overcome the dishonesty and ill-will of the peasant serfs. A steward heard all the grievances and didn't allow troublemakers or beggars to disturb his lord's repose. Zaroy had a small troop of well-armed soldiers, numerous women as well as a wife, beautiful children, and peace. He was the king of all he possessed and only visited the prince of the *nome* when he had to, for the honour of kissing the feet of those higher than himself left him more breathless than proud.

He was a small, stout man who liked nothing better than a delicate skewerful of birds from Punt, accompanied by fine wines and served on alabaster trays, each one of which he had chosen lovingly. His other pleasures included walking about his lands among the bent backs of his people; sitting under the big tamarisk and amusing himself by playing the game of snakes with his favourite, rewarding a good servant, in order to hear the sustained murmur of praise rippling through the palace rooms, and condemning to sudden disgrace another servant who had ceased to please; in short, playing at being Pharaoh.

His steward waited for him to finish his evening bath before telling him that the wife of a simple scribe had craved the honour of a roof for the night for her two servants and herself. Then he reported that he had answered that a building was set aside for the use of distinguished travellers, but that in the eyes of his powerful master a visitor only started to be distinguished if he held the rank of Vizier in a *nome*, and therefore this traveller could only expect to be lodged in the house of his master's scribe. He added that the sky looked down on many unimportant people, swollen with immeasurable pride, whose insolence did not receive the punishment it deserved.

Zaroy smiled at his good servant and nodded his approval. At the New Year he would give him a necklace of enamelled metal, to reward him for his zeal. The steward walked out backwards, his back bent double, his arms outstretched, and inwardly he jubilated, for the heart of his master had been touched and before long his generosity would overwhelm his servant.

Just as the Lord Zaroy was about to make his way to his concubine's apartments and take his meal there to the accompaniment of the songs and dances which gave such pleasure to a lover of the arts, the first scribe entered hastily.

'Forgive me for disturbing you,' he said, eyeing the lordly frown, 'I would rather be castrated than prevent you hurrying to your pleasure, if my worry was caused by the ravages of a canker worm in a grain silo . . . but I come on a serious matter, touching your position as a friend of Pharaoh. On entering my house, I saw my wife, and my wife, though she has a disagreeable voice, is none the less intelligent. She said in my ear: "On the orders of Lord Zaroy, two young girls and a herdsman have come to spend the night with us. The girl's clothes are dirty and her skin brown as if she has journeyed far in the sun. As for her servant, she was born with a coarse yellow skin and is clearly of little importance. It is strange that this scribe's wife travels in a little boat, and on foot across the marshes, when her fortune should be sufficient for passage on a merchant ship to Tanis. It is strange also that she should have dared to travel alone, for she is very young. She seems to be of an age with the daughter of Pharaoh . . . and in spite of her rags, she is very well born. Did you not tell me a runner had come to see the master on behalf of the king (to whom health, life, prosperity)? And that the master

72

advised us to keep an open eye in case the princess Nefertiti should happen to come this way?"'

Zaroy had listened to the beginning of this speech without interest, for he feared he would not reach his skewerful of birds from Punt before they were cold and uneatable; but little by little his interest grew and when the first scribe fell silent he was no longer hungry.

Two days earlier he had received from the prince of his *nome* a message which said: 'The well-beloved daughter of Pharaoh, the divine princess Nefertiti, boarded a papyrus boat with her servant Mischere, and the current carried her far from his eyes, which weep for her. If you see her, treat her with honour, as the future queen of Egypt, for she will soon ascend the throne of the co-regency beside her well-beloved brother Amonhotep. However, the sun may have turned her head and fear dulled her brains, and she might refuse to go aboard one of your ships. Then must you respectfully oblige her so to do, lift anchor at once and bring her back to Thebes, where the royal family waits anxiously for news. Waste no time. Your loyalty will open up the Treasury and give you powerful friends at court.'

If the scribe's wife was right, it wouldn't be long before the steward was going to find himself punished for his insolence! Hadn't he been disrespectful to the divine Princess? Hadn't he, a miserable insect, forbidden her to enter the building reserved for distinguished guests? At the New Year, he would be disgraced. . . .

'What is the servant's name?' Zaroy asked suddenly, struck by this detail.

The first scribe smiled widely.

'My wife has good hearing, even if her voice is disagreeable . . . she told me that by listening outside the door of the traveller's room, she heard her addressed as "Mischere" and there was no mistaking the commanding tone of voice.'

Lord Zaroy wasted no more time: he hurried from the room, his scribe at his heels, excited and happy at the idea of the present which would certainly reward his zeal.

If it had been any other matter, Zaroy would have taken time to think: he would have carefully collected information, he would have listened intently to numerous witnesses, he would have sought the advice of wise men, and thus his final decision would have run less risk of bringing about his downfall; for a man's reputation is like a virgin's hymen; he must protect it carefully if he doesn't want to see it torn to bits by those who wish it harm.

But now Zaroy had no time to think nor to collect statements from witnesses; he was spurred on by the magical words of the prince who had written: 'Waste no time'.

He was the lord of all he surveyed when he was alone, but when the orders of the great ones hung in the very air above his lands, he felt himself morally flat on his face, his back as bent and his soul as servile as the most humble of his servants.

He knocked at the door of the room in which Pharaoh's daughter was resting, was ordered to enter, and advanced, his two arms outstretched, his head bowed. All he could see were two pairs of dirty feet, and there was no way of telling which of them belonged to the future queen of Egypt.

Nefertiti felt her heart stop beating. The man who stood before her in such a respectful position was dressed in fine linen and wore ornaments of costly jewels. Round his neck hung the order of the Golden Fly which was only given to valiant officers or to ex-generals in retirement, and there was a strong smell of best-quality perfume. This man was Lord Zaroy. He was Lord Zaroy and yet he was bending double before the wife of a simple scribe. The pretence was over. Pharaoh had informed the princes of the *nomes*, and the princes their dignitaries. She made an unconvincing effort to fight against fate.

'What is the meaning of this visit by a noble lord to the humble wife of a simple scribe?' she asked in a wavering voice.

The stout man started, suddenly conscious of the fact that if the wife of his scribe had made a mistake he was behaving like an idiot. Luckily, just as he began to feel the pangs of doubt, he remembered that his prince had written: 'The sun may have turned her head and fear dulled her brains. . . .'

'You are the divine princess Nefertiti and the river swept you away from the affection of His Majesty. Pharaoh is worried about you, which is why a boat is moored at my quayside, ready to take you back to Thebes.'

Nefertiti was about to reply ironically that she was surprised but delighted to learn that her clothes and jewels were so similar to those of a princess that a great lord had failed to detect she was a commoner. But she didn't have time. Exhausted by the emotions of the last few days, poor Mischere burst into tears.

Then the young princess knew that she had lost. She shrugged her shoulders wearily and said in a voice which trembled: 'I am Nefertiti the eldest daughter of Pharaoh. You have been ordered to return me to Thebes, so there's no point in asking you to take me on to Tanis. Will you be good enough to reward the herdsman Pikamen who brought me here—my father will repay you, in addition to what he gives you out of gratitude for finding me. Now may I ask of your hospitality a bath and clean clothes for myself and my servant?'

The Lord Zaroy congratulated himself at having conducted the affair so ably, and rejoiced at the idea of going to Thebes and harvesting the honours due to his loyalty, for the heart of Pharaoh would be touched, and his generosity would overwhelm his servant.

CHAPTER EIGHT

THE return journey took twenty days, because of unfavourable currents and the sudden shifting winds, which meant the sailors had the difficult job of hauling the boat along from the tow-path. As well as this it was better not to risk travelling at night, for, though the waters had risen considerably, dangerous sandbanks still broke the surface in many places.

Because of this, New Year's day was celebrated on board, but Lord Zaroy hardly felt any regrets, he was so taken up with the virtuous pleasure of doing his loyal duty.

Nefertiti, though she hadn't fully recovered her lightheartedness, was at least surrounded by some of the luxury and comfort which, though she wouldn't admit it even to herself, she had regretted. Her host did his best to vary the pleasures he offered, so his future queen would not be bored during the long journey. He had found for her two harpists, two singers and a lady-in-waiting in the person of his own youngest daughter.

Because Nefertiti was still a child at heart, she finally forgot she was sulking in order to laugh and enjoy herself. Her obstinate expression only returned when the white cliffs of Thebes appeared in the blinding light of mid-day. She knew what to expect in her father's palace; disagreeable explanations, disapproving whispers, Pharaoh's anger, Tiyi's coldness and above all, her future husband, Amonhotep. . . . Amonhotep from morning till night, at meal-time and in bed, until she died. For Zaroy had said to her: 'Your divine brother has put on the crown of the Two Kingdoms, but he has forbidden any rejoicing until your return for how can Egypt rejoice with her queen in danger?'

Nefertiti had scarcely stepped onto the quay of the royal palace before the lady Ti was bowing ceremoniously before her with a respect which made Nefertiti uneasy.

'I see I'm expected,' murmured the young girl. 'Well Ti, is this the only sign of your affection? Aren't you going to kiss me?'

'You do me too much honour,' said Ti sadly, and she bit her lip so as not to cry. That very morning she had been ordered to behave towards the princess ceremoniously but coldly, and her heart was in imminent danger of breaking at this difficult task. For nineteen days she had wept tears of blood, blamed herself bitterly, prayed and made offerings without number to the gods, beseeching them to protect her foster-child . . . then, when Lord Zaroy's messenger reached the palace, for twelve days she had wept tears of joy, while she considered all the tender reproaches she intended making to her 'Lotus Flower'. She had prayed and made offerings to the gods to thank them for their mercy . . . and then Pharaoh had ordered her to hide her feelings and to receive Nefertiti with nothing more than the respect due to a future queen of Egypt. He had added: 'It is well she should be astonished by our calm.'

Nefertiti smiled, but her lips trembled. She said: 'Are you to take me to my father? Then let us go as soon as possible, for the sooner disagreeable explanations are over, the better.'

Ti quickly took advantage of this excuse to turn her back on her Ewe-Lamb, for she was not certain she could pretend indifference much longer. Silent and dignified, she led Nefertiti to the apartments of the king and left her on the threshold without a word; she was much too close to tears to speak.

Her nurse's welcome saddened Nefertiti. She realized that strict orders must have been given to treat her coldly, and knew that, behind this door, her father and Tiyi were waiting to treat her similarly. Her heart was beating uncomfortably, but she summoned up what courage she had left in order not to let them guess at her discomfiture.

Pharaoh was seated nonchalantly on a high-backed chair, looking quietly bored. From time to time he waved his fly-swatter, made of four jackal tails, with a weary hand. Beside him, on a stool, sat Tiyi, straight-backed, stiff and attentive, her eyes burning with the fire which smouldered beneath her icy attitude. They watched without a word as Nefertiti advanced, her arms outstretched, her head hardly bent at all. When she stood before them, silent and unmoving in the position of respect, Tiyi spoke, and her voice lashed the young girl like a sand wind.

'You are late for your marriage,' she said, 'and your husband was crowned without you. Let's hope the child you give him won't be a bastard whose real father is a herdsman from the Northern swamps.'

Nefertiti went white. She lowered her arms, lifted her head and replied cuttingly: 'When my father married you, you lived with your parents' servants. Must we suppose your eldest son is illegitimate?'

Pharaoh covered his mouth with his hand, for he couldn't help smiling. His daughter had inherited her mother's sharp tongue all right, but she had a quick wit and a splendidly well-bred contemptuousness.

'You insult me in the presence of my husband? You're not afraid his anger will destroy you?' said Tiyi furiously, but without raising her voice.

'You insult me in the presence of my father and you're not afraid he'll repudiate you,' answered Nefertiti in the same furious tone.

'You are impossibly bad-mannered. You stand guilty before us, yet you don't seem to feel any shame at having behaved like a fool before all Egypt. At this very moment, in every *nome*, people are talking about your stupid adventure, laughing at you, and angling for the crown behind your back. Who believes the lie your father told them? Who believes you were accidentally swept away by the flood?'

'You are the guilty one,' replied the young girl bitterly, 'you alone . . . you, with your savage determination that I should marry your son, for you knew quite well that otherwise he wouldn't have the crown. My mother may be in the harem, but she entered it a wife and not a concubine. Well then, aren't you happy now your son is crowned? I'm sure you counted on my "accidental" death to get your own way. And now you're speechless with rage because I'm alive . . . Alive, Tiyi! At this moment, in every *nome*, they are certainly astonished to learn I stand at the foot of my throne, while it is occupied by a usurper. If the respect due to the crown suffers, it's not my fault, but yours.'

Pharaoh decided to interfere before the two women insulted each other unforgivably. In a calm, almost amused voice he said: 'For a moment I thought I was with Osiris in the House of the Dead. You have both spoken as though you had just accompanied my mummy to its grave. One of you insults me by suggesting I've brought a harlot into the world, and the other suspects me of having married one. In my presence! In truth, Nefertiti, you spoke then like a fatherless child. You accused the Great Royal Wife of intrigue, you spoke of *your* usurped throne, as if I were a shadow with nothing to say. But I am alive, Nefertiti, so alive that *I* chose Amonhotep to be co-regent, and you to be his wife. It is *my* will. No one can influence me nor disobey me, I am All-Powerful for as long as I live. Amonhotep has been crowned, and so were you, even though you were on the Nile at the time. It is done, and neither you nor Tiyi can do anything to change it, so why hurt each other? You accuse Tiyi of wishing for your death. But she trembled more for you than I did. She blamed herself for forcing you into a thoughtless act. She said to me in tears: "Nefertiti's mind is so mature I forgot she might act like a fourteen year old." And in truth, your obstinate insistence to be insolent despite your faults shows you are still a naked baby. You lost your head and rebelled against *my* authority. Admit it and take my pardon when you leave. But first kiss the mother of your husband, whom you have doubly grieved: first by your flight, and then by your impertinence. If she is willing to forget the unnecessary harshness of your words, you will owe her gratitude and deep affection, for in her place I wouldn't have accepted the thousandth part of what you said.'

Tiyi stiffened and looked disapproving. Pharaoh wasn't exaggerating, for the young girl's flight had in fact upset her greatly, and if she had lashed Nefertiti with such wounding words, it was only because she was fighting back a wish to weep. But she resented her husband speaking of her anxiety: from now on Nefertiti, who already didn't like her much, would despise her weakness into the bargain.

The young girl glanced quickly at the expression on her mother-in-law's face, and was certain Tiyi was furious to see her alive and well. She curled her lip scornfully, and said coldly, ignoring her father: 'I am back in Thebes, Tiyi! I will sit on the throne beside your son, and if it is true you trembled for my safety, you'd better start trembling now for that of my royal husband.'

This made Amonhotep angry.

'Be quiet!' he ordered severely. 'Don't forget you're still young enough to be spanked. Since you're determined to sulk, return to your apartments. Your mother will prepare you for your coronation. What you need, my girl, is a husband to use up some of your vindictive energy. After your wedding night you'll talk less violently.'

Nefertiti blushed and shut her mouth tightly. She glanced once, furiously, at the woman she hated, and on whose account her father had just insulted her. Then, without another word, she left the room backwards, with outstretched arms, like the most humble of Pharaoh's servants.

So—she was forced to marry her half-brother? So—she was young enough to be spanked? Well then, she'd show them all of what she was made! It wasn't *her* energy which was going to be used up! She remembered the story of the woman who tired her husband to death; the man had been helpless as a child before her, for she had given him a strong love philtre to drink, and each night a little more of his life ran out, as if from a sack with a hole in it and when he was completely empty he had dropped down dead. The co-regent didn't look healthy, it shouldn't be difficult to make him lose what life remained to him. Then Tiyi would weep tears of blood.

Giluhepa was waiting in her daughter's bedroom, reclining languidly upon the bed and eating dates which a servant held out on an alabaster tray. Three Nubian slaves were busy unpacking a big ebony chest from the land of Kush, containing costly fabrics and precious stones; a present from Amonhotep IV to his future wife.

Giluhepa smiled at the young princess and beckoned to her before biting into a date dripping with sugar.

Nefertiti frowned. She would have liked to be alone, the better to plan her vengeance.

'What are you doing here, my mother?' she asked discourteously.

Giluhepa paused to spit the date stone into a cup her servant held, and then said, in the affected voice she used to bleat the latest songs: 'My child doesn't seem glad to see me. And yet, my child has grieved me lately. She has caused me worry and many tears.'

Nefertiti shrugged her shoulders. Her mother had shown little interest in her up to now, and she couldn't imagine her weeping if anything happened to her.

'If I'd known that I wouldn't have run away,' she replied ironically.

Giluhepa might have a shallow and feckless character, but she wasn't a fool. She started to laugh, as only she knew how, throwing back her head in a magnificent and long-studied pose. Her beauty was all the more striking because the fineness of her Aryan features stood out among the heavier Egyptian faces.

'Oh yes, you would,' she said lazily, 'for you are my daughter and my daughter, like myself, has no common sense. Just look at me! A woman who agreed to be second wife, preceded by a commoner! But I'm here to see you don't make the same mistake. I've come to dress you as a Great Royal Wife and to make sure you mount the throne I should have had. Think of the insult to your mother, Nefertiti. Show Tiyi the difference between an upstart and a queen of royal blood.'

'In truth I must have caused you worry and tears,' said the young girl unkindly; 'you would have died of grief if your last hope of a throne was eaten by a crocodile.'

Giluhepa blinked and ate a date before replying: 'My child, only those who wear the crown of the Two Kingdoms have the right to be insolent. If your tongue itches to be rude, you'd better prepare yourself . . . the sooner you're ready, the sooner you can exercise your natural impertinence with impunity.'

81

She signalled to the three watching Nubian girls, who had been biting their lips so as not to laugh.

'Bath your princess, and don't be sparing with the perfumes, for tonight she will receive a visit from the young rising sun, Amonhotep the fourth.'

'Where is Mischere?' asked Nefertiti in a hard voice.

Giluhepa pouted to show she didn't know, and delicately bit into a large date with a preoccupied air which showed how uninterested she was in Mischere's whereabouts.

'I want Mischere. Let her be looked for!' commanded Nefertiti.

In fact, now she had lost everything, Mischere was the only person she wanted by her side. In her eyes she would see sentiments other than hostility, indifference or disapproval. Mischere could not help her, but she could give her the affection which she needed more desperately than ever.

One of the three Nubians went off to find Mischere, and it was some time before she returned, followed by the little Syrian girl. By then Nefertiti was washed, dressed, perfumed, and sitting sulkily on the carpet while the two black slaves put the last touches to her hair and Giluhepa watched, still absently nibbling dates, a half smile on her carefully carmined lips.

Mischere threw herself to the ground before her mistress and crawled to kiss her feet as Nefertiti asked harshly: 'Why weren't you here? Where should you be but at your owner's side? Take care, Mischere, or I might give you away.'

Mischere looked up and two heavy tears trickled down her cheeks.

'She was in the reeds by the washermen's quay,' said the Nubian sharply, furious at having had to search everywhere while her companions handled rich materials and ornaments of gold.

'Silence! She can speak for herself,' interrupted Nefertiti angrily. Then, addressing Mischere in a tone scarcely less annoyed: 'And what were you doing, dreaming there in the reeds?'

'Nothing,' replied Mischere, her voice shaking, 'nothing at all . . . it was so long since you spoke to me and I displeased you at Lord Zaroy's, I thought you didn't want me any longer.'

Nefertiti was moved by Mischere's distress. Suddenly, because

82

the little Syrian had evoked the adventure they had shared alone, lost between the river and the sky, far from the court and the petty world of men, Nefertiti felt like crying on her servant's shoulder, like the two lost children they really were.

She put her hand to Mischere's face and gently, tenderly, wiped away her tears.

'You haven't displeased me, Mischere,' she said, 'and if I had to give away everything I owned, I still wouldn't part with you. You are my first servant and the others will owe you obedience. I would have liked you to dress me and do my hair as usual, that's all. But . . . you've torn your dress in the reeds . . . go then, and let them wash and dress and perfume you; take from my jewel chest the lapis lazuli ear-rings and the necklace of enamel and gold. I give them to you, not as a reward for your devotion, but because I love you like a younger sister.'

Giluhepa's servants turned up their noses at the idea of washing and perfuming this graceless Asiatic girl. They glanced at their mistress, hoping she would use her authority to relieve them of this thankless job, but Giluhepa only said: 'Take care, Nefertiti, that the lapis lazuli ear-rings and the necklace of enamel and gold don't change your slave's devotion into servile hypocrisy. My father, the king of Mitanni, spoke these wise words: "Devotion grows among the briar plants and dung is the only suitable manure; feed it on gold and the devotion will die, while the briars grow stronger".'

Mischere was hurt at the thought her mistress could suspect her, even for an instant, of self-advancement.

'I pray you, give me nothing at all,' she pleaded, 'just let me stay beside you.'

Nefertiti glanced triumphantly at her mother.

'Go, Mischere, let them wash you, dress you, perfume you . . . and don't forget to take the jewels which I have given, for I say again, they do not reward a slave's devotion, but adorn a younger sister.'

Giluhepa shook her head. Nefertiti was young and had plenty of time to learn that slaves were a dangerous, bestial race.

She got up nonchalantly and said: 'Let us go to my apartments,

83

daughter, for I too wish to adorn you as a younger sister. I will give you a necklace from Mitanni, so each time you wear it you will remember that you bring to the crown of Egypt an alliance with the great "Two Rivers" kingdom. That is a fine wedding present for your husband. Better than a chest filled with linens and jewels. Always remember this, my daughter; because you bring much, you may expect much in return.'

Nefertiti knew her mother meant: 'You have the right to demand luxury, possessions, wealth and jewels . . .'

She gave a scornful smile.

CHAPTER NINE

HUDDLED in a corner on a linen mat woven to look like sheepskin, Nefertiti waited for her husband. At the other side of the room, lit faintly by an alabaster lamp, stood the big royal bed, supported by two statues of Thoueris, the hippopotamus goddess, symbol of fertility. New servants had brought her to these apartments, which from now on were her own; they had rubbed her with sweet-smelling oils and left her sitting naked on the bed. Even Mischere had had to go, though she had been promoted: 'First Servant on the Right Hand of the Queen'.

Alone in the bedroom, Nefertiti had suddenly become aware that she was naked, and had been overcome by an obscure feeling of shame. She had left the circle of light and taken refuge in a shadowed corner, hunched up to hide as much of her body as possible from the eyes of the man for whom she waited. During the ceremony in the temple of Karnak, her husband had scarcely glanced at her, and had spoken none but the ritual words. Nefertiti had thought him ugly and graceless, and his face had worn the same expression of austere gravity as Tiyi's. And now, this very evening, he was going to take her in his long, bony arms . . . kiss her with too-thick lips . . . crush her beneath his flabby weight, while his hands, always a little damp, fondled her body: she shivered with distaste.

Silent tears ran down her cheeks. The frogs were croaking down by the artificial lake and the locusts filled the night with their summer chant. There was a light step on the flagstones in the corridor . . . in the distance someone laughed . . . a mosquito buzzed near the young princess's ear and unconsciously she crushed it on her temple with a little slap.

Perhaps Mischere was crouched outside the door? Nefertiti would have liked that; it would have made her feel better on this oppressive summer evening when she was going to know a Man. Though she had been told just what to expect, the sexual act suddenly seemed a terrifying mystery for which she was quite unprepared. Giluhepa, remembering she was her mother, had seen fit to give her some advice of an erotic kind. Among various other curious things, she had said: 'If you don't take your pleasure tonight, it may come tomorrow or the next day, but whatever happens, don't let your husband sense that you're indifferent: for a man is born, like a warrior, with a lance, and like a soldier he must be sure of victory. If he thinks he has been beaten his courage leaves him and he turns to other enemies, easier to vanquish. It is then that he starts to fill his harem, and believe me, a harem means the dissemination of a husband's affection.'

If only my brother could consider himself beaten in advance, thought Nefertiti despairingly. Alas, her mother had also said: 'Nowadays a young man of eighteen has had considerable experience with the many female slaves who convince him of his valour . . . but it seems your husband is the serious type, more given to meditation than to action. If you're lucky he will look at no one else for ages. Make the most of this good fortune.'

Suddenly Nefertiti sensed that someone had entered the room. She glanced up through her tears and saw her husband standing just inside the doorway leading from the terrace, and staring fixedly at her. Instinctively she shrank away and fear took her by the throat.

Amonhotep moved towards her. His feet were bare, but he wore a loincloth round his hips, and his head, shaved right up to the sidelock of youth, gleamed softly in the pale lamplight.

His head must have been anointed with sweet-smelling oil, his body too, on this his wedding night . . . he was going to take off his loincloth and be as naked as Nefertiti . . . he was going to take her in his arms . . . he was going to . . .

Nefertiti's imagination worked feverishly and by the time her brother reached her side, she had to press her hand to her mouth so as not to cry out.

'I've come to say goodnight,' the young man said in a cool, almost severe voice. 'What are you doing on the ground? Don't you want to go to bed?'

Nefertiti said nothing.

'You shouldn't have waited for me, child,' Amonhotep continued. 'Go to sleep and try to forget you married me today. I won't be any less merciful than the crocodiles you faced, rather than share your bed with me. Now the crown of Egypt is assured, the dynasty can wait.'

Nefertiti felt the danger receding, and because of this, she noticed that her husband had called her 'child', and this infuriated her. In an almost steady voice she said: 'Why should I have waited? I was getting cool, that's all. I'm not so young I have to go to bed in daylight. But why aren't you asleep? I heard you don't stay up late at night so you can wake at dawn to worship Amon-Rê when his ship rises in the east.'

'You've been ill-informed if you've heard I worship Amon. I don't worship Amon, I worship the sun-disc which shines above men's heads, the *Aten*, source of happiness and light. . . .'

The young man's voice grew warmer, and Nefertiti was angry with herself for starting a theological discussion. She had heard that her dull brother came to life as soon as anyone raised the question of religion and that all his hidden passions burst forth like the god Hapi* from the Syene cave each year at flood time. Of course she knew the young man didn't worship Amon. Indeed he treated the god with such scorn that the priests of Thebes had complained to Pharaoh. Nefertiti wasn't interested in such problems, considering them boring, but she couldn't help hearing the gossip after her brother had called the High Priest of Amon an 'oppressor of the people', a 'hypocrite' and an 'offerings eater'.

She wanted to put a stop to her husband's sudden and dangerous show of interest, fearing instinctively that in the excitement of discussion he would remember he was a man.

'Forgive me for forgetting that small detail,' she said. 'Of course, you are a fervent worshipper of Aten.'

Amonhotep glanced at the young girl angrily. Still huddled on

* God Hapi: Personification of the Nile.

87

the ground, she was looking up at him with the pointed face of a plover, in which two dark burning eyes stared at him without affection or even understanding. What was she to him? His sister? When they were both naked in the house of the royal children, they had hardly known each other: she was noisy where he was taciturn, she was rude where he was shy, she was authoritative where he was timid. Passions had shaken him inwardly since earliest childhood, but he had quickly learnt to hide them. His mother Tiyi would not have tolerated a son lacking in self-control. So, conscious that he was expected to be different from the other young people in the house of the royal children, Amonhotep had drawn apart from them. He had retired into a shell of silence and of shadows, as an owl fears the bright light of day; he had done without the pleasures and pursuits of adolescence, rather than surprise a look of scorn in his mother's eyes. And he had always been lonely. Yes, what was he to Nefertiti? Her husband? She had preferred to face the crocodiles rather than agree to marry him. When he had learnt of her flight he had gone to his mother and had dared to say to her: 'I know it's the custom for brother to marry sister . . . but under the circumstances, can't I marry a younger one? Must we force Nefertiti to accept a husband, since she is so reluctant we should marry?'

But his mother had replied: 'Nefertiti is made for you as I was made for your father. Don't give in so easily, stand up for yourself. Any woman loves her husband if he treats her in the way a trainer treats an animal. The important thing is not to show you're frightened.'

'I'm not frightened,' he had cried out hastily, for he thought he heard scorn in the voice of this woman he so passionately admired. And he had never again dared to question Tiyi's wishes, for fear she would consider him a faint-hearted youth who trembled before an adolescent girl.

He had married his sister, and he had looked her up and down with majesty and authority, just as if his heart had not been beating wildly in his breast. But he had sworn to overcome her hostility, and, out of respect, not to sleep with her until she asked him to . . . and now here was Nefertiti turning out to be as featherbrained and stupid as any harem woman! For was she not treating lightly the only important subject on earth, which was GOD? And that being the case, overcoming her hostility was no longer important. He preferred solitude to the love of a woman so inferior in every way to his mother, the great Queen Tiyi.

'The Aten isn't "a small detail",' he said scornfully. 'But how can you understand, for you have always been undisciplined and idle? You're just a woman, whose only worries concern clothes and luxury. Your head and your heart are empty.'

Nefertiti was deeply insulted. Forgetting she was naked, that this man was her husband, and that it would be better not to provoke him if she wanted to remain a virgin, she jumped to her feet and stood before him, her arms taut, her little breasts provocative, her fists clenched ready for battle.

'I am a queen, and I think about my kingdom; I don't have barren dreams about the attributes and names of God. For me, Amon, Rê, Aten, all mean SUN, and I worship the sun as my god. He could be called "pig-dung", what does the name matter? I know he rises in the east, blesses the earth and sets in the west. I believe from dusk to dawn he visits the world of the dead and that there also he is a blessing to them. I carry to his altar the fruits that Rê has ripened, I shake sistrums to please him and tell him of my love . . . anything else is a waste of time; I leave useless discussions to those whose job or interest it may be. But to the former I don't say: "You are offering eaters," nor to the latter: "You are the kind of men who quibble over words" . . . What my heart believes is not altered because people like you cavil over the meanings of texts. Anyhow, Amonhotep, doesn't your name mean: "Amon is satisfied"? And again, isn't one of your titles "The Peace of Amon"? And another, "The only Rê"? Why not do away with them in favour of the third you bear, which is "High Priest of the Aten's joyful warmth"? Are you like a lady's lap-dog which barks more than it bites?'

Amonhotep's lips curled and he dug his nails into his palms.

'I'm not going to stay here arguing with you, trying to convince you or even listening to what you have to say, which is all nonsense,' he said condescendingly. 'I see you are only a little girl

89

with no more brains than the harem women who brought you up. In any case, what does it matter to me whether you understand or not? You're just here to give me a son. What a fool I was to think I was talking to a woman as intelligent as my mother. How wise the "Divine Father" was when he said: "Women are like owls, no good except at night".'

The two young people glared at each other like animals about to fight. Nefertiti was too angry to be frightened by the sudden turn her brother's thoughts had taken. She said coldly: 'I quote your own words: "The crown of Egypt is assured, the dynasty can wait." We are both young and can afford to wait before devoting our attention to producing children, because I don't like you well enough to wish for that kind of exercise. But if it's what you want, find some serving woman who will swoon with joy at the honour of your favours! As you so rightly said, there is nothing in my heart . . . this evening you will find it empty, and to take me would be violation.'

'I don't feel like it this evening, Nefertiti,' answered Amonhotep in a voice which shook with fury, 'but when I do I'll come, for you are my wife and I must quicken the seed within you as a bull quickens a heifer, lest she be for ever barren. If the sun's rays do not penetrate the land, the land brings forth famine, and is doomed to perish. . . . I pity you, my sister.'

He turned and left.

'I hate you and I hate your mother,' muttered Nefertiti, who had never been so angry in her life. 'And the day you touch me will be the day that you begin to die!'

During the next three months, Nefertiti had time to discover that the life of a queen wasn't enviable. She, who had been relatively independent for so long, now found herself obliged to do many things which she disliked intensely. She was rarely alone, for her new servants considered it their duty to be in her apartments constantly, the better to amuse and serve her. One played the three-stringed harp, another danced while her companions kept time by clapping, a third sang love songs, accompanying herself on the asiatic lyre . . . and the young servants seemed to enjoy these musical games so much that Nefertiti hadn't the heart to put a stop to them. She watched them absently, usually without a word, and began to understand why her mother ate dates all day, stared into space and daydreamed. Only the presence of Mischere comforted Nefertiti; they never talked about their journey, for the subject was forbidden in the palace, marked with a seal of shame. But they looked at one another and remembered . . . Sometimes, to strengthen the wonderful secret complicity which bound them together, Nefertiti would murmur with a smile: 'Mischere, you are a dead donkey,' and Mischere would chuckle behind her hand. Nefertiti rarely saw her husband, and never alone. He hadn't visited her room again, and not once had he said a word to her in public, contenting himself with giving her severe looks which sent her into a cold rage. She didn't know if the courtiers and palace officials knew she was still a virgin or not. Every evening her servants bathed her, anointed her with perfumed oils and left her naked on her bed as though she were going to spend the night with her husband, and the conversations she had with her mother made her think the harem women suspected nothing.

Only once had Giluhepa questioned her directly: 'Have you taken your pleasure yet? Or are you still pretending?'

'I take my pleasure as it comes,' Nefertiti had replied carefully.

'That's a silly thing to say, my little girl. You mustn't be content to take it as it comes! Practice makes perfect, so if you need any advice, just ask your mother.'

She had laughed loudly, in a way which had displeased her daughter, and fearing her mother would follow up this line of questioning Nefertiti had replied: 'A mother's experience rarely helps her daughter, for children always believe they know everything. So your words would fall on deaf ears.'

Without a doubt this had annoyed Giluhepa: she didn't risk questioning Nefertiti about her conjugal experiences again.

Ti didn't dare to venture onto these shifting sands either. She knew her foster-child well enough to be sure she would never tell her anything unless she wanted to. She contented herself with listening hard to everything she said, in case her words contained some clue to her inner feelings, and she examined Nefertiti's delicate little face closely in the hope that she might read there the first signs of satisfied love. But her foster-child made things very awkward for her: she never mentioned her husband's name and didn't seem to have lost any of her brash arrogance. As for her eyes, they still stared at people and things with that contempt which denotes the awkward age of adolescent girls.

However, Ti's curiosity finally made her life unbearable. After three months of patience, she decided to use artificial means to provoke the confidence of her over-discreet foster-child. Secretly, she mashed some water melons and begged a little milk from the breast of Karen the cook, who had given birth to a boy at the beginning of the floods. Ti mixed these two ingredients, at the same time praying to Isis of the marshes, and then invited Nefertiti to taste the result, assuring her perfidiously that it was a popular Mitanni dish. She even made the sacrifice of eating some herself and found it excellent.

Nefertiti swallowed the mixture of crushed water melon and milk without batting an eyelid, pronounced the dish refreshing, and seemed to feel no ill-effects—certainly no nausea, as poor Ti had so devoutly hoped, the nausea which would at least have shown the queen was pregnant.

On the other hand, Ti was having the greatest difficulty in keeping down the fruit salad herself. She withdrew from her queen's presence hurriedly and was sick in private.

These results astonished her for they proved that, though her foster-child wasn't expecting a baby, she herself had a strong chance of giving birth in nine months' time. She tried to remember the last excesses of her husband Ay, but could reach no satisfactory conclusion. Karen's milk can't be good, it has curdled my magic! she told herself consolingly.

She decided to make a more direct attempt at finding out what she wanted to know, and took from her jewel box a little statue of Thoueris, the fertility goddess who protected pregnant women. Her mother had given her this amulet on her wedding day, and it was carved with her name, but she took it to an engraver and asked him to replace her seal with Nefertiti's, which he did beautifully.

Armed with this present, Ti visited her queen and begged an immediate private audience. Nefertiti dismissed her servants at once. She had noticed her nurse's air of mystery and hoped for an important piece of gossip. In any case, now she saw Ti less often, she took pleasure in her visits: Ti could be amusing when she wanted.

'Now then, what have you got to tell me!' she asked, drawing her knees up under her chin in a position she liked. 'You seem as excited as if you had seen the serpent Apophis attacking the ship of the sun! If that's what it is, come and wake me next time, so that I too can appreciate a rare occurrence. I'm tired of watching my servants dance.'

Ti chuckled happily.

'Let Apophis attack the sun ship every time it rises and sets. You and I know he can never swallow it. I have come on much more urgent business.'

She held out the amulet of painted limestone.

'Look what I've brought to my Gazelle. The magic face of the goddess Thoueris, engraved with your seal. Hang it round your neck and take care not to lose it. It has been made so that your child will come head first, and thus not tear you at your first confinement. A young mother is like a young ostrich, her first egg is often laid in sorrow.'

Disappointed, Nefertiti shrugged her shoulders.

'Listen, Ti, every night I sleep in a bed supported by two images of Thoueris! If she watches over my sleep, she'll watch over my confinement, but I'm not going to bend my neck in two by hanging this heavy thing around it just to please you.'

Ti considered these words a clear allusion to an advanced state of pregnancy. So her nursling was well and truly with child! She had always suspected it: her indolence wasn't natural, neither was her lack of appetite. On the other hand . . . her eyes shone in a special way. Her face was slightly drawn. And wasn't her belly already stretching her linen dress? Poor little lamb, too modest to confide in anybody.

Ti smiled broadly, unable to contain her pride at having found out all on her own.

'My Gazelle,' she said proudly, 'you can't hide anything from the one whose milk you drank. No one breathed a word to me of your condition, yet I knew in my heart you were expecting a child. When will you learn that a foster-mother is bound to her foster-child by secret ties? I had heard nothing, yet I took this amulet to the engraver and told him to be quick about it. I was in a hurry.'

Nefertiti was annoyed by Ti's over-confidence, and had an unkind desire to puncture her pride.

In a detached voice she said: 'Tell me, Ti, you who know everything, do you know how children come into the world? Does the Nile leave them one day on the thresholds of women who have been nine months pregnant?'

Ti blinked rapidly. She didn't know what her nursling meant.

'What's that?' she stammered, frowning, because it occurred to her that Nefertiti might be laughing at her. 'Wasn't it I who taught you that . . . that children . . .'

For a moment or two the young girl laughed inwardly at her good nurse's bewildered expression, and then, as Ti fell silent and perplexed, Nefertiti continued calmly: 'If you don't think the Nile is responsible for bringing children, why give me this amulet? Have I said to you: "I have done this, and I have done that, with my husband, and am now expecting a baby"?'

Ti opened her eyes wide with astonishment. She didn't dare to understand the young queen's words. Nefertiti knew quite well that a man and a woman united blindly, without knowing what moment the gods would choose for their seed to bear fruit. 'Done this and done that', had no reasonable meaning except the one which the unfortunate Ti feared to give it.

She murmured in tones of infinite horror: 'My poor, poor little white Ewe Lamb! Are you still a virgin, that you have done neither this nor that with your husband?'

Nefertiti blushed violently and bit her lip. She had gone too far, and said what she shouldn't have said to the only person to whom she should never have said it. Even if Nefertiti laughed now and said she had been joking, Ti would continue to wonder; she would go away by herself to think things over, and when her imagination was sufficiently heated she would have to get her worries off her chest to someone else.

'Don't look so horrified,' Nefertiti ventured, trying to sound unconcerned. 'Can't you recognize a joke? The simple truth is I'm not pregnant . . . .or if I am, I haven't noticed yet. Perhaps you're right, and a foster-mother is so close to her foster-child that she guesses her secret before she knows it herself.'

Ti forced herself to smile and look relieved, but when she left Nefertiti shortly afterwards, she still felt uneasy. 'He doesn't do what's necessary, he doesn't do what's necessary,' she muttered.

She went off to think things over in the cool solitude of her bedroom, and worked her imagination up to such a pitch that she decided she simply had to confide in her husband or die strangled by anxiety.

Ay was a good man, and did not like complicated or difficult situations. He also believed that if a man wanted peace he should not interfere in the private lives of the Great. On the strength of this principle, he suggested that his wife should worry about her husband's desires rather than those of the co-regent.

Abandoned by her cowardly husband, who had given her neither the comfort nor the counsel which she had a right to expect, Ti determined to find out the truth for herself, using the poor excuse that her foster-child had every right to the pleasures of love.

That night she pretended to go out and watch the Nile rising, but crept instead into the royal gardens and, hidden behind a flowering hedge, saw her Gazelle carefully anointed and perfumed by her devoted servants, garbed in nuptial expectation, and then left sitting on her bed. But then, oh! horrors! Nefertiti pulled a papyrus from a book chest and calmly started reading in the lamplight.

Ti waited in vain for the young husband to join her, but after a while Nefertiti blew out the linen wick and went to sleep.

That night, Ti had to anoint her cheeks and arms and legs with fresh oil and goose-grease, to calm the fiery bites of flies and gnats which, for love of her nursling, she had bravely borne behind her flowery hedge.

Ti made up her mind to put an end to this state of affairs, and used the most effective means she knew. She engaged in conversation with Giluhepa and gave her to understand that the co-regent's foster-father was sufficiently stupid to believe that children were left on pregnant women's thresholds by the Nile, and had been foolish enough to teach his foster-child the same. She made these remarks lightly enough for them to appear jokes, but she knew that neither Giluhepa nor the harem women would miss the chance of spreading such a juicy story.

And the inevitable happened.

The story came to Tiyi's ears. Believing it had been started by her daughter-in-law, she decided to question her son, rather than a bitter Nefertiti. Since the marriage Tiyi had never chosen to face her openly, fearing she would only hear hard and wounding words, but she was sure that in time the young girl would fall in love with her husband. Tiyi was patient and she had faith in herself: she was never mistaken in her judgements, and was certain that Nefertiti was made for her son as she herself was made for Pharaoh.

She therefore told her eldest son of the rumours which were going round the harem and asked him to warn his wife of the dangers of such careless talk, even if she had only spoken jokingly, 'for,' she added, 'she must learn that a queen is like a slave up for sale on the auctioneering block; the customers who limp find her crippled, those who squint cry out they don't want a servant who is cross-eyed. . . . Nefertiti has joked like a child, but those who have evil hearts hear only evil, and are delighting in it.'

Amonhotep frowned. After he had left Nefertiti on the evening of his wedding night he had paced up and down in his room for hours, a prey to grief and fury. At first he had blamed the little girl who had lashed him with such wounding words, and then he had blamed all women, whose insolence and scorn he always feared. Later, exhausted by his bitterness, he had thrown himself onto the linen bed cover and remained prostrate, suffering confusedly from combined remorse and weariness: he was sure he had just destroyed his only chance of winning the sympathy of his young wife. He, who up till that time had been content with solitude, had suddenly felt an eager thirst for love and affection such as he hadn't experienced since childhood. He didn't know Nefertiti, but now he was sure he had lost her he endowed her with all the most desirable qualities and gifts. For the first time in his life, he had even felt a kind of revolt against his God—the God who warmed his heart and threw him breathless to the ground, in glowing ecstasies. It was because of Him that His son had lost his temper with his wife and for ever destroyed his hopes of happiness.

The next day he had gone to repent in his 'secret place' which faced the east on the banks of the Nile. At dawn he had confessed his faults and begged his God not to cease talking to him in secret. To punish himself, Amonhotep had decided not to try and gain his wife's affection: he had treated her with rudeness and indifference, he hadn't visited her apartments in the evenings, he had never spoken to her except when he had to.

And now, though he had done nothing to win her over, his wife was complaining about not having a child. Did that mean that Aten had taken pity on His son? That He was giving him another chance to put his lips to the precious cup of human happiness?

Amonhotep shut his eyes and with all his heart he thanked the God of light for His immense goodness. Then his mind wandered and he imagined Nefertiti as he had last seen her in the nuptial chamber on the evening of their wedding, her perfect little body gleaming like polished stone in the pale lamplight . . . and he desired her.

That evening, Amonhotep had himself anointed with perfume, took his loincloth from his hips and made his way along the main veranda towards his wife's apartments.

When Nefertiti saw him enter, naked, she knew the time had come to face the warrior her mother talked about. She had heard the harem rumours and though she was furious with her nurse, she was honest enough to admit that it was her own fault. One always paid for one's mistakes.

For a moment Amonhotep gazed at the young reclining body, which seemed to quiver nervously before him, like an animal which has been broken, but is still half-wild.

He thought he should start by saying something reassuring, and began gently: 'This evening I learnt my foster-father has deceived me, and though the Nile fertilizes the land it does not put children into their mothers' wombs . . . how you must have laughed at my stupidity!'

Nefertiti felt uneasy. Suddenly the atmosphere in the room seemed strange and heavy, and the change did not come from the last warm summer days. Her throat grew dry, her temples throbbed and her mind became so troubled she could think of nothing to say in reply. If the harem rumours had not prepared her for this misfortune, she might have reacted, but fatalism nailed her limbs to the bed and her tongue to her palate.

Amonhotep smiled and moved closer. Her lips were trembling and her eyes grew big with fear. Amonhotep felt as though he were submerged in happiness . . . no other woman had ever given him this secret joy, this fragile feeling of tenderness which beat inside him like an unfledged bird.

Instinctively he knew that the conquest of Nefertiti would demand the greatest care; but a man could eagerly desire this conquest and yet take his time about it. For the first time in his life, Amonhotep discovered that his soul was not completely filled by Aten; he was trembling now in the presence of another.

He sat on the bed and slowly, almost religiously, stretched out a large hand towards the trembling Nefertiti.

Nefertiti shrank back from the caress; her heart beat wildly and she was breathing fast.

It'll soon be over, she thought frantically: it'll soon be over, he'll take his pleasure and go . . . it's my fault . . . but it'll soon be over . . . so much the worse for me . . . it's my fault . . .

But the young man's hand lingered; it caressed her lips, it smoothed her hair, it moved down her neck and brushed across her breasts as lightly as the feet of flies. The blood had rushed to Nefertiti's head and her eyes were hurting. She shut them, and Amonhotep thought she was offering herself.

He bent down and began to kiss her.

When Nefertiti woke, she was alone; her body felt weary and suddenly she remembered what had happened during the night. She shivered and bit her lip in reaction to the curious feeling of well-being which came over her as she recalled Amonhotep's hands touching her. He was her enemy, she hated him; she only gave herself to him because he had power over her, but next time she wouldn't be frightened and would keep a cool head. He could wear himself out caressing her and she would react with an in-difference which would hurt his soldier's pride. One day, she would give herself to Maï, and Maï could do with her as he pleased. His hand would be soft, soft, his lips warm . . . she trembled as she imagined his kisses on her skin . . . the kisses were like Amon-hotep's but she made an effort and attributed them to Maï, shut-ting her eyes so as to concentrate better.

Ti advanced on tiptoe, wide-eyed and smiling. Her husband had told her Amonhotep hadn't been to greet the sun at dawn, and it was the first morning her Gazelle had stayed in bed so long. Ti was feeling moved to think she had contributed to the happiness of her beloved nursling; she was congratulating herself warmly on her cleverness.

Nefertiti sensed a presence, and opened her eyes hastily, horri-fied at the idea that this silent footstep might be that of her husband.

She was relieved to see that it was only Ti, but all her vengeful anger returned as she thought how Ti must be chortling at her victory.

'I'm no longer a virgin, thanks to you, my dear, good Ti,' she said coolly. 'You'd better run and tell the harem.'

At these last words, for which the grateful introductory phrase had hardly prepared her, Ti stopped short, and the feeling that she was the victim of her own affections depressed her so much she started to cry. Her husband had reproached her sharply, and now her foster-child was turning against her . . . without a word, and smothering her sobs, noble in misfortune, she moved towards the curtain which hung across the veranda entrance, and pulled it aside so the sun could enter the room. Then, still in silence, she bowed before her queen and left the room backwards like a humble servant.

Nefertiti shrugged her shoulders. This show of mock-humility annoyed her, for she knew she couldn't resist the temptation to console her nurse. But this time she would sulk longer than usual. A queen shouldn't be tender-hearted if she desired respect.

Nefertiti didn't realize she was reasoning just like her mother-in-law, whose character she was nevertheless sure she loathed.

CHAPTER TEN

THAT morning Amonhotep hadn't got up at dawn to make his offerings in the temple when the Aten rose, but as soon as he was ready he hurried down to the banks of the Nile and the 'secret place' he consecrated to his lonely meditations. He felt both happy and anxious: happy because he loved with all his being: anxious because from somewhere deep inside his joyful heart a little voice reproached him for his morning's laziness, and the voice was the voice of his god. He recognized it because it came from within him, and yet was distinct from his own thoughts. He had heard it many times, but had never told anyone about it, from a sense of modesty and from the fear of not being understood. The first time he had experienced a state of ecstasy, a doctor had examined him and diagnosed swamp fever. Though Amonhotep had been quite young at the time, he had objected violently, saying: 'I was overwhelmed by a blinding, spinning disc of light, that's not swamp fever. It's the sun inside me.'

His nurse had wiped his damp forehead and the doctor had shaken his head gravely.

The attacks had continued, and Tiyi, deaf to Amonhotep's protests, had insisted on having him nursed as though he were ill. So the young Amonhotep had resigned himself to silence and had no longer refused to take his medicines. But he knew that the glowing, life-giving disc was the image of his God who was trying to talk to him 'in secret'. It was easy to believe that he had seen the spirit of the sun itself, and one memorable day, the morning of his fourteenth birthday, this was confirmed when a majestic voice spoke to him so loudly he had been astonished to find that no one else had heard it.

The voice had said: 'I am Aten, the only God, giver, through the sun, of warmth and life; I am the ONE god who looks on all men with kindness: the noisy and the taciturn, the rude and the shy, the authoritative and the timid. My love alone is worth the seeking. All else is waste of time and vanity.'

Amonhotep had grovelled trembling in the dust, and from that moment on he had started to worship this unique God. Of course he already knew His name, for his father and mother worshipped Him in one of the Karnak temples: but up to the moment of revelation, Amonhotep had paid no more attention to Aten than to the many other gods which crowded the altars of Egypt. But now the unearthly voice had said to him: 'I am the Aten!' From then on the boy had listened closely to the voice of his secret God, who had often said to him: 'I have revealed myself to you, so you can make me known to all the blind who pray to statues which are deaf and dumb.'

Unfortunately Amonhotep hadn't dared to shout the shining truth aloud, in case his mother laughed at him and made him swallow more medicine than ever. He had taken refuge in his weakness and said to himself: 'When I am Pharaoh I will act. Now I am naked before my people and who would listen to me?'

Nonetheless he had asked the High Priest of On for advice, for he thought highly of the old man, and the High Priest had nodded wisely and replied: 'Aten is the bright image of Rê which Lower Egypt worships in its holy sanctuaries. You are greatly blessed, for you have been chosen to proclaim the only God in these dark times when Thebes, our capital, is ruled by the false priests of the false god Amon. In a dream I saw the sun melt the metal heart of this false idol which sucks the lifeblood of the people.'

Shortly afterwards, the Voice had confirmed these wise words, saying: 'Amon is the symbol of the lifeless stone idols which the ignorant worship in vain. What does he know of the peasant sweating on his land, or of the seed shivering in the dew-soaked earth? He will stay in his *naos** until the end of time, as unfeeling as the granite or the precious metal from which he is made. He

* *Naos:* The holy sanctuary which only the High Priest may open.

102

cannot save his faithful from destruction or despair, for the warm blood of divinity does not fill his heart.'

From then on Amonhotep had watched the priests of Amon closely and had noticed their unworthiness. As soon as he was crowned co-regent, he started a secret war against the priests of Karnak: they received from him not one single head of cattle, not one single gold or silver ring, not even a pitcher of spoiled beer or a jar of rotten dates. He refused to attend their services, and when Ken, the High Priest, had insolently reminded him that it was Nefertiti's duty, as first wife to Amon, to preside over the god's harem, Amonhotep had sent him away after calling him a 'hypocritical fornicator' and a 'coward who took advantage of women's credulity'. Ken hadn't swallowed this affront, but had complained to Pharaoh and predicted years of poverty unless Amon the god forgave this sacrilege. After this interview, Pharaoh had sent for his son.

'If Amon forgives you, and refrains from unleashing the fury of lion-headed Sekhmet* on Egypt (but let's hope the 575 statues in her effigy which adorn my funeral temple and that of Mut will help to spare us this misfortune), believe me, Ken the High Priest will make up for the god's indulgence: he'll use sorcery against you. My son, you make things awkward for me. By refusing to give your queen to the divine harem, you are casting public doubt on the honour of your grandmother and my relationship with Amon. Don't forget that the friezes in the great Luxor temple say I resulted from this god's love for my mother.'

But as he spoke Pharaoh had smiled knowingly and added: 'However! Perhaps you prefer to keep your wife for Aten? After all, the solar disc might be jealous of a sacred concubinage in which he took no part, since he is your protector. Which is what I told Ken. . . . I said this important matter was out of our jurisdiction and in the hands of the gods, and that Amon and the Aten will certainly not revive the great struggle between Osiris and Seth, on account of a humble woman.'

The young man realized from his father's tone of voice that the religious aspect of the question didn't interest him, but he had

* Sekhmet: Goddess of war.

decided to follow the wise old Lower Egyptian proverb: 'Offend neither your field nor yet the sacred ibis.' But Amonhotep wasn't interested in sparing the feelings of the priests of Amon. On the contrary, he made a point of being honest enough not to hide either his scorn or his enmity. No one at court could ignore the fact that all his efforts were for the one god, Aten. He had taken advantage of the flood waters to bring huge blocks of sandstone from the Khenu quarries to complete Aten's temple; he covered Aten's priests with gold and privileges; he never attended services at Karnak and the name of Amon never crossed his lips.

The young man squatted down on the large stone at the top of the steps leading to the river. The Nile flowed past almost on a level with his bare feet, for the floods had been heavy that year, reaching the sixteen cubit mark, and Kha'emhet, director of the royal granaries, would certainly be publicly anointed with perfumes and receive the 'presentation of gold' for telling Pharaoh how good the harvest had been. And this in spite of the fury of Amon and the magic of his priests.

Amonhotep smiled derisively; then he thought of Nefertiti's fragile, tender body in Ken's hairy hands. . . . Wife of the god! Prostitute, rather! Given up to all those bald priests, the very ones who dared condemn an adulterous wife to death. Aten made no such demands. He was the God of purity, the God of love. The only offerings He claimed were the fruits which He Himself had ripened and the beautiful flowers which He Himself had made. He rejoiced in the hymns of gladness which rose from His innocent believers' hearts.

Aten's 'inner voice' spoke to his well-beloved son, saying: 'I didn't ask you for your wife, yet you neglected to come and see me rise this morning.'

But His son wasn't listening: He had allowed his gaze to wander across the flooded countryside, which looked like Nun, the primordial ocean out of which life in the form of a lotus had first emerged: he contemplated the villages, spread out on their hillocks of mud like water lilies, and he marvelled at the many petals of Karnak and Luxor. He gazed at the watery wastes which boiled with red mud and murmured in a kind of dream: 'The god Hapi quickened the land of Egypt as I have quickened Nefertiti. . . .'

Suddenly Amonhotep woke from his reverie and was filled with shame and remorse; not only had he just voiced the kind of popular superstitious belief which it was his job to fight against; worse still his mind was filled with thoughts of lust when it should have been concentrating on prayer and adoration.

He held up his palms towards the sky and said: 'Forgive me, God of beauty, forgive me, for Thou art the God of love and Thy son lovest the wife which Thou in thy great goodness hast given to him, for I am ugly and she is beautiful, I am deformed and her body is a precious vessel, I am dull and she is filled with understanding! This night did I caress her with hands which trembled, and my kisses were unsure, yet she did not reject me . . . Oh! God of love! Let her heart be filled with mine! Let her hand tremble on my neck with tenderness and her lips move under my lips! Make her love resemble mine, fearful as an unfledged bird which dares not try to fly! Thus we will be like twin brother and sister: she will see my reflection in the mirror of her soul, and by the greatness of her own love she will be able to measure mine, for words do not exist for me to tell her of it!'

Aten, whose light shines in the hearts of men, was satisfied by this prayer, for the heart of his well-beloved son was pure and zealous and knew no jealousy. He said: 'Love your wife, she is worthy of it, but tomorrow rise to worship my boat when it emerges in the East.'

'I will be there at dawn,' promised Amonhotep joyfully.

And in turns, his day was one of thanksgiving and elation.

However, he took care not to meet his wife. A confused sense of decorum kept him from coming face to face with her in daylight . . . or perhaps a vague fear that he would not see the longed-for affection in her eyes.

When night came he had himself anointed, took off his loincloth and, with beating heart, went to the queen's bedroom.

When he saw her, naked on her bed, his throat muscles contracted and his body grew damp. He couldn't speak, and moved

105

towards her with the same gravity and religious fervour which he felt before the sanctuary of God.

Every night for a week Amonhotep made silent visits to his silent wife. Every day for a week he avoided meeting her and she didn't seek him out. It was as if they were postponing the explanations for fear of being disappointed.

Nefertiti always felt strangely troubled when night fell. She became like a gazelle which starts at the slightest sound: her senses alert, her eyes wide, she watched the shadows deepen and her throat grew dry. Then, when her servants had left her naked on the bed, she would hear light footsteps on the veranda flagstones, the curtain would be pushed aside and the man would advance slowly, staring at her with eyes which glowed like two linen wicks . . . there would be a buzzing in her ears, a pulse beat at her temples, her breathing would quicken and long shivers ran up and down her body. She desired this man and gave herself to him without giving his face a name.

Next morning, in the bright light of day, she would remember he was called Amonhotep, he was her husband and she hated him. Her heart would fill with bitterness and anger and she would speak Maï's name as that of a warrior who would avenge her humiliation. Then she would decide to act that very evening, and send her husband off before he touched her.

No, she didn't want to meet Amonhotep during the day. She didn't want to see the look of victorious satisfaction in his eyes. Once she had refused herself to him she would find the courage to tell him he was ugly and she could never love him.

However, on the eighth day the two young people met face to face in Pharaoh's library, where Nefertiti had gone to fetch a casket of books. The library was a big building, composed of four rooms in which, for generations, all the Egyptian and Mesopotamian literature had been housed; novels, poems, religious and scientific histories, even the royal correspondence and the reports from scribes accredited to the many administrative services. When Nefertiti saw her husband she lost her head and stepped quickly backwards, bumping into Mischere. This shock restored her wits: she turned on her servant and said sharply: 'Look where you're going, can't you!'

After which she felt sufficiently recovered to face her husband. She stared him straight in the eye, searching for the insolent gleam of victory.

But Amonhotep was like a child of three before her; his mouth trembled, and his eyes only shone in the strange way which fascinated her so in the hot darkness of the night and which she now put down to a lack of intelligence. She had to make an effort not to laugh at her own stupidity, which for eight days had kept her at this man's mercy. He didn't look at all like the victorious warrior about whom her mother had spoken—she felt almost indulgent towards him. She could give thanks to the gods, who had for ever set her free! Her husband loved her, as romantically as the lovers in poetry books. She was sure that if she gave him the slightest encouragement he would start reciting the latest fashionable poem:

> *My heart is filled with many joys*
> *Because we're walking cheek to cheek*
> *'Tis wine to me to hear your voice*
> *I only live to hear you speak*
> *And when you come in sight I think*
> *'Tis better far than meat and drink.*

She was filled with a kind of despising pity. For eight nights she had given herself to her husband and that had been sufficient to make him her slave. From now on she would have power over His Royal Person, and if she were clever she could turn this to her great advantage. She had always heard that her brother had a difficult, secretive, stubborn nature, and she was proud to think that she had conquered his heart. In consequence she sounded just a little condescending as she asked him: 'What is my brother doing in the library? I have never seen him here before. Has he come to feed his soul on poetry?'

Amonhotep was seized by a terrible fit of shyness. He heard neither mockery nor harshness in his wife's voice, and was troubled.

107

'I have come to file away some letters from Svtarna, your grandfather, the king of the land of Naharina*, and also letters from the king of Alasa** who asks from me a golden bed, a costly chariot, silver and linen in exchange for the jar of precious oil he gave me as a coronation present.'

He felt impelled to talk about anything and everything in order to postpone the burning declaration of love which had dried up his mouth.

Nefertiti laughed lightly.

'What a good friend, this king of Alasa!' she said in worldly tones. 'I'm sure he'd give you sanctuary in his "sea island" if our people rose against you. He would feed you free of charge and cover you with riches. After all, he's given you a plover in exchange for a herd of fat cows. What did you do? Send him a clay tablet inscribed with your gratitude, and a hundred women loaded down with presents, in exchange for his little oil jar? Or did you answer that he was your vassal and had nothing to expect from you except indulgence?'

Amonhotep looked bewildered.

'This king is my brother,' he said quietly. 'He rules a little kingdom which doesn't yield abundant riches . . . that jar may have cost him much, and what he asks for costs me hardly anything. Why grieve him, for we are all brothers under the sun.'

Nefertiti was shocked by this reasoning.

'And what do my father and your mother say about this remarkable transaction?' she asked dryly. 'Did they beg you to add on their behalf a collection of ostrich feathers and a pack of cheetahs from the land of Punt?'

Amonhotep realized his wife was disapproving of his action, and was annoyed at having started a conversation on such a subject.

'The king of Alasa wrote direct to me, and I have sent him these presents from my personal treasure. In so doing I have neither cheated nor impoverished anyone but myself.'

'I hope you won't be so prodigal with your people's wealth,' said Nefertiti in much sharper tones.

* Naharina: 'Kingdom of the two rivers', one of the names for Mitanni.
** Alasa: The island of Cyprus.

108

There was a sudden silence, during which the two young people stared at each other. Amonhotep was shaken by the hard voice of a Nefertiti he no longer recognized, for he had built her up in his imagination to be the essence of tenderness and love. As for Nefertiti, she was furious with herself for saying too much. She still had a lot to learn before she would be as clever as her mother-in-law Tiyi.

This thought stimulated her. She made an effort to soften her voice, and said:

'I see you so seldom, and you seem to forget I am the queen, whose love for Egypt's glory is equal to your own. But I am still a child and understand so little of affairs of State; would it be asking too much if you instructed me yourself on what to do and not to do in the administration of a kingdom? Perhaps I spoke unwisely when I reproached you for sending presents to the king of Alasa? If that is so, excuse my ignorance and blame only yourself, for you have not thought to teach me.'

These words were balm to the young man's wounded pride.

'Certainly, certainly you spoke wisely,' he hurriedly consoled her; 'you spoke wisely because you didn't know the jar was costly. . . . I didn't dare to hope affairs of State would interest you, but I'm happy that they do, for often a woman sees more clearly than a man and her mind is naturally attuned to justice. I am still young and ignorant of many matters; like you, there is much left for me to learn; but what I know I'll teach you. When shall I begin?'

Nefertiti made an effort not to smile.

'I don't feel like settling down to serious matters just at present. What would you say to a game of hounds and jackals?'

'I'd like nothing better,' replied the young man quickly. 'It so happens I have a magnificent set which I've been meaning to give you as a present: the board is of ebony and oliban wood, the hounds are lapis lazuli enamel and the jackals black laminated schist inset with gold . . . it was a present from the viceroy of Nubia.'

'In exchange for what?' asked Nefertiti. But her smile softened the irony and Amonhotep laughed.

One of Nefertiti's attendants ran all the way to the harem with the news: the co-regent and his wife were playing hounds and jackals on a magnificent board of ebony and oliban, and this in the middle of the afternoon . . . in the queen's bedroom! It was certainly the first time that such a thing had happened since their marriage. Giluhepa shrugged her shoulders and said that it was better than to play at dog and cat.

The news flew round the royal palace and from there to the apartments of the nobles, and thus came to the ears of poor Ti, who had found herself to be a gifted housewife since the heart of her foster-child was closed to her: now Ay always found her waiting for him when he came home. Whatever time it was, she would be there, surrounded by her servants in her bedroom and eating her heart out, or in the courtyard outside the kitchen talking to old Nefret, who had brought her up and who, at the age of seventy-three, could still pluck geese 'like a young thing'.

The news reached her just as she was about to bite into a cake. Without a moment's hesitation she put the cake back on the tray and threw herself on the ground to pray to the goddess Nut, protector of conjugal bliss.

'All thanks and glory be to thee, oh Nut! For thy power has once again been proved! My Gazelle plays hounds and jackals with her husband in the middle of the afternoon! Tomorrow she'll go with him to the temple . . . the next day she will receive Ambassadors by his side . . . and the day after that she will give him a child. For if they play hounds and jackals in the middle of the afternoon, they must certainly play Nut and Geb* at night, as the sky and the earth did before Shu** interfered. Watch over this union, Great Nut! For if my little bird is tamed by the bird-catcher, your devoted Ti won't be forever in disgrace.'

The servants, an impertinent lot, hid their smiles, for they feared the anger of their mistress. Then Ti got to her feet and ate her cake happily. She was certain that soon she would be called back from her sorry exile in apartments so distant that rumours

* Nut and Geb: god and goddess personifying the sky and earth.
** Shu: God personifying the air.

from the royal harem only reached her three hours after being started.

As for Tiyi, when she heard the news she just nodded her head and smiled.

CHAPTER ELEVEN

N<small>UT</small> must have listened indulgently to the good Ti's prayers. Nefertiti often accompanied her husband to the temple of Aten; stood at his side when he received the Ambassadors of Syria, of Nubia, and of the 'Islands-of-the-sea'; in addition, she was carrying his child. As for the game of Nut and Geb, she played it more enthusiastically than she had intended. She argued:

Night and Day are like a Negro and an Egyptian who are travelling together. Each has a different way of life, worships the god of his tribe and eats the food he is used to. Peace exists between men if they aren't aggressive, and don't try to impose laws on each other; my husband explained this to me when he talked of peace among peoples, but it is the same for Day and Night! At Night, a man enters my bedchamber; I can't see him, for I put out the lamp before he comes; he speaks words of love to me and I listen without replying; when he leaves me, I am weary and go to sleep, maybe even with a smile. Next day, I wake in the royal bedroom, meet my half-brother, and speak to him concerning matters of State; I preside over meetings; I am clear-headed, wary and watchful. But my Day and my Night are separate, and to live peacefully they must not use the same laws to judge each other.

She still held a grudge against her nurse, however, so the great goddess Nut hadn't fully manifested her goodness after all; Ti didn't return to favour but continued to bewail her banishment.

The Nile had regained its original bed, and the time for sowing, fishing and decomposition had arrived. All over the vast 'Black Land of Kemet' peasants broke up the lumps of mud, ploughed and sowed with eager jubilation: the spectre of famine faded, for the harvest would be plentiful and enough grain stored in the silos to relieve a future drought. The air was full of shouts and laughter, clamour and songs. From the Northern to the Southernmost horizon, men rediscovered the pleasure of walking on their lands, and pacing the boundaries of their properties. And yet the atmosphere 'smelt stronger than fish spawn', near the numerous pools of stagnant water which the Nile had left behind. It had always been thus, ever since Nun* had given birth to Egypt.

It was the time of the mosquitoes and the good season for oil and goose-grease merchants.

It was the time for Royal festivities, boating, tournaments and hunting in the marshes. Pharaoh willingly relegated to his son affairs of State, but he would let no one organize his hunts. Water birds were not important game for a man who had killed hundreds of lions, wild bulls, leopards and other dangerous animals, but he didn't despise them when they were flying to the shelter of the green and tufted marshes.

The day before the great opening hunt, Maï arrived from Tanis with letters from his father. He had insisted on carrying them himself, for he was beginning to be bored by provincial life. He could remember the splendours of his childhood, when he lived in the 'house of the young suns', and now that Amonhotep was co-regent on the throne, Maï dreamed of being part of his personal suite. With all the assurance of his fifteen years, he was sure he would get what he wanted if he presented his request himself. Hadn't he been the best friend of Nefertiti? And hadn't Nefertiti become all-powerful queen?

He advanced resolutely towards the throne, his head high, his glance assured, and at the sight of his pleasant face and well-built, muscular body, Nefertiti felt herself deeply moved. Now she had known desire, and could tell the difference between a woman and a man. Maï was a man; the man she should have married and for whom, in moments of passion, her body yearned.

* Nun: The primordial ocean.

With him there would have been no frontier between day and night, they would have run together in the tender anarchy of love. She listened as his voice rang loud and clear and compared it to her husband's, dull and low. Suddenly she hated Maï seeing her beside this ugly, deformed man to whom, now she was carrying his child, she was indissolubly tied. She felt besmirched; it seemed to her the stigma of her shame must show on her face . . . like a spot on her nose. She pretended to be taken ill, and only reopened her eyes when they laid her on her bed. Above her she saw her servants' frightened faces through a mist of tears.

'Leave me alone . . . !' she murmured in a shaking voice.

The servants glanced at each other hesitatingly and left regretfully, their curiosity unsatisfied. Then Amonhotep stepped from the shadowed corner where he had been waiting, uneasy and unhappy, until the slaves revived their queen.

When Nefertiti saw him it was all she could do not to scream.

'What's the matter?' asked Amonhotep, anxiously, 'Shall I send for Pentu?'

Nefertiti choked, but she controlled the sobs which were forcing themselves into her throat.

'I'm not sick to see a doctor,' she managed to say. 'I'm expecting a child. I'm expecting a child, that's all. Leave me alone, alone, ALONE!'

She shouted the last word and then, burying her face in her arms, burst into tears.

Amonhotep was struck dumb with amazement.

His wife was expecting a baby . . . his baby! His son! Inside his wife there lay a tiny germ of love, and this seed was his son. Up to that moment, Amonhotep had thought little about this divine miracle of transmitted life; he had not been struck by the wonder of this act, he hadn't been deeply conscious of its astonishing truth.

After a while Amonhotep silently left, his heart filled with a quiet, glowing happiness. He returned to the audience chamber, greeted Maï like a brother and invited him to join the grand opening hunt which was to take place next day.

Queen Tiyi watched her son carefully. He had reassured the

court as to his wife's health, explaining that the strong seasonal smells had upset her and all she needed was rest in an incense-perfumed room. But Tiyi wasn't satisfied. She remembered something the Lord Zaroy had said; he who had stopped Nefertiti when she was going, so it seemed, to see her grandfather in Mitanni.

'. . . the divine Nefertiti said: "You have been ordered to return me to Thebes, so there's no point in asking you to take me on to Tanis".'

When Maï was a child he had been the favourite of the little princess . . . and Maï lived in Tanis. And on the morning of her flight, hadn't Nefertiti said to her stepmother: 'Why should I be saddled with your son? Especially as I love someone else.'

Tiyi remembered these words clearly; they had worried her for some time.

Why should Nefertiti choose the moment of Maï's audience to faint? Her fears increased when she heard from a servant that her daughter-in-law was weeping on her bed.

Yet her son seemed quite unworried, and his quiet voice expressed a peaceful heart.

Tiyi sent a message to her first born announcing her arrival. She didn't want to share her suspicions, only to question him. Had she acted foolishly in forcing Nefertiti to marry her half-brother, in the belief that a virgin will fall in love with the man who awakens her senses? For three months now, Amonhotep had worn the satisfied air of a happy husband, but Tiyi knew from experience that men were sufficiently vain and stupid to be taken in by their wives' satisfied expressions.

Her son was in his study, as he was every afternoon between the fifth and the sixth hours. Before him, a low table was covered with clay tablets and rolls of papyrus, but the young man wasn't studying them; his eyes were fixed on an invisible world of beauty and round his mouth hovered a gentle smile.

He came back to earth with a start as his mother entered, and looked up with an expression which clearly told her of the joy within his heart.

She motioned to him not to rise, and sat down opposite him on a stool.

115

'I've come to see you about Nefertiti,' she said, 'I hope she isn't ill. I didn't dare disturb her, for you said she needed rest. Is it really the smell of decomposition which has upset her? That's strange, for every year since babyhood she has smelt it without coming to any harm. I fear rather sickness in her head or heart. You should call Pentu to her bedside and let him prescribe a medicine.'

Amonhotep laughed. His mother hadn't believed his lie; she had a sharp eye, a quick mind . . . and she was as curious as only a woman could be.

'Her head is in place,' he said, 'and to use the wise language of Pentu, her heart "speaks in all her limbs with regularity". So, in truth, it seems that only the smell is responsible for her swoon.'

Tiyi shook her head.

'I have been told her eyes are damp as if she were in a smoke-filled room. Is not that a sign her body is overheated, and producing an irritating moisture? Perhaps the new date wine doesn't agree with her? My eldest son, you do not seem fond of your wife, for she suffers on her bed while you laugh and care nothing.'

Amonhotep's expression became grave.

'My mother, my mother,' he said gently, 'certainly my wife is ill. She is ill from carrying a child — my child. And if she weeps, it is because she is troubled by life's mystery.'

Tiyi sighed with relief. Nefertiti pregnant explained almost everything. However she decided to clear the whole matter up once and for all, and dispel any doubts she still retained.

'I am happy for you, my eldest son, for children bind a couple closer. But do not be angry with your mother if she asks you a direct question. Indiscretion is a weapon in the hands of a common person, the better to direct his arrows, but it does not exist between a mother and her son. Nefertiti is young, and I didn't hide from you the fact that your marriage was decided without her consent. You have lived together for half a year now and for three months she has seemed steadier, more ready to consider you her husband. Tell me, my son, does your wife love you?'

Amonhotep hesitated, because his mother had knocked on a secret door which he obstinately wanted to keep closed. During

116

the day, Nefertiti never gave him any tender caresses, secret glances or loving smiles . . . she never reached for his hand and squeezed it secretly during the long audiences; she never handed him her cup to drink from: she never gave him furtive kisses behind the pillars . . . and when he reached for her hand, she withdrew it; when he gave her his cup, she put it down without drinking; when his lips neared her cheek, she moved away. And yet, at night, she became a different person; she returned his kisses, her body welcomed him and loved him. So he chose not to remember that she stayed silent as a shadow from the invisible world. He only knew that desire radiated from every pore of her body and that the warmth of her slender hand burnt his damp neck.

No, he didn't want to open the door of doubt.

'My wife loves me,' he replied in a low voice, 'I'm sure of it.'

Tiyi had noticed her son's hesitation, and was sorry for it. Her son had spoken as though to persuade himself about this love, and she was filled with pity for him.

'Of course she loves you,' she went on with a smile, 'I have seen how she has changed these last three months. However, remember this: a woman is a fragile object and must be handled gently . . . she is like metal which must be polished long before it shines. Don't take your pleasure before the metal gleams, for if it is dull you will not see your reflection.'

Amonhotep replied brusquely: 'Nefertiti has no need to complain of me in that respect, nor I of her!'

Tiyi smiled knowingly. This time her eldest son had spoken the truth, as the warmth in his voice proved. Nefertiti might affect coldness and indifference in public, but her husband had known how to awaken her senses, and the rest would follow.

But it would be a mistake to neglect the possibility of a secret love for Maï; it would be necessary to act as if the latter were responsible for the young queen's fainting and her tears.

'Maï is a good young man,' Tiyi said in a casual voice. 'I am happy to see how handsome and able he has grown, for his father is a friend of your father and his joys are ours. I think we should watch over his future and use his loyalty as a shield against traitors. Ask him what would please him. Perhaps he would like to go as Pharaoh's Ambassador to the land of Punt?* Another thing, has Ramose told you that the workers are complaining in the City of the Dead? It appears that rations of corn, vegetables, fish and beer have been insufficient. I expect it is the scribes embezzling again. I don't like Neferi, he's sly, one sees the skin on his head more often than the colour of his eyes, he is so bent over with respect.'

Amonhotep smiled.

'Ramose has spoken to me and I will visit the Necropolis myself. As for Maï, I would be happy to grant him what he wishes, for he is my brother, and I have seen him naked in the house of the royal children.'

When Tiyi left her son, she felt reassured. Amonhotep had spoken of Maï warmly, and without fear; so long as jealousy did not dwell within his heart, there was less chance of his behaving clumsily towards his wife and losing what little affection he might have won in the last six months.

* Land of Punt: land of incense . . . perhaps the coast of Somaliland.

CHAPTER TWELVE

MISCHERE was half asleep outside the door to her mistress' room. Nefertiti had said to her: 'Stay there, and if anyone wants to see me, say that I'm resting.'

A thankless task. It wasn't difficult to stop the other servants from entering, but one needed to be very skilful indeed to make the great ones listen to reason without wounding their susceptibilities. And though Mischere had been promoted First Servant on the Right Hand of the Queen, her heart was no braver in consequence. She hated giving orders, for her natural humility prevented her from believing in her own authority. And when, in addition, it was necessary to deal with the nobility . . .!

All afternoon she had had to say: 'My mistress sleeps and will be better when she wakes . . . she must not be disturbed.'

She had said exactly the same words to the slaves, the ladies and the noble lords, for she couldn't shake with fear and invent a new phrase at the same time.

Towards evening the visits had become less frequent, and Mischere had passed the time in a beneficial doze. However, her Ka was keeping watch for her. It heard a step in the corridor and shook her awake. She pulled herself together, made a big effort to open her eyes, and saw standing before her the Great Royal Wife. Mischere had a moment's pure panic: she was a heap of dust before the Great Royal Wife! How could she ever find her voice and forbid her to enter the bedroom? Her mistress had said to her: 'You will let no one enter . . . no one, you understand? Neither slaves nor masters.'

The Great Royal Wife didn't belong in either category, she was the Goddess, she was the moon in the sky! Who could say to the moon: 'Light my orchard but don't let your gaze wander into my house! Stay outside!'?

Throwing herself flat on the flagstones, her face pressed against the cold alabaster, she stammered out a few new phrases to suit the occasion: 'If I am impertinent, have my head cut off at once, O Great Royal Wife, but I cannot let you see my mistress, for she ordered me to watch her door so that none should disturb her rest. Must I displease her to please you, or displease you to please her?'

Tiyi took advantage of the fact that the little slave wasn't looking at her to smile good-humouredly. She had weighed Mischere's heart and found it heavy with devotion and innocence.

'If I must cut off your head before entering my daughter's room, I prefer not to enter, for the sight of blood makes me feel unwell,' she said, amused. 'I will thus choose the—cleanest solution, and retire after receiving an assurance that my daughter has recovered.'

'She told me she would be better when she woke,' replied Mischere, happy to get off so lightly.

'That is good news. And don't be frightened, little one, the loyalty of a servant never displeases.'

When the noise of Tiyi's footsteps could no longer be heard, Mischere resumed her original position.

'O Great Royal Wife,' she murmured with the tender pity of an old man for the artlessness of a child, 'you are good but very innocent. Today my loyalty has displeased many people. But you are the moon, O Tiyi! And you are set too high to see what happens on the earth. Yes, I have displeased many people, truly!'

At last Nefertiti called to her and she hurried into the room, relieved that her torture had come to an end. Alas! Her mistress gave her another mission even more alarming than the first.

'Listen,' said Nefertiti, without even asking the names of those who had sought news of her, 'you must go to my father and tell him I am too tired to take part in the feast tonight. Say to him: "The Great Nefertiti wishes to regain her strength in solitude for it would grieve her greatly if she could not join the opening hunt

120

tomorrow. She is sure that, if she rests, she will kill twenty more birds than her father. She requests him to prepare himself as best he can for this loyal challenge so that the honours will not be only for the winner".'

Nefertiti knew that on receiving such a message, Pharaoh would be blinded by his hunter's pride and no longer think it important that his daughter was bad-mannered enough to be absent from the feast given in Maï's honour. She could see him now, arriving like a warrior in the great harem banqueting hall, his eye bright, his carriage assured, for Pharaoh kept his indolence for affairs of State and his energy for hunting.

'The co-regent's wife has sent me a loyal challenge,' he would announce ironically. 'She claims she will bring down twenty more birds than I! And she bids me to prepare myself well for this competition, as if I needed to husband my strength the evening before a hunt. It is the young things who take the precaution of resting before exertion. She faints today because of the smell, but she is certain that tomorrow she will throw her boomerang true!' And he would smile fatuously.

Mischere trembled as she heard this inflammatory message. As she trotted off to Pharaoh's apartments she repeated to herself the consoling words of the Great Royal Wife: '. . . the loyalty of a servant never displeases.' And she added quickly: 'Let's hope the Sun remembers this!'

Nefertiti felt calmer, for she had wept all the tears from her body, and slept for five hours running. But she still had to decide what she was going to do. Tomorrow she would meet Maï under the piercing gaze of Tiyi and she would have to be very careful. Tanis, Maï, her daughter-in-law's sudden fainting fit, her incomprehensible tears, her refusal to see anyone, her absence from the festivities—Tiyi might put two and two together. It was always a mistake to lose control of one's emotions.

'Behave naturally, I must behave naturally,' murmured Nefertiti. 'If I greet Maï warmly, as a dear childhood friend, Tiyi will do all she can to have him kept away from Thebes for good. And

121

if I pretend coldness, she will be surprised and suspicious. . . . I must be simple and friendly, but not too much so, as though all that remains of my childhood affection is a vague memory of innocence and laughter. But can I do this? Can I?'

Perhaps after all she was worrying about nothing. Could Tiyi really be so clear-sighted? Her son had surely told her that his wife was pregnant, and a pregnant woman has every excuse to faint, to cry, or to do any other capricious thing she chooses. Especially if she was going to give birth to a Sun. And the message to her father had been clever. It came from a girl who had more important things to worry about than the wish to avoid a meeting.

The bad smell! Mischere had told her the co-regent had said his wife was ill because of the smell. What a stupid excuse! Every year since her birth, Nefertiti had been exposed to the pestilential miasmas which followed the floods and all that Amonhotep had been able to invent was: 'My wife is ill because of the smell.'

'What an idiot he is!' murmured Nefertiti, all the more bitterly because she was picturing the handsome, intelligent face of Maï. How could she have given herself to Amonhotep with such abandon? How could she have let him believe for an instant that he excited her? She shivered with disgust and self contempt. She would never again think of Maï with tenderness, she was unworthy of him. He must never for a single instant know of her love, for he would be unable to prevent himself from considering her with scorn and shame. Yes, because of Maï, because of her love for Maï, she must pretend cool indifference. He would get married and be weighed down with honours while she—perhaps she'd commit suicide? No, she couldn't do that, she had a duty to watch over her husband to prevent him harming the people. For she was sure that once his mother died, Amonhotep would make mistake after mistake. He needed a counsellor. No! Egypt should not suffer because her queen was sorrowful. She must bravely forget her troubles and think only of the destiny of the kingdom; then, when her husband's son was old enough to reign, she would retire. . . . Perhaps she would commit suicide then. The idea of killing herself soothed her aching heart. She was no longer bitter, she was majestically, royally, heart-broken. . . . Poor Amonhotep!

122

'I wish to speak to you about something important,' she replied shortly, 'otherwise I wouldn't have disturbed you before you were ready.'

Tiyi was silent for a moment, and then said in her deep voice: 'The noble Ladies Nacha and Kheti have spent much time with me, despite their eagerness for the refreshments which are waiting on the banks of the artificial lake: if they would like to go on now without me, I will follow shortly.'

'Sit down beside me,' said Tiyi after her ladies-in-waiting had gone, 'and tell me what's worrying you.'

Nefertiti squatted down on the carpet, wondering how she should phrase what she wanted to say. Tiyi wasn't her nurse, to be intimidated by insolence or by a show of authority, for she was insolent herself and the supreme authority was hers anyway. On the other hand she was extremely intelligent and could sense the truth under any amount of complicated phraseology. With her it would be better not to waste time, but to be honest and truthful. Only — too much honesty could do Nefertiti's cause harm; for though Tiyi liked to hear the truth about herself, her deep, instinctive love for her eldest son impaired her judgement and anyone tactless enough not to consider him handsome and faultless in every way had to resign themselves to court disfavour.

The young girl decided to resort to guile.

'I have heard my father wishes to make his son Amonhotep co-regent on the throne of Egypt,' she said quietly.

Tiyi smiled.

'You heard well,' she replied, 'and your ears are as sharp as is to be expected at your age ... for they hear in the desert something whispered secretly inside a room. Whose voice did you recognize among those who discussed the news? Or is it already harem gossip and must everyone be beaten indiscriminately? For nothing has been announced officially and we must punish the indiscreet person with the long tongue, lest one day he give away important secrets.'

She spoke thus to frighten the princess. In truth it mattered little that news of the co-regency was already known.

31

Nefertiti shut her mouth tightly. She didn't want to denounce either Houia or her good Ti, for whom she suddenly felt considerable affection.

'Gossip is like the smell of onions frying . . . the onions are cooked in the kitchen yet the smell spreads through all the palace,' she said carefully.

Tiyi's equine features expressed amusement.

'That's a clever simile, child. Well then, I will reply frankly: it is true that my eldest son will mount the throne beside your father. But does that news interest you so greatly that you've gone to all this trouble so early in the morning just to confirm it? Or do you really want me to tell you the name of the co-regent's wife?'

Nefertiti bit her lip. This was where things got difficult.

'I hope it's not me,' she said shakily.

Tiyi thought the young girl was lying in order to dis·over the truth, and she saw, in this indirect approach, a habit picked up from the harem women whose success often depended on that kind of trickery.

'Of course it's you,' she replied abruptly, 'as you know quite well, since you're the eldest daughter.'

Tiyi's abruptness made Nefertiti angry. She stopped pretending and said violently:

'I know it's me . . . that's why I've come to see you. Because in truth I am my father's eldest daughter and that one fact is sufficient, I believe, for me to be queen one day; I don't need to marry your son for it. The crown passes through the female line in Egypt, when Pharaoh is lucky enough to have an eldest daughter. So why should I be saddled with your son? Especially as I love someone else.'

She stopped abruptly, realizing she had said too much.

Tiyi had paled, but her face showed no trace of her inner anger. She said coldly: 'You are not the daughter of the Great Royal Wife, Nefertiti . . . you seem to forget that. If you had been my child, you might have had the right to claim the throne, but you are only the daughter of a harem woman, and if I wanted you to stay in the women's quarters with your mother, I could give orders for Amonhotep to marry a younger sister, and who would reproach me?'

These words made Nefertiti furious. She remembered her mother's cutting remarks about Tiyi's lowly origins, and used them now to hurt her as much as possible.

'You are the Great Royal Wife,' she said, her voice shaking, 'but from which humble village do you come? You loll about on soft cushions, woven in Nubia, but onto what sand dune were you delivered from your mother's womb? Who has the purest blood, your son or I? I came when my father Pharaoh quickened the seed of a Mitanni princess, the eldest daughter of a Hurrian king, but your rank has not made your blood any nobler, and though your fruit ripened in a royal hot-house it has kept the sourness of a fruit grown wild. I was not born the third of the month of Choiak to be deaf nor the twentieth of the same month to be blind! In my father's palace you are feared because when you speak you are aloof and cold, but I hear and see you are not loved, and many think your pride is only vanity fulfilled. They say pride is a noble quality, and vanity only its common caricature. Do you think that those who say that, and they are many, do you think they will let your son mount the throne? I have only to raise my voice, and they will raise theirs also, believe me. I do not fear to speak thus to you. Even if at present you are all-powerful and I am still only a naked child.'

Tiyi was a forthright woman who admired courage above all other qualities. She knew that Nefertiti had spoken thus through anger, but she admired the straightforward honesty, the pride and the contempt which showed her royal blood. That was what she wanted in her son's wife. Neither for him nor for the throne of Egypt did she want one of those affected princesses with heavy ear pendants, who wallowed in self-indulgence and bowed before authority for favours. Tiyi had never asked a favour from her husband, and when she had mounted the throne, she had not hidden her parents away in a dark corner; she had installed them among the nobility and had never shown Pharaoh any servile gratitude. If he had given her the choice, she would never have loved him and would never have married him . . . but Pharaoh was not small-minded like most of those around him: he had had the courage to impose Tiyi on his court without hiding her humble origins behind an imaginary nobility.

Suddenly Tiyi wanted to know what Nefertiti thought. If she scorned her for being a commoner, it would mean she was too weak to stand against the slander of the harem women in general and of her mother in particular, in which case she wouldn't be worth as much as Tiyi thought, and perhaps in the end she wouldn't be wife to the co-regent either.

'You have talked well,' she said coldly, after a long silence during which she had examined the young girl's angry face attentively, 'and I know that your words are not completely lacking in truth, because, as you said and as I have already noticed, you weren't born deaf. However, you have only repeated things you have heard, opinions which are held in the women's quarters. Have you no personal opinion of me? Are you still too frightened to leave your mother's skirts and have views of your own? You have shown courage in telling me what others think . . . now speak in your own name: I am curious to know with what *you* reproach me?'

Tiyi's calmness threw the young girl off balance. As soon as she had attacked Amonhotep she had expected shouting, insults, violence even; but the cold dignity with which Tiyi had countered her rudeness left her surprised and almost ashamed. She suddenly felt like a little girl who had been spanked for being headstrong and rude.

'What does it matter what I think?' she said obstinately.

'It matters a lot to me. At least try and be brave. There's no need to be frightened: I won't punish you for what I hear.'

Nefertiti was annoyed that her step-mother thought she was trembling before her authority, and she answered furiously: 'I have no reason to complain of you up to now, so why should I think badly of you? But I have no reason to praise you either, so why should I think well? Whether you are a commoner or of noble birth is my father's affair and nothing to do with me. Don't think I'm jealous you're on the throne and not my mother, or that I've come here to plead her cause. My mother is like you, she

It wasn't his fault he was so repulsive. He wasn't wicked, only weak, indecisive, stupid . . . he was like a child of three before his wife and would be as faithful to her as a dog. At this moment of disillusioned magnanimity she forgave him and even accused herself of having grieved him.

She ate alone in her room, and refused to allow herself to be washed and anointed, for she took a strange pleasure in feeling that her dirty body was a symbol of her sombre soul. Amonhotep could come or not come, what did it matter to her? If he came, she would offer herself for his pleasure, but she would be like a corpse, empty and absent in his arms. In this state of impressive indifference, she slept, the lamp still burning.

Amonhotep entered the room and for a long time, lovingly, he gazed at his wife's fresh and childlike face; then he covered her gently, for the nights were damp, blew out the linen wick and returned to the feast in the banqueting hall. Perhaps Nefertiti didn't love him yet, but he had immense patience and inexhaustible reserves of obstinate will-power. Aten would take pity on his servant, and give him the lifegiving warmth of mutual love.

Dawn had scarcely coloured the eastern sky before the palace was humming like a beehive, for on the day of the big hunt, the women disregarded their practice of sleeping long after sunrise, and in the dwelling of the king, as in the house of his humblest servant, it is well known that where there are women, there is noise.

Nefertiti awoke much refreshed. She no longer feared she wouldn't know how to behave towards Maï; she even felt a kind of impatience to meet him, and to anger Tiyi by reducing her suspicions to nothingness.

As her servants hadn't yet arrived, she rose, rubbed herself with perfumed oils and put on a long robe, wide enough to give her ease of movement, very necessary for her competition with her father. It had been a clever move to challenge Pharaoh. Now the energy she devoted to hunting would seem natural and would excuse her apparent neglect of Maï, Tiyi and her husband. For, though her heart beat faster at the idea of seeing Maï again, she couldn't help shivering at the idea of meeting Amonhotep after

123

the confession she had made to him the day before. He wouldn't hesitate to look at her in front of everyone with that moonstruck expression of his which shamed and sickened her.

When she was ready she went out by the veranda, down through the garden and on to the western quay where the great royal *dahabiyeh** were moored. The bustle and noise hadn't reached that far as yet, and the three boats slept, bursting with provisions and vintage wines.

Nefertiti boarded the one on which a purple canopy for the use of Pharaoh had been placed, and sat down in the bows, her legs dangling over the side, to watch the water flow by. It was a mild day, and during the night the smell of mud and rotting vegetation had disappeared, though the heat of the sun would soon bring it back again. Nefertiti felt a vague nostalgia sweep over her: how happy she had been on the little papyrus boat! Remembering it, she felt she would have liked to glide on for ever, even beyond Tanis; on and on in her tiny floating kingdom, towards an ever-receding horizon, travelling hopefully, but never reaching her destination.

It was at this point in her reflections that the royal party arrived. She turned at the sound and watched calmly as an enthusiastic Maï appeared with Pharaoh and Amonhotep.

As soon as her husband saw her, he left the others and joined her.

'We were worried about you,' he said reproachfully. 'Your servants didn't see you this morning and you weren't in the temple of the Aten.'

'I saw you chatting away as you came down here,' said Nefertiti rudely. 'You didn't look worried then, so why worry now that you've found me?'

Amonhotep hadn't time to reply, for Pharaoh came on board and said gaily: 'I told you, my son, my daughter rose early to work my throw-sticks out of true, and make sure of winning.'

Nefertiti smiled.

'I have rasped them all with shark-skin, on one side only, so they will be unbalanced and miss their targets. But as you have

* *Dahabiyeh:* Pleasure boats.

124

surely done the same to my boomerangs, it doesn't matter, for we will still start equal and the most skilful will still win the competition.'

Pharaoh laughed and so did all the courtiers.

'If we ever dedicate an animal to you, my daughter, I suggest we choose the viper.'

'And you the A. . . . .'

Nefertiti bit back the word. She had been going to say: the Achech, that fabulous animal, half bird, half lion, which exactly resembled her father: careless as a bird regarding affairs of state, yet splendid as a lion when it came to hunting.

'The what, my daughter?' asked Pharaoh pleasantly, in the sudden silence.

Nefertiti started to laugh.

'Come close, so I can whisper in your ear, for there are jokes which you, the Sun, can understand, but which others might consider treasonable.'

Pharaoh approached with a frown, and Nefertiti stretched up on tiptoe to whisper to him. The court held its breath, silent and nervous. Nefertiti's forked tongue! Pharaoh had described her exactly. She might nip the king's good-humour in the bud, and fill the clear skies of this hunting party with menacing storm clouds.

But Pharaoh broke into a great guffaw of laughter and everyone sighed with relief.

Giluhepa murmured to her first lady-in-waiting: 'She has surely compared him to that bird which prefers to stay in the nest and hatch the eggs while the female bustles about giving the orders for both of them.'

This acid remark went the rounds of the delighted ladies, for they feared Tiyi's authority and liked nothing better than good jokes about it.

The opening hunt was starting well.

Nefertiti turned towards Maï and said in a natural voice: 'Maï, Maï, what must you think of me, you who knew me when I didn't mind smells! I would have liked to be a better friend and not affront you by being absent from the feast given in your honour, for I remember well that we have played together in the house of the royal children. But forgive me and be happy. For I also remember the throwing lessons which you gave me and soon you will be proud of your pupil. Pharaoh thinks I am boasting, but he has never seen me at work.'

'My queen throws better than I,' replied Maï cautiously, with a graceful bow.

'A flatterer's phrase!' thought Nefertiti, with pain. 'Maï, Maï! You, too!'

She drew herself up, the lines of her mouth bitter, and her eyes met Tiyi's. So she said politely: 'I hope we will see you often at the court of Thebes.'

Then she turned towards her husband: 'I have no throw-sticks, brother, will you lend me yours?'

Tiyi smiled. She admired the natural way Nefertiti had greeted the young man, but she had seen the expression on her face when he had bowed before her. Now she knew she had been right: Nefertiti was still fond of Maï.

The stench grew stronger with the sun. The three great *dahabiyeh* were anchored in a backwater, two hours downstream from Thebes, surrounded by a bed of white and violet waterlilies. Complete silence reigned on board, for before leaving with the hunters in lighter papyrus skiffs Pharaoh had warned: 'Let those who wish to remain here refrain from moving; let those who wish to sleep, do so without snoring; for the birds take fright easily and will fly off at the sound of a tooth hitting against a tooth.'

So the women who hadn't wanted to leave the comfort of the boats had lain down to continue their interrupted sleep, and in the holds the servants plucked fowl for the feast, while the sailors teased them in whispers.

The air was hot and heavy. The huge marsh lay motionless, silent, drained of life. The only moving things were the swarms of mosquitoes which circled above the tall papyrus stalks.

Suddenly, cutting through the long-drawn-out, attenuated song of the insects, came the rustle of wings . . . a high whistle . . .

126

followed by a splash. Then the forest of reeds and papyrus mysteriously came to life, swaying creakingly from side to side, as countless crawling things rustled past. A crane gave voice, a frog dived, the waterlilies bobbed in the ripples like a fleet of small boats, and a flight of wild geese rose against the blue porcelain sky.

Nefertiti, standing in her skiff, was looking for some throwsticks she had lost in the reeds. Her trained cat had brought back only a goose and a thin plover . . . she was glad she wasn't with the others, for her father would surely have laughed at her.

'Surely I hit that other goose,' she muttered to herself, 'and this plover isn't mine . . . I must hunt well away from the others, or my imbecile cat will bring me all the throw-outs.'

She found her two boomerangs, picked them up and signalled Mischere to paddle towards the right.

'Shouldn't we keep nearer the others?' suggested the little Syrian weakly; she was still unhappy whenever she went near water. No one would guess she had once been right down to the delta of the Nile.

'Be quiet!' ordered Nefertiti, her eyes and ears straining to catch the least movement. She was no longer thinking about Maï: her mind was wholly given up to the hunt and her only worry was over the missed goose. Strangely, she wasn't frightened they might meet a crocodile; it was as though the fact they were surrounded by hunters was enough to keep danger away.

She managed to kill two ducks and a magnificent heron, but the sun was at its zenith and she knew it was time to rejoin the others. There was a sound from behind some clumps of papyrus down-river. A crane rose suddenly from the rushes, its wing brushing past so close to Nefertiti's face that she stepped back in an involuntary movement which almost sent her into the water. Annoyed, she blamed Mischere: 'Give me that oar! My poor Mischere, always so clumsy. You look after the game, and don't lose the cat. Next time I'll come alone, it'll be easier.'

The boat moved forward silently, guided by the noise down-river.

Suddenly Nefertiti heard a laugh quite close to her and recognized the voice of Ourel, daughter of Ramose, the Vizier.

Ourel had been brought up in the house of the royal children with Nefertiti and Maï, but she had hardly ever taken part in their games because she was a slow-moving, rather dull child with what Maï used to call a suety character. But that morning she and Maï had never stopped laughing; it seemed that 'suety characters' no longer displeased him. He hadn't joined her in her skiff, for that would have been improper, but he had manoeuvred in such a way that his boat was always beside Ourel's. Even now they must still be together.

Nefertiti was suddenly furious. Before she had time to think what she was doing, she had sent her boat nosing through the thick curtain of papyrus which separated her from Ourel's laugh.

Maï and the young girl, sitting decorously in the prows of their respective boats, were amusing themselves by pelting each other with lotus flowers while their servants paddled from the sterns, uninterested and incurious.

'May this waterlily speak my admiration for your beauty!' Maï said.

'And this one wound you as you have wounded my modesty,' laughed Ourel.

'If you want to play games,' cried Nefertiti in a furious voice, 'go back to the *dahabiyeh*! This is hunting territory!'

The young people froze, their arms in the air. Maï saw clearly from his queen's expression how annoyed she was.

'Forgive us,' he said, abashed, 'we thought we were a long way from the hunters. We left them when they turned towards the south.'

'Your hunting doesn't seem to have been fruitful, my brother,' Nefertiti said derisively. 'Has your eye become less sharp and your arm flabby amid the numerous delights of Tanis?'

'Yours doesn't seem much better!' replied the young man with spirit; and then, wishing to recall these unfortunate words which he had addressed to Nefertiti rather than to the queen, he added quickly: 'But no doubt that is because we have frightened off the game. If you continue towards the west you will find many blue teal nests, and the birds will surely soon return to them, to protect their eggs.'

Ourel said nothing. She was not fond of Nefertiti and envied her rank and beauty. As for intelligence, she didn't think Nefertiti had any, for hadn't she always ignored Ourel?

The young queen knew she must stay no longer; Maï's new polite reserve and acquiescence sickened her. He was no longer a friend, but had become a courtier; his expression was no longer candid, his speech no longer honest.

She turned quickly so that Maï and Ourel wouldn't see her expression, and sent her little boat gliding towards the west without another word. She and Mischere were scarcely out of sight among the papyrus before she heard Ourel's laugh ring out again like an insult.

They're making fun of me, she thought, torn between sorrow and anger, and I behaved like an idiot.

Nefertiti remained in the depths of the marshes for what seemed like hours. She tried to concentrate on the hunt, but her thoughts were in the reed-filled creek where Maï and Ourel were pelting each other with lotus flowers, and she only managed to kill two teal.

She didn't want to go back to the *dahabiyeh*. She even took a kind of pleasure from the thought that people were probably worrying about her. All the other hunters had certainly returned to the boats by now, loaded down with their spoils. They would have waited for her for a while, laughing and joking, and her father would have said: 'She is ashamed to face me with so little game.'

Then Maï would have spoken of their meeting and Pharaoh would have laughed louder than ever . . . because of the plover.

She knew they had called her, for she had heard their voices, and been careful not to reply; she had moved further away, out of spite, fury and a desire to shake Maï's new self-control, so that, in his anxiety, he would at last realize how much he loved her.

Suddenly, not far away, Nefertiti heard her name called in a voice on the verge of panic. At first, she thought it might be Maï and her heart started to beat wildly . . . but alas, it was only her husband.

Mischere resorted to a stratagem. She had noticed her mistress's bad temper, but without trying to analyse it, for the duty of a servant is to love her queen and not to understand the secrets of her heart; but she felt that if she didn't do something, they both stood a good chance of losing themselves in the forests of reeds and being surprised by nightfall in this den of crocodiles. In a loud voice which she hoped sounded natural she said: 'Mistress, I think someone is calling you!'

'Be quiet, can't you!' said Nefertiti angrily.

But Amonhotep had heard. He seized the oar from his servant's hands and paddled vigorously through the thick vegetation. He reached his wife's small boat without difficulty and called out as soon as he saw her: 'Come back, Nefertiti! They are all waiting to start the feast, and our father is displeased!'

Nefertiti didn't reply, but she turned her boat to follow her husband's, her expression furious and her mouth shut tightly.

Greetings and laughter met them as soon as they came in sight of the creek where the royal *dahabiyeh* were anchored. Pharaoh himself said nothing, but went to sit under the purple canopy, the result of his morning's hunting laid out on the deck in front of him.

Servants approached and placed his daughter's birds beside his own, and Pharaoh pretended to have difficulty in counting them. Then, sensing that his daughter was standing near, he lifted his head, and smiled ironically, saying: 'I'm sure you are honest enough to have placed before me only the result of your morning's hunt, for a contest must last the same time for each competitor. In this case I have won easily. But I wish to be a fair opponent, and after all, we hadn't decided on a length of time, so I can only blame myself for having preferred to come back here rather than continue hunting. You may therefore order your servants to bring forth the many birds you must have killed this afternoon.'

Nefertiti knew that her father was laughing at her, but as she wasn't in a mood to jest, she shrugged her shoulders: 'That's all I've killed, except for a big goose which my cat couldn't find, but left to yours,' she said pointedly.

130

Pharaoh pretended surprise: 'If this goose is yours, you may take it,' he said with a smile, 'but that still doesn't give you enough.'

Then, believing that his daughter's sulks were only due to wounded pride, he added paternally: 'Now then! Now then! Don't look like that! The honour is not only for the winner, for in fact you have killed more than I thought. Of all the women who hunted today you are by far the best shot. In truth I'm proud of you. However, next time don't go so far away, for the swamps can be dangerous.'

The incident was closed; everyone regained their good tempers and their appetites. Nefertiti made a great effort to be pleasant and not once did she seem to notice the way Maï and Ourel were behaving.

However, to keep up her spirits she drank a lot, and Ti, who knew her foster-child better than anyone, knew this to be the sign of an aching heart. In consequence she felt it was her duty to be near to her Gazelle, even if she did get snubbed for her pains. But, for the first time in months, Nefertiti greeted her joyfully, saying, in a slightly blurred voice: 'My good Ti, were you ill, that I have not seen you? Come close that I may kiss you, for in all the world you are the nearest to my heart.'

Thus Nut rewarded the patience of her servant: Ti was back in favour, before the eyes of the whole court, and the jealous could die of vexation, for she had been called, 'nearest to the heart of the queen'.

CHAPTER THIRTEEN

As the effect of the wine wore off, Nefertiti began to brood. The words exchanged by Maï and Ourel on the way home still echoed in her ears. 'What am I going to do at Tanis, so far from your charms?' Maï had said. 'Tss! Honeyed words from a bitter heart!' Ourel had replied. 'If my heart is bitter, it is because it fears it will never gain yours,' answered Maï. 'Nonetheless you have pierced it with lotus flowers,' continued Ourel. 'May I aim better with arrows of love,' Maï countered gallantly. 'My heart is well protected from them,' said Ourel with a silly laugh.

Lying on her bed in the dark, Nefertiti thought surely Maï was more intelligent, more subtle than that! True, Ourel was an idiot and would not have understood greater finesse. 'A suety character . . . a suety brain!' murmured Nefertiti with scorn. Did she not realize Maï was making fun of her? And that soon he would come to the queen and laugh at Ourel's stupidity, as he used to on their little sacred ibis island?

Certainly, Maï didn't seem to be paying much attention to his childhood friend, but that was because he was troubled by the new respect which he owed her. Perhaps he was trying to make her jealous by forcing himself to flirt with Ourel? At least he couldn't have found a better way of allaying the suspicions of Amonhotep and his mother. Perhaps even now he was in his room, crying for his lost love. Perhaps he dreamed of taking her in his arms, of kissing her, of fondling her . . . she quivered with longing, and didn't even try to fight against her guilty thoughts.

It was at this moment that Amonhotep pushed aside the veranda curtain. He had been unhappy all day; he hoped that a night of tender love would reassure him as to his wife's affection; that pregnancy was the only reason for her sudden strange behaviour.

'Are you asleep?' he asked timidly.

Nefertiti held her breath.

Go away, go away, she willed, with a loathing which would have stunned the young man if he had been able to see into her heart.

Amonhotep stood for a moment uncertainly. He was reluctant to wake his wife, for he knew she was tired from the day's hunting, yet he felt himself incapable of living any longer in uncertainty. He decided to approach the bed, and ran his hands gently over the naked body he adored.

'You aren't covered and the nights are cool,' he murmured, as if to excuse himself for his insistence.

Nefertiti's mouth had gone dry, and already she felt the strange unease which preluded pleasure, but she made an effort to fight against desire, and because the effort was great. her words were similarly out of proportion.

'Leave me alone!' she said furiously. 'I didn't answer you because I want to be alone. Why is it always me you want? Haven't you a harem like your father? Do I have to be the only victim of your lust?'

Amonhotep's heart stopped beating.

'I thought . . . I thought it pleased you,' he stammered, 'I thought. . . .'

Nefertiti envisaged the silly expression he always had when he looked at her, and she wanted to hurt him, to crush his folly like some harmful insect.

'You *thought* it pleased me!' she said bitingly. 'No, you're so arrogant you were *sure* of it. You, the Sun, did me the honour of visiting me often, and you thought this favour filled me with joy and pride! Remember what I said to you the first evening: "There is nothing in my heart . . . you will find it empty." And you have never held it otherwise. I submitted to you, for you are Pharaoh, the God . . . and the duty of a courtier who wishes to live in peace, is not to go against the wishes of his king! My sighs were lies, my kisses were more lies . . . because, in the land of Egypt, only

133

Pharaoh is powerful enough to speak the truth. Once the others leave the house of the royal children, they can only hope for life, wealth and respect if they are sly and hypocritical.'

She thought of Maï as she said this, for he had lost both his candid expression and his honest speech, and this hurt her more than ever.

'But I'm sick of having played so long at being a happy woman. I despise myself for having pandered to your vanity. I don't love you, Amonhotep, I've never loved you! Only your mother thinks you're irresistible and it's her own fault if I'm speaking to you now like this. Do you think I would have faced the Nile in flood if I hadn't wanted to escape a marriage which disgusts me? You're ugly, Amonhotep, ugly and not very intelligent. You have eyes like a toad; when you look at me, I want to be sick. The touch of your hands makes me want to be sick. I'm going to give birth to your son . . . but don't touch me again. Don't touch me!'

She shouted the last words, and they echoed in the deathly silence.

Amonhotep had begun to tremble as he listened. His world was falling apart. Slowly, clenching his jaws to keep back the sobs which rose and stifled him, he left his wife's room. He didn't go back to his own, but went to take refuge in his 'secret place' on the river bank. It was there that Aten talked to him and he badly needed divine consolation. He was suffering as he had never believed it possible to suffer. He felt each fibre of his being had been bruised and that only the great mercy of his God could help him. He tried to concentrate on Aten so as not to plunge into the depths of despair.

'Thou alone art good . . .' he murmured. 'Thou alone art good. . . . Thou alone art love; Thou dost not feel aversion for a human being. I turned away from Thee and gave to my wife that which I should have given only to my God. I adored her as Thine image, I respected her as Thyself. I trembled at her voice as at the sound of Thine. And all this love I took from Thee. For three whole months I have thought of my wife as I sung Thy praises. I ran to her arms and forgot to praise Thy name. I thought I was a simple mortal but I am Thy son! And Thou hast cruelly punished me. But Thy punishment is just. I thank Thee for having given it so soon, for my despair will be the less. And this is a proof of Thy great Goodness. Strengthen my heart! Take pity on my weakness, for I have only just been born into Thy splendour. O Aten! I will live for nothing but Thy Glory!'

Though these words gave him strength, Amonhotep still ached all over like a fighter after a hard battle. He stayed all night beside the river, waiting impatiently for sunrise, for he had an almost desperate faith in that magic instant when the eye of Aten would flood him with radiant light. Then courage would come back to his aching heart, force to his tired limbs, and joy to his miserable soul. And he would be cured for ever of the torturing memory of his wife.

Nefertiti was feeling uncomfortable now she had spoken out. But she was making a determined effort to find excuses for herself: 'All the same, sooner or later I had to tell him what I thought,' she mused. 'It wasn't honest to let him believe I loved him. The only pity is I waited so long; that was weakness on my part. He must be suffering, but he would have suffered even more if I had postponed my confession. In any case, I'm going to give him a son, so he won't have anything to reproach me for. I'll stay by his side and no one will know anything about how I've just abused him . . . I may even be nicer to him in public. Naturally I shouldn't have told him straight out that he was ugly, but he got on my nerves. He knew quite well I was tired out by the hunt! No, he is too stupid, too. . . . Now he's probably crying like a girl . . . in any case, this time he'll have understood and stop looking at me with his frogs' eyes! How the courtiers must have laughed at his languishing airs — a king can't expect obedience from a people if they're laughing at him. Amonhotep isn't conscious enough that he is king, and it's all Tiyi's fault!'

At last Nefertiti had found someone on whom to vent her anger. Yes, it was Tiyi's fault. She played at being queen, but she hadn't bothered to give her eldest son the character of a king. Nefertiti would not neglect *her* son, she'd teach him how to wear the crown!

All of which excellent reasoning failed to dispel her uneasiness, and her sleep was troubled.

Remorse and uneasiness waited patiently for her to wake up in order to swoop down on her again. At early dawn Nefertiti was already sitting up in bed, her forehead stubborn, her mouth sulky, like a child who has done wrong and won't admit it.

She told herself she wanted to meet her husband and see in his face the traces of the pain she had inflicted on him. Without a doubt his eyes would be swollen with weeping, and grief would have etched deep lines in his forehead . . . he would be disagreeable and cross and the nobles would crowd round him anxiously, each one fearing to have unknowingly displeased him.

But Amonhotep's face was not ravaged by grief, sorrow could hardly be detected in his eyes. . . . Nefertiti heard him speaking in the Audience Chamber and he was as controlled and calm as ever. He rose at her approach and only sat down again when she did. But he said not a word to her; he acted as if she wasn't there. By a curious reflex, Nefertiti felt hurt by this lack of attention. All day she forced herself to laugh and joke with everyone, but she couldn't help glancing quickly at her husband from time to time to see how he was taking it, and not once did she catch him looking at her. During the feast, Amonhotep started a long discussion with Maï on the affairs of Lower Egypt, and even smiled once or twice, just as if his heart hadn't been broken in pieces.

The harem women have consoled him, thought Nefertiti contemptuously. Men were like that: all they wanted from a woman was pleasure. As it happened, Maï too was all man in this respect. The night before he had received, by royal favour, a concubine from Pharaoh's harem, which was why, though his eyes had dark shadows under them, his morale seemed excellent. He flirted with Ourel outrageously and seemed to enjoy her company. Nefertiti was as disappointed in him as with the rest of the human race. She didn't know how she could have thought of him, even for a moment, with affection.

By the end of the day she was so disgusted that in the middle of the feast she suddenly fell into a haughty silence. She stopped glancing furtively towards her husband and completely lost interest in the affairs of Maï and Ourel.

As soon as the dancers had finished their ballet, she pretended to be exhausted, and asked Pharaoh for permission to retire.

The days which followed were all very much the same, and after a while the young queen didn't even make an effort to behave politely to the people in her entourage. She didn't go back to the audience chamber and didn't try to see either her husband or Maï again, but sulked with a mixture of indolence, boredom and resignation. Sometimes, in the evening, she found herself listening to the night noises and her mouth would grow dry at the least stirring in the bushes or the faintest footfall in the corridor . . . then a vague feeling of unhappiness would sweep over her and she would go to sleep with tears in her eyes.

Tiyi was worried. The behaviour of Nefertiti and her son bewildered her. She decided to find out what was wrong, in order to save whatever remained to be saved; for she was wary of the extreme inflexibility of the young, knowing they often preferred to die where they stood, rather than to make concessions. She went one afternoon to her son's study at an hour when she knew he would be there. Amonhotep greeted her with a sad smile which told her of the sorrow in his heart.

'I come to you because I'm worried,' Tiyi said abruptly.

Instinct warned the young man what was bothering his mother, and he immediately tried to avoid a discussion which he did not yet feel strong enough to face; for, though the days went by, his pain hadn't grown less, despite the goodness of his God.

'Let's see,' he said lightly, 'is it the scribe Neferi who has displeased you? Has he again embezzled the necropolis workers' food? I haven't had time to investigate these men's complaints, but I will do so as soon as Maï leaves. By the way, I asked him which would please him most, a trip to Nubia or to the land of Punt. The thought of leading a mission to the incense shores delights him. He is young, enthusiastic, honest and trustworthy. . . . I couldn't choose a better Ambassador to instil the Empire's neighbours with respect. In him they can admire the vitality of Egypt in all its vigorous honesty. It is good that foreigners should turn towards us confidently, thus they will understand that the One God shines for everybody.'

He finished his speech absentmindedly, as if to signify to his mother that their discussion was over. But Tiyi didn't see it that way. She thought to herself: my son has spoken of young Maï with real affection . . . he knows nothing about his wife's secret attraction; so it can't be jealousy which makes him sad.

'Listen, my eldest son.' she said, 'I know you well, and you cannot distract my attention from the thoughts which occupy my mind, for your happiness, and that of Nefertiti, is very dear to me. Not long ago, you told me joyfully of Nefertiti's pregnancy, yet in the last few days you have scarcely noticed the efforts which your wife has made to withdraw from Court life! I fear a stupid quarrel between a young married couple, and have come to see if I can put things right.'

Amonhotep quivered as his mother spoke, and his expression hardened.

'Mother, this subject is a painful one, and I desire you not to touch on it again. However, you should know that it is not a stupid quarrel between a young married couple. Nefertiti and I have spoken together, and, by common consent, have decided that we feel no love for one another . . . only a deep friendship, and a brotherly affection. As we no longer force ourselves to a display of sentiments we don't feel, we have naturally returned to our private occupations. I don't know those of my wife, but as for mine, you know they concern Aten, my God. This won't stop us from helping one another as the occasion demands. And my happiness is still as great at the prospect of a son.'

Tiyi frowned, but she replied calmly: 'An impressive speech, my eldest son! And more impressive still if you hadn't started by saying: "this subject is a painful one, and I desire you not to touch on it again." Truly a curious way to start a speech expressing peace of mind!'

Amonhotep's mouth trembled. He rose and started pacing up and down. After a silence, he said: 'There are subjects a respectful son doesn't wish to discuss with his mother, for fear of having to be rude . . . but I find myself obliged to, to put your uneasy mind at rest. I both love you and respect you, and I ask your advice in governing the kingdom, for before my people I am still a child. But, though it pains me to say it, I wish you to concern yourself no longer with my private life. I know you wish us happiness, but our conception of happiness is not the same as yours. We don't believe in passion. For us, love is a word used by story-tellers. We believe in affection, in friendship . . . in mutual understanding. . . . So, by Aten! Don't try to unite us according to standards of your own! Don't try to reason with us! We are old enough to know what we like. And don't be hurt, my mother . . . though I regret it, I have had to speak like this so that your troubled mind would not accuse Nefertiti of bringing me unhappiness. In fact, she has made me very happy; I would not have wished for any other wife. Don't raise this question again, for there will always be a difference between our reply and yours.'

Because Tiyi was deeply hurt by her son's words, she believed they were sincere.

'Very well,' she said dryly, 'it is possible that youth feels differently from us older ones. I only insisted in the interests of you both, but as that doesn't please you, I would blame myself for troubling you further. Do as you wish . . . but allow me to say you are depriving yourself of a great many joys.'

Amonhotep laughed, so sadly that Tiyi surely would have noticed if she hadn't been wrapped in her own grief.

'Go in peace . . . our joys are as great as yours,' said Amonhotep.

CHAPTER FOURTEEN

ONCE Maï's visit to the land of Punt had been decided on, Amonhotep had plenty to do, and was thankful; it prevented him falling victim to a hopeless pessimism. He wrote to the commander of the fortress of Saw on the Red Sea, ordering him to construct five solid *goubliyeh** of cedar wood, each built for thirty oars and carrying a large sail. He supervised personally all the correspondence with the Great Ruler of Punt and his well-beloved wife. He carefully drew up the inventory of the numerous battle-axes, sharp daggers and precious jewels which he was sending in exchange for Punt's annual tribute of electrum, wood, spices, ivory, cosmetics, greyhounds, female and Kiou monkeys, which was due to all-powerful Egypt. Amonhotep wrote that the floods had been favourable and that the Black Land of Kemet's grain stores were open to their brothers from across the sea if Aten had seen fit to dry up their lands. He filled several rolls of papyrus with descriptions of the Goodness of the Only God and he drew the word signs with care so that the patient occupation of his hand would distract him from the sorrow in his heart. When he had finished this work, he found another outlet for his sorrow in preparing for his own departure, for he felt the need to get away from Thebes for a while, and had decided to accompany Maï as far as the town of Saw.

As soon as all was ready, he went to Pharaoh and said: 'I am returning all the responsibility of government to your wise hands. After I have seen Egypt's envoy set out from Saw to show our glory to a vassal country, I will journey to On, the town of the sun. I plan to found a "house of life" there, a sacred college with

* *Goubliyeh:* Fighting ships.

140

a High Priest, scholars and young aspirants to priesthood. The High Priest of the temple of Rê, my venerable teacher, will advise me on this matter: I will listen to him with respect, and when I have carried out his recommendations I will return to Thebes.'

Pharaoh wasn't too pleased with this arrangement, for he had no wish to be once more saddled with work in the study and the audience chamber; however he knew his son's character too well to try to hold him back when the 'God fever' was on him. Pharaoh deplored, and had often cursed, his eldest son's religious fanaticism. To Pharaoh, all the gods were worth worshipping, even the foreign gods like Ishtar (of whom he thought highly since she had cured him three times of terrible tooth-ache). In his view, heavenly affairs resembled earthly ones, and needed specialists for each administration.

Pharaoh had nothing against Aten, he had even built a magnificent temple for him, but his admiration wasn't exclusive, and he was clear-headed enough to believe that a state of balance comes from divided loyalties, and that peace comes from a state of balance: he would never have been able to keep his kingdom peaceful if he had amused himself, like his son, by alienating the priests of Amon. They had much power over the people and their anger could be dangerous. Amonhotep would realize this when he was older and his enthusiasms were blunted by the years.

Because he believed this Pharaoh did nothing to keep his son at Thebes.

The evening before he left, the young king went to the studio of Bek the sculptor, to order the huge statues which were to stand against the square pillars in the courtyard of Aten's temple.

Upon his entrance, the workers dropped whatever they were doing and flung themselves to the ground, their noses buried in the carpet of multi-coloured dust which covered the beaten-earth floor: white limestone dust, yellow sandstone dust, green from the lumps of serpentine, black from the basalt; dust from grey and pink granite, red quartzite and all the precious and richly nuanced chippings of alabaster, diorite, marble and porphyry.

Amonhotep didn't order them to rise: he knew that, far from disliking such a position, which allowed them to rest their muscles,.

141

the workers were delighted to have such a good excuse to laze at ease. So he sat down in front of Bek and said: 'I don't know when I'll be back in Thebes, and I don't want Aten's temple to suffer by my absence. You had better begin work on the guardian statues of the Sun.'

Bek nodded several times respectfully. 'I know exactly how I'll make them,' he said obsequiously. 'Eight cubits high and in your image. You will have one foot forward as if walking towards the rising Sun, and your features will contain all the nobility and beauty of the well-beloved of Aten.'

These last words pierced Amonhotep's heart like enemy arrows, clearly recalling to mind his wife's cruel words, which he had been trying so desperately to forget: 'Only your mother thinks you're irresistible . . . YOU'RE UGLY . . . YOU HAVE EYES LIKE A TOAD; WHEN YOU LOOK AT ME, I WANT TO BE SICK! YOU ARE UGLY! UGLY! UGLY!'

Bek was a flatterer, all those who surrounded him were flatterers. Their mouths praised the 'nobility and beauty of the well-beloved of Aten,' but in their hearts they laughed at his ugliness.

Amonhotep had turned whiter than limestone from the mines of Tourah and his prominent eyes glared fixedly at the unfortunate Bek, who felt his confidence in himself melting like a honey cake in the sun. Bek had plenty of self-assurance. His gifts as a sculptor had been recognized and appreciated before he himself had begun to doubt them, and no setback had come since to teach him modesty, which was why he considered he had every right to behave tyranically towards the humble workers who took orders from him.

The present strange mood of his sovereign made him feel, for the first time in his life, uncertain and alarmed. In vain he racked his brains, trying to find what fault he had committed, but could think of nothing.

'Have I features of nobility and beauty?' Amonhotep finally asked. His voice was so hoarse, so different from usual that Bek understood instinctively that vulgar flattery would not do.

'Your *soul* has the most noble, beautiful features I have ever seen, your Majesty,' he stammered.

142

This phrase seemed to restore the co-regent to near normality.

'And what form are you going to give my soul, if it is the soul you wish to reproduce?' he asked with irony.

For a moment Bek didn't know how to answer. Finally he said: 'The features of your face, made godlike, illuminated by your inner light,' and he was pleased with his subtle reply.

But Amonhotep was determined to be difficult.

'I have eyes like a toad and a face like a horse,' he said dryly. 'If my soul has nobility and beauty it doesn't show in my features. My face is like a thick wall, more useful than elegant, set up to protect me from the enmity and ugliness of the outside world. My soul, my only precious possession, is hidden deep inside me, and no profane eyes may penetrate my sanctuary. Which is why I am ordering you, Bek, to make the statues of me just as I am: ugly, repulsive even, but with my lips sealed on my secret. Make me uglier than I really am, if such a thing is possible, the better to protect my sanctuary. Standing thus against the temple pillars I will symbolize the mystery of God which only the pure in heart can understand. For those who listen hear, those who look see, and the door stands open for those who wish to enter. As for the others, they stay outside and no one can help them except themselves.'

As he spoke the young man thought of Nefertiti: he had given her his immense love but she hadn't tried to understand him, and no one could help her except herself.

Bek was bewildered by all this abstract talk. He decided that his king hadn't recovered from his strange attack after all, and that once the crisis was over, he would see things from a more reasonable point of view. And if, when that time came, the co-regent forgot that one day his artistic taste had been, to say the least, curious, Bek might be severely punished. They might even cut off his hands, which hadn't known how to carve respectfully. The underdog was always in the wrong.

So Bek told himself he would be faithful to tradition, and in spite of everything he would give Amonhotep's unfortunate face the harmonious features of a god. After all, wasn't Pharaoh God in the land of Egypt?

143

The young sovereign saw from Bek's expression what he was thinking, and realized he wasn't going to be obeyed. All at once he lost his temper.

'Take up a piece of limestone, Bek,' he said furiously, 'and sketch me as I've ordered, or I'll give the job to someone else; if you don't want to do as I command, say so, and I will praise your honesty . . . it is not true that in the land of Egypt, only Pharaoh is powerful enough to speak the truth. It is not true that it is the duty of a courtier who wishes to live in peace, not to go against the wishes of his king. But if you assure me of your good faith and then deceive me in spite of it . . . I will be merciless. I hate deceit as much as I hate lies.'

Bek felt the blood rise to his face at being found out.

'No, no,' he said hastily, 'look, I've got a piece of limestone here.'

'Rise, workers, and ask for a ration of beer from the palace,' said Amonhotep, taking pity on his servants who, their faces pressed to the ground, had swallowed too much dust not to be thirsty.

They went off promptly, after shouting out a very sincere: 'To you life, health, prosperity.'

For two long hours Bek sweated over his work. He thought bitterly of his underlings who were probably laughing at him, warmed and cheered by the excellent beer from the royal cellars, and he promised himself they would pay for it later by doing their work over and over again till his anger was appeased.

Twenty times the sculptor had to recommence his sketches, but Amonhotep was never satisfied. His face was drawn too full, his nose too fine, his eyes too shapely; his mouth wasn't fleshy enough, and his chin should be heavier. His body was too well proportioned, his shoulders too broad, his stomach too flat, his legs too shapely, his hips too slender. Here the sketch was too weak, there too strong. . . .

Poor Bek was in such a state of nerves he could have wept. He was a good artist, a sought-after, praised, considered artist! During his long years of apprenticeship he had been beaten to teach him how to give a human body divine proportions. He had

144

swallowed bushels of dust without being invited to drink best quality beer. He had torn his fingers on granite while trying to learn the golden rules of his art. At last, he had been 'inspired', he had won fame and at the same time a fortune. and now here were all his cherished beliefs crumbling . . . all his hopes too! When possible future clients passed the temple of the Aten they would cry out: 'Who is responsible for these horrors?'—'The famous Bek,' would sneer his jealous subordinates. 'Then we won't order our statues from Bek,' people would say.

The more Bek's hand shook with nerves the more his sketches resembled drawings done by a two-year-old. At last, filled with the bitterness of despair, and with the gloomy irony of those who have no more to lose, he made a sketch which showed an ugly, long-legged person, with distended stomach, worn-out body, bow legs, narrow shoulders and swollen hips, a face like an up-turned gourd, a chin which hung down like a false beard, lips which pouted in the centre and curved up on either side into a grotesque smile, eyes slitted like a knife blade and strangely raised towards the temples. . . .

It didn't take him long to do this caricature for, once the cult of beauty was forgotten, once the rules of harmony and balance were abandoned, it wasn't difficult to sink to disproportionate repulsiveness.

Amonhotep the fourth looked at this perfection of the horrible, and said: 'That's just as I am, just as others see me. Let it not be said that I feel less repulsion than they when looking at my ugliness. An ugliness I will never forget again. . . . I wish to see it standing eight cubits high, backed against each pillar in the court-yard of Aten's temple. The symbol of man whose shapeless clay contains the sanctuary of God. Bek, your skill will be rewarded. But don't be tempted to change my features, for to draw me as I am is an act of honesty, which will be glorified. Those who see these colossi in their place will cry out: "In the land of Egypt, it is not only Pharaoh who is powerful enough to speak the truth. Bek has carved truth from stone and instead of losing his hands he has been named 'Great Friend of the King'. Let us find Pharaoh and unburden our hearts without fear; let us banish hypocrisy and lies and become so pure that Aten will take pity on us and let us penetrate his sanctuary".'

Amonhotep's face seemed to light up from inside and Bek felt an obscure and almost superstitious fear take hold of him, as if he were a mortal who had suddenly seen the infinite power of God. It was only after his lord had left that he recovered his wits sufficiently to take pleasure from the fact that he had been called: 'Great Friend of the King'. Then he forgot the strange fear brought on by his brief mystical insight and regained his common sense, which advised him not to fight the madness of the great, but rather to draw profit from it.

Amonhotep's new feeling of exaltation gave him the courage to say goodbye to his wife, and his surprise visit made Nefertiti's heart beat strangely.

For the first time in a month, Amonhotep spoke to her: 'We leave early tomorrow morning and I would blame myself for waking you before the usual hour, which is why I interrupt your revels now to greet you.'

The ladies-in-waiting were dying to stay during this interview, which might at last throw some light on the curious relationship between the married couple; but they were all too well brought up to pretend they didn't know the rules of good behaviour, and they rose reluctantly to leave.

Nefertiti and her husband waited in silence until the last servant had disappeared behind the last lady-in-waiting. Then she said in a tired voice: 'I wish you a good journey and a swift return.'

'I'll be back in time to see my son born,' replied Amonhotep calmly. 'However, I have something else to say to you: I have thought over your words, I have considered your ideas, and I have realized that they were full of common sense. I honour and respect you for not fearing to make me understand that the first duty of a king is to encourage honesty among his people. Thank you for being truthful in the midst of flatterers. I owe my first virtue to you and will try to remain worthy of my teacher. Fearing to tire you in your present state, I have left the affairs of the king-

146

dom in the hands of Pharaoh, but I would be pleased and re-assured to know that your intelligence and your ability are keeping watch. Once more, may Aten bless you, for you are as flawless as a carnelian from Nubia.'

Nefertiti was embarrassed by her husband's compliments. She saw in his eyes that he was sincere, and faced with his honesty and simplicity which spoke so clearly of his nobility of character, she was ashamed that she had been unkind. . . . A viper! Her father had been right! She was a viper! She wanted to cry, to confess her faults to someone and regain her self-respect, but she had no friends to help her justify her actions in her own eyes. Ti would never understand: Mischere wasn't old enough; she couldn't hope for help from either of them. She shrugged her shoulders wearily and her mouth trembled as she said: 'Don't thank me for something I didn't mean; I don't deserve respect, for it was my intention to hurt you, not teach you wisdom. Your indifference would be less difficult to bear than undeserved esteem. Go, and I sincerely wish you a pleasant journey.'

Each human being is alone, thought Amonhotep with exasperation, each human being is separated from his brother by a thick, smooth wall; he is a prisoner in his cell. Sorrow and joy, hope and despair, all come from within himself. The strong find food, and the weak die of starvation. I have so much love, and Nefertiti has not enough . . . but though I have too much I cannot give her any.

Conscious of his helplessness, he turned and left.

Nefertiti misunderstood the reason for his sudden departure, and thought her husband had been hurt by her words. She shrugged her shoulders, her mouth and her heart bitter.

To allay her boredom, she picked up a small lyre which a lady-in-waiting had left lying on the ground, and drew from it an uncertain melody. The sadness of the tune reminded her of a poem whose melancholy she had never understood, and suddenly its disenchanted lines roused an unsuspected echo in her heart:

> *Death is as near*
> *As the perfume of myrrh.*
> *Death is as real*

As a path in the rain;
Death has drawn nearer today
Like a man sailing home from war,
Like a slave freed after many years,
Eager to find his family again.

CHAPTER FIFTEEN

EVERY year, in the hot season, Pharaoh
and his court crossed the Nile to the summer residence: a palace
of verandas, cool rooms, shady gardens and basins of clear
water in which the women liked to bathe naked. It was the time
of lazy mornings and long siestas, of meals and games in the open
air when the sun drew its heat behind the dusty cliffs and away
towards the western horizon. Then it was pleasant to sit under
the big sycamores, and the air was filled with joyful chatter, songs
and laughter, until late in the jasmine and lotus perfumed night.
'The time of the summer residence' was the happiest of the year;
the women's sharp tongues were too lazy to repeat slanderous
gossip, the men's hard hearts melted into benevolence, the slave's
insolence grew less, the whole atmosphere breathed cordiality.

Nefertiti had always loved the hot season, for the long, idle
days had allowed her to escape to the wild solitude of her sacred
ibis island . . . but that was in the time of her careless youth. She
was an adult now; worse, a pregnant adult, and the great heat
tired her. Pentu had warned her not to treat her first pregnancy
lightly. He often came to visit her and prescribe medicines:
'Honey so the child would slip from side to side without hitting
its mother's abdominal walls too hard;' 'a mixture of slops, beer
and green dates to draw water from the body and prevent a thin-
ning of the blood;' 'massaging with perfumed oils to chase the
male and female pains from the forty-six vessels of the body.'

Nefertiti allowed herself to be ministered to without protest.
It was true that, since she had started taking the honey, she
thought she could feel the seed which grew within her moving
like oil in a goat-skin; as for the massages, they seemed effective

against the male and female pains, for each time that she had them a feeling of well-being filled all her weary body. If only Pentu had been able to cure the weariness in her soul! Since her husband's departure, Nefertiti had lived in a kind of dream. The days passed, but nothing interested her. Often she was surprised to hear herself murmuring: 'Death is as near as the perfume of myrrh.' Then she would shake herself angrily and fight against the apathy which was pushing her gently towards the acceptance of nothingness.

She didn't understand the reason for her strange lassitude, but said to herself: 'It's because of my pregnancy; a child is like a sand devil; it feeds on its mother, eating her from inside, and as it grows larger she grows smaller.' But deep down inside her, she knew this wasn't the real reason for her boredom.

It was the good Ti who, unsuspectingly, helped to solve her problem.

Knowing her passion for reading, Ti ventured into the library of her little summer residence, a room in which she had never before set foot, believing that in the hot season it was unhealthy to feed the mind with controversial matters which might bring on painful swellings. She chose a book casket with what she considered a particularly hopeful title. It was *The Book of Estimable Joys*, and though she herself would never have read such a thing, she thought its contents might be comforting.

Triumphantly she brought it to Nefertiti.

'Here,' she said, 'since you have decided it is cooler indoors in the shade, you can permit yourself an exercise which won't overheat your blood.'

The gods had been good to their loyal servant, and had directed Ti's hand to the right anthology. For, among the poems which made up the work, Nefertiti read:

> *In my youth when I was naked*
> *My belly held my only joys*
> *For thirst I had both wine and beer,*
> *For hunger, geese and graceful quail;*
> *With happiness I laughed aloud*
> *And then one day my serious eyes*

150

Opened to find that drink and food
No longer gave me any joy.
Thirst in my head, hunger in my heart!
I said: 'Of knowledge let me drink,
And women's hearts be all my food,
Browned on a skewer like birds from Punt!
Then I will find my joy again.'
And thus I knew I was a man
And wore a loincloth round my waist.

Suddenly Nefertiti understood the real reason for her boredom: she no longer enjoyed the pleasures of her youth, because she had become a woman. A woman like Tiyi, like her mother. . . .

Certainly, she had considered herself grown-up ever since her marriage and the moment when she had felt desire for a man, but only unconsciously; she hadn't been really aware of it, in all the fibres of her being, until this moment.

This discovery astonished her. She went to her mirror and contemplated her transformation. She saw that her eyes had become expressive, that her plump cheeks had narrowed, that her mouth had lost its sulky, childish pout and had filled out like a fruit, full of eager sap, and finally ripe . . . and a tranquil joy swept over her as she saw that she was beautiful. For a long time she gazed at her reflection in the polished metal, smiling at herself to make quite sure that her smile too had acquired the mysterious grace, the secret fulfilment which she considered to be the expression of a soul come to maturity. She had a sudden urge to underline her eyes with *mesdemet*; then she smeared her upper eyelids with a cream made from malachite, painted her lips bright red and put on her ceremonial crown, an elegant head-dress which covered her hair and set off the delicacy of her face and graceful neck.

'I'm beautiful . . .' she heard herself murmur with astonishment.

Then her eyes fell to her swollen body and she turned away angrily. She couldn't show herself as she was, despite her eagerness to appear before the courtiers in all the radiance of her new beauty. She still had a whole month to wait.

Suddenly she realized that soon her husband would be back

151

from On, and was seized with disgust at the idea that he would see her with her deformed body, on which even the prettiest tunic looked like a lumpy grain sack.

If he comes before the baby arrives I shall refuse to see him, she told herself, frowning. And I told him he was ugly! He could ask Bek to sketch me now, and make a statue eight cubits high, out of vengeance!

For Nefertiti, as indeed everyone at court, had heard about the co-regent and the royal sculptor. Bek had been careful to repeat the story in order to escape a reputation for bad taste. The court had been astonished, but Nefertiti had just shrugged wearily; she recognized only too well the kind of foolish extreme to which her husband went. When he returned from On, he would say, like an angry child, in order to calm his mother's anger: 'Since Nefertiti told me I was ugly, I had myself made uglier than I am, to satisfy her.'

And Nefertiti decided she would annoy him still more by saying, when he asked for her opinion: 'Really, a very good likeness.'

But under no circumstances must Amonhotep see her in this stage of advanced pregnancy. . . . No, she would refuse to receive him.

When the good Ti came to ask her how she was feeling, the young woman told her she had decided to see no one till her confinement, except for Mischere, her slaves. her dear nurse and Pentu. She excused herself by saying she was tired, and too bad-tempered to be agreeable company to anyone.

So for three weeks the young queen remained invisible, killing time with the help of books from the noble Ti's library, and above all with her mirror, which she would sit in front of for hours, lost in contemplation of her new womanly beauty. And she promised herself that once the baby had come and she was slender and graceful again she would know how to make the best of the privileges which went with being an adult.

Pentu had been to visit her and had said: 'Two more weeks and the child will be born without difficulty. It will come into the world with the New Year.'

But five days before her time, Nefertiti's pains began. Pentu hurried to her bedside and frowned, as though he found this advance worrying, but a display of anxiety was part of his job. In order to be respected, a doctor has to be categorical; then, if his predictions are not carried out, he has to feign astonishment.

'Strange, strange!' he murmured. 'I suppose the star Sirius is rising earlier this year. Otherwise I don't understand it. I expect the flood will come before the 19th of the month. Things aren't what they used to be.'

Having thus reassured his listeners as to his competence, he prescribed a draught of poppy and went away again, but not before advising Ti to prepare the bricks in case the birth was premature.

Sure enough, no sooner had Ti placed the two unbaked bricks upon the mohair carpet than Nefertiti felt the need to squat down, a foot on each brick and her legs well apart to leave room for the child.

A servant ran to fetch the doctor, but before he could arrive, Nefertiti cried out twice and the baby slipped from its mother's womb into the outstretched hands of Ti.

The good nurse bit her lip with vexation when she saw it was a girl: a month before she had taken a grain of spelt and one of wheat, and according to a well-tried recipe had soaked them in her nursling's urine and put them in two little bags; of the two seeds, the wheat had germinated and Ti had quite naturally concluded that her Gazelle's first-born would be a boy. Because of this she had told everyone they could rejoice in advance at the birth of a young Sun. Now the court would be sure to laugh at Ti's expense, and the sharp-tongued would say: 'The Great Royal Nurse's eyesight is failing as quickly as the waters drop after the flood. She has taken spelt for wheat and wheat for spelt. Soon she will mistake her excrement for honey cakes!'

Pentu arrived when it was all over, Nefertiti lying down and the child washed.

'Things aren't what they used to be,' he murmured, and Ti agreed with him.

With expert and respectful fingers he examined his queen's colostrum, sniffed it and pronounced it of excellent quality, a

153

certain promise of rich milk to come. Then he bent over the wailing mite, felt it carefully and asked: 'On coming from its mother's womb, did it cry NI or MBI?'

'If my eyes are failing, my hearing's still all right!' said Ti crossly. 'It cried NI, and I dare anyone to contradict me!'

'Yes, yes . . . it cried NI,' chorused the servants.

'Glory to the Gods, the daughter of the Sun will live!' said Pentu in pompous tones. 'I have done my part, the rest is up to the priests. Let the child's body be rubbed with oil of lilies and the mother's with myrrh.'

'I know all that,' muttered Ti, who thought Pentu was making game of her because of the spelt and the wheat.

Three hours later Pharaoh, Tiyi, the High Priest of Amon and the High Priest of Aten, followed by all the court in ceremonial dress, came to bow before the young queen and her first-born.

Pharaoh was annoyed by his son's absence and had taken it upon himself to bring together at Nefertiti's bedside the representatives of the two enemy religions. He didn't want to appear biased, and if Amonhotep didn't approve, he had only himself to blame.

'Merit-Aten . . . let your name be to the glory of the solar disc!' said Pa-Houa, the High Priest of Aten, lifting his palms towards the eastern sky.

'Merit-Amon . . . let your name be to the glory of god the magnificent!' said Ken, the High Priest of Amon, lifting his palms towards the western sky.

And throughout the ceremony the two men, back to back, pretended to ignore each other as they recited their prayers to the four cardinal points.

'You were shaped by Khnum, the potter god!' said Ken.

'Your body is filled with the light of Aten!' recited Pa-Houa.

'Hekt the frog-headed gave you breath!' said Ken.

'Aten breathed radiant life upon you!' chanted Pa-Houa.

'Amon held his hand between the bricks and received you before the midwife!' said Ken.

'Aten was the first to see you at your birth!' droned Pa-Houa.

'Hathor will suckle you and Mut anoint you!' said Ken.

154

'Aten will turn your mother's milk to honey in your mouth!' cried Pa-Houa.

When the ceremony was over, the two High Priests deigned to notice one another, and exchanged spiteful glances which said: Luckily I was here to save the child from your malignancy . . . if it weren't for me she would be dead and her blood on the head of Pharaoh. May you die like a dog, devoured by your own vermin!

Amonhotep got back from On the day before the New Year. The court had returned to winter quarters, in the palace on the eastern bank.

When Nefertiti heard that the great royal *dahabiyeh* was in sight, her heart beat painfully. The time had come to appear in all her womanly splendour. She bathed, had herself rubbed with myrrh, made up her face carefully, bound her stomach tightly with a strong linen band, dressed in a long pleated tunic which showed off her figure, perfect once again, to the best advantage, put on her golden head-dress and all her most precious jewels, then joined her father and her mother-in-law in the throne room to await the ceremonial arrival of her husband and his followers.

When Tiyi saw Nefertiti enter, she was amazed at the change which had taken place. All at once Nefertiti had lost the slim awkward air of adolescence; her firm breasts stood out under the fine material of her garment, her hips were rounded and her figure well-formed, she moved with the supple grace of a full-grown cat and there radiated from her face a womanly beauty and nobility which the cosmetics only served to emphasize. She even seemed to have grown, she held her long, graceful neck so straight.

'Motherhood suits her,' thought Tiyi. 'When my eldest son sees her like that, may I be consumed with fire from the solar disc if his conception of love doesn't undergo a change and become like ours!'

And she smiled contentedly.

Pharaoh himself appeared impressed by his daughter's new splendour.

'Your husband is lucky to have a goddess waiting for him,' he said gallantly, and a curious lump rose in his throat.

'You are very beautiful,' Tiyi said with sincerity.

Nefertiti felt herself swell with pride and joy. She was beautiful. Pharaoh and Tiyi had noticed it, the whole court must have noticed it, and she was impatient to see her husband's face when he saw her.

But Amonhotep didn't seem to notice his wife's beauty. He hardly looked at her . . . only just long enough to ask if she wasn't too tired after her confinement, to congratulate her and to express a wish to see his daughter. Then he went off with Pharaoh to discuss the situation in the delta.

Tiyi saw the vexation which her daughter-in-law was trying to hide behind tightly shut lips and a haughty air, and she was pleased, for she believed vexation was often the forerunner of love.

CHAPTER SIXTEEN

AMONHOTEP was uneasy. He had been at
On for almost five months, and during those months he had
banished his wife from his thoughts, concerning himself exclusively
with his religious duties and with founding a sacerdotal college
where the priests of Aten could be trained and where he himself
intended to teach the doctrine of life. Day by day his mystic zeal
had grown stronger, and there had been moments of ecstasy during
which his body had seemed to weigh no more than a feather. He
had thought himself cured of Nefertiti for ever.

Then he had returned to Thebes, and when his eyes had seen
the beauty of his wife, his body had trembled and his brain had
boiled with violent thoughts and disordered passions. He had left
in love; he had come back insane and delirious.

Amonhotep hardly slept at all, but spent most of his time in the
temple of Aten or his own 'secret place', trying to recover his
moments of ecstasy. Alas, Aten no longer talked to him, but left
him to fight alone against the fury in his blood.

One morning, as he was praying to the rising sun, he heard a
voice inside him murmur: 'Your wife has only had a daughter. . .
it would be well that she should have a son.'

Amonhotep stood up, his eyes wild. No! It wasn't possible! It
couldn't be Aten who had said that. Aten knew very well that if
Amonhotep once touched his wife he could no longer fight against
her fatal fascination.

But each morning, when the sun rose, each evening in his
chamber, the small inner voice murmured: 'Your wife has only
had a daughter . . . it would be well that she should have a son.'

What upset Amonhotep even more was that Nefertiti, superbly

gowned and more beautiful than ever, also rose at dawn and made offerings in the temple of Aten. When he was in his study, she would join him and discuss affairs of state; when he went to the work-site where the slaves were setting up his statues, she accompanied him, and there the young man suffered more than ever as he contemplated, side by side, his wife's beauty and his own eight cubits worth of ugliness. She had said nothing when she saw the statues, and he was convinced her silence signified: That's exactly what you look like.

He had vaguely hoped she would exclaim: 'You're not *so* ugly! Why order such horrors?'

But she hadn't said a word, and grief had filled Amonhotep's heart like molten gold, burning and insupportable.

Unable to bear it any longer, he decided to go away again, using as a pretext the temple he wanted to build in the province of Syria. He began preparing for his journey, despite the reproaches of his father, who was annoyed at the idea of once more having to assume the full responsibility.

Nefertiti's nerves were on edge. For two months she had used her charm to flirt in a way she had never believed possible. She had got great satisfaction from the fact that all the young courtiers had fluttered round her like moths attracted by the light, paying her more compliments in sixty days than they had ever done in sixteen years . . . but her husband hadn't seemed affected in the least. He had remained cold and distant, secret and silent. He appeared to have returned from On full of religious zeal, and the service of his God prevented him from undertaking any other duties. And now he was planning to leave and build a temple to Aten in Syria!

I don't care if he doesn't pay me any attention, reflected Nefertiti with a shrug, I'd be embarrassed if he thought my efforts were to please him. But I married a king, not a High Priest. His mother should tell him the good of the people comes first. If this goes on, I shall have to reign alone!

She forgot that every evening for two months she had jumped at the least sound which seemed to come from the veranda, and her body had grown tense each time her husband had approached her.

When he came to say goodbye, she couldn't help remarking sourly: 'If I am not mistaken, I must consider that my reign is like my ancestor Hatshepsut's, who watched over the riches of the kingdom without a husband. I am honoured by your confidence. Well then, go in peace! I no longer carry a child and I am no longer feeding it, so I am free to rule instead of you. But don't reproach me later for acting against your wishes.'

Amonhotep laughed bitterly. 'I have more confidence in you than in myself,' he replied, 'for it is you who have taught me that Pharaoh must rule over a people of men and not of flatterers. Your eye is as sharp as my mother's, and I am sure you will choose none but worthy counsellors. Do as you wish, I will approve. There is however one subject on which I want to state my views: not only are the priests of Amon cheats and hypocrites, but they are also dangerous. They profit from the people's ignorance, and if we don't wish to see them ruling Egypt one day, we must destroy their wealth, for wealth in impure hands is a deadly weapon. It can buy jealous hearts, impetuous arms, and hands holding daggers.'

Amonhotep spoke coldly and he looked at Nefertiti with a kind of hate, as if she, she with her radiant beauty, her desirable body and her lips which he would have liked to crush with all the force of his great passion, was the living embodiment of the hated sect's infamy.

Nefertiti recoiled before his expression. It annoyed her to think she had inspired nothing but indifference or anger in this man.

'Why don't you stay and watch over the priests of Amon, if you are so frightened of them?' she asked dryly. 'Go without giving me orders, or remain and do as you will. But know that if I am alone I will act as I see fit.'

Amonhotep clenched his fists.

'At least I've warned you, Nefertiti! Open your eyes and don't let yourself be taken in by superstition and stupidity.'

And before she could answer, he left the room.

Nefertiti didn't see him again before he went, and indeed she didn't try to. He had wounded her pride and she promised herself

159

that when he returned, her husband would be astonished at the results obtained by his wife.

Pharaoh was agreeably surprised to find his daughter prepared to accept all the responsibilities he had once more feared would be his. As for Tiyi, she was delighted to see that her daughter-in-law possessed ability and common sense. The two women saw each other more often than before, and little by little, the views they shared and the similarity of their characters brought them closer together. They never talked of Amonhotep: Tiyi had sense enough to realize that the subject irritated the young woman and might upset their new relationship.

Maï came back to Thebes one *khamsin* storm sooner than Amonhotep, and this apparently unimportant fact changed Nefertiti's destiny.

When Maï arrived from the far land of Punt, his boats loaded with riches from the incense shores, Tiyi was annoyed that her eldest son wasn't there to defend the heart of his young wife, deprived of affection, and her body, deprived of caresses . . . If Nefertiti gave in to temptation she wouldn't be entirely to blame, and it wouldn't be Tiyi who ordered her head to be cut off for adultery!

With anguish, the Great Royal Wife watched her daughter-in-law paying far too much attention to Maï. In his company Nefertiti joked, chatted, laughed and flirted dangerously. As for Maï, he might never have courted Ourel: he only had eyes for his queen, visited her in her study, went with her to the temple of Aten, and indeed followed her almost everywhere.

But Nefertiti didn't seem to find her own behaviour strange. She was even curiously at ease with Maï; she liked to talk to him about their childhood and drew endless satisfaction from the knowledge of how much her presence troubled him. Only once had he annoyed her, and that was the day they had gone to the temple of Aten.

'Whatever made Amonhotep order such curious statues?' he had said, with an ironic smile. 'Couldn't you dissuade him? Are not you, who are so beautiful, all powerful over the heart of your husband?'

'It was I who advised him to ignore tradition,' she had replied shortly, 'for Aten is a new and unusual god, and his temple should be in his image, new and unusual.'

Maï had replied with a courtier's speech which had displeased Nefertiti greatly.

'Put like that,' he had said with enthusiasm, 'the idea seems excellent and worthy of your great intelligence! Studying these statues more closely, I see they have considerable value as works of art. The stone really comes to life! You have created a new artform! How I admire you for this, my queen!'

Nefertiti had shrugged her shoulders without replying, but it had taken some time for the disagreeable effect of the words to fade.

However, Maï's good looks spoke much in his favour, and just as she was beginning to wonder if she would be able to resist him, if he ever dared to make a bid for his queen's heart, Amonhotep returned from Syria.

As soon as his burning gaze fell on Nefertiti, she felt the same trouble which had paralysed her on her bed during his visits to her bedroom, and she withdrew as quickly as good manners allowed.

That evening, at the feast, she heard Maï say: 'Lord, if you have visited your harem, you will have seen the ten splendid girls I brought back to you from the kingdom of Punt, and tonight, you will learn that the women of Punt have skins perfumed with incense.'

These words were like daggers in Nefertiti's heart, and she asked violently: 'Have you tasted them before your Lord, to know so much about their skins?'

Maï laughed as if at a good joke, and replied, 'When I was in Punt, I ate the birds of Punt, drank the beer of Punt and knew the women of Punt! But I brought back to my lord live birds to grace his aviaries, and jars of unopened beer. . . . Such is my reply. Need I say more?'

Amonhotep gave a half-smile.

'You are loyal, Maï, let my friendship recompense you.'

You're mad, mad! thought Nefertiti angrily. If you hadn't come back Maï would have taken me in his arms without a qualm and I'd have let him because I love him and I don't love you.

161

She laughed nervously and recited:

> '*I said: "Of knowledge let me drink!*
> *And women's hearts be all my food,*
> *Browned on a skewer like birds from Punt!*
> *Then I will find my joy again."* '

'Sing, oh queen,' said Maï, 'and rejoice your husband's heart.'

'A queen is not a harem woman,' Nefertiti answered sharply. 'She doesn't know how to sing, dance or be agreeable. She is there to help her husband with affairs of State and for the good of the people.'

'I have heard that you know how to do that very well!' Amonhotep said gravely.

'And how to play hounds and jackals!' riposted Nefertiti quickly, in what she hoped was an off-hand tone.

'It is a game of intelligence and you shine at games of intelligence,' said Amonhotep calmly.

Nefertiti laughed rather too loudly.

'My intelligence has eaten up my heart,' she said.

And suddenly she very badly wanted to cry, just like that, for no good reason. She was silent for the rest of the meal, and if anyone spoke to her, she replied in monosyllables.

It was late that night before she went to sleep: she kept thinking of her husband kissing the perfumed bodies of the girls from Punt, and tears rolled down her cheeks. Tomorrow she would give herself to Maï, she decided, because she didn't see why her husband could commit adultery and she couldn't.

She never had the chance to give herself to Maï.

Next day a sandstorm blew in from the south-west.

Afterwards old men would say, shaking their heads, that they couldn't remember having seen or heard about a worse *khamsin* storm.

It started with a loud murmuring sound which seemed to come from everywhere at once like the muttering of an angry crowd, and the noise grew until it became a savage shriek vibrating with menaces and death. Then suddenly the red sky fell in on Thebes. The whole population had sought shelter in their houses and had stuffed the cracks with pieces of linen soaked in water, but the wind was so burning hot that the linen dried quickly and sprang from the cracks like corks from jars in which beer has over-fermented. Sand devils beat against the doors, the hangings cracked like whip-lashes, and big palm leaves, torn from the trees, swept along the ground like immense brooms, activated by invisible and furious hands. In Pharaoh's palace the doors and windows had been shut, caulked, and secured by strong cords which cracked and groaned. In the harem buildings the women huddled against each other, their hands pressed to their fluttering hearts, as if to make sure they still continued beating, and the children hid under the beds. Only the slaves were active, running to strengthen a fastening, block up a crack, or tighten a cord, their bare feet squeaking on the sand which slowly but surely invaded all the rooms.

Even though Nefertiti despised unreasoning fears, she felt anxiety paralysing her limbs. Suddenly she remembered the little princess, alone in her bedchamber. She rose from the corner in which she had taken shelter and ran towards the royal apartments.

The room was in semi-darkness, and the little girl wasn't crying: a tall figure was rocking her in his arms and murmuring words which the young woman couldn't make out, so loudly was the wind whistling and the doors and windows creaking.

Then Nefertiti knew she loved her husband with a strong, yet strangely tender passion.

Later, when she thought back to that instant of revelation, she could never decide exactly what had made her conscious of her love: she had seen Amonhotep, holding in his arms a fragile little life, and there radiated out from him an immense tenderness, a feeling of security which seemeo to create an oasis of peace and calm at the centre of the noise and anger of the elements. Suddenly she wanted to feel his strong arms around her, to rest her anxious head against his solid chest, to hear soft words whispered in her ear, cool as fresh water on her burning skin. She stood motionless, watching the man she had once thought ugly, and saw that now each detail of his face in the dark, shadowed room was dear to her. If Maï hadn't arrived before Amonhotep, perhaps she would never have understood that her desire to be consoled like a little girl was part of her love; she might have put it down to her own weakness. But for fifteen days she had been face to face with Maï and she knew now that the desire she had felt to be in his arms had sprung from an unquiet mind, yes, even the day they had visited the western bank and sheltered from the tail end of a *khamsin* in the Necropolis. They had shut themselves into the house of the Building Overseer while the sandstorm raged outside the door. They had been joking as usual and Maï had said: 'Women are always afraid of the noise made by the south-west wind. It's a good moment for a man to hold his arms open.'

'Keep yours closed, I'm not frightened of anything,' Nefertiti had replied with a laugh, but she had been ashamed of her secret thoughts.

And now here she was longing to be in her husband's arms, and her desire was one of overpowering tenderness.

Amonhotep took no notice of her; when Nefertiti went up to him he simply handed the child to her and left without a word.

Nefertiti too remained silent; it would have been necessary to shout to be heard above the storm and her heart was full of whispered gentleness. She kissed her little daughter's cheeks and continued to cradle her, singing:

> *I am with you in the garden,*
> *I have planted it with flowers*
> *And with all sweet-smelling herbs.*
> *Charming is the lily pond*
> *Which was dug by my own hand.*
> *In the cool of the north wind*
> *Walk we in this happy place*
> *While your hand is holding mine.*
> *My heart is filled with every joy*
> *Because we're walking side by side.*

And as she sang, Nefertiti thought of her husband, and was carried away on the strong tide of her love.

164

CHAPTER SEVENTEEN

Mischere was frightened of loud noises, strong winds, open spaces, and solitude, but when she thought her mistress might be in danger, her heart filled with a courage that caused her to do foolish things. When the fury of the *khamsin* started to shake the palace, she had crouched down in a dark corner, near a large and solid pillar, and from there she had kept an eye on her mistress, in order to save her, or if necessary die with her, when the sky fell in on their heads. But when the door of the northern chamber had blown in with a rending crash she couldn't help burying her head in her hands and crying: 'We're done for! We're done for!' . . . and when she looked up again, she could no longer see her queen.

A mortal terror seized her already overburdened heart. Terrified at leaving her safe refuge she ran into the corridors, crying out to the passing slaves: 'Have you seen the queen?'

And the slaves, seeing her so distraught, became anxious themselves and replied anxiously: 'She's nowhere here.'

In spite of the storm which was howling like the demon Gebga himself, Mischere forced herself to search through the dark rooms, filled with unknown and terrifying sounds, vomited up, it seemed, by hordes of evil spirits, all after her little body.

Finally she reached the royal chamber and almost fainted with relief at finding her mistress there unharmed.

Nefertiti smiled at her gently. 'You've come at the right moment,' she shouted, above the roaring of the wind. 'I can't leave Merit-Aten alone and I have things to do. Stay close beside her, the sand wind frightens her.'

Mischere trembled, but she didn't want to appear less brave

165

than Nefertiti, so she took the child in her arms and chose a solid pillar which she hoped would provide adequate protection. Then, when her mistress had gone, she crouched down, the baby pressed to her heart, both of them reassuringly covered by her cloak.

Nefertiti wanted to see her husband again at once, to make sure that love was the name for what she felt for him with all her being. She was so astonished at what had happened that she didn't for a moment doubt the happy outcome of their meeting: she forgot she had wounded the young man deeply and told herself: When he knows I love him, he will take me in his arms and kiss me. I will beg his pardon for having been so stubborn, but he will kiss the words from my lips . . .

When she reached her husband's study, her eyes were bright and her face shining.

Amonhotep was there all right, slumped in a chair, his hands grasping the arms, lost in a kind of sad dream. He was startled by her approach and at first he didn't recognize her because of the darkness.

'What is it?' he asked sharply, as if he were talking to a servant who had interrupted him at a bad moment.

Nefertiti's heart leapt in her breast like a puppy at the voice of its master, and then she knew that she was really in love.

'It's me, your wife,' she said gently.

Amonhotep frowned. He dreaded being alone with his wife. He had left for On and his love had grown stronger . . . he had crossed the Syrian frontier and his love had multiplied . . . he had tried to stifle his passion with prayers and religious preoccupations, but the prayers and preoccupations seemed only to have nourished his love, which had grown taller and stronger than ever.

'What do you want?' he asked roughly, 'and why have you left Merit-Aten alone? Don't you know she's afraid of the sand wind?'

Nefertiti sat down on the Vizier's stool.

'Mischere is with her, and if I have confidence in anyone, it is in Mischere. She is the only person here who loves me for myself.

166

You can appreciate that, because you too have faithful servants. A good man is rarely alone.'

Amonhotep was startled by this unusual compliment from his wife, and thought she was making fun of him.

'I know you have often reproached me for giving to all who ask,' he said dryly, 'and that you consider it weakness; so why call it goodness now? It is easy to laugh at things one doesn't understand.'

'Once you were too young to know certain things yourself,' replied Nefertiti calmly, 'and then one day your mind grew and understanding came to you. Do you blame your youth for believing what was not true? Do you accuse yourself of laughing at things you couldn't understand? I have grown, too, Amonhotep, my husband; I am no longer the little girl who floated down the Nile and refused to enter the world of adults. At last I have opened my eyes to look around me and life in the world of men has taught me a new lesson each day. So now I can say simply: "You are good".'

Nefertiti's obvious sincerity impressed Amonhotep, but because he had forced himself to disregard the feelings of his heart for so long he replied roughly: 'All right. I'm good . . . now what is it you want from me?'

Nefertiti ignored the insult.

'I haven't seen you much alone since you returned from Syria, and as I took your place beside our father, I thought it only right to give you an accounting of my actions.'

'I have talked with my mother and with Pharaoh, and they have both been full of praise for your intelligence. The Vizier told me of your decisions and decrees, and I know you are too sensible to act unreasonably,' said Amonhotep gruffly, angry with himself for having spoken sharply at a moment when his wife seemed filled with patience and goodwill. 'So, as everyone seems pleased with you, I don't see why you shouldn't continue in power. I would feel like a stranger on the throne of Egypt until I have carried the worship of Aten to the four horizons, for peace will reign between all men on earth when they understand that the divine Sun shines equally for all; the Egyptian will no longer say to the Negro: "You

167

are a miserable man from the miserable land of Kush . . . you are not worthy to kiss the sole of my sandal;" nor to the Asiatics: "You are slaves whom we trample underfoot!" But every morning each one of them will kneel in the dust, crying: "Before you, Aten, we are as nothing." And among all those who are as nothing, what eye is sharp enough to discern the greatest from the least. I have founded a temple in the province of Syria. I intend to found another in the province of Nubia. I will go from east to west as Aten tells me. Here in Egypt the people have no need of me, for you are watching over them. And who better than you can teach them how to love the truth?'

At the thought that her husband was about to go away again Nefertiti felt desperate. She cried out in a shaking voice: 'Can you not forget the words I spoke one day in a fit of childish anger? You praise my honesty because I once said to your face "You are ugly!" but at that time what did I know of ugliness or beauty? What do I know even now? What can anyone know? Ugliness and beauty are terms which each one uses as he thinks fit; they have no fixed meaning. A sandstorm can be harmonious in its power . . . a wild swamp in its savagery . . . an ugly face, because of its expression. Yes, I believe now that beauty is not analysed, it is sensed, it is breathed like a perfume . . . Did not Maï say to you "The women of Punt are beautiful because their skin smells of incense?" Last night, didn't you desire those Asiatics because of their perfume?'

She spoke the last few words with violence. Suddenly all her gentleness had been swept away by a burning wind of jealousy, leaving behind only anger.

Amonhotep couldn't understand the sudden change in her; but the tone of her last words made him forget the rest of her speech. He searched for a hidden reason for her outburst of fury against the women of Punt, and the only one he could find annoyed him.

'Asiatics!' he cried, sitting up suddenly. 'Why speak that word with scorn? Are they any less than you, before the Sun? They don't have your pride, that's all. They are humble because they have been brought up to believe in the superiority of Egypt. They have the humility of those who pay tribute. But in my palace they will not be any less well treated than the proud Egyptian women. They will learn that the only race in the eyes of Aten is that of the pure in heart. Yes, the skin of the pure smells of incense, you have spoken truly!'

Nefertiti's heart beat like a summer rain storm, repeating incessantly: women of Punt, women of Punt.

The sound seemed to deafen her. She only understood one thing: her husband had sampled the girls from Punt! He was comparing her to them, and to her disadvantage! Grief made her deaf to the real sense of her husband's words. Amonhotep had stopped loving her, perhaps he had never loved her. The truth stared her in the face: her husband had never loved her! She was certain of it now, for if he had, he would have fought to make her love him, instead of spending his time running to all four corners of the provinces. He had the soul of a caravan leader who spends his life upon the desert routes, stops when his donkey stops and sleeps with the innkeeper's daughter. Propagate the worship of Aten, indeed! A pretext to sample the women of the provinces in peace. While his wife was left at home to mind the shop, to weep for her absent husband and to shed tears of remorse at having grieved him during his last visit.

She got up furiously.

'Go to Punt then, and found a temple to Aten,' she cried tearfully: 'you'll have more than a skewerful of birds from Punt then, you'll have the whole aviary! But when you take them in your arms, ask yourself whether it is your beauty which makes them swoon or whether they are just paying tribute to the Pharaoh of all-powerful Egypt.'

She ran quickly out of the room, so her husband should not see her eyes were full of tears.

Amonhotep's anger was such that he took hold of his table in both hands and sent it, and all the clay tablets and papyrus rolls lying on it, flying.

'. . . ask yourself whether it is your beauty which makes them swoon or whether they are just paying tribute!' He could think of nothing but these words, which had lashed him as a leather thong lashes raw flesh. Why was he so ugly? Why? Why?

An immense despair swept over him, and with his head on his clenched fists he began to cry like a still-naked child.

If Nefertiti's new love for her husband hadn't been so passionate, she might have been content to suffer in silence . . . but the strength of her love drove her to increase her suffering. She had an irresistible desire to see the women of Punt, to learn from their own lips that her husband had spent the night dispensing his royal favours to them, to see on their lips the smiles of victory.

Hiding her feelings as best she could, she went to the harem.

Amonhotep's harem wasn't a big one. Before the arrival of the ten Asiatic girls it had consisted of twelve Egyptians who were vaguely dancers and three Nubians who were vaguely musicians, with a few slaves and five girls of marriageable age who officiated as harpists. It was an open secret that the co-regent didn't have his father's taste for 'gadding about', as Giluhepa termed it . . . she had also made it fashionable to refer to the women in the co-regent's harem as the 'poor unfortunates'.

Until then Nefertiti had rarely visited her husband's harem, because it contained no woman she would have wished for as a companion, and she knew from experience that a harem was the worst place of all for flattery and slander.

The wind had dropped by this time and the slaves had lit the lamps.

When Nefertiti entered, her head high and her expression haughty, the women stopped laughing and chattering and greeted her with the respect due to a Great Royal Wife who was reputed not to lend a complaisant ear to the obscene jokes which made life in a harem worth living.

The young queen looked closely at the ten girls from Asia, and didn't think them beautiful at all, judging them over-plump and stolid — but she remembered something Ti had said about well-covered women: 'A man is like a pig, in that he loves sows. If he goes to sleep with his hands full, he feels he hasn't been cheated on the deal.'

Nefertiti questioned the girls about the land of Punt, and

170

modesty didn't prevent her from asking them if the women there pleased their men. She told them the co-regent had noticed them favourably and begged them to content his desires to the best of their ability so he would remember their eagerness to serve him. At which point she added in a detached voice: 'My husband much admires the perfumed incense of your armpits! But I forget the name of her among you whom he praised most highly . . . is it you? Or you? Which of you was favoured by my husband last night?'

Her question was greeted by silence.

'Have the daughters of Punt so much modesty they dare not congratulate themselves aloud at having found favour in the eyes of the Sun?'

One of the Nubians shook her head and replied in a deep, musical voice: 'The lord did not come last night. Not even to listen to my singing, though I know he likes it.'

For a moment Nefertiti didn't understand. Then, suddenly, she realized how foolish she had been: she had just offered up her jealousy as a subject for harem slander. She knew she would hardly have left the women before they would be whispering among themselves.

She felt the blood rise to her face and tried to make good her mistake.

'My husband talked of you so warmly, O daughters of Punt, that I was sure he had come on to you after his visit to me.'

The women didn't reply and Nefertiti knew that their little brains were busy inventing obscene jokes to amuse their lonely evenings once their queen had left them. She didn't dare to go immediately; she didn't want it to look as if the only reason she had visited them was to get information about her husband's love affairs. Consequently she sat down on a cushion and asked the Nubian to sing, and drown with the beauty of her voice the sad sounds of the receding sandstorm.

And as the Nubian's voice rose, warm and full, Nefertiti thought over what she had just learned.

Amonhotep hadn't sampled the daughters of Punt.

Because she couldn't remember all he had said, she finally came to the conclusion he had wanted to make her jealous. And if that were the reason . . . he must still love her! For he had loved her, there could be no doubt about it. The care he had taken of her at the beginning of their marriage, the burning glances he had given her, the words he had so often murmured on their nights of love. His departures too! Departures which could surely be interpreted as flight! What madness had made her ruin everything, with her sudden flare of jealousy over the girls from Punt? It was Maï's fault! No, it was entirely her own fault. She had listened to the voice of anger, and in her grief, she had again tried to hurt Amonhotep.

She was ashamed of herself. Before the song was finished she briefly congratulated the Nubian and went off to try and mend what her blind jealousy had so nearly destroyed.

Preferring to eat alone in her apartments, she sent Mischere with her excuses to her father and mother-in-law — and she also entrusted her with a personal message for Amonhotep: 'My mistress has something so important to say to you that it cannot wait until tomorrow. She will stay awake until you come, but she begs you not to cut short your enjoyment of the feast.'

Amonhotep was disturbed by these words, for he feared his wife's bedchamber more than any other place of temptation, especially during the hours when the mind begins to sleep and thus gives free rein to the natural violence of the senses.

He prolonged his stay in the banqueting hall as long as possible, hoping that Nefertiti would go to sleep while waiting for him: he bolstered up his courage by means of wine, taking care, however, not to drink too much and find himself deprived of common sense; finally, from the depths of his heart he begged Aten not to abandon him at this hour of trial and, bravely, headed for his wife's apartments.

Nefertiti wasn't asleep; she wasn't even considering sleep. She had herself bathed and anointed, sent her servants away and now she waited, in the pale lamplight, attentive to the least sound, her nerves on edge, her throat dry, as at the start of her marriage. A kind of modesty had made her cover her nakedness with a fine white shawl, while a thousand times she had repeated the words she meant to say, a thousand times she had imagined her husband's replies, her story ending with a kiss which filled her mind until her body trembled with desire.

Suddenly she heard her husband's footsteps. Her assurance and her imagination left her. She sat up on the bed, her eyes frightened, her mouth open, her two hands clutching the shawl. She couldn't remember the gracious phrases she had chosen while she was alone; only one idea filled her mind: her husband was about to come in.

Amonhotep entered, silent and severe, and they stared at each other without moving, both of them concentrating on their fear. Then, as the silence looked like continuing indefinitely, Amonhotep took it upon himself to put an end to the anxiety which gripped his heart. He said coldly: 'You have something important to say to me, so here I am. I didn't wait till morning.'

Nefertiti's lips trembled.

'Come nearer, for though the south-west wind has dropped, the storm still growls above us and I cannot shout what I have to say.'

The young man approached unwillingly and stopped three paces from the bed.

'There . . . I am nearer,' he murmured.

'I couldn't sleep without asking your forgiveness for what I said earlier this evening,' said Nefertiti in a small voice.

Amonhotep's breath came more quickly. Her words were so unexpected that he stammered: 'I was angry too . . . I . . .'

His embarrassment gave back to Nefertiti some of her presence of mind. She rose from the bed and walked towards her husband, who backed away.

'It wasn't really what I meant to say at all, but . . . I . . . remembered the women Maï brought back to you from Punt and I let myself give way to . . .'

She hesitated over the word 'jealousy' because she was afraid of appearing ridiculous in the eyes of the man she loved, and who, suddenly, she was not at all sure loved her in return.

'. . . to jealousy,' she said finally, blushing with shame.

173

Amonhotep stared at her with the thunderstruck expression of a goat spared by the lioness from whom it expected nothing less than a savage bite. Fearing he had not heard properly because of the storm which, in fact, did still rumble above them and was capable of deforming sounds, he repeated: 'Jealousy?'

Nefertiti took a deep breath: her husband wasn't angry and he wasn't laughing at her. . . . She smiled with new-found confidence.

'Yes. . . . I meant to tell you that I love you, not a little as a stranger loves a stranger, nor much, as a sister loves her brother, but completely, as a wife loves her husband. Perhaps even more than that . . . I love you with love . . . I . . .'

She hesitated as she saw the stupefied expression on Amonhotep's face. He didn't look at all like a lover gratified at last, but more like a child terrified by some nameless fear.

Perhaps she was mistaken after all. She bit her lip and tears sprang to her eyes. There was a long silence. Then, convinced she had made a fool of herself, and overcome by grief, Nefertiti cried out in a voice which shook with sobs:

'Yes, it's true! I love you with love . . . why don't you laugh? It's ridiculous enough!'

As she turned to flee, Amonhotep seemed to come to life. An immense joy surged through him; he caught hold of his wife almost brutally, pulled her close and held her tightly in his arms while she sobbed. His big frame trembled like a papyrus umbel in the north-west wind and happiness surged through his limbs with such vigour that he almost hugged his young wife to suffocation point. The goodness of his God was at last visible to his servant's eyes. . . . Aten hadn't let Amonhotep destroy his love because He had seen further than the suffering in His servant's heart, and if He had permitted this suffering, it was so that his love should be cleansed of all impurities, like fine Nubian gold after smelting.

With a gentle hand Amonhotep raised his young wife's face. How beautiful she was, despite the *mesdemet* which streaked her cheeks, despite her reddened nose and swollen eyes. . . .

Nefertiti sniffed, and smiled up shyly at him.

Then the blood beat in Amonhotep's ears, he grasped her

shawl with a burning hand and pulled it slowly down the quivering back of this body which belonged to him—to him, the ugly man to whom, up till that moment, women had only paid tribute.

And, as at the end of Nefertiti's thousand stories, their lips met in a kiss which lasted as long as their desire.

That night, Nefertiti conceived in fervour and in happiness.

Nine months later, she gave birth to a daughter whose first cry was 'MBI'. But no one heard this wail of death.

The little princess was called: Meket-Aten.

PART TWO

AKHENATEN

CHAPTER ONE

AMONHOTEP IV was in his study, seated
on an ebony chair, his mouth hard and his eyes angry as he
stared at the four wax images which were spread out like so many
deadly scorpions upon his table. Servants had found them that
very morning, hidden at the four cardinal points of the palace:
the first two by chance and the two others because of the suspicions of Ramose, the Vizier. In his youth Ramose had spent
three years in the service of the priests of Amon and had learnt,
among other things, that objects of witchcraft were always placed
at the four cardinal points so no help could penetrate the enclosed
area. The poor man had been especially shaken when he saw that
the images represented two Oxyrhyncha, a Tiger Fish and a
Barbus, for these fish were of the species which had eaten Osiris's
reproductive organs at the beginning of time, when Isis was trying
to reassemble the scattered fragments of her husband cut to
pieces by his brother Seth . . . and this meant that an enemy of
the king wished to see him stricken with impotence and sterility.

Weighed down by fear, Ramose had gone in person to the co-
regent, carrying the wax objects as though they burnt his fingers.
He had said in a shaking voice: 'Majesty whose light shines in
the east, the south and the west, today we are in the fourth year
of your reign, the sixteenth day of the first month of the summer
season. Your light has made Egypt prosperous, your wisdom and
that of your well-beloved wife, the mistress of the Two Kingdoms,
has led your people along the paths of righteousness and truth.
You are good and generous to your friends, magnanimous and
just to your enemies . . . and yet an evil heart has flourished in the
shadow of the land, as a viper gains strength in the dark places

under the stones. Its poison sacs have swelled, and it has opened its jaws to bite. It has cast upon you the spell of sterility, so you will have no male children.'

As he spoke, the Vizier hadn't been able to resist a quick though respectful glance towards that part of the royal loin-cloth hiding the organ which engendered Suns, with the distressing idea that he ought to ascertain whether the spell had already achieved any unfortunate effects. For who could say how long the evil fish had lain at the cardinal points of the palace before being discovered?

Amonhotep was troubled as he reflected on all the hate and hostility the images represented.

He only knew of one real enemy: the priests of Amon. The priests of Amon were the only people who had reason to desire his fall. For four years Ken-Amon and his priests had suffered from their king's public indifference; every morning for four years they had been forced to listen to the choir of fifty singers in the temple of Aten, quite near to their own, and the hymn to the Sun, bursting from fifty vigorous throats, had offended their ears. They had also had to bear the knowledge that their own faithful and lucrative flock was growing smaller, and that offerings were being rationed. The hearts of the priests of Amon had grown bitter.

Amonhotep's tight mouth relaxed into a smile: from now on, he had the excuse he needed to punish these oppressors of the people severely.

Until then he had never directly attacked the priests of Amon; not from weakness, but out of respect for his father, who disliked trouble. Amonhotep had contented himself with ignoring both their insolence and the hands they stretched towards the treasures of the crown. Parallel with this public scorn, he had worked actively to spread the holy doctrine of Aten: he had founded many 'houses of life', sacerdotal colleges where he himself often taught. He had discussed his theories with the court nobles and with foreign visitors and, for the more simple-minded masses, he had adopted a system of charity and justice: to this end he had made regular distributions of corn, vegetables, fish

180

and beer to the workers in the mines and the cities of the dead, taking care that the heads of the work-gangs and the scribes put nothing aside for personal profit. He had also done away with the gangs of Nubians, armed with rods made from the central ribs of palm leaves, who had accompanied the tax collectors on their journeys to induce the peasants to pay up. Nowadays tax collectors were instructed to ask politely for the tributes of grain, and were told not to be too severe with farmers who had had a bad harvest, but rather to express the wish that Aten grant them a better one next time. In the Hall of Justice, dominated by a picture of the Sun, whose long rays ended in compassionate hands, plaintiffs were listened to with attention and impartiality; errors and ill-will no longer crept into the judgements. As for the offerings which the priests of Aten asked from their faithful, these mostly consisted of purity and uprightness, with, according to the means of the worshipper, fruits and flowers, the symbols of life's fecundity and beauty under the Sun.

In short, Amonhotep had taken the greatest care to inculcate into his people the conviction that the adoration of Aten only demanded gifts from the heart, that it made masters honest and eased the lives of the poor.

Equally anxious to underline the Universality of Divine love, the young king took special pleasure in enrolling foreigners in his service. Though he knew how fiercely sectarian his courtiers were, he had named an Asiatic, Dudu, as First Servant, High Chamberlain, Mouthpiece of the Land, Commander in Chief and Head of all Inspectors of Works. He had gone further: he had made Mahu, the head of the Medjai* police force, 'Great Friend of the King'. He had even granted him the war-axe and the fan, insignia of those favoured posts, so that the Nubians could hold their heads up among the noblest of the Egyptians.

A storm of scandal had threatened, but it had not broken, because the co-regent had said in public: 'I honour highly the man who is intelligent enough to understand that races are like guilds: they are formed, not by men of the same colour, but by men with the same skills. Thus there is a race of wise men and a

* Medjai: A Nubian tribe from which Pharaoh recruited his police.

181

race of fools, a race of the educated and a race of the simple. I honour the intelligent man who understands this, I esteem him and desire his company, but I despise stupid vanity, swollen with self-conceit, I disdain it and wish to see it exiled far from the world of real men who live in the sight of Aten!'

Hearing this, those who were vain and swollen with self-conceit had granted themselves enough intelligence to applaud a theory dear to the heart of their open-handed king. They had pursed their lips, laughed among themselves and said: 'Let those who think differently be counted among the unintelligent! We of good sense have no difficulty in grasping the point of this argument. In truth, we find it quite natural that races are like guilds.'

In this way Amonhotep had muzzled the fools who, as he knew from experience, were far more dangerous than horned vipers.

All that remained now was to pull the sting from the priests of Amon; then the immense peace of God would anoint His peoples as if with perfumed oils, from one end of the earth to the other; brother would smile at brother, the Great would take pity on the Small and the Humble would no longer fear the Powerful.

When Amonhotep thought of this glorious era, he was filled with a mystic exaltation which swelled his chest and lit up his face with an inner flame which frightened the uninitiated. Even his mother was worried.

'You have certainly caught swamp fever,' she would say. 'You had better see Pentu about it.'

Amonhotep would smile without replying. What was the good? His mother was a woman full of common sense, but not subject to religious fervour. Only his wife understood; she had received the Teaching with an eagerness which equalled his own. Because Nefertiti approved his actions so completely, he felt capable of overcoming all difficulties, forcing all retreats, conquering all strongholds.

And now the priests of Amon had taken the last step which separated them from the abyss which was going to swallow them up. These magic images would turn against those who had moulded them.

'I'll close their temples,' murmured the young man with concentrated rage. 'I'll distribute their goods to their stupid followers who ruined themselves to make the priests rich. I'll have the name of Amon and of his wife Mut hammered off the monuments and tombs . . . then, when they are no longer among the living, they will disappear for ever, for their name will be forgotten. They want war? They will learn to their cost that I am not afraid of that!'

He rose suddenly, determined not to waste any more time. With long, nervous strides he crossed the rooms and courtyards to his stables, where the stableboys were only pretending to groom the horses while they reflected happily that the midday sun would soon indicate the hour of rest.

When they saw their sovereign's approach they were so unpleasantly surprised by the unusual privilege of contemplating Supreme Authority face to face in the simplicity of a place reserved for horses and their miserable selves, that they flung themselves spontaneously down onto the manure, the curry combs still clutched in their outstretched hands, their noses buried in horsedung and their hearts beating with remorse at having been caught shirking their work. Amonhotep's voice stimulated their zeal in a way remarkable at that hour above all others unlucky for a display of energy, and while they busied themselves with harnessing the royal coursers to the superb gold chariot, they were overcome by a superstitious respect for the co-regent, who, even at the hottest moment of the day, showed such determination and vigour.

Amonhotep did not send for his bodyguard. He mounted his chariot, cracked his whip and left the town with the rapidity of a waterspout in the direction of the great temple of Amon at Karnak. At high speed, he turned into the paved avenue which ran beside the temple of Mut, reached the alley of the sphinx which led to the south gate and burst into the enclosure of unbaked bricks, much to the terror of the guards who were brutally woken from their happy midday snooze. His entry into the courtyard had the effect of a stone thrown into a calm pool. The idlers were seized with feverish activity. The *Kheriheb**, informed hastily, ran out to greet his sovereign, his back parallel to the ground,

* *Kheriheb:* Lector-Priest.

183

his head between his outstretched arms. His emotion was so great, his field of vision so restricted, and his pace so rapid that he only just avoided bumping into the sacred person of the co-regent, who was standing aggressively near his chariot.

'This is an unmerited honour which you do us, O radiant Horus-of-the-glory-of-the-Sun! But the star, your father, who sets light to the sky, has a burning gaze at this midday hour. Forgive my presumption in suggesting to you the cool shade of the inner rooms. I . . .'

With the handle of his whip, Amonhotep pushed the troublesome fellow aside and headed, his face hard, his mouth a thin line, towards the apartments of Ken. He was certain to find him, if not at table, at least being anointed with perfume, an indispensable operation before a meal in this season of dog days when the body so quickly became sticky with evil-smelling sweat.

Without pausing Amonhotep entered the High Priest's magnificent chamber, and found him just being draped in his pleated robes.

Ken was a tall man, still strong and muscular at an age when flesh usually falls in around the bones like the pulp of a dried fruit. He had a hard mouth, an experienced eye, tightly pinched nostrils and a forehead scored with lines of meditation. His innate sense of power gave him a proud bearing which he didn't drop even before Pharaoh himself, for he believed that the sacred character of his rank necessitated a high carriage of the head and a majestic insolence. This attitude made him cold and unfriendly to lesser mortals; he rarely smiled and never wasted words. The terror he inspired seemed natural to him, and it frustrated him that he could not make the same impression on the royal family as on the rest of his followers. He detested the Amonhoteps in general because their position gave them the self-confidence to treat him haughtily and fearlessly; more particularly he hated the young co-regent, whose actions he contemplated with scorn, telling himself that one day, when he was tired of being magnanimous, he would slap down Amonhotep's pride like that of a spoilt child, and show him who was the real master of Egypt.

184

Ken was not impatient like a peasant so eager for profit he would teach monkeys to climb into fig trees and gather the fruit before it was ripe. His refined tastes led him to prefer the quality of pleasure rather than the premature satiation of desire. The moment for settling accounts would come. And then—woe betide the co-regent!

The High Priest looked at Amonhotep as a scribe looks at a peasant, with a kind of scornful pity. This fool, taking advantage of his rank to enter as though he had come to find a slave in his hovel! Without a herald, without a procession, abruptly and insolently, and now he was standing there with his legs apart, like a commoner, arrogant as a freed slave.

The High Priest forced himself to bow before the man who was still his lord, but not until he had taken the time to fix to his belt the leopard skin head which was part of his insignia of office.

With an angry and discourteous gesture, the co-regent dismissed the servants, as well as the poor *kheriheb* who stood, undecided and terrified, on the threshold.

'I am sorry to delay the moment of your meal,' he said in a hard voice in which dislike and irony could be heard, 'for I know that since the sun rose you have been rejoicing at the thought of meeting face to face the roast fowl, the sliced beef, the cakes of fine flour, the delicious fruit, the excellent wine and the first quality beer which the god Amon sends you for your midday meal by the pious hands of his worshippers. But urgency dictates my incivility.'

Ken's eyes flashed dangerously.

'The king is the only one on earth who can never be uncivil,' he replied.

Amonhotep's lip twisted scornfully.

'You're right, Ken, he is the only one on earth who can show his feelings honestly, for he is not held back by the fear of being accused and condemned by men more powerful than himself. The words you have just spoken may save your life, for they make me think that perhaps those images which you hid at the cardinal points of my palace were only put there as an interesting experiment: perhaps, you wanted to find out if, once I had become

185

impotent, I would keep my straight-forward character, or whether I would start to crawl, resort to cunning, turn this way and that with fear in my heart and deceit in my soul, like everyone else on earth? But I have come to reassure you, Ken, I have come to proclaim that my reign will be one of virtue and honesty. Don't fear any longer to tell me what you think. To the man who has the courage to say to me: "You are ugly," I will reply: "You speak the truth. Let this honest man be given recompense in gold!" To the man who looks me in the eyes and says: "I hate you and I spit on Aten," I will reply: "That is your right, for you were born free. My servants, give this honest man sufficient provisions and rings of gold to take him to some corner of the earth where the solar disc does not shine." For a man who demands justice is listened to with sympathy, and no one, not even Pharaoh, can force him to support a yoke which irks him.'

Having said this, Amonhotep placed on the ebony table the four white wax images.

'I give you back your property, Ken,' he said, 'count them, make sure I haven't kept for myself a single one of these works of art.'

Ken frowned.

'I don't know what you're talking about,' he said. 'These objects are not mine.'

Amonhotep shook his head and said in scornful tones: 'Didn't you hear what I said? Why do you tremble before me? Don't you understand I honour frankness and hate hypocrisy? If you admit: "These objects of sorcery are mine, I had them moulded with you in mind and I myself engraved the magic formulae," I will ask you, "Why did you do that, my brother?" And if you answer: "To experiment upon your character," I will appreciate your scientific mind. If you reply: "It is because I desire that you shall lose your virility before you have a son; I want to dethrone you, save the people from paying so few taxes, and rescue the priests of Amon from their increasing misery. God created the world so man has a chance to buy for himself joys, peace and riches in heaven. And he has instituted the priest to sell them" — If you say that, Ken, I will admire your honesty; instead of cutting off

186

your head, I will give you provisions and gold rings. You have nothing to fear by being honest.'

Ken thought quickly. He had had nothing to do with the ridiculous affair of the wax images. Thank Amon, his methods were more subtle than that! There was no time to find the guilty man and assuage the co-regent's wrath by handing him over, but perhaps a display of wounded dignity would work. He would not have to feign much: he was enraged with whoever had risked spoiling his own ripening vengeance in order to satisfy a vulgar, personal hate. For Ken didn't believe that his own hate was dictated by personal feelings; he ruled over his kingdom and was persuaded that he thought, spoke and worked for his subjects.

'I am happy to learn I can talk from my heart without running the risk of disgrace,' he said, making an effort to speak calmly; 'happy also for this occasion which will allow me to clear up with your Majesty certain misunderstandings which have created enmity and suspicion between us.'

His flashing eyes looked straight into Amonhotep's, the better to persuade him of his honesty.

'These objects are not mine,' he continued forcefully. 'I have no idea to whom they belong and I beg your All-seeing Divinity to understand that I am not lying, that I have no need to lie. The High Priest of Amon, chosen by the gods, instituted by your divine father, has not, and cannot have, a base nature capable of carrying out such a vile, and above all such a stupid action. This is the act of a man frightened of your power, and I am not frightened; what should I fear when I carry out to the letter the tasks for which I was elected? This is the act of a fool, and I do not have the right to be a fool, for I am responsible for Amon and his faithful followers, and I know only too well you are not sympathetic towards us. Would I risk my flock's freedom to worship Amon in order to satisfy a personal resentment? Anyway, you know how much respect and affection I have for the royal family. . . .'

This made Amonhotep lose his temper completely.

'I almost believed you, Ken,' he interrupted, 'fool that I am, I was beginning to agree with your reasoning! But you make the mistake of lying too impudently. "The respect and the affection I have for the royal family" indeed! Base flattery! The flattery of a paid employee!'

Ken drew himself up and said in a voice which shook with repressed rage: 'I am no longer paid. I get nothing from the crown.'

'You are right. Not only do you get nothing from me, but I teach the worshippers of Amon to give you nothing. Daily you see your fortune and your power grow less. Today, you possess what is necessary to have yourself anointed before a meal; tomorrow, you will have to eat with the smell of your sweat in your nostrils, and this distresses you, for your stink is rank. I am no seer, but I have a sharp sense of smell, and beneath the perfumed oils with which you cover your body I sniff the spawn of the Oxyrhyncha, the Barbus and the Tiger Fish. On the pediment of the temple to your god is written: "Let he who comes into this sanctuary be pure, be pure, be pure, be pure!" Do you think the injunction to "be pure", four times repeated, was a deranged sculptor's error? Is that why you greet your god morning and evening with such evil-smelling anger and hate in your heart? Are you not afraid of his displeasure? No, you are not afraid, and I will tell you why: because your soul is dry and shrivelled . . . you believe in nothing, neither in Amon nor in any other god. You impose your authority by whipping, by cutting off ears, by pulling out tongues, without reference to the Hall of Justice, for your pride would suffer if a slave won his case against you. You keep up the barbarous custom of Amon's sacred harem, for your lust drives you to possess virgins before their husbands, although hypocrisy makes you hide these evil desires from the eyes of men, who still believe in your purity as a priest. Now Ken, the time has come to reply to the accusations which I make against you. I am judging you now, you and your god, who ask and ask from men and give them nothing in exchange. Yes, tell me, what do you bring to men in exchange for their offerings? Even if I judge you as a merchant, you cannot win, for as a merchant you have robbed your clients. You have sold them nothing but wind against good gold! Suffering, my people come to you; suffering, they return

188

home again. As a merchant, you have robbed them; as a priest, you have not fulfilled your office. What have you to say in your defence and in defence of Amon who is as much a cheat as you are, for after all this time he hasn't seen fit to put an end to the damage you cause?'

Ken's skin had taken on the dirty yellow of a papyrus roll too long hidden from the light. But his eyes burned like the red metal of a dagger when the blacksmith hammers it, flashing with thoughts of death.

'What can I say in defence of myself and of my god,' he stormed, forgetting it was a time for cunning and calm, 'when whatever I say will be turned against us, for you have come here to accuse me, not to listen! These wax objects are a pretext . . . perhaps the High Priest of Aten made them to your orders because you need a pretext to attack me? "Ken has committed a crime against the king! Ken deserves exile or death and his goods will be confiscated by the crown!" But I will cry aloud to Egypt these words from the book of *Precepts for Merikara*. . . . "The poor do not speak impartially," for he who says: "I want . . ." is not impartial, he is biased in favour of those who give!'

Amonhotep sneered: 'Your riches would be to my treasure as a drop of water is to the sea. I would as soon touch them as I would the cursed gold of a criminal. I will return them to those you have defrauded, I will distribute them to those you have terrorized. The world will know I am not poor and do not say: "I want . . .", and your defence will disappear. I too will invoke *Precepts for Merikara*, saying to all men: "God is more pleased to receive the virtue of an honest man than the ox of the iniquitous." I will remind my people of that passage in *Admonitions of Ipoour* which follows a description of the evils of a society given up to crime, hypocrisy and debauchery because their priests no longer believe in anything: "The Saviour, the kindly conqueror comes. . . . It is He who will throw water on the flames. He is called the shepherd of men. There is no evil in His heart".'

'Ipoour also says: "His flocks are not numerous",' shouted Ken, 'and that I can confirm, for the night of your birth I studied the stars, I saw the signs of the gods and I grieved over your destiny; when you were a child I wished you no harm, and I wept when I saw that the heavenly powers had named you "Criminal, heretic, madman, madman, madman!" '

A sudden silence fell, like that which precedes the *khamsin:* pregnant with anticipation and fear, heavy with concentrated menace and violence to come. Then Amonhotep spoke again, strangely calm.

'Perhaps the gods are against me, Ken, but Aten is with me. Therefore I am going to test your honour and that of your god Amon, for at present it is Aten and his eldest son Amonhotep who have the right to speak in the name of Egypt. Clench your teeth, while you wait for your hour of vengeance, because I am going to give orders for the temples of Amon to be closed and his name to be hammered from the stones. I believe that an empty house must be knocked down, for fear its shadows serve to shelter vipers, scorpions, centipedes and other unclean beasts whose hate turns to poison in their fangs. Yes, Ken, your life hangs by a thread.'

Amonhotep watched the High Priest carefully as he said this, trying to discern the shiver of fear which would have increased his scorn for the disciples of Amon, but Ken was too angry to be frightened.

'Your father isn't yet in his sarcophagus, and you to make decisions without him!' he replied in stinging tones. 'You are only co-regent, not Pharaoh. Remember that your father has built a great gateway here at Karnak, that his name includes the sacred name of Amon and that he has chosen to call you, his eldest son, likewise. You are not named "Glory-of-Sebek" or "Horus-watched-over-his-Birth", but AMONHOTEP. Will you also hammer your father's name from the temples? You must, if you want Amon to disappear from the world of the living! Then, when your father dies, his Ka will vanish in smoke as surely as if it were devoured. Selfish, irrespectful son, who would deprive his father of eternal life.'

Amonhotep laughed shortly.

'Selfish, irrespectful, criminal, guilty, yes I would be all these things if I believed I could take life from my father by hammering his name from the statues. But I don't believe it, Ken. I will efface the name of Amon from the stones, the better to efface it from the hearts of men, but such an act could never kill the god himself, if he existed. And you know as well as I do that it is ignorant and superstitious nonsense to think otherwise. No, Ken, my father has nothing to fear. His reign has been a just one: he hasn't stolen from the people, nor killed his enemies; his laugh is joyful as a child's, and if he has honoured the multiple deities of Egypt it is because he believes in none of them . . . he is still searching for the truth. When I have convinced my father he will rejoice to know at last the answer to his inner problems.'

Amonhotep drew himself up, kinglike and noble; his face no longer bore the signs of anger and the half-smile on his lips reflected the inner peace of his heart. There radiated from him such calm assurance, such strong faith, that even Ken was impressed. Suddenly a strange anxiety took hold of him, and for the first time since the start of his secret fight against the co-regent, he feared he might not win. Amonhotep was not mad, nor weak, nor a degenerate and fanatical tyrant, but a dangerous adversary, gifted with intelligence, lucidity, moral strength and will-power. Ken had under-estimated his adversary, and because of that he ran a good risk of losing all he fought for: his authority, his riches, his life perhaps.

'You have forced me to be insolent, your Majesty,' he said in a shaking voice, 'so you can have the excuse of another crime against the king to put me legally to death. Who will defend me before you? You said to me: "Be honest and fear nothing," and because I had confidence in you, I forgot the teaching of Phtah-hetep: "Silence is more profitable than too many words".'

'It is not he who quotes the wise men who is full of wisdom, but he who meditates their teachings and makes their words the essence of his soul,' replied the young man calmly. 'If you had assimilated the sayings of the philosophers, you might have forgotten the words they used to formulate them, but certainly not their deeper meaning. But have no fear, Ken, I will not accuse you of a crime against the king. Your faults are too numerous already. In fact, if it reassures you at all, I have already forgiven

191

your offences to my royal person. I have no wish to add the pebble of my personal spite to the bushel of stones which will bury you.'

Amonhotep's ironic smile wounded Ken's dignity more than the words which followed: 'Don't be afraid,' the young man added. 'I speak in images. I don't take life from those who tremble to lose it, for I believe that to tremble at the thought of death is to begin to be aware of one's evil actions . . . and it is wrong to take from a man the chance to mend his ways at the very moment when he is conscious of the weight of his faults.'

Ken felt a relief flood through his veins.

You are a fool, he thought, his eyes glinting dangerously; one should always draw the fangs and claws of a lion freed after a beating.

Aloud he said, unsmilingly: 'Your magnanimity is great. Let Amon pity you because your heart is honest.'

Amonhotep frowned, annoyed by the insolence behind the High Priest's words. However he didn't want their argument to descend to the level of personal spite, so he controlled his temper and said before he left: 'Eat your fill, spare neither goose nor wine nor music nor perfume. For what you spend will be your only profit.'

Ken was no longer hungry, and his thirst was not of the kind which can be slaked with wine: he thirsted after vengeance.

That very day he ordered a thorough search to be made for the priest who had taken it upon himself to breathe his solitary hate into the four magic images. When the young priest was found, Ken said to him: 'The co-regent arrived here in a fury this morning. He said that if I didn't punish the culprit, the heads of all the priests of Amon would fly like quails in summer. He added: "Let the man responsible be castrated, let him be beaten, let his tongue be torn out, let the skin be flayed from his back, let his own magic spells make him impotent." I am not going to have you castrated, nor flayed alive, for I pity you, even though you have endangered all your brothers in Amon. But I must have your tongue pulled out and order you a beating, for fear the co-regent's anger spreads among us all. Thank me for my clemency and let no one know you still have skin upon your back and have kept your manhood. That would be lack of gratitude for my affection.'

The young priest's tongue was pulled out, and he was beaten soundly. Hate flooded his heart, and his mind throbbed with murderous thoughts towards his sovereign. The third day Ken went to see how he was, and said to him: 'Your eyes are too bright. Amonhotep will suspect I hadn't the courage to have you castrated. I beg you, out of gratitude to me, out of pity for your brothers, pretend to be a eunuch. For one can expect anything from a bloody madman like the co-regent.'

Then he sighed with infinite sadness: 'Alas! If I wasn't so weak and old I would sacrifice my worthless life and assassinate that degenerate tyrant. But my hand shakes. . . . Old age! Great god Amon, what times we live in, when men allow themselves to be castrated like common rams, without one of them brave enough to risk everything to save his brothers.'

Ken saw the young priest's mouth tighten, his fists clench and his eyes fill with hate.

He was satisfied. His words hadn't fallen into the ears of a eunuch or a cripple. Once the man had recovered sufficiently the stupid fellow would waste no more time in creating magic images; anger would make him rash, impatience for vengeance would impel him to reach for a dagger, fanaticism would send him running to the palace to thrust the murderous blade deep into Amonhotep's heart. And he would do this in sight of everyone, without fearing to lose his life, secure in the belief that he was the only one of his generation worthy to rise up and save his brothers. And without a tongue, how could he waste his energy in useless words and dangerous accusations? For Ken understood men; he knew that a fanatic will proclaim his motives, to convince the victim he has been justly killed.

One should always draw the fangs and claws of a lion freed after a beating, thought Ken jubilantly. If your Majesty had assimilated this philosophic saying you would not have forgotten its deeper meaning.

193

CHAPTER TWO

IF Amonhotep was assassinated, the High Priest of Amon would not hesitate to recognize the assassin publicly as the evil man who had dared to cast a spell on the co-regent, and whom he himself had cruelly punished; the executioners and several members of the priesthood could bear witness to that. If Amonhotep escaped with his life, Ken would affirm that he himself was to blame for the attack because he had not beheaded the wild beast in the sheepfold of Amon, the traitor in the flock where the royal family was so deeply venerated. Then he would take the opportunity of saying to the co-regent: 'You accused me and I couldn't defend myself, but look how I punished the enemy who wished you harm! What further proof of my innocence do you need?' Perhaps Amonhotep would swallow it. In any case he could no longer use the wax images as an excuse to close the temples of Amon and distribute the priest's possessions.

It was to be hoped, however, that the dagger would reach its target. That would be the simpler solution, and if it happened, Ken was sure he could retain the power of the priesthood.

But fate was against his secret hope.

Amonhotep had gone to his 'secret place' for meditation. The sky was a dark, deep blue and the last stars still shone directly overhead, while a pale light from behind the eastern cliffs announced that the morning star was soon to rise from the hostile ocean which surrounds the land of men. It was the hour when silence seems to hold its breath, the hour when the soul reels before God's

194

infinity and trembles on the verge of discovering life's mystery. Amonhotep believed that God in His wisdom gave man this transitory moment of intuition, so he should not sink too deeply into the thick mud of his beginnings, but should remember that he was born with the seed of the infinite buried in his heart. Whenever he could, the young man hurried to his 'secret place' before going on to the temple of Aten for the service to the rising Sun. There, looking out across the river, surrounded by a barrier of reeds, he let his mind dwell on the immensity of the vault above his head, felt himself drawn up into the endless azure pastures from which his secret being took its nourishment, and he came back from these dizzy contemplations purified, exalted, strengthened.

For three days he had been going there earlier than usual, for the rest of the royal family had already moved to the summer residence on the western bank. Nefertiti had tried to insist on staying with him, but, though it cost him an effort, he had refused. What he had to do now was dangerous, as dangerous as big game hunting; it called for flexibility, caution, concentration and quick reflexes, qualities necessary for the survival of a man who hunts to kill. Amonhotep did not under-estimate his adversary; he knew Ken was of the breed who creep up to bite the heel. It was now three days since he had left the High Priest standing in his chamber, raging inwardly, and the man would not have remained idle, waiting for the moment of his public disgrace. In vain, during these three days, Amonhotep had racked his brains to imagine what move his enemy would make. He had asked Ramose to keep quiet about the business of the magic fishes, for he didn't want to alarm anyone.

Luckily Ramose was of a placid nature and little given to losing his head, and he had therefore agreed not to mention the affair before it was necessary. It was possible that Ken had had nothing to do with the magic fishes; at any rate he was quite capable of denying such a crime vehemently before a court; and he was certainly sufficiently clever to produce a real or false culprit, some young fanatic priest who would be exalted at the idea of sacrificing himself as a pure victim on the altar of Amon.

Amonhotep regretted that anger had made him say too much

to Ken; he had spoken too soon of his secret intentions, which, though they hung in the air like a threatening storm, had none the less retained up to then the reassuring power of hidden danger. If he did close the great temple of Amon, distribute the riches of the priests and erase the name of the god from the stones and the hearts of the faithful, he would rather do it at the start of the New Year, so his action would take on an aspect of renewal, a sense of regeneration. But now he had opened Ken's eyes to his own reserves of strength and will, and the High Priest would see the urgent necessity of taking action; there was a good chance it would become necessary not to postpone the announcement of the royal decision.

The royal decision! The co-regent's, anyway, as Ken would be pleased to point out. He would say to everyone: 'Pharaoh built a gateway to the temple of Karnak. Pharaoh gave us flocks and lands. Pharaoh called his son by his first name: Amon. Pharaoh worships Amon. The co-regent is only the first subject so long as his father is not in his tomb. Surely, in his folly, this irrespectful son has put pressure on the person of his sacred father. The priests of On have made the king drink bewitching potions which have destroyed his royal will. Who knows if he is not moving gently towards his death, his thirst quenched by some slow poison which dries up his strong heart like a solution of natron. Take care, O people! Remember the priests of Amon saved this country from the bloody claws of the Hyksos. Remember this, and reflect that to blaspheme against this great god could bring about your fall. The frontiers seethe with impatient hordes of nomad tribes and those of the shepherd kings . . . only the hand of Amon holds them back. But the hand of Amon can release them! Then they will descend on Thebes, like a *khamsin*, burning and ravaging, setting on fire and killing. Your women will be raped, your children gutted.'

Such speeches would certainly impress the superstitious ignorants who feared nothing more than to be castrated, and the cowards who preferred slavery to death.

Amonhotep sighed and felt a strange despair: 'Aten! Aten!' he murmured humbly, 'give me the strength not to doubt Thee.

196

Speak to me at dawn, tell me Thy reign will not begin bathed by the blood of a people in revolt. As Thy coming is heralded by this redness in the eastern sky, so, if blood must be spilt, let it be that of a single person. Mine, O father! For only the blood of Thy son can flow with enough passion to colour Thy Dawn.'

He prostrated himself on the dried mud, and silently prepared his soul to hear the voice of God.

At that very moment, God spoke.

There was the crackling of broken reeds . . . a cry . . . a death rattle. . . .

Amonhotep leapt to his feet and stared without understanding at the sight which met his eyes: two paces behind him lay a man, his mouth open, his eyes turned up in death. His head-dress had fallen off, uncovering a shaven skull which shone in the first light of dawn; near him, another man was frozen on his knees, gazing at Amonhotep with fear and a kind of horror. Finally a toneless voice broke the long silence.

'My master, he was crawling through the reeds, a dagger between his teeth . . . I come from On with a message from the High Priest, and because no profane person can know what his holy mouth says to your sacred ear, Dudu, The First under the King, said to me: "Follow the alley of sycamores to the spot where the river turns towards the south, for there is the 'secret place' of the lord." And as I came walking, my soul in peace, my heart joyful, I saw this thing moving noiselessly, and some magic turned him into a marsh monster before my eyes. I seized the war axe slung upon my shoulder, I sprang, I struck . . . and as I struck, he cried out and broke the spell. I saw the dagger fall from his teeth, I felt the scales become flesh beneath my hands.'

Amonhotep rose and walked towards the man. He saw the knife lying on the dry mud, and the axe buried between the fallen body's shoulder blades: he said: 'His skull is shaven like a priest's.'

Ignoring the High Priest's messenger, who remained kneeling, Amonhotep lifted the dead man's head and saw the seal of Amon hanging round his neck.

'He is a priest of Amon come to sacrifice me to the sun,' he said.

Then he remembered his prayer to Aten, and knew his God had sent him a sign. His soul was filled with wonder, and raising the palms of his hands towards the eastern horizon, he murmured: 'Aten, Thy power is infinite! This man has paid the blood-price! His love must have been great for Thou hast chosen him to be the expiatory victim. Take pity on his blindness and let the purity of his love for Amon dispose Thee to treat him as one of Thine own sons. For, in Thine eyes, pure love is a quality which knows no boundaries. He has coloured Thy rising. On the walls of his tomb we will engrave his new name: Dawn-of-God. But I, Thine eldest, have gravely offended Thee by doubting Thy reign!'

Amonhotep turned to the messenger from the High Priest of Aten, and asked gently: 'What is your name, you whom Aten loves sufficiently to make you the priest of his dawn?'

'Marire, Lord.'

'Marire, if the High Priest, the all-seeing saint, chose your heart to guard the secret which his mouth sends to my ear, it is because he knows you have a heart which can guard such a secret from On to Thebes. So I say unto you: "Seal your lips on that which you have seen and done this morning. Let your eyes forget, let your ears never have heard. For this holy sacrifice must be kept a secret. No one shall curse this man's name nor say: 'Let him be thrown to the scavengers, he has committed a crime against the person of the co-regent.' For in truth, this man is blessed, he is my twin brother in his love for god. Remove his robe and the seal he wears around his neck. You see this boat moored to the bank? Put him into it, cover him with my cloak and take him to the embalmers in the City of the Dead. Say unto them: 'My lord Amonhotep sends you his twin brother to be mummified with respect; here is the seal of my Lord; Let all be done in secret'".'

Saying which, Amonhotep gave Marire his gold ring and his cloak. Then he added: 'I need no pretext to close Amon's temples. Aten has spoken and has reassured me. See! the east is red, the disc of light is about to rise on Egypt and spread out its warmth to the people. Never again will it set on the world of men!'

Marire didn't understand what his sovereign meant, for he

knew the sun appeared in the east, set fire to midday and disappeared in the west 365 times a year; but he could tell by the
exalted way the co-regent spoke that something important was
about to happen. Joy flooded his heart, for he had confidence in
his king.

What would happen he did not know, nor when it would come,
but he was sure it would be soon, now that such extraordinary
things were taking place: a priest of Amon attempting to assassinate the king, and being called 'blessed, twin brother in his love
for god'! If an assassin is thus honoured by his holy victim, how
much more so the assassin's killer, he thought. And visions of
riches swam before his eyes.

However, as Aten rose in the sky, He cast an oblique and kindly
glance upon Marire. He could read deep in the hearts of men,
He knew His servant's new-found ambitions, but He also knew
they were only due to the greediness of extreme youth, and would
not continue past the 'time of decomposition', for a rich and fertile
land can always absorb the evil-breeding pools of stagnant water
which the river leaves behind after the flood. Then is the time to
plough and sow, to trample in the seed with the sharp hooves of
pigs, and to watch over it well to ensure a prosperous harvest.

For in truth, Marire was the man chosen to be High Priest of
Aten.

CHAPTER THREE

NEFERTITI sat up in bed, her forehead damp with sweat, her eyes frightened. While she was asleep her Ka had shaken her and whispered: 'Schhh! Schhh! Schhh!' She didn't know what it meant, but fear had awakened her.

Amonhotep came towards her, smiling, as he said: 'You have slept late, my queen, the sun already forms an angle with the eastern cliffs!'

She gave a little cry of joy as she recognized him, and threw herself into his arms.

'In my sleep I heard "Schhh!" And I didn't recognize your step, my love,' she said, laughing. 'That it should be *you* who made me tremble! You, whom I have longed for all the week! Here you come at last, and I think you are an evil spirit from my nightmare.'

Then, taking her husband's head in her hands, and gazing tenderly into his eyes, she continued: 'Is it only a week? It seems more like the whole summer season. The days pass slowly and wearily without you. Oh my love, tell me you couldn't live without me either.'

Amonhotep held her tightly and buried his face in the soft warmth of her neck. His wife was his secret place of peace, the spring from which he drew his strength, and when he held her in his arms he had the feeling that he was surrounded by a wall which isolated him from the noise and fury of the world; when he pressed his lips to her close-grained golden skin, he had the physical sensation of breathing in a warm, life-giving substance which nourished his blood and circulated through the forty-six vessels of his body, like strong wine in the veins of a hungry man.

Usually this excess of energy was expended immediately; he would carry his wife to their bed and share with her the intoxication she had given him. But on this morning of weighty events and decisions, Amonhotep was like a miser, determined to hoard both necessary and surplus energy.

When he had drunk deeply of his wife's loving warmth, and his invigorated blood was beating at his temples and singing in his ears, he pushed Nefertiti gently away and said: 'When you are not with me I am like a dead man. Each day I wandered in the palace of Thebes like a lost soul in the Necropolis. But I have crossed the river, not because I was impatient to live again, but because I had to: things are moving swiftly, I no longer have time to remain in loving contemplation of you and of my God. Nefertiti, my joy, my dearest love, Dawn has coloured the eastern sky. The sun has risen!'

As Amonhotep told her about his interview with Ken, the wax images, and the sacrifice of the priest sent to assassinate him, Nefertiti's astonishment turned to fear. Amonhotep reassured her: 'There is nothing to fear! Do you not see in this abortive crime the all-powerful and all-kindly hand of Aten? He has made His wishes clear enough. My death will wait until my work is over. At present you and I have only sharpened our tools and must work in our field for many seasons; and remember this, my love, a lord only throws his slaves to the scavengers when his lands are yielding well. The more acres he has, the more chance his servants have to make old bones, and our field is the infinite land of Egypt and the Provinces. Perhaps we will only die when we are two centuries old! The embalmers won't need to soak us in natron, we shall already be so dried up! They will lay us in our tomb just as we are, saying: "Blessed be Pharaoh and his well-beloved wife who have given us gold for doing nothing." '

Amonhotep's good humour reassured his wife. How I love him! How I love him! she thought. Since the evening of the terrible *khamsin*, her life, her body and her heart were filled to overflowing with happiness; sometimes she felt her joy was so great, her happiness so tangible, that something inside her would give under the pressure. One day she had said jokingly to her husband:

'I believe that terrible *khamsin* filled me up with hot sand, as it filled all the places insufficiently protected against its fury. I am bursting with love; take care not to hang me up by the feet, for fear that it all empties out and you find me as before, as hollow as a dried-up wineskin.'

Amonhotep, gazing into his wife's adoring eyes, feared he would not be able to husband his energy after all, but would give way to his desire. He suggested therefore that it was time for them to join Pharaoh and Tiyi.

'Go, and I will join you later,' replied Nefertiti. 'My body is sticky after the hot night, and I am no longer a child to appear naked before my father and mother.'

Amonhotep left regretfully. I will sleep here at the summer palace tonight, he told himself; in any case, it is too late to do anything today, Aten will soon be at his zenith.

In fact, Aten had scarcely risen above the eastern plateau. Ipoour knew all about men's bad faith when he wrote: 'The hungry stomach cries: "Midday", at any hour; it does not hesitate to call the sun a liar.'

As Nefertiti reached the corridor leading to her mother-in-law's apartments she heard Pharaoh shouting with unusual energy:

'Magic fishes and an attempt on your life! How can you expect us to keep quiet about this?'

Nefertiti paused to listen.

'My father, it is too easy for Ken to deny these two crimes,' replied Amonhotep in an irritated voice; 'what is the good of starting a long trial? Justice demands many witnesses and those who will bear witness in favour of the High Priest of Amon will be more numerous than those who will bear witness in favour of us, for Ken won't hesitate to pay voices to clear his name. In any case, I left the wax fish with him, and by now the young priest's body has been emptied of its intestines, stuffed with pure myrrh, and is soaking in salts of natron.'

'You're mad, my son!' exclaimed Pharaoh. 'You hear what he

says, Tiyi? The images are destroyed and the assassin is being embalmed!'

'What were you thinking of, my eldest?' questioned Tiyi in worried tones.

'Once and for all,' cried Amonhotep, 'understand that an honest man's proof turns against him when he is dealing with a liar. In any case, those cursed fish were too dangerous in the palace.'

Pharaoh's laugh rang out, loud and scornful.

'Does my son fear the works of magic! Tiyi, your first-born has relieved himself of all the good sense he drank in with your milk!'

'The priests of On have shown me many wonders brought about by magic,' shouted Amonhotep furiously. 'Even this morning, before he crossed the river to the Necropolis, Marire gave me this message from Aten's High Priest: "Take care, for Ken wishes your death! His treachery has been revealed to me and I send you a talisman I have made myself, more powerful than all the works of Ken, for Ken is a fool." Is the power of this talisman not proved, when the moment it came near me, the assassin's dagger fell from his jaws?'

Nefertiti remembered the blue enamel amulet her husband had been wearing, representing an *oujda** in the centre of a looped cross.

'The dagger fell from the jaws of that cursed slave because he had an axe-blade in his back,' growled Pharaoh. 'The open eye set in this cross of life can see no more than the eye of a dead fish. The High Priest has no need of magic to tell him Ken wants to be rid of you, nor to know he is a fool. Each time you go to On, you speak of your grievances against the priests of Amon, and tell him what you think of Ken's intelligence. Do you think he is fool enough to ignore your tastes and enmities? Is it not the priests in On who will benefit most from the ruin of those in Thebes and who will inherit their riches?'

'The Ur Ma is a holy old man,' cried Amonhotep, his voice shaking with anger. 'It is he who taught me to love purity and

* *Oujda:* Protective amulet representing an eye outlined in black.

truth. His simplicity laughs at lands and riches, and he prefers prayer to a soft bed. I know that. . . .'

Nefertiti thought it was time to make her entrance. She pushed open the door and advanced with a smile. There was a sudden silence, and she took her time about greeting her father and kissing her mother-in-law.

For a moment Amonhotep was lost in contemplation of his wife's beauty. Then he turned towards Pharaoh again and took up the threads of his speech with an enthusiasm which escaped no one. Tiyi said to herself: my son is much helped by his wife. She is better for him than the *oujda* from Ur-Ma, for she gives him strength and a sense of fulfilment. Now no one will ever be able to vanquish him.

Her husband's voice brought her back to reality.

'So be it,' said Pharaoh, 'I spoke of Ur-Ma too hastily; I know him as well as you. He is a man of great honesty, and what is more, of great common sense. But don't talk to me of magic! I am not a dreamer, I am a hunter! What do you intend to do, now you have destroyed the proofs you needed if you were to convict Ken of the crime? Cast a spell on him?'

Amonhotep allowed himself to smile. His heart was full of happiness as he remembered his decision to spend the night in the summer palace.

'I shall carry out a *coup d'état* — if I can call it that. I shall assemble the police and the army. The generals will close the temples of Amon and parade on horseback in the streets of Thebes, so the people will see them, and say: "The town is full of generals armed for battle; they have come back from the frontier posts, so the enemy cannot be at the border, but here!" Their ignorance will breed fear, and because they will be afraid, they will approve this show of force; they will shut themselves into their homes, and once they are in safety they will say: "The sooner the enemy is punished the sooner will we be in security. Pharaoh knows what he is doing and in his great wisdom he has seen the danger before it fell on us, his people." When they come out of their houses again they will see that the name of Amon has been erased from the stones, that the priests of Karnak have been disbanded and that the temples of Amon have been closed. They will be surprised to learn the name of the "enemy", but they will not complain, for they will be too relieved not to have been counted among the trouble-makers.'

Pharaoh gnawed the handle of his fly swatter and looked thoughtful.

'That's all very well,' he said after a while; 'certainly the people eat the food we give them and never fail to look contented for fear of running the risk of punishment, but the nobility are not so easily handled. There is always a prince of noble birth among them, born with the feeling he has been cheated of the crown. He will seize any opportunity of collecting supporters, promising them everything if they will help him to usurp the throne. And many will join him, persuaded that everything is just what they need! And are you sure the generals will obey your orders? Suppose they profit from the presence of troops under their control, to try and seize power? Don't forget that among our people there are many worshippers of Amon.'

'My father, in the name of my people's liberty I scorn the power and self-interest of the rich. If a landowner will not be converted to Aten, I will dispossess him and divide his goods among his servants; I will accuse him publicly, loud enough for the other recalcitrants to hear and take heed, lest they too lose their flocks and lands. For, though it saddens me to say so, most of the rich worship only their fortunes. Abundance is a god which no one will make them deny! And you can be sure that I won't give them time to reflect; I will act like lightning, which strikes at the same time as the thunder.'

Pharaoh shrugged his shoulders.

'Execute Ken, weed out the priests of Amon, muzzle their power, put one of your strongest supporters at their head, I agree. So be it! But why blame the god Amon, who has done nothing? What difference does it make to you if he is worshipped in his temples? After all, a god does the work for which he was created when he draws men's eyes up to heaven, whether he is called Amon, Aten, Ptah or Rê! The important thing is that the people believe he reads their innermost hearts. The gods are Pharaoh's

205

best police force! If you take their belief in Amon from those who worship him, you run the risk of making unbelievers. And then you will regret it, for those unbelievers will feel sufficiently alone to do evil. They will regret it, too, for their eyes will be turned towards the earth, they will see only their own selfish souls, and their miserable serfs and slaves will suffer in consequence.'

Amonhotep's eyes were shining.

'My father,' he said energetically, 'if I were alone in wanting this fight, certainly I would be guilty of monstrous pride, of stupid and dangerous fanaticism. But I am not speaking for myself, I am speaking for Aten, the one and only God, who has taken pity on the superstition and misery of men. He talks to me in a voice which is not my own inner voice, and this is the reason why I believe. If He guides my steps, then He is sure of victory.'

Pharaoh sighed: his son had decided not to be convinced.

'You are as deaf as a child born the third day of the month of Choiak,' he said gloomily. 'But you are co-regent, do as you please. If I had wished to continue watching over Egypt's good, I wouldn't have called upon your strength. Only, when you make your decisions, don't come asking for counsel if you don't intend to take my advice. You make me waste saliva and precious time.'

He smiled at his wife: 'Isn't that right, Tiyi?' he asked.

Tiyi nodded her head.

'Let us rest our old bones,' she said calmly, 'let us stay in the stable and munch hay while the young ones labour at the plough under the burning sun. You are right, my husband.'

Amonhotep slept that night at the palace, and in the delirium of their love, his wife conceived another child.

CHAPTER FOUR

AMONHOTEP moved with the speed of lightning, 'which strikes at the same time as the thunder'.

While the generals, hastily recalled from the frontiers, paraded their troops and chariots up and down the streets of Thebes, armed as though to attack an enemy fortress, the police went to Karnak and closed all the temples dedicated to Amon, accompanied by workers with instructions to hammer his cursed name from the stones. The occupants of the sacred enclosure were evicted and the gates were sealed with the royal arms.

A wind of fear blew through the city and the neighbouring countryside: town dwellers and peasants alike shut themselves up in their houses, astonished and uneasy. Army officers were to be seen everywhere, proclaiming the words of the king: 'Hear me, Egyptians, hear me strangers from the Provinces and the confines of the world! The time of justice, truth and love, has come. Serfs, slaves, all those most miserable among you, the time has come to hold up your heads and see the rising Sun, Aten, the only God, who is waiting to warm your hearts. Such is His loving-kindness that He orders your masters to be gentle and just. The lords will love their servants, they will not treat their dependants harshly. The unjust priest will no longer demand offerings by dishonest or false means, or by threats of violence, for the unjust priest has been destituted; his goods have been confiscated and will be distributed among you; the temples of his god, whom he called Amon but whom I call "Cursed Wealth, Evil Power, and Shameful Lust" have been closed; from now on they will be arid wastes, the lairs of poisonous reptiles, and their sealed doors will be named: "Forgetfulness", "Abandon", "Emptiness", "Solitude". Hold up your palms towards the east, where the disc of God rises. The day which has begun will have no end. Justice, truth and love proclaim the reign of Aten — the reign which shall last for ever.'

The nervous citizens came out of their hiding-places hesitantly. At first they didn't believe what they were told, for they had often heard promises of justice — an abstract term if ever there was one. But soon they became brave enough to hope, because it certainly seemed that the immense wealth of the priests of Amon had been confiscated. And finally, when they received their share of the booty, they recanted joyfully and were converted to Aten.

The court of Thebes reacted with less simplicity and indifference. The *coup d'état* had shaken them brutally from the lazy lethargy which characterized the summer season. From high on the 'balcony of appearances' the co-regent had addressed the nobles in these terms.

'I have been born with the dawn and am now called AKHENATEN, he who pleases Aten. At this moment, on the eastern bank, the divine rays of sunlight are transpiercing the city's wickedness, burning and cleansing the market places and the buildings, so that Akhenaten, his wife, his family and his friends can instal themselves in a purified town. But only my family and my friends will be welcome on my lands. And my friends are those who believe as I do: "Aten is the only God, the others are inventions of men and Amon is the symbol of evil." Let those who have ears hear! Let those who have brains understand! But I am willing to instruct those who do not understand. Each day I will be at the disposal of those men of good-will who do not condemn what they do not know.'

Courtiers who considered this a good opportunity to win royal favour, or who coveted the title 'Friend of Akhenaten', with all the wealth and honour which it carried, lost no time in recognizing the supreme divinity of the Sun; but they thought it unnecessary to listen to the Teaching, for they did not want to be taken for waverers and imbeciles who had neither zeal nor intuitive understanding.

Lords who were well-disposed towards the co-regent and his wife, and who were already familiar with their beliefs, were glad

208

of the success of the enterprise. They had no difficulty in becoming fervent worshippers of Aten and took pleasure in hearing their young king talk so well of the brotherhood of man and the unity of God.

But many were discontent: those who were averse to change, the eternal criticizers of any régime, the stubborn, the families and friends of the priests of Amon, the landowners who traded with Karnak, the members of families who had paid fortunes to the priests of Amon to ensure food and consideration for their dead, and also those who sincerely believed.

Tongues wagged as each of them put his point of view.

'Pharaoh has made no mention of his son's insolent action in changing the name given to him at birth. The co-regent can't behead half Egypt. Let's protest to Pharaoh.'

'Let us demand justice and freedom of worship.'

'Let's return to our country estates and oppose him with passive resistance.'

'How long must we support this tyrant's yoke?'

'Amonhotep is mad and his wife puts on airs.'

'It's an open secret that Maï is welcome in the queen's apartments.'

The smothered grumbles which shook the summer residence left the young king indifferent. He was busy teaching, praying, organizing the reign of his God and travelling around the countryside to gauge and encourage the new-found fervour of Aten's worshippers.

Nefertiti never left her husband's side. Certainly she believed his God was watching over him, but her faith wasn't strong enough for her to bear separation without anxiety: if an assassin's knife was going to strike, let it strike the two of them. When she and her husband drove through the crowds in their chariot, she held her body in front of his like a living shield, and her inner certainty that she could deflect any blow intended for her husband, exalted her and made her forget her fear.

One day, on a visit to the lands of Lord Mose, not far from Thebes, the co-regent saw Maï coming fast towards him in his chariot, followed by a small band of jog-trotting Nubians.

'Majesty,' said Maï hurriedly, 'you must return to the palace, for this morning a delegation of nobles, all unbelievers in Aten, have sought out your divine father, their mouths full of menaces. Ken, whose life you were generous enough to spare, has organized a revolt, and the lands which you were magnanimous enough to give him are the centre of a whispering campaign against you and your wife.'

He who would for ever afterwards be known as AKHENATEN, smiled scornfully.

'They are brave when I don't look them in the eyes, these beasts of shadows and of darkness,' he said. 'Go back, Maï; I will follow. Since you will arrive first, announce that the co-regent comes in person to listen to their grievances. Let them prepare a list of their claims and let their arguments be strong enough to stand up against my justice.'

When Akhenaten entered the room where his wife was resting, he seemed worried and even sad. Nefertiti sent away the servants and questioned him anxiously: 'My love is tired? Let him refresh himself in my arms.'

Akhenaten sketched a smile and sat down on the bed.

'Yes, perhaps you're right, Nefertiti,' he said, 'perhaps I am tired. My limbs are as weak as if I had been in a long fight. This morning I was full of enthusiasm, sure of winning; I saw, stretching from the eastern to the western horizon, nothing but fields, the seed sown and already beginning to sprout. But I went to sleep . . . yes, I went to sleep and didn't see the tares spring up. When I opened my eyes, the tares were trying to strangle the young wheat and I am discouraged at the thought of having to take up my tools again to fight them.'

Akhenaten told Nefertiti what was happening at Thebes and ended by saying: 'I thought that there was nothing left to add in order to convince them of the dazzling truth of Aten. I thought the shame of the priests of Amon was so evident that I only had to speak of it for everyone to understand. But I was like a child, taking desires for realities. Now I must find new words, new arguments, new defences. I must grub up the tares, and destroy them . . . destroy . . . destroy . . . when I had thought the work of

210

destruction was over and rejoiced in building, planting, growing. Thebes is rotten! So many, many centuries of rottenness, the town is leprous through and through. I will never be able to do more than amputate its sick limbs, never be able to purify it. If only I had been born at the start of the world! I would have built God's city in a healthy place.'

Nefertiti was distressed to see lines of bitterness in her husband's face. She wanted to cry out to him: What does all this matter! I love you, nothing counts except our love!

But she knew that her husband's infirmity came from God; already in his mother's womb he had suffered from it, and only death would set him free. In his life she was only a well-shaded dwelling place to which he came to build up his strength in order to fight better in the sun.

She searched for a solution, and suddenly her face lit up: 'Thebes is rotten!' she cried, 'but what does that matter? Why not act as though you had been born at the start of the world? Why not choose a healthy place and found another capital? A new unblemished site, where you can build a city to Aten's glory. Those who enter can be carefully chosen. They. . . .'

Akhenaten's face brightened.

'Of course!' he interrupted her eagerly, 'why didn't I think of that? Thebes must no longer be the capital, for a capital is its people's heart, and if the heart is rotten, in the end the limbs will die too. I will give Egypt a new heart and the blood of my people will be renewed.'

He rose to his feet and started pacing up and down as he spoke. 'Akhet-Aten, the Horizon of the Disc . . . from there the Disc will rise upon the world!'

His anxieties vanished . . . he felt more enthusiastic, more optimistic than ever. Aten hadn't spoken to him directly because He had been annoyed by His son's discouragement, but He had taken pity on him, and had suggested His will to the pure Nefertiti. Akhenaten looked at his wife and thought her more beautiful than ever, so he took her in his arms and said with humility: 'My love, my love, you are the shining child of the Sun, His first-born, even before myself. Yours is the mouth chosen by Aten to show

211

His sovereign will. I am as nothing before you, my good fortune is that you have loved me, that you do love me. My astonished heart misses a beat when I realize you are mine.'

Nefertiti held her husband closely to her and her eyes filled with tears as she thought: it was not Aten who inspired me with the necessary words, my love. When I spoke I didn't for one moment think of Aten. But a woman's love is often as powerful as a God's, and I love you so much! No, I am not the first-born of the Sun, I am she who wishes to remain in your shadow and who would throw herself under your feet to prevent them being scratched by thorns. Go forward without fear, your eyes fixed on the Sun. I am here to make sure no earthly evil does you harm.

When they reached Thebes, the royal couple felt as though they were diving into a boiling cauldron. The whole court had crossed over to the eastern bank and Akhenaten found his father very worried.

'My son,' he said without anger, 'you should have had Ken killed. Now it is too late, for the people have been worked up into a dangerous mood. If Ken's head fell now the rebels would put it on the end of a spear and march under its bloody banner. They came before me and I could not answer them. Even your mother was silent!'

Akhenaten began to laugh.

'I know how to punish their proud hearts, my father,' he exclaimed. 'I will speak to them from the "balcony of appearances" and, believe me, you will be agreeably surprised.'

Pharaoh shrugged his shoulders. Nevertheless he went with his wife and daughter to the 'balcony of appearances', and, like everyone else, listened to his eldest son's speech with astonishment.

'When I was here in Thebes, you didn't dare to challenge me openly. You muttered in dark corners, you preferred to spit out your hate in secret. I thought you had understood, I was proud of your intelligence and my heart was filled to overflowing with affection. But when I went away, your courage came back to you. You have rebelled, and it was Ken, whose life I spared, who urged

212

you on. If I am dethroned, Ken will regain his power, and with it the freedom to oppress the poor and sell all you clever people something which doesn't exist. Well then, stay in ignorance. Do what you like. Pray to Amon in your private chapels and hide the smell of rottenness with incense. Thebes is no longer the capital. Ambassadors from neighbouring nations will no longer be received here, nor bring their tribute. Soon Thebes will be nothing but a straggling village, its temples closed and its palaces abandoned. Its great gardens will fall under the plough and its ruins will be overgrown with wheat. No more feasts, festivals or entertainments. And when you say: "I am a citizen of Thebes of a hundred gates," people will laugh and reply: "The hundred gates hang open, the sand wind blows through them and makes their rusty hinges creak. Are you an outlaw or a beggar to live in that dead place?" The well-beloved of Aten will follow me to Akhet-Aten, city of the Horizon-of-the Sun . . . the new capital which will rise upon a sound, unsullied hill. In their company I will live out my days joyfully. However, I do not bear you any grudge. Let those who love truth question me openly and I will answer them.'

A deathly silence followed this speech.

Pharaoh thought the co-regent was carrying eccentricity too far, but Tiyi realized her son and daughter-in-law's deep sincerity and knew it was no use trying to reason with them; she would have to come out of retirement to look after the details which, in his grandiose plans, her first-born would be sure to forget.

She instructed her faithful servants to keep their eyes open, and one morning Ken, the High Priest of Amon, was bitten by a viper coiled in the reeds at the spot where he usually went down to take his bath. Ten people witnessed the event, and there were so many poisonous snakes about at that time of year that no one could accuse a criminal hand of committing the crime. Akhenaten took advantage of this opportune death to talk of the finger of God, of the vengeance of Aten, and of the victory of the Sun over the world of darkness, and many superstitious unbelievers were shaken and asked for the Teaching. Tiyi held her peace. And after that it dawned on many proud nobles, who had long boasted of belonging to the richest and pleasantest city in the world, that to linger on in Thebes when it had been deserted by Court and Government would be humiliating and disagreeable. What did religious convictions matter when honour, pleasure and comfort were at stake!

CHAPTER FIVE

In the second month of the summer season, during the fourth year of his reign, Akhenaten and his wife Nefertiti, mistress of the Two Kingdoms, together with members of their court, boarded the great royal *dahabiyeh* so that the hand of God could lead them to the sacred site of their new capital.

Messengers had been sent to all the riverside villages, ordering the local officials to decorate the banks with flower-garlands and to prepare thousands of loaves of *zeret* wheat and jars of good wine to rejoice the heart of the king at the stopping places. This splendid journey down the Nile took place in an atmosphere of song, entertainment and festivity.

Morning and evening Akhenaten asked Aten to lead him to the sanctified ground chosen for his future residence. On the sixth day, the voice of God spoke to him, saying: 'My horizon shall be here, in the centre of the land of Egypt.'

It was midday and the *dahabiyeh* had reached a spot where the cliffs fell back attractively on the eastern bank to form a kind of loop, five miles long, two and a half miles wide.

Akhenaten's heart filled with joy and gratitude.

He gave orders to halt the rowers, furl the sails and for a rope to be thrown to the papyrus-covered bank. It was a beautiful spot, and completely deserted. In the distance the limestone cliffs showed their teeth in a dazzling smile. Everything was peaceful, silent under the burning sun. The spirit of God hovered in the bright sky, over this sacred expanse of rolling ground He had chosen for His dwelling place.

First the delimitation rites were carried out.

In solemn procession, the co-regent, his well-beloved wife

215

Nefertiti, Ay the Divine Father and Ti the royal nurse, followed by the priests of Aten, the nobles in ceremonial dress and the officials shimmering with gold, all moved off humbly, on foot, in the full heat of the sun. Slowly the cortège moved along the foot of the limestone cliffs, passed the open mouths of dried-up *wadis*, and crossed the sandy waste from south to north, following the natural bend in the river. Every so often Akhenaten would call a halt and sing a hymn to his God as he pointed out which rock face was to be engraved with: 'Here, the foundation *stelae*', or 'Here the city limits for the Horizon-of-the-Sun'.

By the time the procession had reached the northernmost point, the importance of the occasion had impressed everyone. Poor Ti had tears in her eyes. She had never suspected that the worship of Aten could contain so much majesty and beauty. Certainly she was dripping with perspiration and her feet hurt, but not for the greatest honours in the world would she have given up her place on the right of the queen. At first, when her young sovereign had carried out his *coup d'état*, she had been disapproving: mainly because she was a creature of habit, and didn't like change, but also because when the worship of Amon was done away with she saw herself being deprived of many enjoyable ceremonies, such as 'The-beautiful-festival-of-the-sacred-Harem'. On the day of 'The-beautiful-festival-of-the-sacred-Harem', all Thebes boarded flower-garlanded pleasure boats and joyfully escorted Amon's statue from Karnak to Luxor, with much festivity and feasting. On that day the gallants were allowed to tease the young maidens and in the resulting atmosphere of love and lasciviousness Ay regained the ardour of his youth, looked at his wife with unusual interest and gave many signs of new-found vigour. Alas! One of the many charming old customs which would disappear for ever.

But Ti hadn't sulked for long. She had discussed the question with her foster-child, and Nefertiti's enthusiasm had soon convinced Ti's affectionate old heart. At the same time her husband had found a weighty argument to combat her hostility. He had said: 'Akhenaten has honest eyes, and an upright soul. He believes what he says, and acts as he believes. From a nest of scorpions, one can only expect poison, but when something radiates

216

beauty, one can assume it is not dangerous. I know little about the co-regent's god, but from his acts I conclude that he is worthy and only ask to learn more.'

So Ti was converted to the worship of Aten and consequently found herself on the queen's right hand during the delimitation ritual.

Papyrus huts had been quickly set up at the northernmost point. Servants unpacked the food and a feast was improvised. The noble ladies danced, sang and made music, while everyone drank, laughed and joked with each other, for the impressiveness of the occasion had given way to merrymaking.

Akhenaten was in a particularly good mood. He proposed the construction of a small-scale model of the new city. The excitement reached its height as, with the end of his long ebony cane, the king traced the course of the river with its expanse of sand, then added the wall of cliffs, running round the back in a graceful curve. Finally he planted his stick more or less in the centre of the river bank and said: 'Here we will build the temple of Aten. And as I have chosen the dwelling place of my God, let each one now choose his own. You first, my queen.'

Nefertiti had drunk a considerable amount of wine and her throat was full of laughter. 'There, there, to the south, I see the pleasure palace, with a lake and the summer verandas. I will call it Maru-Aten. In the centre, near the temple, will be the great palace with the royal apartments, and here in the north, another palace, a palace to relax in. . . . Yes, yes, three palaces: in the south, at midday and in the north. For once the Sun will rise in the north and set in the south.'

She threw back her head and laughed. Akhenaten looked at her affectionately. 'My queen's wishes are my commands. Let my friends be content with what remains.'

Then, in an atmosphere of gaiety and laughter, each one pointed out the place where he wished his house to stand.

Afterwards, Akhenaten said to the vizier Nakht: 'Take note of this plan, for it has been drawn up in joy and happiness. Let nothing be changed.'

Because Akhenaten was impatient to reign over his new capital, he hurried on the architects and builders. Old Hatiay, the Works Inspector who supervised the hundreds of workers brought in to do the job, permitted himself to remark one day, since frankness was the latest law: 'If Amenhotep, son of Hapu, your father's architect saw how these buildings are going up, he would be grieved. No good solid stone! Bricks of raw mud mixed with pebbles, alleyways and temple roofs filled with pressed sand and hastily covered by paving stones, clay gateways reinforced by wood, pebble walls slapped with whitewash, whispy avenues of acacias! Nothing lasting, nothing strong! The first big flood could tear the city of the Sun away from its hillside like a clump of papyrus from the banks. Will you not order granite and sandstone?'

Akhenaten laughed.

'I'm in a hurry, my good Hatiay; in any case, what does the weakness of the material matter if the foundations are strong? The foundations of this capital are built of faith, love and purity; components more indestructible than stones from the Coptos quarries. Also, I wish Akhet-Aten to be a city as delicate, charming, beautiful as queen Nefertiti herself. Heavy buildings symbolize stubbornness, brutality, tyranny . . . they are good for frontier towns, against a neighbour's possible enmity. But the city of Aten reaches up towards the sky, its columns graceful, its walls permeable, its construction delicate, like a bird poised on the banks of the Nile, about to fly off into the sunlight.'

Hatiay shook his head without replying. Poetic ideas were all very well, but they didn't give much solidity to a building.

The city of the Horizon continued to rise towards the vault of God. Countless sacks of fertile earth had been transported to its arid banks so a pleasure garden could be planted; gingerbread trees, acacias, sycamores, pomegranates, olives, tamarisks, date palms, fig trees, jujube trees, sweet-smelling shrubs, seeds and plants of all descriptions were brought from the parks of Thebes and laid down in a wonderful design of pathways, shrubberies, orchards and miniature forests.

At the court of Thebes, the new capital was the fashionable

subject of conversation. Those who had been lucky enough to choose a site for their home talked of its future splendour, described how they would decorate its walls and what they would lay down for flooring, discussed the way the rooms would face and where the courtyards would lie. Some even had a model constructed and placed in a prominent position so they could show their friends around it in anticipation.

The women talked of nothing but the wonders of the city of the 'Disc', the whiteness of the cliffs, the originality of the position, the coolness and the splendour of the future gardens. The 'sun-pleated' dress came into fashion and wives advised their husbands to wear their loincloth full around the hips and low in front, thus elegantly underlining the roundness of the stomach; this showed the delicate beauty of the navel to best advantage, indeed from that time on affected speakers referred to it as 'the midday star'.

In short, the excitement came at just the right moment to encourage the religious fervour of the court and turn the indifferent into faithful worshippers of Aten. The few rebels, no longer listened to, resigned themselves to nursing their grievances in silence. And since the High Priest of Amon was no longer there to fan the flames of their revolt, they finally got used to not setting aside a tenth of all their goods for the priests, and in time were surprised, and indeed delighted, to find what a difference this made.

When the good weather came, excursions were organized down to the site of the new capital. Each one was an excuse for festivity and pleasure, hunts and water games. The women exclaimed: 'Thebes has become so boring! Oh, the pleasures of living the simple, peasant life! We sleep hard, eat simply, our hair is full of sand, our skin is rough, our eyes ache, we are dirty and sticky with sweat—just like the simple, happy peasant!'

This new form of snobbery lasted for some time and was then replaced by another: the affectation of honesty as ordered by Aten.

It became the fashion to say exactly what one thought of one's neighbour, and the gossip-sessions always began with the same words, a hymn to truth: 'By the One God who honours frankness,

219

I couldn't keep what I am about to say to myself without feeling a hypocrite!' And when one wanted to criticize one's friends to their faces: 'You, who are a zealous believer in honesty, won't blame me for telling you that. . . .'

The only ones who were more or less spared were the members of the royal family, for those with power to inflict disgrace can always react unexpectedly.

It also became usual to show one's affection in public; the young people no longer hid themselves away to pay court to the ladies of their choice, and an atmosphere of joyful dissipation filled the air, presided over the festivities and even penetrated the most surprising and unsuitable places.

What the young king and his wife did with simplicity, the neophytes of the new cult exaggerated, as though only excess could give the measure of their zeal. To those used to falsehood and hypocritical evasiveness, practising sincerity meant going to extremes of rudeness.

Tiyi was not taken in by all this, and one day said to her son: 'Don't you realize the falsity of the courtiers' candour? Their frank speech, their free manners, the way they exaggerate everything is a fashion, a way of flattering you by imitation. Honesty means nothing more to them than the permission to follow their instincts. And woe betide the nation, my son, if the young people become shameless.'

'What's this, my mother?' replied Akhenaten with a smile. 'Do you, of all people, accuse someone of showing too much honesty? You who have always taught me that sincerity made a good man.'

'In truth, my eldest son, I will say again: "Sincerity makes a good man", for that means a good man is always sincere. But let me point out to you that your courtiers are using "sincerity" as an excuse to satisfy their worst instincts without danger, as an arm to wound each other, and as a means of pleasing you. Does not sincerity thus become a form of falsehood and lying?'

Akhenaten shook his head.

'I will discourage no one,' he said. 'Who knows, perhaps if they pretend long enough they will end up by being sincere.'

220

In the fifth year of the co-regent's reign, in the last month of the winter season, queen Nefertiti was brought to bed of a third daughter, whom they named Ankhes-en-Pa-Aten.

On the first day of the sixth year, the thirty-year jubilees of both Amonhotep III and Aten were celebrated. To his surprised people the young king explained: 'Pharaoh is in the thirtieth year of his reign, and from the moment he mounted the throne, the One God has been worshipped. My father built him a temple, and it was my father who spoke to me of Aten's greatness. It is only justice that Pharaoh's jubilee should be coupled with that of the sacred Disc.'

Akhenaten had really combined the jubilees for two secret reasons. First, because he wanted to show the scandal-mongers his profound respect for his father, even though he had ordered his name to be erased from the temples of Amon, and also because he desired that this honour to his God should coincide with the court's installation in the city of the Horizon.

In the last month of the winter season of the same year, Akhenaten, his wife and his three daughters, followed by all those of the court who believed in Aten, the priests and the servants, set off for the new capital. It wasn't finished yet, but none of them had the patience to wait any longer.

A magnificent entertainment preceded the departure, and the journey passed happily. When at last they arrived in sight of the new city, gleaming with white, gold and bright-coloured enamels, a cry of admiration rose from the throats of nobles and commoners alike. The city was certainly worthy of the Horizon of the Glorious Star.

Above their heads, Aten rejoiced at all this enthusiasm in His honour, and gave His blessing.

In solemn procession the crowd marched to the temple, in the full heat of the midday sun. They crossed the entrance of Per-hai, the 'house of jubilation', whose proud gateposts stood like majestic sentinels, holding in their fists flagpoles from which multi-coloured streamers floated in the north-west wind. They crossed the uncovered ceremonial alleyway, flooded with sunlight and lined with low offering tables, engraved with scenes of

221

the king and queen at prayer. They entered Gem-Aten, the 'meeting of Aten', by a third gateway, its archway brilliantly enamelled, and came out onto a vast lawn from which one could see a covered courtyard, surrounded by flat roofs. They descended the steps which led to a big altar, loaded with gleaming fruits and quarters of meat which shone as though they had been glazed.

Then Akhenaten halted and said in solemn, moving tones: 'The secret sanctuary of Aten is not yet finished, so we will worship Him here today. My well-beloved brothers, go on up the raised corridor behind the altar; there you will find tables on which to offer up your hearts and innocent souls to the kindly gaze of God. My wife, my children and the priests will stay here to pray.'

The procession went off in the direction Akhenaten had indicated and solemnly took their places.

Then, in a cry of love and faith, the deep voice of their High Priest king rose towards the vaulted sky:

> *'Your rising is beautiful at the Horizon of heaven,*
> *Oh living Aten, giver of life. . . .'*

The 133 lines of the holy psalm took wing towards the sun like a covey of phoenix at the dawn of their first day.

And such was the beauty of the moment that even those who bowed their heads without believing were uneasy and, for a moment, were conscious of the hollow emptiness of their hearts.

In the thrilling silence which followed the prayers, Akhenaten consecrated his capital: 'You are the Horizon from which the divine Star rises,' he said, 'you are the dawn of the day which will never end for men. Your name is Akhet-Aten, the glorious, the radiant, the pure. May evil never cross your threshold.'

The months which followed were filled with excitement and joys. Each family moved into its new home, and paid inquisitive visits to friends. Party followed party, everything was an excuse for rejoicing and festivity.

Akhenaten, wishing to reward his subjects' zeal, granted them all 'houses of eternity' in the northern cliffs, distributed gold and

222

riches, honours and dignity, received them with affection and listened to them with indulgence. The foreigners who visited the city returned home marvelling, and exclaimed: 'A charming city; mistress of pleasure and entertainment, filled with every luxury. Great is the city of the Horizon of Aten! When one looks upon it one is dazzled as by the summer sun.'

Life was uncomplicated and joyful in this isolated community, with pleasure and beauty flowing like milk and honey. Akhenaten passed the days happily in the company of his wife and his beloved children. He believed he had found peace of mind at last, because he had time to laze in the sun and contemplate the marvels of his God without being interrupted by his duties as a king and the demands of his people; he was lulled by a strange peacefulness, a sense of timelessness which was the forerunner of eternity. . . . As for the tiresome duties of kingship, he left them to his Vizier, old Nakht, in whom he had complete confidence. If Nakht, after reading the letters from the Provinces, told him that such-and-such a vassal was asking for gold, sweet-smelling oil and other presents, Akhenaten answered: 'Granted, my good Nakht! If they ask this from me, it is surely because they have a need of it, and my treasure is large enough to content them.'

If the Vizier presented a request from the workers in the quarries or the mines for more and better food he said: 'Why worry me? Are my grain stores and my cellars closed? Take and distribute! Let it be known that the most humble of my subjects lacked for nothing during the days of my reign.'

Nefertiti loved her husband so much that after six years of marriage she still trembled when he neared her. She never worried about affairs of state. In the velvet palace atmosphere, where all was grace and beauty, affection and tenderness, she had once more become 'Queen of the sacred ibis country', her soul was happy and at peace—for was not her dwelling place a remote island where nothing mattered except love, the sun and her silent dreams?

In the seventh year she presented her husband with another daughter. At the same time Tiyi conceived and nine months later brought into the world a boy who was called Tut-ankh-Aten.

When this news reached Akhet-Aten, there were many who laughed and made the usual jokes about this late maternity: 'Pharaoh was so bored in his Theban palace there was nothing for it but his wife!'—'If Pharaoh has so much energy after ruling for thirty-three years he'll see us all into our sarcophagi!'—'Old men are like children. Leave them a moment without supervision and they do something stupid.'

Tiyi had stayed on in the old capital with Pharaoh, the harem women and those of the courtiers too old or too conservative to change the habits of a lifetime. Giluhepa had remarked, with the bitterness of frustration: 'What are we doing, in this decrepit old palace? Since the young ones left everything smells of boredom and decay; Our singers have no teeth, our dancers are crippled and our gallants are in their dotage.'

Alas, the secret wish of her heart hadn't been granted. Never yet had Pharaoh and his wives embarked for the magnificent, glorious, joyous city of Akhet-Aten, and the echoes of festivity and laughter which visitors brought back with them made Giluhepa bitterer than ever.

If Tiyi hadn't visited the city of her first-born son, it was because she had no time to spare. She considered that he was living in a dangerous apathy. Not daring to interfere too much, for she loved him and Nefertiti enough to be pleased by their happiness, she told herself that danger was not imminent; she still had a good head upon her shoulders and had once more taken up the reins of government. She sent spies to the provinces to ward off the revolt which without doubt threatened there, fore-shadowed by the princes' insolent demands. She knew of her son's generosity and deplored it. She had told him a hundred times that wild animals only respect a whip.

She worked two hours a day in the palace study, instructed the generals to inform her about the state of the frontiers, sent police patrols out after the sand runners, reminded the vassals of the amount of their annual tributes, and inspected the troops and the mines, accompanied by an unwilling, grumbling husband. For age hadn't increased Pharaoh's energy and he missed no opportunity of showing his displeasure. He said: 'My eldest son is wailing in the "house of the royal children" at Akhet-Aten, and I have younger sons wailing here under the sycamores. What a lucky man I am! Soon I will be able to shift the burden of government onto their shoulders and warm my old bones in peace in the sun. Another twenty years' hard work, and on the day before my death I'll finally be able to devote myself to the pleasures of living.'

Tiyi smiled and didn't reply. May we be granted another twenty years of happiness, my dearest love, she thought.

CHAPTER SIX

T**IYI** feared the Hittites and detested the Amorites. She judged the latter from the character of the many Amorite women in her husband's harem; they were all cowardly, spiteful and hypocritical.

She feared the Hittites because she knew they were violent, cruel, unsettled, barbarous and as uncivilized as the sand runners and the nomad tribes of the Khabirus*, who wandered on the north-east frontiers. Since they had decided to extend their territories they were a constant menace to Egypt, whose provinces they coveted. It was impossible to negotiate with them for they killed envoys without listening to them. The Kingdom of Mitanni was the only obstacle in the path of their destructive fury: it lay between the two rivers which flowed in the opposite direction to the Nile, and had a sea coast just north of the provinces of Syria. Already during the reign of Amonhotep II it had been important to conclude alliances with the Kings of Mitanni. Later Thutmose IV had even gone so far as to make the daughter of Artatama I a Great Royal Wife; she had been Tiyi's mother-in-law and Pharaoh's mother. As well as this, Pharaoh himself had reluctantly agreed to marry Giluhepa in the tenth year of his reign. There were many close ties between Egypt and the country 'of the two rivers'. When things went badly for one, the other was affected. Since the death of Sutarna, Mitanni had had more than its share of worries. Anxiously, Egypt had watched from a distance as a civil war had torn their allied kingdom apart; Egypt had trembled for the younger son, Tusratta, Giluhepa's brother, carried off by the traitor Pirkhi after the assassination of the elder

* Khabirus: Probably Hebrews.

226

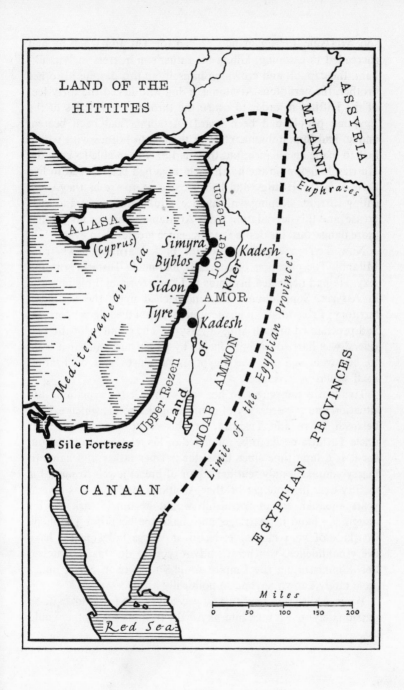

LAND OF THE
HITTITES

ASSYRIA

MITANNI

Euphrates

ALASA
(Cyprus)

Mediterranean Sea

Simyra

Byblos

Lower Rezen

Kadesh

Kher

Sidon

AMOR

Tyre

Kadesh

of

Upper Rezen

Land

MOAB AMMON

■ Sile Fortress

Limit of the Egyptian provinces

EGYPTIAN PROVINCES

CANAAN

Miles

0   50   100   150   200

Red Sea

son Artassumara; Egypt had prayed for Tusratta when he had succeeded in escaping, killing his father's murderers in Wassukkani, the capital, and crowning himself, all this despite his other brother, the perfidious Artatama, a dog who licked the dirty feet of the Hittites in order to usurp the throne. The prayers of the Egyptian people had been heard: Artatama had been beaten, and so had Suppiluliuma, chief of the bandit hordes with whom he had made an alliance; but they had only been able to keep the Hurrian kingdom in the north. Artatama had been forced to live there with the Hittites, and had become as savage as they were, eating carrion, sleeping with his lice, stinking of sweat and goat grease, and this degradation made Artatama's hate for his brother more dangerous, his desire for vengeance greater than ever.

Now Tiyi's messengers brought back alarming news from Mitanni. The pleasures of court life had made Tusratta soft and lazy. He had neglected his lands in Upper Syria and his interests in Assyria. Suppiluliuma had encroached upon the adjoining territory; Erba-adad, an adventurer, a jackal feeding on corpses, had proclaimed himself king of Assyria. The country 'of the two rivers' was harried on both flanks by its enemies, and if it were to be swallowed up, the Egyptian provinces and civilization itself would be in danger.

Tiyi sent a messenger to her son with a letter explaining the situation and the necessity of reinforcing the bonds which existed between Egypt and Tusratta. To this effect she wrote: 'Your uncle Tusratta needs to be reminded of his relationship with you, for it is a long time since his sister left her father and came to marry yours. He only sent her a pair of breast jewels to mark his victory over his younger brother Artatama, and that was several years ago. An act of friendship would be timely: ask for his daughter's hand in marriage, and make the beautiful Taduhepa first lady of your harem. Nefertiti, in whose judgement I have every confidence, will herself advise you to do this; I watched her administrating the Empire while you were in Syria, and I have rarely known anyone so politically astute.'

When Akhenaten read this he was angry. He loved his wife so passionately that it hurt him physically to think his mother could

228

even consider proposing a second wife. Taduhepa was a princess. She wouldn't be like the few unhappy women in his scanty harem who had long ago resigned themselves to being no more than their lord's harp players, singers and dancers. She would expect a married life and he had no wish to give her one. How could Tiyi think for a single moment he would offer to another woman something which belonged by rights to Nefertiti, however beautiful the other woman was? Akhenaten remembered with affectionate amusement his wife's reaction to the ten girls from the land of Punt. Not for all the gold in Egypt would he cause her such sorrow again. She had given him a fifth daughter, but what did that matter? They had all eternity ahead of them in which to 'meet together' and the time would certainly come when a boy would slip between the bricks, into the hands held ready to receive him.

He decided not to worry Nefertiti and replied to his mother that if an act of friendship was necessary to reassure his uncle, he would rather send him the best horses from his stables; and that if a political action was called for, he preferred to strengthen the frontier troops, but he didn't want to hear another word about his cousin from Mitanni.

Tiyi frowned as she read.

'The young are selfish and stupid,' she murmured, 'they think only of their pleasures and their joys. Are Pharaoh and I never to be able to rest?'

So once again, Pharaoh's goodwill was put to the test. Tiyi explained to her husband that the security of the Two Kingdoms called for further self-sacrifice, and he allowed himself to be convinced without too much trouble when he learnt that the sacrifice consisted of marrying a young Mitanni girl. He knew by experience that Mitanni women were beautiful, fine-boned, sensitive, sensual and extremely well-versed in the arts of love: quite different from the savage Nubians, the stolid girls from Punt, the passive Syrians or even the over-proud Egyptians.

He sighed, however, for the look of the thing, and said: 'My son is the guilty one. Doesn't he know I need a rest? Am I to give in to him right up to my death?'

Tiyi urged her husband to send an Ambassador to Tusratta, loaded with presents, wishes of prosperity and an elegant request for the hand of his daughter, the very beautiful Taduhepa.

It is a custom with rulers and merchants not to hand over their goods until their value has been appreciated to the full. Following this principle, Tusratta began by making difficulties. 'You are no longer young,' he wrote, 'and my daughter has a young girl's appetite; she is a filly dreaming of a vigorous thoroughbred whose teeth are not worn down by the bit. Surely I must give her what she needs. Shall I present her to a stallion who prefers to rest in the stable?'

Though at first sight such words might appear harsh, they didn't worry Pharaoh, for he knew his brother-in-law wrote thus to give him a chance of boasting about his merits. By return of messenger, he assured Tusratta of his vigour, described his prowess and stated the age of his last-born child, who still took pleasure from nothing but its foster-mother's milk.

'So far so good,' replied Tusratta, 'but I remember your second marriage was to my sister the exquisite Giluhepa. By giving to Egypt the grace and beauty of a second Mitanni princess will I not be showing her too much favour, and risk displeasing other friendly nations? This could make me dangerous enemies among the other people with whom I have alliances.'

'Beautiful and desirable women are as numerous in Mitanni as the magnificent lotus flower in Egypt,' wrote Pharaoh. 'Any sovereign would lay his kingdom at the feet of the most humble girl from your country. In any case, why fear your neighbours? Are not you and I together more powerful than they? Are we not brothers, dividing the world of men?'

'Without a doubt,' replied Tusratta, 'but I am sorry for Tiyi, the Great Royal Wife, whom I hold in much respect . . . will she not be jealous? Is it right for me to set against her the freshness and energy of a young girl?'

'She is happy to think she is to be relieved of half my vigour and hopes your daughter has a strong constitution.'

When Tusratta had exhausted all his arguments and Pharaoh had refuted them one by one (which took five months, including

230

the Ambassador's journeys; the poor man was resigned to having no rest until his mission was brought to a successful close), the king of Mitanni granted the hand of his daughter, with the usual show of unwillingness which good manners demanded.

Then the tone of the letters changed.

'What can I hope from you in exchange for my daughter's great beauty?' asked Tusratta.

'My support, my friendship, the strength of my right arm.'

'I have heard that in your country gold is as common as dust on the roads.'

'I will send you many bushels full. Don't hesitate to ask.'

'Dare I demand another couple of bushels, then, for two cubits of my palace passages are still uncovered.'

In reality these exchanges were only an elegant way of settling a contractual price already agreed upon at the time when Pharaoh had married Giluhepa, for Tusratta was honest enough not to ask for more than his father for the same commodity. The old king of Egypt appreciated this respectful indication of straight dealing and thought highly of such a wise and moderate man.

At last, when all had been discussed, concluded and paid for, the beautiful Taduhepa set out for her husband's harem, accompanied by a suite of 246 servants and followed by 100 slaves carrying her trousseau and presents from her father to Pharaoh, these last being by way of a bonus for an esteemed client. She was escorted by a company of soldiers and also by the Ambassador, rejoicing at the thought that his long peregrinations were over and that he would finally be able to settle down on the new lands which his lord would certainly not fail to give him as a reward for his obstinate and worthy efforts.

Thebes welcomed the princess from Mitanni with magnificent celebrations. Only Giluhepa managed to introduce a discordant note into the general goodwill. She remarked in acid tones: 'We are going to have a gad-fly at our heels. This young woman will try to dominate us on the pretext that she is the ear of corn and we the straw. So what? The hay is no less useful to the donkey than the ear . . . and Pharaoh is a donkey! Doesn't he know that on a stormy sea, an old *dahabiyeh* splits at the seams, fills with

231

water and sinks? Does he think he is just out of the shipyards to risk himself thus on the waves?'

Giluhepa's wise words didn't come to the ears of Pharaoh, or if they did he paid no attention to them; which may well have been the reason why it wasn't long before the old king 'split at the seams and filled with water'.

He had welcomed his young wife with the energy of a youth, and in order not to disappoint her too soon, he had resorted to drugs made from plants which the gods created expressly to give man vigour when all else has failed: a misleading expedient which hides from the taker the real state of his resources. When Pharaoh's natural energy was used up, his health failed suddenly and no drugs on earth could give him back what he had lost.

One morning he couldn't get up, and Pentu, who had remained at the court of Thebes in order to supervise his nearby lands, was respectful enough to pretend not to understand what was wrong with him.

Rather than give the impression he was abandoning his royal patient to his sad fate, Pentu prescribed a mixture of dry flour soaked in mild beer, a remedy for those with swollen stomachs. He prepared poultices from a mixture of wax, grease, date wine, honey and cooked wheat, and applied them at random; the more so since their purpose was normally to draw blood from a wound. He administered a draught against worms, and a concoction of Te'em plant in date wine, recommended for nursing mothers. He even tried some of the mixtures in which suffering humanity had put its faith before the advent of scientific medicine. He applied to his patient's skin scarab wings cooked in oil, and obliged him to swallow the head and wings of the same insects simmered in snake fat. It was a remedy reported efficacious with piles, and could hardly harm a healthy anus.

Pentu didn't put fly-droppings into his ointments and medicines, for fly-droppings were an ingredient mainly suitable for the poor, who could thus, thanks to the foresight of the gods, procure a pharmaceutical product cheaply by scraping their walls.

In short, Pentu acted with sufficient energy to allay any suspicion of negligence. And when he had finally worked right through his considerable collection of formulae, he could at least announce that there was nothing for it but to rely on divine intervention.

'Alas, Majesty,' he exclaimed despairingly, 'you have beaten science, certainly because of your divinity. You need pills of earth pounded with the holy saliva of Semsou, the sacred magician. If I spit on clay, I just spit on clay, like a miserable mortal.'

Then suddenly his face lit up, and so intent was he to be helpful that he forgot one of the most simple tenets of his new faith in Aten. He spoke the name of a goddess belonging to the contemptible pagan religion, and a foreign goddess into the bargain. He said: 'Remember the statue of Ishtar which king Tusratta sent some years ago, when I could do nothing for you? She cured you then, and you rose from your sick bed healthier than ever.'

Pharaoh's dull eyes, already filled with visions of death, brightened.

'Let my Mitanni father-in-law be requested to send me the holy statue of Ishtar,' he whispered. 'She will save me.'

Ishtar came at once from her temple at Wassukkani, accompanied by many of her priests, who were the only ones who knew how to recite the mysterious healing prayers. They placed the precious statue in Pharaoh's room and for the whole of one day they chanted words which were all the more impressive because no one could understand them. They sounded like:

> *Edera, edesana,*
> *Ederagaha edesana,*
> *Marmou edesana . . .*

A strange and moving litany which buzzed like a swarm of dung flies on rotting matter in the season of decomposition.

At sunset the priests stopped for a rest. They came gravely from the room and went off to relax and joke among themselves in the apartment reserved for them in the quarters of the priests of Aten. Tiyi remained alone with her husband. She saw him, collapsed and only half-conscious, and in her heart she knew it was the end. It was the end, and afterwards perhaps there was only nothingness, a mummy which stared with empty orbits at the dumb walls of its sarcophagus, in a silent, never-ending night.

233

Tears trickled down her tired face. She felt herself weary, beaten, exhausted and the desperate consciousness of her unimportance, faced with the immensity of time, made her shrink in upon herself and look shrivelled. She remembered the thirty-four happy years spent at this man's side, as a leaf burned by the *khamsin* remembers the north-west breeze: memory made grief all the sharper, and the feeling of loss more unbearable.

Pharaoh opened his eyes and smiled; a smile of complicity which said: 'My old love, we've seen life together, haven't we!'

Tiyi took his hand and pressed it to her lips with a gesture of infinite tenderness. She had never known how to show her husband the extent of her love, for she had been born ill-endowed for such a task: her voice was authoritative, the lines of her mouth hard, her eyes were sharp and her bone structure such that all her movements were angular, lacking the rounded grace which so often seems the outward sign of an affectionate soul.

Now, for the first time in thirty-four years, she found the secret of transmitting the feelings of her heart, for the strength of her despair had broken the hard shell with which she had entered the world, as others are born clothed with fat or with a caul.

Pharaoh died in the early morning, before Aten opened his eye above the eastern cliffs.

It was the thirty-sixth year of his reign, the eleventh year of his eldest son's co-regency, in the pale dawn of the twenty-eighth day of the second month of the summer season: a time when the wild south-east winds swept down with their great winding sheets of sand, tributes from the dry regions to the Master of the Two Kingdoms.

CHAPTER SEVEN

T IYI sent her son a laconic letter: 'Your father is dead and being embalmed. Waste no time, for the natron bath only lasts seventy days.'

Akhenaten quickly gathered together his suite and embarked for the old capital, which he hadn't visited for five years. Nefertiti didn't accompany him for she was six months gone with child and tired easily.

When the *dahabiyeh* came in sight of Thebes the young sovereign knew in his heart that he had never stopped loving this majestic city, despite its evil, despite the decay in its stony heart. Almost shyly he trod the soil of the alleyways and the flagstones of the corridors which led to his mother's apartments. Tiyi was waiting for him, sitting bolt upright on a chair in the lotus boudoir. She had aged, and in her face, devoid of all cosmetics, he could see the lines of bitterness and dark despair.

A wave of tenderness swept over Akhenaten as he realized that this hard woman also had her weaknesses; he was about to run to her and take her in his arms when she made a gesture which stopped him in his tracks.

'You have come quicker than I thought,' she said dryly, 'I didn't know you were so fond of your father.'

Akhenaten stared at her in surprise.

'Mother, you must know how dear my father was to me,' he cried, 'why speak such hurtful words?'

Tiyi's lip curled.

'Can one believe a son loves his father when he is responsible for his death?'

In the silence which followed Akhenaten tried vainly to understand his mother's animosity and the sense of her strange words.

Finally he asked in a puzzled and anxious voice: 'What have I done wrong?'

Then Tiyi could no longer contain the violence of her grief.

'What have you done wrong?' she cried. 'You refused to marry Tusratta's daughter when it was your duty, yours, the co-regent's. Your father didn't appoint you co-regent to live in sloth and pleasure like a harem woman. He had confidence in you, but he was wrong—and so was I. And wrong about Nefertiti, too. She is like her mother! Her arrogance is not that of authority, but of foolish pride. Neither of you is worthy to sit upon the throne of Egypt. Taduhepa was *your* duty . . . you are the ruling prince. Because you refused to undertake your obligations as king, your father sacrificed himself. *He* strengthened the alliances with Tusratta to secure *your* kingdom.'

She laughed mirthlessly. 'The kingdom you are going to ruin, and finally to lose! He died for nothing. Not only do you now have the power to wreck Egypt, but like it or not you also inherit Taduhepa.'

She leant back in her chair and tried to laugh.

'Yes, and she won't leave you in peace. She'll throw herself at you as she threw herself at your ageing father. She is a man-eater, a lioness at the time of the full moon. And when, although you still love Nefertiti, you can't stop yourself running to Taduhepa, drawn by violent desire for her young body . . . then perhaps you will realize that love, real love, is something more than the satisfaction of one's desires. Perhaps your father won't have died in vain, perhaps your mother's grief won't be for nothing. Who knows? Perhaps you and Nefertiti, learning more about the nature of love, will be cured of this blindness which binds you together with no thought for the rest of the world, will at last become conscious of the heavy burden for which you were born. Woe betide those who are born on a throne! Their bread is bitterer than a peasant's. If they forget that, they become tyrants, sons of Seth, enemies of their people and, on the day of judgement, their punishment will be that of those who have not accomplished the work for which they were born.'

Akhenaten listened to this tirade with astonishment and fury.

236

He told himself his mother was deranged by grief and talking wildly, but he blamed her for attacking Nefertiti so violently and he wondered if perhaps she had always been secretly jealous of Nefertiti's beauty. At this thought, he felt scorn, and said in a cold, hard voice: 'Nefertiti shows me more affection than you ever did; that's why I love her so passionately. I believe you love me, because I have always wanted to believe it . . . but in truth, you have never proved it to me. Certainly you watched over my upbringing, saw I was well fed and cared for . . . but did you sing me lullabies in bed at night when I was a child and afraid of the dark? Did you take me in your arms to caress me, kiss me, say the foolish words all little children need as surely as they need their wet nurse's milk? No . . . you always said goodnight coldly, and told me not to disturb my nurse with my stupid fear of the dark . . . you never kissed me except on the forehead. I trembled at the idea of displeasing you and suffered at having emotions in a world where it seemed that dignity was expressed by coldness. I venerated you, I admired your intelligence and I cried secretly because I was not as you expected me to be; I dreaded your disapproval. That is why I forced myself to be inflexible and reserved. That is also why I turned passionately towards a God who spoke to me with words of love. In time I grew up. I became more reasonable, knew once and for all that you loved me in your way and no longer minded the coldness in your voice. I expected nothing more from anyone, except from God. Then . . . then Nefertiti came into my life, and at first she seemed like you. I who loved her, who admired her, found myself like a child before her, trembling at the thought I might displease her, fearful of her scorn. Until the miraculous day when she took my face in her beautiful hands, she held me close to her, she smiled at me and in her eyes I saw all the gentleness of her affection, and the burning fire of her love. I was no longer alone. I was drawn irresistibly towards this human being who was so like myself. I no longer care about the rest of the world, I am not grudging in my love, for all the world, except for Nefertiti, has wounded me, and I have suffered too much from reserve. You cannot teach *me* that love is more than the satisfaction of desire. But I can tell you this: love is the perfect creation

237

of God, the perfect emotion in man; it expects the body to be faithful as well as the heart and the mind. If one breaks this harmony and unity, if one loves many women, one becomes impure, as surely as gold smelted with copper.'

Tiyi made a tremendous effort of will not to cry out in pain. Sweat bathed her forehead and the cold seemed to run down into all her limbs. She shivered as though she were suffering from swamp fever, but not one face muscle moved. There was a long silence, during which Akhenaten felt the tardy uneasiness of those who, once they have voiced their grievances, are afraid they have gone too far and given themselves away. Then Tiyi said in a level voice: 'I won't try to justify myself in your eyes, my son; I need not account for my actions to you. He who governs is always alone when he carries out his duties, otherwise he will confuse those duties with his feelings. You can have a warm heart for just so long as you keep a cool head, for those it is your mission to lead have greater need of your good sense than of your friendly gestures; they will lose their respect and obedience if they know they can count on your indulgence. It is thus with a king towards his subjects . . . and thus I think it should be with the master towards his pupil, and with the parent towards his child. Perhaps I was mistaken . . . I can't tell. You might be even softer now, if I had spent my time kissing you, being sorry for you and letting you believe that your mistakes were not serious. You are the one on trial here, not I. I regret that I was carried away just now, for I failed to follow my own rule of moderation. However, calmly this time, I will repeat my advice: get it into your head that you are not a common mortal who can allow himself weaknesses. You are a God in the eyes of thousands, and you are responsible for your creatures. You are the Sun incarnate and must light up thousands of lives. Your lot is not enviable, but if you admire honesty, admit honestly that you must submit because it is your destiny. Do what you will about Taduhepa; but her brother is our only shield against the Hittites, remember that. I have spoken. Go now, and see your father's body. Your apartments have been prepared . . . they are your father's old ones. Now leave me alone, Pharaoh.'

Akhenaten would have liked to go down at his mother's knees and ask her pardon for all the things he had said. He hesitated, worried and uneasy, with the guilty look of a child whose conscience is not at ease. But his mother's expression was forbidding and he feared that she would consider his repentance weakness, so he turned to leave the boudoir. As he was crossing the threshold, Tiyi called after him: 'I should warn you that the embalming and burial rites will be those of the God Osiris. I wrote to Abydos and asked the priests to come. I don't know if you have discussed the question of funerals with your God. It seems to be missing from your dogma and you should consider filling the gap, for the harvest time has come for Aten's faithful of my generation. Your father is the first to be reaped . . . the sickle isn't far away from Ay, Nakht, Ti, Ramose and others. Don't make a scandal in my city and blame only yourself if your father's body is prepared in the old way. However, Amon's name will not be mentioned and the engravers will not take up their chisels to put back on the royal *hypogeum* the inscriptions you have erased. Now leave.'

Akhenaten said nothing, but went, suddenly feeling tired and very sad. If only his wife were with him! He wanted to lay his head in the hollow of her neck, to drink her life through parted lips from her soft skin . . . he needed someone to say to him affectionately: 'You haven't been bad, you spoke the truth in your heart, and your mother, who respects honesty, will respect you even more because you did not hide from her the secret sufferings of your childhood.' Yes, if Nefertiti had been there, that is what she would have said; he would have drunk in her words eagerly and would have felt better, as a feverish man feels cooler after a drink of water: a misleading feeling no doubt, but how good! With his own hands he had thrust a dagger in his mother's heart, deliberately meaning to hurt her, forgetting that she was already prostrate with grief. That had been an ignoble and cowardly act.

His sense of his own cruelty was such that despair trickled, drop by bitter drop, into his soul. Akhenaten crossed the river to the City of the Dead, where he was received with the respect due to the Great King of the Two Kingdoms which he would become as soon as his father was buried. The prince of the Western

Necropolis accompanied him into the silent room where the royal corpse lay submerged in a bath of natron; the prince waited, passive and indifferent, until his young sovereign finished meditating on the dead man. He had been governing the City of the Dead long enough to be accustomed to such things. He no longer wondered at the terrible enigma of the rigid corpse's silent lips, closed eternally on the secret of the invisible regions in which the Ka lives on. Because the priests believed in the hypothesis of survival, he had decided to believe the same thing and thus his soul had nothing to worry about. For, from that moment of decision, death took on a joyous aspect of new life, confirmed by the relaxed, rested, peaceful faces of the dead given into the embalmer's hands.

Akhenaten remained for a long time in contemplation of his father's naked body; the process of drying made it appear larger than ever. But he looked without seeing, for his thoughts were centred on himself, and he was too busy despising himself to recognize in this corpse, already made anonymous by the deformation of its features, the father he had venerated and deeply loved.

There were still forty days to go before the burial; forty days in which to live with his guilty conscience, to face the scorn and bitterness of his mother and to harden himself not to weep in front of her. Forty days of boredom because his uneasy mind refused to allow itself to be diverted. . . .

Akhenaten tried turning to his God for help and spent long hours in his old 'secret place', but all his thoughts were confused and bitter, and he was not comforted.

On the tenth day, not knowing what else to do, he entered his father's harem, which was now his, and met Taduhepa.

She didn't bow before him, but stared at him with bright, lively eyes, straight and proud as a wild animal from the desert lands where a hunter's net has never been spread. Akhenaten felt a shock which jolted him abruptly from his depression, and he saw that she was beautiful. Her voice throbbed with life and all her body quivered with the kind of nervous energy which runs under the skin of a racing mare.

The blood beat in his temples, and the young man said to himself, with unconscious hypocrisy: if my mother sees me with Taduhepa, she will triumph; and the impression that she has won a victory will be like salve on the bitter pain of her wound. She will be happy to have predicted rightly that I can desire a body other than Nefertiti's; she will be more indulgent towards me and in the end may even forget the harshness of my words. I will know she has pardoned me when I see in her eyes something other than grief and loneliness.

Thereafter he often went to the harem to visit Taduhepa, and found sufficient charm in her conversation to persuade himself that she could be a friend at a time when he badly needed one. Certainly she couldn't hold a candle to Nefertiti either for beauty or intelligence, but he was grateful to her for being a refuge for his boredom and his solitude.

She is a charming child, radiating candour and youth; she will be a friend for Nefertiti, he said to himself, to still his small inner voice which whispered: 'Take care!'

The reality, which he preferred to ignore, was: 'You are taking your father's harem back to Akhet-Aten. Despite your great love for your wife, you must resign yourself to considering Taduhepa as a second wife you have no right to ignore. You like her, and mustn't hurt her feelings. Remember you cannot incur her father's anger.'

On the seventy-first day, Amonhotep III was taken from his natron bath, washed, carefully bandaged with fine gauze, loaded with amulets, precious stones and magic formulae, placed in sarcophagi of gold incrusted with carnelians, lapis lazuli and coloured glass, and at last, decked for eternity in this brilliant and incorruptible god-like form, he was transported on a ceremonial bed to the throne room where the royal family, the great lords and ladies of the kingdom and the professional mourners, chosen for their powers of mime, were waiting for him.

The High Priests of Abydos, Akhet-Aten and On lifted their palms towards the ceiling and cried in chorus: 'You live again, you live again for ever, now you are young again for ever.'

241

That was the signal for the lamentations; a hallucinatory performance on the part of the professional mourners, all artists in heart-rending sorrow, agonizing cries and despairing gestures; they rolled on the ground, sobbing, suddenly jumped to their feet with the cry of an animal wounded to death, beat their breasts, slapped their cheeks vigorously, threw themselves to the ground again to knock their heads against the flagstones, and covered themselves with dust which they had taken the precaution to bring with them in a little bag. They acted according to the inspiration of the moment, each one trying to outdo the other. Many of them showed great talent; some, the youngest in the profession, who hadn't had time to perfect their methods, threw themselves round with a certain clumsiness and showed no imagination in the phrasing of their lamentations. The most gifted could easily make themselves weep, and their tearful faces, streaked with *mesdemet*, their red, swollen eyes, and their dripping noses gave an atmosphere of tragedy of which they were particularly proud. In the evening they met to compare notes, to joke and to congratulate each other, relaxing with peals of healthy laughter, for theirs was a difficult profession. It required great physical endurance and an exceptionally well-balanced nature, to stand up to the nervous exhaustion induced by the long hours of hysteria.

After a while, when the atmosphere was filled with electricity from the cries and the convulsions, the more emotional spectators were affected and sobbed without pretence or simulation.

Then the moment came to form the procession which would accompany Pharaoh to his eternal home. Akhenaten, straight-backed and stern, took the lead, escorted by the High Priests, the *kheriheb* who chanted the ritual formulae with the aid of the sacred Book, the princes of the royal house, the generals, the lords and friends of the king; then came the richly decorated raised platform with, on either side, two *oudja* eyes painted wide open, so the deceased would not miss any of the ceremony. Then the harem women, headed by Tiyi, pale and exhausted, and the noble ladies in tears, followed by the mourners, still hard at work. These latter profited from the abundance of sand on the pathways

242

to make generous use of the particularly evocative gesture of wild despair which consisted of covering themselves with dust.

When they reached the river bank, the crowd embarked on several *dahabiyeh* decorated for the occasion. Slowly the funeral boats moved off towards the western bank, where eternity began. There the catafalque was placed on a boat completely covered with gold, which in its turn was put onto a sleigh pulled by four oxen, groomed until they shone, their horns ornamented with precious stones.

The procession formed up again, still to the accompaniment of piercing cries, and moved off towards the western gully where the great *hypogeum* which Amonhotep III had had built by his architect, the son of Hapu, gaped dark and silent.

The road led upwards under the burning summer sun, through a landscape of baking hot cliffs and enormous piles of rock, motionless under a layer of fine white limestone dust. The heat dried up the throats; soon the wails and groans died away; the mourners straggled, wilted and slowed down. Only Tiyi continued to walk quickly and unhesitatingly, just as if sweat did not weigh down her ankles like everyone else's. Her eyes were dry, her expression lifeless, her mouth shut tightly on a grief jealously hidden away in her secret heart, where all her being cried with tears of blood. Even when they reached the door of the tomb, and according to custom she had to throw her arms around the gleaming golden feet of the sarcophagus and bewail her misery aloud, her cries of sorrow and her sobs were unconvincing, much to the disappointment of the professional mourners, who liked to pick up tips from the widow's solo with the mummy, hoping to add to their repertoire such wails and gestures as suggested real grief.

The three High Priests proceeded to open the mouth of the death mask, anointing, fumigating, lustrating, and tapping the massive mask with a small axe and a flint fork, while in a voice hoarse with all the dust he had swallowed on the way up, the *kheriheb* chanted passages from the *Book of the Two Ways*, the *Book of the Caverns* and the *Book of the Night*.

When the ceremony was over, and it was quite certain that the powerful Pharaoh had been filled with all the vital energy necessary to permit him to enjoy life in the Land of Shades, a silence fell so the Great Royal Wife could say her last goodbye. Tiyi raised her head and mechanically spoke the words of a speech written for the occasion.

Everything had been done, everything had been said. The body of Amonhotep III slipped down into the darkness. It would lie inside an interminable succession of chambers, the walls of which swarmed with innumerable slaves of darkness, right inside the great 'Golden Room' among a river of riches: arms, chariots, coffers filled with embroidered clothes, plates, dishes, furniture, arks, precious ointments, statues of his best loved wives and children, statues made of various precious materials which represented Tiyi and himself kissing each other with ceremonial stiffness . . . and finally *shawabtis* by the thousand: those servants who would answer his call and carry out his orders, work his lands, care for him and feed him, dress him and amuse him in that world where the splendid sun-boat only glided for one hour every night. Nearby, four alabaster urns containing his intestines would wait until the children of Horus* ordered them to throb again with powerful life. Amset would say to the liver: 'Press out your bile'; Hâpi to the lungs: 'Breathe, don't hold your breath'; Duamutef to the stomach: 'Chew the food'; Qebehsenuf to the intestines: 'Empty like an irrigation canal' . . . then, in the silence of the tomb and until the end of time, the viscera would start to beat like organs fed by blood, and the grave robbers would halt terrified at the mouth of the black well from which came the muffled rhythm of a life at work.

When the entrance was sealed, the cliff looked like polished stone. The next sand wind would powder its wounded flank and hide the last marks of the scar.

Silent and anxious now that all was over, the mouth of eternity sealed and the mind left knocking vainly at the entrance to the terrible unknown, the living sat down to share the funeral feast.

Akhenaten's eyes met his mother's; the terror and the bewilderment which he saw in them made him feel an immense pity for

---

* Each of the four Canopic jars was under the protection of one of the four sons of Horus: Amset, Hâpi, Duamutef and Qebehsenuf.

this woman emptied of her strength as a sacred victim is emptied of its blood on the sacrificial altar. He went up to her and said as gently as he could: 'Mother, don't stay in Thebes. Come back with me to Akhet-Aten. Your place is there among affectionate hearts.'

Tiyi shook her head slowly.

'Not yet,' she murmured. 'No, not yet . . . I have something to do. . . .'

Her voice sounded so strange that suddenly, without knowing why, Akhenaten remembered an old story which a Keftiou slave from the Islands-of-the-sea had told him when he was still a child and frightened by the strange night noises in his room. She had said: 'What you hear is the souls of the dead come back to the places they have loved. Their voice is quieter than a mosquito's, but if you listen well you can hear what they say. . . .'

When he had told his mother this she had replied brusquely: 'Nonsense! It is the night wind which makes the wood creak, the curtains whisper and the linen hangings sigh.'

Akhenaten wondered if his mother wanted to stay in the palace of her happiness, her ears strained to catch her husband's voice among those of all the dead spirits which the night breeze carried through the corridors and the empty rooms. How can one know what wild hopes spring from a tortured mind, a troubled soul and a headstrong determination not to believe in the worst?

He didn't stay long at Thebes. Having extracted from Tiyi a promise to visit the new capital after the season of the floods, he left with Taduhepa and his father's harem.

The time had come to shave his sidelock of youth and put on the crown of the Two Kingdoms. He was Pharaoh, and only the Sun was more powerful than he in all the land of Egypt and the Provinces.

CHAPTER EIGHT

THE return journey was uncomfortable, because Akhenaten spent most of the time fighting a desire to visit Taduhepa in the solitude of her cabin. He had finally realized that she was his wife and he had been celibate fifty days since leaving Akhet-Aten. But he told himself he wouldn't touch her until Nefertiti was convinced that it was necessary. He spent a lot of time deciding what he would say to her so that she would be obliged to answer: 'It's obvious you cannot do otherwise than content Tusratta's daughter. We mustn't overlook the Hittite menace.'

Then he would no longer feel guilty and with his conscience at rest he would succumb to the charms of the beautiful Mitanni girl. He would probably tire of her quickly . . . but for the moment it was in his interest not to hurt the feelings of a princess with such an ardent temperament.

He was impatient for the journey to end; impatient to talk to his wife, impatient to be delivered from the madness which stirred his blood and kept him awake at night.

Nefertiti didn't come to meet him at the landing-place; for the last two weeks she had been feeling very tired and kept to her room, not even taking her meals in public.

Akhenaten went to his wife's apartments as soon as he had received the homage of the many princes from the different *nomes* who had come to take part in his coronation.

When he saw how his wife's tired little face lit up with joy and tenderness at seeing him, he was filled with remorse and fell to his knees near her bed, without worrying about the servants. They withdrew, but not before taking a last look back, to feast their eyes on the manifestations of love from a god to a goddess. Certainly they had caught them kissing before, but they never tired of the wonderful sight of their affection. This time they had their money's worth: the last thing they saw was their sovereign's head buried in the woolly coverlet, while Nefertiti stroked the back of his neck with a shaking hand.

Seeing his wife's condition, Akhenaten didn't dare to speak to her at once about Taduhepa, and decided to put off the conversation until later, after his coronation.

By a lucky chance, the coronation festival coincided with the first day of the New Year, and this fact gave it more splendour and prestige than ever in the eyes of the superstitious people, who considered it to be the luckiest date of all.

Akhenaten took advantage of this particular belief on the part of his subjects to reaffirm his faith in Aten, the Only God. He majestically abolished many of the old customs relating to the ceremony of the 'Sun rising on Egypt' in which the sacred drama was played out by a multitude of major divinities. The two High Priests who placed on his head the red crown of the Delta and the white mitre of Upper Egypt, did not wear the masks of Seth and Horus, but were draped in yellow and caparisoned in gold to symbolize two rays of the sacred Disc. At the same time, the secondary ceremony to the god Min was replaced by a service which took place at midday in the great temple. Sixty-eight blind harpists, thirty-seven flautists, and forty-five trumpeters, a hundred male singers and as many women, took part in a ceremony during which a sheaf of spelt was cut by a golden sickle, to symbolize the richness of future harvests. However Akhenaten kept the old custom of a procession headed by the bull Mnevis and the priests whose duty it was to look after this sacred beast, for the young sovereign had not abolished the custom of worshipping Mnevis (he even had tombs dug in the cliffs for the mummified bulls). He had agreed to this out of respect for the priests of On, whom he venerated and in whose wisdom he had confidence.

Finally, in place of the four geese of Horus which should have been freed at the four cardinal points to carry the Good News to the furthest corners of the earth, he had chosen to free four ash-coloured phoenix, for this bird symbolized the sun and was considered by the people as 'he who watches over the festivals of everlasting life'.

The great pageantry of the coronation and its many attendant ceremonies filled all the spectators with admiration and respect. The princes from the *nomes* and the ambassadors from vassal and friendly countries, returned home deeply impressed.

Letters of congratulation poured in from everywhere, even from the land of the Hittites. The most moving one came from Tusratta. He asked for no bushels of gold, precious vases, oils or perfumes, as did all the minor kings who never lost an opportunity of filling their coffers with Egypt's riches. He simply said: 'When my brother Amonhotep III went to meet his fate, I wept for days. I slept not, and in my great sorrow took neither food nor drink. But now that Amonhotep IV, the great son of Amonhotep III and of Tiyi his wife, has written to me saying, "I will be king", I answer: "Amonhotep III is not dead, for his noble son, born of Tiyi, takes his place, and he will change nothing of our past relationship".'

Akhenaten was touched and willingly forgave his father-in-law for forgetting the new name of the sovereign of the Two Kingdoms. Not for a moment did he suspect him of having done it on purpose, following an old principle which was never to get mixed up in his allies' internal affairs, and also to avoid complicating his own filing system. Tusratta is a just man, Akhenaten thought affectionately, I will try not to make trouble for him, but will back up his frontier defences so his enemies will not triumph.

While thinking of his father-in-law, he remembered the beautiful Taduhepa, and made up his mind to wait no longer before contenting the young girl's impatience, thus honouring the friendship of his Mitanni ally and sparing him the affront of hearing remarks like: 'Taduhepa is not good enough for Pharaoh.'

Akhenaten, like everyone else, knew that the women of the harem often had to make do with each other, but it had never worried him; on the contrary, he preferred this solution to the introduction in his women's quarters of an energetic lover, capable of begetting bastards who would stain the dynasty. But now, thinking of the beautiful Mitanni girl, he found the thought disagreeable . . . and felt cheated, like a merchant when some expensive article is stolen.

So, plucking up his courage, he decided to speak to his well-beloved wife. He had never yet been unfaithful to her; he had never wanted to be, even during the last months of her pregnancy when he couldn't touch her. But now the situation was different. Taduhepa was a simple state duty.

Not for a moment did Akhenaten reflect that his wife had had plenty of time to talk with her mother Giluhepa, who, together with the other harem women he had inherited, had accompanied him to the court of Akhet-Aten.

Giluhepa wasn't unkind by nature, and she loved her daughter with all the affection of which her selfish and flighty character was capable, but the dull life she led in the royal harem had given her a taste for savoury gossip and smutty stories; when it was her turn to tell them she took an artistic pleasure in livening them up with piquant and personal remarks. This gave her a reputation for wit among her companions, a reputation she valued all the more now that her age ruled out the possibility of any other kind.

She hadn't meant to cause trouble when she told her daughter about the many visits Akhenaten had paid Taduhepa. On the contrary, she had thought it would amuse her and take her mind off her tiring pregnancy; she had gone to great pains to turn the dull reality into an amusing little work of art at which she herself laughed till she cried.

Nefertiti had listened with a sad expression which Giluhepa had put down to fatigue. Finally convinced she couldn't make her daughter laugh, she had concluded somewhat peevishly: 'I see you aren't in the mood for joking. But there, you're in the last stages of pregnancy. I was like that too before my confinement. And by the burning Disc, you have borne five daughters!'

Then, suddenly seeing a chance to make a witty remark, she

249

added: 'Pray Aten you have a son this time! Your poor husband will be really disappointed if you give him another princess. He will turn towards a wife who has not yet borne children, hoping not to fail again . . . like a bad player who thinks that by changing the checker board he will change his skill.'

Nefertiti had understood the allusion to Taduhepa and had suffered as she had never thought it possible to suffer. If only she had been able to have her baby earlier and present a slim, desirable body to her husband on his return from Thebes. Then she would have feared no one! But she was carrying his child . . . she was deformed and ill and her husband couldn't come near her.

When Akhenaten approached Nefertiti, she knew from his air of embarrassment that he was going to talk to her about Tusratta's daughter, and her heart ached. Was he going to confess he had already broken their unspoken pact of reciprocal faithfulness? Perhaps he no longer loved his wife; a wife who had only given him daughters.

At this unbearable thought Nefertiti felt she might slip into death, like a woman who faints at the time of her confinement. Perhaps her time had come to die. She shut her eyes, the better to hear the words which would free her from life. She no longer desired to live if the world of her love was collapsing.

Akhenaten thought she was dizzy. Glad of the excuse to postpone a painful conversation, which he didn't know how to start anyway, he said hurriedly: 'I came to ask how you are, but I see you are not well . . . I will go and fetch the doctor.'

How badly he lies! Nefertiti said to herself; has he ever sent my servants away before, when he came just to ask how I am? She made an effort to stop her voice shaking and replied as calmly as possible: 'It's nothing. I'm better now. I haven't had the pleasure of seeing you alone recently.'

'You know . . . I . . . with all these ceremonies and the coronation festivities. How I wish you had been beside me, my love.'

Nefertiti smiled sadly.

'I too . . .' she murmured. 'But in any case, even if I had been feeling well, I would never have presumed to appear at your side, deformed as I am.'

250

'You know quite well you are the most beautiful of all,' Akhenaten said hastily.

Nefertiti shook her head slowly.

'I have heard Taduhepa is very beautiful and that you take much pleasure in her company,' she said, hoping to precipitate matters.

'Who told you?' he asked angrily.

Nefertiti shrugged her shoulders and tried to smile.

'What does it matter? Everyone knows everything here. But why be angry? Is Taduhepa not your second wife?'

When he heard this, Akhenaten was so relieved that he didn't hear the bitterness and grief in his wife's voice. He regained his good temper and said in joyful tones which hurt Nefertiti more than ever: 'That is exactly why I came to see you! You know I have never been unfaithful to you, you are my one and only love and I care nothing for anyone who is not you. When my mother wrote to propose that we strengthen our alliances with the Mitanni, because the Hittite danger menaces our Syrian frontiers, I refused. I know a princess cannot be treated as one would treat a commoner. I didn't talk to you of this affair in order not to worry you; above all I feared you would insist that I sacrifice our love to my kingly duty.'

Nefertiti almost started to hope again at the news that her husband had preferred to annoy his mother rather than consent to take a second wife. But Akhenaten quickly took it upon himself to shatter her weak illusions. With the brutality of a man who wants to get a difficult task over as quickly as possible, he continued: 'Now, however, my father is dead, and it is the custom for me to inherit his harem. What I feared has happened: Taduhepa is proud and cannot be treated lightly. I cannot insult Tusratta by refusing to visit his daughter. First, because Tusratta is our ally and his Empire borders on the Hittite frontier, then because he is the only one of the kings who sent me a really friendly letter of congratulation. If Taduhepa tells her father she receives no favours from Pharaoh, I fear there will be war. War which I loathe, for it kills men created by Aten to live in happiness and peace. Tusratta loves his daughter dearly (she's a nice girl,

251

by the way, quiet and full of good qualities . . . you'll like her, I'm sure), such an affront would wound him deeply, especially as he is not so civilized as we Egyptians. What do you advise me to do?'

Akhenaten was so certain he had stated his case in such a way that Nefertiti would be obliged to give him a satisfactory answer, that he could hardly believe his ears when she replied calmly: 'I hear you freed phoenix, instead of geese, at the four cardinal points. I hear also that you have altered many of the coronation ceremonies. As well as this I have with my own eyes seen how many customs you have overthrown in Thebes. Why conserve here in your capital a stupid practice which is in contradiction with the intelligence which characterizes your new institutions? "To inherit your father's harem" can very well be classed with the other archaic customs based on symbolism which have no more significance for anyone. Write and tell Tusratta that his daughter is a widow, that we are sorry for her and that we treat her with the honours due to her. Let her return to Thebes and rule over the women of her husband's household, with my mother Giluhepa and the Great Royal Wife Tiyi, *both* in the same deplorable position as she. You are not so cruel as to impose a husband on her by force, for in Egypt a widow has the right to remarry according to her own choice. You know that many worthy royal princes aspire to her beautiful and desirable hand. I think Tusratta would be touched by your delicacy, especially if you send with your letter enough gifts to give him the feeling he has made a good bargain.'

Nefertiti looked closely at her husband and saw the consternation in his face. Then she knew she had lost and that her husband would not send Taduhepa away. He desired her. Bitterness swept over her . . . a dry bitterness, without tears, which burnt up her heart, but left her mind cold as ice. Before she was certain that her love was to be discarded she had thought she would die; now it had been, she found herself stronger, and her brain was clear, but her body seemed drained of life like a gutted mummy. She looked at the man in front of her as if he were a stranger, and the words he spoke didn't move her at all . . . they broke to pieces against her stone scarab heart.

Akhenaten had pulled himself together and was walking up and down with a frown, annoyed by his wife's lack of understanding. Without realizing it, he repeated his mother's words, which he himself had rejected so forcefully. He said dryly: 'You don't seem to realize the importance of a royal couple's duties. To be king is not to live for pleasure, riches, comfort, self-indulgence, indolence . . . it is to sacrifice oneself for the people, to be their slave. To forget that, is to become a tyrant, and the enemy of one's subjects. Then, on the day of judgement, one is punished for not having carried out the work for which one was born. It doesn't please me any more than you to have to consider the feelings of Taduhepa and her father . . . but it is our duty, as it was the duty of my mother to welcome your mother, Giluhepa, into her husband's harem, despite her love, despite her suffering. How can I write to our Mitanni ally that I plan to give his daughter to a mere prince? She, the widow of Pharaoh! It would be a public disgrace. Let us silence our unworthy jealousy . . . above all unworthy of your common sense. The time has come to wake from our apathy. Have you forgotten you are the Mistress of the Two Kingdoms?'

Nefertiti heard herself reply in a light, detached voice which seemed to echo deep down in the empty sanctuary which was her body: 'You asked for my advice, but you don't need it; you know quite well what you want to do, so why question me?'

Akhenaten felt himself growing angry and replied: 'I thought that I owed it to you, because I respect the love which joins us. For you are the only Great Royal Wife; no one will ever replace you.'

'I am too weary to see where my duty lies. What you do will be well done. Nothing which comes from you can be suspected of being cowardly or false, for you are the living truth.'

Akhenaten stepped back as if he had been slapped. Because he had a guilty conscience, he was stung by his wife's quiet faith in him, and replied: 'You're making fun of me, trying to make me look foolish . . . you're jealous! Jealous, like any ordinary woman! After all, why should I consult you about what I have to do? I'm not answerable to you, to you or anyone. I'm Pharaoh!'

He strode away, his footsteps echoing on the flagstones, and

253

went straight to the harem to refresh his soul with Taduhepa's simplicity . . . a dear child, who as yet knew nothing of adult selfishness.

That night he took Taduhepa with all the violence of a man whose fires of desire are activated by vengeful anger. But the ardent Mitanni girl was the last person likely to complain. As Tiyi had said, she was a lioness at the time of the full moon.

CHAPTER NINE

NEFERTITI spent the fifty days which separated her from her confinement in a state of gloomy resignation. She remained cloistered in her apartments, and refused to see anyone, even the good Ti, and above all her mother Giluhepa, whose acid remarks she wouldn't have been able to bear. She didn't need to be told about what was going on between Taduhepa and her husband. When Akhenaten visited her he showed the guilty nervousness and the irritated impatience of a man whose thoughts are with another woman. He spoke to her sharply and always seemed ready to leave . . . without doubt in order to run to the arms of the girl who had so cleverly driven him mad with an as yet unsated desire. Sometimes at night, when Nefertiti was lying awake in the darkness, unable to find that healing sleep which obliterates thought as surely as death, she felt her stone scarab stirring in her chest as if blood had suddenly flowed into it; then grief would wash over her like waves of life and she would weep. At these moments her mind would become troubled and feverish, filled with wild dreams of fury and vengeance. While this delirium lasted, one phrase kept haunting her: When I'm no longer pregnant, I'll show my husband!

In the third month of the season of floods, on the morning of the seventeenth day, Nefertiti gave birth to a sixth daughter, who was named Setep-en-Rê. She should have been distressed at not having a son, for she more than ever wanted to give her husband a male heir. But the feeling of relief at being delivered from her ugliness was so great that it drowned all her other emotions — disillusion, grief, lassitude and the pain of disenchantment. She studied herself carefully in the mirror to make sure her beauty hadn't suffered too much, and what she saw reassured her. Certainly her features were drawn and her skin still looked a bit like an old papyrus left lying in a damp cellar . . . but her eyes were bright again and her smile was as beautiful as ever.

Nevertheless, she waited a few more days before reappearing at court: she didn't want her stretched stomach muscles to appear flabby under her thin fitted dress, so in the secrecy of her room she had herself thoroughly massaged by Mischere. Mischere was the only person from whom she hid nothing, for among all those who served Nefertiti, she was the only one who didn't speak out of turn. Of all the people in the world, her husband included, the little Syrian was the only one who hadn't disappointed her. Mischere loved her mistress with an absolute and undivided love. Nefertiti had often wanted to free her, marry her off and install her on lands where, in her turn, she could live served by others, but Mischere had always refused. She had grown older, but her soul had retained the innocence and purity of youth. She always said with a smile: 'I wouldn't know how to order my husband or my servants about, for I was not born courageous. My husband and my servants would soon find this out and it wouldn't be long before they were giving me orders; I would be forced to run from one to the other and die of exhaustion before my time. Here I don't have many masters, I only have one: you, my queen. Thus my work is not heavy. That is a good reason for not getting married. But if it doesn't appear sufficient to you, know that my heart is too small to love more than one person at a time. I love you, for you were the first to teach me that life could be pleasant. So how could I love a husband? Leave me where I am happy; beside you. The day you no longer need me there will be nothing left for me to do but die, for I will have fulfilled my destiny, which is to serve you as well as I am able.'

Nefertiti knew Mischere well enough to realize she spoke the truth without expecting gratitude or gifts from her mistress. Mischere wasn't out for what she could get like the other servants. She claimed none of the privileges which were hers by right, as first servant to the queen; she wore little jewellery, dressed simply and refused to be honoured in public. Several times Nefertiti had wanted to give her the 'Presentation of Gold', with a ceremony in front of the assembled people, but on each occasion the little Syrian had shaken her head and said unhappily: 'Please don't make me, mistress! I would die of shame in front of everyone, for the people would say: "What has that humble girl done to be exalted in this way?" '

No, Mischere hadn't rendered important services to the state, she hadn't saved the queen's life or won victories, but she had done much more: in spite of all the temptations, in the midst of the vain and worldly vortex of court life, she had remained pure, honest and sincere.

And Nefertiti knew that, even if she had to give away all her possessions until she went naked under the Sun, without a place to lay her head, she would not part with Mischere.

It so happened that at about this time, Maï came back from his tour of the provinces, just as though Aten had sent him to the rescue of his royal servant. Akhenaten was very fond of Maï, and had shown his affection by making him Chancellor, Inspector of Troops, Fan Bearer on his right hand, a Prince of On, and, when he was in residence at the court of Akhet-Aten: 'Personal Levee Attendant'. This last charge was a sign of exceptional favour, for it gave Maï the right to assist at his lord's awakening, to anoint him with his own hands and to speak to him far from indiscreet ears, in the solitude of the bed-chamber. This position was greatly sought after, for it allowed the man thus honoured to keep the king well-disposed towards himself, and sometimes to discredit other people.

Maï didn't indulge in such scheming, however; he had the proud insolence of those who have never been short of money, and though he was by nature selfish, he had the generosity of a great lord conscious of his superiority and desirous of maintaining it by avoiding small and common faults. His marriage to Ourel, the beloved daughter of Ramose, had been partly to further his own interests, certainly, for at that time he was freshly arrived from his father's *nome* and hadn't known that ambitions could be realized by more noble actions. However, from then on, he had always behaved in such a way as not to lose his self-esteem. He made it a point of honour to fulfil loyally, honestly and to the best of his ability whatever task he was given.

Three months before Pharaoh's death he had been sent to inspect the troops on the Syrian frontier, and to counsel prudence to the vassal princes. He had worked his way conscientiously through all the Khabirus tribes who camped in the frontier desert oases near the bitter lakes, and whose submission to Egypt was questionable, and he had made sufficient threats of Egyptian retaliation for their chiefs to have banished from their minds any future project save that of grazing their flocks in the permitted places . . . for the fertile prairies of the Delta were a perpetual temptation to these wild shepherd peoples who kept alive their dreams of seizing them by reminding each other of the brave Hyksos, nomads like themselves, who had descended like a swarm of locusts and succeeded in taking over all the rich lands of Lower Egypt which lay beyond the well-defended fortress of Sile*.

Maï arrived at Akhet-Aten on the very day Nefertiti decided to enter the lists and vanquish Taduhepa on equal terms.

Nefertiti took this to be a sign that Aten was watching over her, and felt certain of final victory. Maï could now be the ibex used to bait the trap into which the lion inevitably falls. Hearing he was in conference in her husband's study, she dressed carefully but without too much jewellery, so her own beauty would not be eclipsed by the sparkle of gold; she put on a head-dress which covered all her hair and thus brought into relief the delicacy of her features and the grace of her neck, she perfumed herself discreetly, so as not to drown completely the smell of her armpits, which she knew had a powerful aphrodisiac effect on the man she wished to fascinate, and finally, after working herself up by remembering all her grievances, like a soldier who gets drunk on bad wine before facing an enemy too strong for him, she went off alone towards the royal study.

She entered without knocking and pretended a joyful surprise

* Sile: Fortress situated on the north-east frontier of Egypt.

258

when she saw Maï. Neglecting to greet her husband, she hurried towards the young man, her hands held out palms downward in the friendly gesture reserved for close friends, which was a permission not to bow to the ground. Consequently Maï contented himself with a slight bow from the waist and murmured with unfeigned admiration: 'On all the earth I have seen no one so beautiful as you, your Majesty.'

'Your compliment gives me all the more pleasure because I haven't heard one for some time,' said Nefertiti with a carefully calculated and throaty laugh. 'A short while ago you couldn't have said that without the risk of being taken for a low flatterer. In truth, I wasn't much to look at! I was shapeless, colourless and graceless.'

'The perfect oval of your face couldn't alter, nor the sparkle of your smile, nor the light in your eyes,' answered Maï, who didn't for a moment suspect that his sincerity could damage his relationship with his sovereign, because when he had left for the Provinces the royal couple's love had been as strong as ever and he hadn't been back long enough to hear the gossip and learn that Akhenaten was neglecting his wife for Taduhepa.

Nefertiti smiled gratefully at him.

'Maï, my dear childhood friend,' she said, emphasizing the last words, 'you should have been here to alleviate my boredom while I was pregnant. I was so disheartened by my ugliness that I shut myself away and refused to see anyone, not even my husband.'

These words made Maï realize with astonishment that something must be wrong. For the first time he wondered if the royal couple weren't getting along together as well as on the morning of his departure for the frontiers: never before, even when she was pregnant, had Nefertiti refused to see her husband. Maï turned to Akhenaten uneasily and tried to repair any blunders he might unwittingly have made.

'My wife Ourel was just the same,' he lied hastily. 'I couldn't manage to convince her that a husband is miserable if he cannot look upon his wife.'

Then, hurrying on, he continued: 'It is nearly nine months

since I saw my well-beloved wife; I didn't take her with me for fear she would find the rough desert life too tiring. Before my departure I left her with her parents on the outskirts of Thebes. I am impatient to see her again; when his Majesty no longer needs me here, may I hope to rejoin her?'

'Poor Maï!' Nefertiti exclaimed kindly. 'Nine months of fidelity! That deserves a reward. I have a suggestion: bring your wife here to Akhet-Aten without delay. Thus you will waste no time and dear Ourel can profit from the pleasures of the capital. For she has certainly been bored to death with nothing but fields and grain silos on the horizon.'

It was only then that she turned towards Akhenaten and gave him a brilliant smile: 'Isn't that so, my husband?' she asked, as coolly as though she hadn't omitted to greet him.

Akhenaten frowned at her, the line of his jaw angry. When Nefertiti had entered he had been struck by her delicate beauty, for, in the constant company of another woman, he had forgotten how lovely his wife could be. While she had kept to her room, he had usually visited her in the evenings, before going on to Taduhepa's apartments, and the ageing of the one had shown up more sharply in contrast to the sparkling youth of the other. Because he was an ugly man, unaccustomed to success with women, Akhenaten was flattered by the unquenchable appetite for love, and the spontaneous admiration he aroused in an adolescent girl still young enough to be sincere, and because of this he had forgotten the years of happiness spent with his wife. For, despite the reassurance of Nefertiti's tenderness, Akhenaten never forgot his ugliness. Taduhepa had thrown herself voluntarily into his arms, without even a shiver at the sight of the features which he knew to be repulsive, and her acceptance made him remember Nefertiti's violent rejection in the early days of their marriage. To quieten his guilty conscience he nursed this memory, telling himself bitterly: 'How generous Nefertiti must have felt in those days, when she granted me her favours. Used she to make a joke of it with her friends, to excuse herself for her lack of taste?'

This painful thought eclipsed the tenderness he might have felt at the sight of his wife's tired face; with a kind of spiteful joy he had even reflected that she was getting old, and that it was time she realized it.

And now Nefertiti had come in, more beautiful, more radiant than ever. Like the Boinu* bird which rises, new and splendid, every morning from the primordial waters into which it fell, old and exhausted, the night before, she now appeared regenerated, graceful and magnificent as in the shining days of her early youth. In her presence the beauty of others paled like night-lamps in the radiant morning Sun, and Taduhepa's pretty face faded away and merged into the faces of all the other harem women.

But she hadn't greeted him, hadn't even looked at him; it was towards Maï she had turned with delight. Her first smile had been for this man who was nothing but a childhood friend, as though it were Maï who had given her her happiest memories. Not for a moment did Akhenaten suspect Maï of disloyalty, but he couldn't help being annoyed by his noble bearing and good looks.

He said sharply to his wife: 'How kind of you to notice me! I thought I must have died suddenly and only my Ka was floating in the room.'

Nefertiti laughed, her lips curling back from her teeth.

'So it really is you?' she asked ironically. 'I have lived so long without a husband I thought I must be a widow. I'm happy to know I was wrong, and greet you, O Sun.'

Saying which, she held out her cheek for her husband to kiss, but Akhenaten, sensing contempt in the gesture, pushed her roughly away.

'We're not alone!' he growled, his voice shaking with anger.

Nefertiti opened her eyes wide with surprise.

'Have the laws of freedom been revoked in Akhet-Aten?' she exclaimed with pretended innocence. 'Do we no longer have the right to show our feelings? Are lovers once again condemned to gaze at each other from a distance, like wild beasts shut into separate cages?'

Maï was beginning to feel more and more uneasy. He would rather have been surrounded by an army of Hittites than caught here between a jealous husband and a flirtatious wife, for in the

* Boinu: Phoenix.

latter situation he had not the slightest chance of getting out alive. What must his king be thinking of him? If he thought the worst, who could persuade him he was wrong? No one is deafer than a jealous man.

'I shouldn't have come here so unceremoniously,' he managed to say. 'Please excuse me. I. . . .'

Akhenaten interrupted him vehemently.

'It was not you who came without ceremony; we were discussing urgent affairs of state when my wife entered.'

Nefertiti drew herself up proudly.

'I am the queen,' she said. 'I am never out of place when affairs of state are under discussion. They concern me as much as Pharaoh.'

Then, turning towards Maï, she asked in authoritative and queenly tones: 'Well Maï, what news do you bring back from your survey of the Provinces? Has Aziru the Amorite seen sense? Or must we send him a schoolteacher in armour followed by scribes with whips? There is a proverb which says: "The pupil's ear is on his back".'

Akhenaten took a deep breath to calm the wild beating of his heart, and having thus regained his self-control he said, more sharply than was necessary in a political discussion: 'Tell the queen what you told me this morning, so we can take a decision, for she is no longer indisposed and I can see her mind is working well.'

Maï lost no time in taking advantage of this opportunity to get onto less dangerous ground, where his chances of defending himself were greater. He was loyal in everything, but especially in politics, and he knew that this loyalty, at least, was not open to question by anyone.

CHAPTER TEN

NEFERTITI'S counter-attack on her husband's affections was only partly successful. Though Akhenaten was jealous, and obsessed by the beauty of his wife, he was still determined not to visit her at night.

In spite of his resolve to hold out, all day his longing for Nefertiti grew as he watched the dazzling charm which she dispensed so lavishly to everyone and anyone, and above all to Maï. For Maï she reserved her most bewitching smiles and her wittiest remarks. In his honour she had ordered lavish entertainments and feasts at which only the most delicate wines and best-quality beers flowed. The court revelled in a state of permanent intoxication and Nefertiti reacted with a light-hearted enjoyment which her disillusioned husband considered bad taste, since her happiness appeared to be in no way connected with himself.

To begin with he had tried to laugh it off, saying to himself: Nefertiti is jealous, she wants to punish me for Taduhepa, and drive me to repudiate her. But I won't harm that innocent child who can't defend herself like the Great Royal Wife. When Nefertiti finds her plan hasn't worked, she will stop making herself ridiculous. Doesn't she realize how embarrassed Maï is by all this sudden favour? The poor boy only wants to run to Thebes and see his beloved Ourel again.

Akhenaten forced himself to visit Taduhepa regularly, but he no longer took any pleasure in this obligation and found the beautiful Mitanni girl's energy exhausting. Suddenly he realized that her mind was neither intelligent nor mature and that, except in bed, she was good for nothing. All at once her innocence seemed childishness; her sensuality, an affliction. For the first time he remembered she was the unbroken filly who had driven his father to his death, and he feared for his own life. Wasn't his face already showing signs of exhaustion?

But he didn't want to give Nefertiti an easy victory, and refused to return repentantly to his wife's bed.

Nefertiti finally became worried by her lack of success, and decided to try another method. She went to the harem, in which she hadn't set foot since her pregnancy, declaring loudly that she had come to pay a visit to her mother Giluhepa; in reality she had been seized by a perverse longing to hurt herself by contemplating Taduhepa's beauty, which seemed to have separated her from her husband for good. And indeed, as soon as she saw her, she couldn't help despairing all over again. Tusratta's daughter was a splendid animal. Nevertheless, Nefertiti forced herself to be charming. She took a personal interest in her, and from then on there were no feasts to which Taduhepa was not invited, the queen paid her husband's second wife the most friendly attention, the most affectionate solicitude. She presented her with some of her own jewels, especially the ones her husband preferred; she made her sit beside her when they ate, spoke kindly to her, didn't permit the young princess to bow before her, and poured out her wine with her own hands. In short, seeing them together, they seemed like two loving sisters, for the one's happiness was the other's joy.

Nefertiti acted her part so well that soon the court stopped gossiping about the misunderstandings between the royal couple.

Akhenaten was taken in by his wife's behaviour. Because a man resents a desirable situation for which he himself is not responsible, he was annoyed when he saw how well the two women got on together. Nefertiti's new behaviour seemed certain proof of her indifference towards himself, the man she had said she loved so much . . . and he concluded that her present attitude came, not from wild jealousy, but from the death of love.

Then his soul filled with sadness and despair.

Now, with the obstinacy of someone who doesn't wish to be consoled because he considers his sin is unforgivable, Akhenaten persuaded himself that he had failed in Aten's final trial. God had decided to test His son's purity; He had brought him face to face with the sensuous Taduhepa, and His son had succumbed to the sins of the flesh. Henceforth he no longer had the right to worship the Sun in the heart of man, nor to hope for the love of the beautiful Nefertiti, dazzling and flawless as a disc of gold, before whom he could only prostrate himself with humility. He tried to rejoice at the idea that she no longer felt any affection for him; he considered she was right to scorn him and promised himself never to speak to her again except with the respect due to one who deserves to shine for ever on the world. He knew then that he would soon die, for he had become useless, and he decided to pass his last days in prayer, not in order to gain his God's forgiveness, but with the intention of lessening the grief he had caused Him.

Once again he assiduously attended the services he had neglected during the period of his blindness; he personally supervised the men working on the temple he was building for his mother; he abandoned the beautiful Taduhepa to the dull life of the harem, and behaved towards Nefertiti with a gentle gravity, an attentive and silent deference tinged with dignity and sadness. Though his heart felt like a young greyhound's, savaged by a lion but still beating with agonizing life, not a word of complaint passed his lips.

Nefertiti was frightened by this new and inexplicable attitude; fearing she had carried her pretence too far she decided not to continue with it. But because pride urged her not to be the first to make honourable amends, she hesitated for a long time as to what she should do, and forced herself to go on pretending lighthearted joy. She also forced herself not to neglect the Mitanni girl, though she no longer seemed to be a danger, and she refrained with difficulty from returning to Ourel the unfortunate Maï, whose job as ibex bait seemed over.

While she was still uncertain how to act, Tiyi arrived from Thebes on a visit to the capital.

It was the nineteenth day of the second month of winter.

Tiyi disembarked, accompanied by her two youngest children;

her daughter Baket-Aten, thirteen, and her youngest son, Tut-ankh-Ate , who was four.

The queen mother was now an old woman, more brusque and soured than ever. Her voice was like the sand wind and her eyes like dried-up wells, for she had become an arid country haunted by thoughts of death, a desert in which cool winds no longer blew.

The court was delighted at the idea of prolonging in her honour the festivities which had lasted since Maï's arrival, but when they saw her they knew that Akhet-Aten was about to be frozen into a long period of mourning in which laughter and games would have no place. The nobles hurried to greet their old sovereign with grave respect, then retired to their homes and hoped that the echoes of their laughter wouldn't carry as far as the royal apartment.

Only Akhenaten and Nefertiti were glad to see Tiyi.

Certainly, when she thought about it, Nefertiti blamed Tiyi for having introduced Taduhepa into her calm existence, but she was too honest to accuse her for long of having destroyed her happiness. Tiyi wasn't responsible for her son's actions. If it hadn't been the Mitanni girl who monopolized Akhenaten's attention it might have been some other woman, for when a man is deaf to his own conscience, he may act foolishly at any moment.

However she couldn't stop herself from replying acidly to one of her mother-in-law's questions, when she had the chance: 'Don't worry about Taduhepa. She is well looked after here. She is stuffed with corn cake like a fattening goose; your son has his hands full, she has put on so much weight.'

Tiyi didn't say anything, but later on she remarked to Akhenaten: 'Your wife is jealous. Beat her or console her, but don't leave her to brood; a woman who broods loses her sense of balance like a faulty pair of scales.'

Akhenaten shook his head sadly, and answered: 'No Mother, my wife doesn't love me any longer, and she is right. I have stained the purity of our love and of my heart for ever.'

Then, humbly, he confessed his fault. He spoke much of his own baseness, in order to convince his mother that nothing could

266

make him pure in the eyes of God. Tiyi listened in silence and, when he had, as he put it, vomited up all his putrefaction, she said brusquely: 'Rubbish! I am going to find your wife and see if she is as foolish as you are. If she is, the crown of Egypt has gone to the wrong person and Tut-Ankh-Aten wouldn't find it difficult to wear it better than you, despite the fact that he is only four.'

Akhenaten begged her not to increase his shame by talking to Nefertiti; when he saw she was unmoved by his arguments and his prayers, he became angry, and told her not to interfere, and that she had done enough harm already. Finally he said it was all her fault anyway and instead of adding to her misdeeds she would do better to repent of them.

Tiyi shrugged her shoulders. No insults could hurt her now, and she went to find her daughter-in-law as she had intended. She told Nefertiti of her interview with her son and ended: 'That should quieten your foolish jealousy. If you love your husband, shake him out of this dangerous stupidity, otherwise, get ready to see him die, and look forward to choosing another husband more to your liking; for a man cannot live long with a feeling of irremediable guilt; he is too eager for the peace he hopes to find in his tomb.'

Nefertiti cried in a shaking voice: 'I love him, I love him, Tiyi! But how can I make him listen to me? He punishes himself more stubbornly than he would punish someone who attacked him.'

'That's it, my daughter, use that tone, use that voice, weep, press a dagger to your breast. Your grief is the only argument to which he will listen. Because of it, perhaps he will forget his selfishness. Anyway, get this stupid quarrel over quickly, for the kingdom cares nothing for your personal squabbles.'

Nefertiti wasted no time in finding her husband alone. She came upon him under the vine pergola which ran beside the river. He was waiting there for the moment when his God would set behind the western horizon.

When Akhenaten saw her, he knew by her loving gaze that his mother had talked to her, and he was bitter.

267

'What do you want?' he asked rudely, forgetting the new deference with which he treated the pure daughter of Aten. 'Can't you see I'm busy?'

Nefertiti could restrain her tears no longer. She threw herself into his arms sobbing.

Akhenaten felt uncomfortable; not knowing what else to do, he patted his wife's shoulder clumsily.

When the worst of her grief had passed, Nefertiti, still sniffing, sobbed into the hollow of her husband's neck, to which she still clung tightly: 'I love you . . . I love you so much and I was so unhappy. I wanted to make you jealous, I wanted to get my own back . . . I was so afraid I didn't please you any longer.'

Akhenaten continued to pat her shoulder silently, as a nurse will cradle a child woken by a nightmare. He didn't know what to make of things any longer, and the blood in his temples was beating so loudly he couldn't concentrate.

For a long time, the breath of Nefertiti's love was warm against his skin. She told him of her distress, her disappointment at giving him another daughter . . . she begged him to forgive her, to give her back the happiness without which she couldn't live, she swore she would love him more than ever now she had been so frightened of losing him, and that if he loved her in return she would be grateful for it hour by hour, and never let habit dull the edge of her happiness. At last she fell silent, her lips busily engaged in kissing the shoulder of this man she so desperately wanted to convince.

Towards the west the God was lowering his eye, reddened with the strain of staring for so long at the sparkling water and burning deserts which formed the greater part of his lands.

Akhenaten's gaze met Aten's, and drew strength from it. Then the young man pushed his wife gently aside and said in a low voice: 'Between you and me, there will always be Taduhepa. When I take you in my arms I will remember that my arms are impure and this thought will cloud my mind; when you put your mouth to mine, you will remember that the girl from Mitanni has drunk from the same source, and you will draw back in horror. A scribe cannot enumerate his master's geese and boinus

268

on the same tablet, but must take a separate one to number each species, lest he confuse their worth. You are the Boinu.'

Then Nefertiti cried impetuously: 'If you don't want to be inscribed on my tablet, I will arrange to be inscribed on yours. I will take a lover for a night. He will tear off my ash-coloured Boinu feathers, then you can no longer refuse me. We love each other! Can you say you no longer love me, that you are indifferent? Tell me! I want to hear it from your own lips. If it's true. . . .' Her voice faltered. '. . . If it's true, I will bother you no longer. I will go and die in the desert, like a traveller without water.'

Akhenaten remained silent. On the western horizon, the Sun slid rapidly down into the world of the dead.

'You don't understand,' he said at last, 'I am like an instrument of music whose sound box has been cracked. I can never again play a note in tune. And it was I who gave the orchestra the key! How can I demand from others what I cannot give myself? How can I exile the wicked when it is I who have introduced evil here?'

'Everyone here has many wives, and no one waited for your example to make use of them!' sobbed Nefertiti in despair. 'Tell me how that makes you impure? You love me and I love you. That is the perfect thing we have accomplished. If it's no longer true, then it has never been true; you have lied for eleven years and for eleven years you have sinned against your God.'

'But I do love you!' cried Akhenaten, determined to defend himself against this accusation at least. 'I have never stopped loving you, not for a single instant.'

Nefertiti threw herself into his arms again, wild with a still tearful happiness. 'You love me! There, you've said it! Oh, my love! My love!'

She took his face in her hands and emphasized her words with a burning kiss.

This was too much for Akhenaten. With the violence of a river too long dammed up he broke through the dykes which he himself had so laboriously constructed, and drowned his wife in love.

Nefertiti believed she had won back her happiness. She was too joyful to remember that man is impetuous when he hears nothing

269

but the blood beating in his ears, but later, when his passions are assuaged, he will listen to his inner voice again.

Once more Akhenaten and Nefertiti lived together as man and wife, and not once did he mention Taduhepa or his inner doubts. But, when he was alone, the small voice of conscience would reproach him, and he never tried to quieten it. He persisted in thinking of himself as a cracked sound box and he believed he was no longer worthy to lead the orchestra. He had lost faith in himself . . . and slowly because life held no more interest, he began to die.

CHAPTER ELEVEN

M AÏ had scarcely reached Thebes for his well-deserved rest in the arms of his wife, before a messenger arrived from the country 'of the two rivers' with disturbing news: Tusratta had been assassinated by his eldest son, and brother was shedding the blood of brother in a civil war, Egypt's friends against Syria's friends. Aki-Tesup, an old pro-Egyptian chieftain, had managed to rescue Mattiwaza, Tusratta's younger son, and in order to save him from his elder brother was fleeing with him in the direction of Babylon.

'The imbecile!' thundered Tiyi, shaken out of her grief by the news. 'Babylon, that nest of scorpions! Everyone knows Assuru-ballit is hand in glove with Artatama the Hurrian! They are like two scavengers hovering on the frontiers ready to devour the corpse of Mitanni. What is the old fool thinking of? Why didn't he seek refuge on the coast, in the land of Hor where our vassals are in control?'

Akhenaten shrugged his shoulders.

'If rumours of the revolt against Tusratta had reached us earlier we could have taken action and saved the victim. But now it's too late. We have many supporters in Wassukkani . . . we must wait and see what happens.'

'Wait' . . . Tiyi interrupted unceremoniously. 'Don't you understand what has happened? Does the word "scavenger" mean nothing to you? Mitanni will be torn to pieces by their beaks! And what of the Hittites who are pouring down into our outlying Provinces, and Suppiluliuma who is taking advantage of the general unrest to extend his frontiers? Have you thought of that? Send Horem-Heb and Maï into our vassal lands, have tongues pulled out and heads cut off, punish the traitors who feel rebellion in the air. Starting with Aziru the Amorite. You heard what Maï said about him: "Aziru is unreliable, he has eyes which slid etowards the east when one talks to him from the south".'

'I have warned Aziru that I will not tolerate his insults . . . that I would rather kill him with my own hands.'

Tiyi laughed scornfully and turned to her daughter-in-law: 'In the season of fleas, he prefers to be bitten rather than crush a single one of them, and now he threatens to crush a traitor! Tell your husband the vassal chiefs laugh at words; what they respect is deeds. They are all nibbling at Egypt's treasure as impertinently as rats in a faulty silo. Rub the silo walls with cat-grease, so they will smell it and be frightened.'

Nefertiti said calmly: 'That's it, we'll organize a ceremonial procession from the Provinces to Akhet-Aten; the vassals can bring their tribute with them, they haven't done that for some time . . . it will give us a chance to display the strength of our army and let it be known what punishments await the guilty.'

'A procession—a procession at a moment which calls for action!' said Tiyi scornfully. 'I tell you, Pharaoh must put on his war armour. It is *he* who is going in procession *to* the Provinces.'

'You know quite well, Mother, that I refuse to intimidate people to whom I have cried: "Fraternity!" We are all brothers under the sun. If they see me arrayed for war they will lose their new found faith in Aten.'

'The Provinces belong to you,' cried Tiyi, 'your forefathers conquered them, you should sacrifice everything to keep them.'

For a long moment Akhenaten stared at his mother. Finally he said in a voice which shook a little, but which was strangely calm and powerful: 'My forefathers made war and conquered kingdoms for which they were not born, as a robber takes goods which don't belong to him. Each year, these annexed lands pour their riches into Egypt and become correspondingly poorer. I have tried to compensate my vassals' losses by gifts of gold and Teaching. I will not make a show of military force in their streets, nor will my war horses trample down their harvests. If my love for

272

them does not bind them to me, I will not use force. My wife has spoken wisely. Once more I will unite the peoples under Egypt's laws. They will come with their goods, not to pay tribute, but to exchange their riches as in a market place. I will sound out their thoughts, I will try again to win them over by persuasion. I do not fear the Hittites, for I do not hate them. Let them come here freely! They only arm because they think that Egypt hates them, like a child whom disappointment makes angry.'

Tiyi laughed mirthlessly.

'You're mad, both of you,' she cried bitterly. 'With my own hands I have crowned those who would reduce the kingdom to the size of an islet lost in the Nile, confused by their visions of God. They no longer know they live in a world of men where the weak are eaten by the strong, and their forgetfulness will cause the death of millions.'

But the old queen was speaking to herself, for neither Akhenaten nor Nefertiti listened. She was old, they thought; her tired mind could no longer assimilate new ideas.

So on the first day of the thirteenth year of his reign, Akhenaten, his wife and his six daughters went in state to a splendid, specially constructed building, in order to receive the homage of their vassals. Sitting beneath the gold and ebony canopy, they reviewed the march-past of the princes: the Nubians from Erzet, Meza, Yam, Wawat and Ka'ou, resplendent with bright robes and jewels, and preceded by enormous and comically dignified baboons, monkeys 'red of ear and violet of buttock', with majestic manes and huge tufted crests of fur, all carefully de-loused; the proud desert Nomads, their eyes screwed up against the sun, their mouths thin as knife blades, magnificent in their ceremonial dress; those from Punt, Canaan, Lower Renzen and the Islands-of-the-sea; Fenekhs, Asiatics, Libyans, Negroes, Egyptians from the *nomes*, all loaded down with riches which they displayed to the indulgent gaze of their king: young incense trees, jars of cedar oil, rare animals, ceremonial vases of costly metals, casks of precious woods, gems, thoroughbred horses, chariots, arms, musical instruments, dogs, cheetahs, dwarfs, cosmetics, perfumes, splendid bulls, rams, male antelopes, coffers bursting with gold and jewels, rich silks, skins, leather, dried fruit, cakes and sweet-meats. . . .

They all came except Aziru, the sly Amorite who lent an ear to the subtle hints of the Hittites. He sent word by his Ambassador that he was ill and would certainly die at not being able to see the wonders of Akhet-Aten, and he apologized for his scanty tribute with the words: 'I have emptied my treasury in order to place well-armed warriors on the frontiers of Khatti, and in so doing I have served the interests of my sovereign better than all the princelings softened by easy living, who tremble with fear.'

Akhenaten put off till later the epistolary chastisement such insolence deserved. He made a speech to his assembled vassals and his voice throbbed with feeling. He reminded them of the friendship which united them all under the eye of God, and exhorted them to peace, happiness and love.

The princes listened respectfully. Those among them who valued peace said: 'In truth, Akhenaten is the greatest of Egypt's Pharaohs, and it is good to belong to his kingdom and benefit from his advice.'

Those among them who had come violent from their mother's wombs remained silent, but they thought: Uncivilized liberty is better than paying tribute. Akhenaten is weak and mad, now is the time to shake off the Egyptian yoke and to seize the wealth of the land of the Two Kingdoms, so rich it flows with honey.

The former went back to their homes, pleased and grateful for the magnificent gifts they had received. The latter returned rebelliously to their little kingdoms, envious of all Pharaoh's treasures they left behind them.

One memorable day, when Amonhotep had been younger, he had said to Bek: 'The mystery of God can only be understood by the pure in heart . . . as for the others, they stay outside and no one can help them except themselves.'

No one could do anything for these bitter chieftains, committed to violence and evil. They were the rotten fruit in the world of men.

To consolidate his work, Akhenaten undertook a tour of Egypt.

He spread the message of hope, lightened the already diminished taxes, and showed himself to the people in order to get it into their hard heads that though he was Pharaoh, he was none the less a being of flesh and blood, accessible even to the most miserable among them. He visited the mines and quarries and distributed perfumed oil to the workers 'so they would not be troubled by the smell of their sweat'; he pardoned prisoners, 'for,' he said, 'in the darkness of a cell, a heart will harden, and come out more wicked than it entered.' He listened to complaints and tempered justice with mercy.

Nefertiti went with him everywhere, as a miser accompanies his gold. Since the Taduhepa affair, she was frightened even when her husband's eyes fell on another woman's shadow. But they had to cut short their journey and hurry back to Akhet-Aten, for an exhausted runner arrived to say that Meket-Aten, their second daughter, was moaning on her bed, struck down by a malignant fever.

They came home to see anxiety and despair on every face. Pentu, who had come from Thebes with Tiyi, was exhausted and at a loss. Once again his science was helpless; he had decided to call the child's disease a malignant fever, but he didn't know what the curious symptoms indicated; the fatigue, the shivering, the cold sweats, the bloody froth which trickled from the little girl's lips. At first he had treated her for a cold, because she was coughing; then for swamp fever, because she was shivering; then for ophthalmia, because her eyes were inflamed . . . but each day life sank a little lower in the young body which had scarcely begun the task of living. Meket-Aten was only eleven and a half.

Nefertiti never left her daughter's bedside. She sponged her damp body, caressed her, cradled her, sang to her in a voice which often broke on a sob. Sometimes, in the evening, worn out by fatigue and grief, she was surprised to hear herself murmuring an old incantation which Ti had chanted at Nefertiti's own bedside when she was a child: 'Go away, you who come in darkness, you who enter by stealth. Do you come to kiss this child? I won't let you kiss her. Do you come to take her? I won't let you take her. She is protected from you by the Efet herb to

275

hurt you, by onions to trouble you, by honey which is sweet to the living but bitter to the dead, by the harmful parts of the Ebdu fish, by the backbone of the perch.'

She repeated these words mechanically, without thinking what they meant, for they sprang unconsciously from the secret fear she obstinately refused to admit.

One evening her husband heard her as she tonelessly chanted the magic spell, and cried out: 'Stop! You'll frighten the child if she wakes. No one and nothing can take away my little daughter, do you hear me!'

Then Nefertiti woke from her daze and understood at last the real meaning of what she had said: she had been speaking of death. She glanced fearfully at her husband and burst into tears.

Akhenaten sat down beside her and took her in his arms. Meket-Aten's poor little face was shining with sweat. She was shivering with fever and her breathing was shallow and fast as if she had to make a determined effort not to let herself be separated from life.

Death . . . the most terrible and most mysterious word of all! Who has ever come back from it, who can say what it is? A body eaten by decay whose ultimate task is to fertilize the soil? A Ka thrown into the currents of the invisible world, into a life of sound waves without thoughts or dreams, while the double of the dead man appears before Osiris, submits to judgement and gains a life in the Shades, surrounded by the silent silhouettes of slaves? A soul delivered of its bonds, dazzling in the sunlight, reaching towards the frontiers of infinity in a wholly abstract sensation of limitless joy and love?

Akhenaten held Nefertiti closer, for she was his only reason for living . . . and the day would come when she too would vanish into nothingness. In his despair he formulated a heretic prayer: 'Let the gods exist! Let them judge us and assign us lands where we will meet again with those whom we have loved. Let it be true!'

Two days later Meket-Aten died. Fate hadn't intended her to reach maturity . . . hadn't she cried MBI at her birth?

Akhenaten abandoned his wife to her grief and went with

Meket-Aten's body to the Necropolis. He watched the embalmers extracting through the nostrils by means of a metal hook the grey matter which had been the home of thought; he saw the viscera loosened and pulled out through an incision in the side made by a cutting stone from Nubia; he watched his daughter closely while they filled the vessel of her body with pure myrrh, cassia and other aromatics . . . but her face didn't quiver with a new and secret life.

Day after day he contemplated her in her bath of natron . . . but all he could see was the progressive drying-up of her features, the falling-in of her flesh . . . Meket-Aten was turning into a shrivelled wine-skin which would be shut into a tomb as one leaves an old sack in a shed.

And instead of emerging from this experience convinced of resurrection, Akhenaten returned to the capital more despairing than ever.

The burial took place a month after the embalming, for the workers couldn't finish the young princess's burial chambers in time.

Akhenaten had the grave which contained his daughter's mummy sealed up, and forbade the engravers to finish their work in the rooms intended for the other members of the royal family.

He didn't want to think of death again. He wanted to live, to hold his wife in his arms, to laugh, sing, look eagerly towards the light, drink in the smell of perfumes with all the strength of his lungs, listen with open ears to the marvellous sounds of life, to touch the things he loved, walk over his lands, not let his attention wander for an instant from what little life was left, not to cease revelling in the dear presences which wove his existence. God, good, evil, metaphysical problems, politics, austere morality, all became so many abstractions on which man wasted precious time, time taken from the 'happiness of being alive'. For a long time Akhenaten had tortured himself unnecessarily because he was ugly, for the last year he had grieved bitterly at having stained his purity, and the madness which had induced him to consider such small misfortunes as important had caused him to let slip through his fingers days he could never recapture again. To live! That was the great truth of man.

Nefertiti didn't understand the reason for her husband's new energy, because she knew him mainly as solemn and rather melancholy, but she thanked Aten for this delightful transformation. She and Akhenaten never spoke the name of their dead daughter; instinctively the young woman knew it was the key to a door she mustn't open, for fear of letting in the desert wind.

this, he turned his attention to the wealth of Pharaoh and brought his spies and trouble-makers into action.

The princes who had come violent from their mothers' wombs rose in Canaan, pillaging and massacring.

With offensive contemptuousness, Aziru took possession of the coastal towns of Syria and Phoenicia, then marched calmly towards Simyra, hoping to continue victoriously right down the sea coast to Gozan, the narrow passageway to the Delta.

Aziru moved confidently because he had a sure friend at Akhenaten's own court, and this friend was Dudu, the High Chamberlain, Mouthpiece of the Land, Commander in Chief and Chief of all Inspectors of Works. Aziru had met him in the tenth year of Pharaoh's reign, in the palace of his father, where Dudu had gone as an ambassador, and the two men had come to an understanding immediately, for they were of the same breed and had the same aspirations. The Amorite and his accomplice had discussed Egyptian affairs at length and had decided that the Black Land of Kemet was a ripening fruit which it would soon be time to pick.

Dudu was a man with complete confidence in his own ability. It hadn't been difficult for him to rise to power under young Amonhotep, for his method was always to play on his adversary's weaknesses. A cunning psychologist, he had at once seen the advantages to be gained from the co-regent's ideas of justice. With pretended bitterness, he had said to him one day: 'Certainly you preach equality, yet a Syrian or a Nubian could never become, for example, "Mouthpiece of the Land" in your kingdom. The noble Egyptians would be shocked if you granted such a signal favour to a despised foreigner.' Not long afterwards, he had been named 'Mouthpiece of the Land'.

Before he met Aziru, he had coveted the title of plenipotentiary prince in the province of Syria, like his compatriot Yankhamou, and had toyed with the dream of shaking off the yoke of Egypt and then founding a dynasty there. Aziru came at just the right moment to back up his hopes. Together they planned co-operation, agreed to divide in brotherly fashion the coastal country from north to south, spoke of colonizing the land of the Nile, of swallowing up Mitanni, of demanding tribute from the 'Island of the Sea' and in addition swore not to harm each other. After which they watered the foundations of their association with an excellent beer from Kede, one which rejoiced the heart and fortified the courage.

When the time came, Aziru would march off with his father's army and plunder the Provinces. Dudu would be responsible for giving the signal for this move, for handling the messages from the victims in such a way as to censor their lamentations, and for speaking his mind to Pharaoh regarding the cowardice of the provincial kings who made mountains out of molehills in order to gain sympathy.

Dudu didn't have the pleasure of giving the signal, for Suppiluliuma gave it before him, but he didn't feel resentful and cheerfully undertook the second part of the programme, which consisted of confusing the issue.

Thanks to his skill, Akhenaten soon couldn't tell true from false in the innumerable letters which arrived from the Provinces, filled with accusations and appeals to Pharaoh's justice.

He said wearily: 'How nervous these people are. How can we make them understand that these preoccupations destroy their joy in living?'

'You have been too gentle with them, you have made them too accustomed to receiving gold and presents,' exclaimed Dudu, with the indignation of a foster-father towards the persecutors of his foster-son. 'They are like spoilt children indulging in little tantrums. Send them the gift of a precious dagger, delivered by your messenger into their hearts.' Things were going well for him and his accomplice.

Then trouble came and from a source which the over-confident Syrian had not suspected. The priests of Amon, laymen for the last twelve years, took off the wigs with which they had hidden their shaven heads, pulled from the coffers their leopard skins, a little moth-eaten, certainly, but still quite presentable, and began to move through the country preaching rebellion. Their letters from the Provinces were not censored, they had spies throughout the Empire, and they had sensed that the time was ripe. They cried aloud: 'The madness of Amonhotep IV has become clear to all, thanks to the watchfulness of holy Amon. Egypt's proud empire is falling about our ears. The Asiatic hordes will swoop down upon our land, as did the Hyksos, guided by the vengeful gods, furious at their worshippers' impiety. Remember that in those tragic days, only the priests of Amon saved the country! Akhenaten, heretic and criminal, the unworthy son who erased his father's name from his tomb; Akhenaten, the traitor who gives your country's gold to vassal states, yet lets his own people starve; Akhenaten has lived long enough to show he is unworthy of his subjects' consideration. Before it is too late, before the gods weary of the indulgent way they have been watching over the greatness of the Black Land of Kemet, repent and rise up!'

The superstitious masses had in fact never stopped sacrificing to many of the less important household gods. They listened to these speeches with approving nods of the head, and the argument which finally convinced them was: 'Akhenaten, the unworthy son who had his father's name erased from his tomb'. As for the princes of the *nomes*, they were more worried about the collapse of the Empire and Aziru's insolent behaviour than by the speeches of the priests of Amon. They had their wealth to protect at all costs and had no intention of losing it by a gratuitous show of friendship for a sovereign in such a dangerous position.

The land of Egypt stirred uneasily, the air was filled with discontent. General Horem-Heb, supreme army chief, was loyal to Queen Tiyi, but he hated Akhenaten because of his leanings towards peace and universal equality. Out of consideration for the old queen he wrote her a respectful letter and told her he had decided to engage his troops on the side of the priests of Amon. He said that if she wanted to calm the heated minds of those ready for rebellion, she must convince her son of the necessity of a reconciliation: 'Let him name a co-regent to reign in Thebes. Let him make public apology and open up the temples of Amon. Then perhaps the dynasty of Amonhotep III, the Great, beloved of the gods, will retain its power and escape the destruction which the angry people are demanding.'

Tiyi sought her son in his apartments and found him eating in company with his wife. Without a word, unbending and austere, she threw the papyrus roll onto the table.

There was a long silence and the servants moved furtively towards the door. Calmly Akhenaten signalled one of them to pour some perfumed water from a ewer onto Tiyi's hands. Then he rose to his feet and dismissed them with a movement of his head.

Nefertiti looked from the drawn face of her mother-in-law to that of her husband, strangely peaceful, and then at the roll of papyrus, which seemed more dangerous suddenly than a nest of horned vipers. She didn't know what it contained, but from Tiyi's attitude she imagined it must be clear proof that her worst fears had come true. For the last year, Nefertiti knew no more about political events than what she had learned through idle palace rumour and gossip. Her husband had asked her not to waste her time on such a troublesome and thankless task. He had said to her: 'For the moment it is all routine matters . . . one of us is quite sufficient for the boring study sessions. Get the best out of life and don't worry . . . you know that if I have any difficulties I will ask you for advice.'

Now suddenly she found she was trembling anxiously at the sight of this roll of papyrus lying on a table.

Akhenaten calmly picked up the letter from Horem-Heb and slowly read it through. Then he put it down, looked at his mother and said with a smile: 'This general has shown proof of great loyalty, he deserves the "Golden Fly" for his moral courage. So! The people are angry? For sixteen years they have acclaimed me . . . not so long ago they threw themselves to the dust, wild with gratitude towards the king who had reduced their taxes, they praised his justice, his goodness; and now suddenly they rise up in fury and demand the destruction of the dynasty. They call down the predatory greed of Amon on their heads! Faced with this example, what must one think of human reason?'

'Words are useless,' said Tiyi dryly. 'There is no time for useless talk, but only for action, and swift action. What are you going to do?'

Akhenaten took a deep breath and thought hard in the silence

283

which followed his mother's question. While reading the letter from Horem-Heb he had tried to retain the calm indifference he had displayed ever since Meket-Aten's death, but his heart was bitter and his body weary; the terrible truth, which he had half realized for some time, and always refused to face, this hateful truth was now staring him in the face: his life had been a failure, and he knew why. He had been born with an obstinate heart and an irresolute mind: he had loved desperately and he had doubted that he could be loved; he had wished passionately for his people's happiness but he hadn't dared to impose his will with sufficient ruthlessness; he had desired perfection, but had lost his way among the thousands of different considerations and uncertainties. This combination of strong ambition and hesitant perplexity had prevented him from finishing his temple before the season of the sand winds, and from harvesting his crops before the time of the locusts. Now his temple was about to collapse and his harvest was going to be eaten.

And how could he prevent it? Because suddenly, coldly, with his whole mind, he knew that he was going to die. He had known it, perhaps, ever since he had first sensed the depths of his own failings. When his daughter had disappeared into her tomb, the knowledge had become too much to face: desperately he had tried to deny it and to stop the leaks through which he had been allowing his life to seep away. But now he saw that this ultimate effort was in vain. He had no more strength on which to draw; already his body was emptying slowly, like a badly caulked well; already he was without energy, ill; in a little while the smell of death would be proclaiming that soon he would be nothing but carrion.

And Nefertiti, her eyes wide with fear, would see the chasm open beneath the feet of the man she loved. She would grovel on the ground, claw at the silent sand, howl his beloved name, and the spectre of solitude would strike terror into her heart. Never again would his beloved be glad to be alive . . . never.

That must not be! Somehow his love must be great enough, somehow he must contrive a sacrifice which would leave Nefertiti in happiness, purity and peace.

A quiet despair filled his being like the cold waters of a winter stream; it cooled his feverish heart and refreshed his mind, so that for the first time since his birth the one was in harmony with the other. He began to see what he could do, and he knew that he would do it.

He turned towards his wife and said: 'Nefertiti, you who have given proof of so much wisdom in your decisions, can you advise me?'

Nefertiti had just finished reading the papyrus and she was hurt by Horem-Heb's contempt. She answered at once: 'It would be shameful to consider the suggestions of this rebellious and treasonable general. The trouble-makers are only a handful. Bring back Maï from On, recall your armies from the frontiers, and destroy this crawling nest of vermin.'

'The army is necessary on the frontiers,' interrupted Tiyi brusquely, 'especially now the Hittites are getting ready to fall on the corpses of our coastal provinces. As for the rebels, they are no longer a handful, but form three quarters of the country's population, and a civil war would only weaken us for good. Then you would see the scavengers in their thousands fall upon bleeding Egypt.'

'Aten is the great and only God,' cried Nefertiti. 'He will give us victory, He won't let our people be blinded to the truth and live again in misery. Birth is a painful process, but one must not be cowardly and refuse to give birth. We will fight not only for the people of Egypt, but for the whole world.'

The old queen laughed.

'The lioness awakes too late,' she said with irony. 'She suddenly shows energy when the time for it has passed. Tell me what you have done, my daughter, since I put the crown upon your head? You have looked in your husband's eyes and you have borne him daughters. Like the common wife of a peasant! From the day you had the misfortune to fall in love with your husband, you forgot you were insolent and proud, clear-headed and energetic — qualities which I chose in you to compensate my first-born's weakness. And all this because you are selfish. I knew you were selfish, but I had the misfortune to think it was a youthful fault.

I thought you were intelligent. Intelligent! You are as mad as your husband. Fight for the whole world indeed! You should have done it when the vassal princes first began to stir. Then you would have maintained Egypt's influence over the greater part of the earth and could have begun to think of establishing your new beliefs in foreign lands. But now your universal god is only worshipped here at Akhet-Aten. Why? Because you were sunk in your own contentment, you, your husband and your children. If you have any sense left, and I've had my doubts on that score for some time, stop talking like a fanatical priestess. You are not a priestess, but a queen, so try for once to act like one.'

Nefertiti was so angry she couldn't speak, but when Tiyi paused she made a tremendous effort and said hoarsely: 'Strength of character means not to deny what one's heart believes, to die rather than give in. But what can you know of such a pride, you who pushed your husband into the arms of his concubines! You who tried to give my husband to Taduhepa! Yes, I am a priestess of Aten. Yes, I love my husband. I am not idle in serving the one or in loving the other, and I will take their part against you and against the whole world if necessary. What do I care for your opinion? You have never liked me; I have been only a pawn you thought you could move as you liked. You tried to destroy my marriage, through jealousy, because you resented your son's love for me. You are selfish too, Tiyi, but in a petty, sordid, common way!'

As she spoke, Nefertiti's tight throat had gradually relaxed so that she shouted the last words as though she were addressing a public meeting.

Akhenaten judged his wife sufficiently heated for the words he was about to speak to have the same effect as cold water thrown in her face. Then, like the blade of a dagger reddened in the black-smith's fire and afterwards plunged brutally into a tub of water, her soul would come out of the process hard and inflexible, dangerous and strengthened for ever.

He said, taking care to keep his voice calm and expressionless: 'Nefertiti, I am obliged to remind you that you are talking to my mother, and I cannot allow such offensive words, even if you

286

think you are in the right. As it happens, you know perfectly well you are in the wrong; your insults were born of anger and my mother in no way deserves them; she has sacrificed her life, her love and her simple happiness as a woman to the obligations of the kingdom, and in this she has shown strength of character and courage worthy of praise. You are still young and she has done much for you, she has every right to tell you her opinion of yourself. I listened well to what she said and in truth I do not find that her common sense has aged. It is true that we have been lulled by the pleasures of palace life and that we have acted like two irresponsible children. Curb your immature reactions and your childish outbursts. Civil war must be avoided at all costs.'

Nefertiti listened to her husband with stupefaction. It was the first time he had ever insulted her by accusing her of childishness . . . and in front of his mother into the bargain, making her look ridiculous.

Lifting her head proudly, she struck back, saying acidly: 'You're right. If you have lost the provinces through your inertia, the least you can now do is to avoid civil war. I am guilty for not having encouraged you to punish the vassals' insolence . . . but I won't be guilty again. Put on your armour, Pharaoh, and scatter this handful of rebels who bark more than they bite. Why should you fear them? But if you are afraid, send for Maï. At least he will know what should be done. Then I can promise you that Horem-Heb will be punished as he deserves for his treachery, and the jackals and the trouble-makers will be quickly dispersed into the desert. If I have forgotten I am queen, to become your wife instead, you had better remember you are Pharaoh. You rule the land of Egypt and you are the first-born of the Sun. Rise up and all will be well again.'

Maï's name thrown at him like an insult shook Akhenaten, but he remembered the part he was playing, and replied sharply: 'Maï is like you, he acts first and thinks afterwards, and your partiality for him displeases me. But that is beside the point. It is not a matter of trouble-makers and jackals, but as my mother has been trying to get into your head, of the dynasty's being in danger. I will not be obstinate like you, because of pride; I will

287

admit my faults. I have failed in the government of my country, I haven't known how to win the people's affection. It is justice that I abdicate and name a co-regent. My young brother, Smenkh-ka-Rê, is an honest and energetic youth. I will marry him to my daughter Merit-Aten; they can return to Thebes and see how matters can be arranged.'

'*Your* daughter!' cried Nefertiti, pained at this sudden display of cowardice by the man she loved. '*Your* daughter? She is also my daughter and I refuse to consent to such a marriage. You cannot believe that the rebellious priests of Amon will accept a co-regent who worships Aten? They will force her to renounce her faith. Do you understand? Your daughter sacrificing to Amon, the idol you hated so much you erased your father's name from the walls of his own tomb!'

Akhenaten feigned a look of apology.

'I was wrong,' he said wearily, 'and my father was right. Any god will do for the heart of man. Let Smenkh-ka-Rê sacrifice to Amon, let my daughter carry him offerings, let Thebes become the capital again . . . only leave me in peace.'

Nefertiti stared at this new husband: weak, worthless, cowardly. She suddenly wanted to weep like a widow over the corpse of all she has loved. What was happening to the esteem which had led her to love, the boundless admiration which had unceasingly fed the fires of her passion? It was ebbing, and shame was flooding in — shame and pity, which tore at her heart, for she knew how dangerous an emotion it was.

Her voice shook as she said: 'Leave you in peace . . . yes, that's all you deserve. You are a lizard on the warm stone and you have only one wish, that your last breath be a sigh of content. I believed in you, Akhenaten. Others believed in you. We would have died for you willingly. . . . And now you say: "Leave me in peace!" So be it, we will leave you in peace, Akhenaten. But find another wife for your co-regent, for as long as I live Merit-Aten will not renounce her faith.'

Akhenaten turned quickly away to hide his face. He remained silent until he had regained his self-control, and then said, in a voice which scarcely shook at all: 'Unfortunately for you, my wife, I don't think the priests of Amon will be content with an arbitrary choice of co-regent. Merit-Aten, the daughter of Akhenaten, will seem the obvious choice to represent at Thebes the total surrender of their enemy. Obviously I cannot force you to follow your husband in his disavowals and his defeat, and I will quite understand if you retire to the northern palace with your suite and your children—except, of course, for Merit-Aten, who will obey her father's orders and marry her young uncle. Perhaps it will console you to know that Smenkh-ka-Rê is not indifferent to our first-born. I have spoken. That is all WE have to say to you, my mother and I.'

Nefertiti went white. Her husband had just announced her disgrace, and to make it clearer he had joined his mother to himself in the royal We, which till then had been reserved for Nefertiti and himself. Straight-backed, dignified, heart-broken, she left the room without another glance at Tiyi and her son.

The old queen had witnessed the scene with interest and astonishment. The ease with which her son had appeared to take the decision to abandon all for which he had fought struck her as very strange, for she was naturally suspicious and understood human nature well. Instinctively she knew he had been acting a part, and she tried to understand why.

'Was it really necessary to banish Nefertiti?' she asked. 'She loves you deeply . . . will she not suffer? I believe that once this affair is settled you could very well live together happily again.'

'Leave me, Mother, I beg of you,' replied Akhenaten in a curiously broken voice.

As he spoke he turned towards Tiyi and she was shocked to see that his face was the face of an old man.

Then, in the deep distress of her heart, there sprang up a real feeling of respect for this man whom she had believed weak and who, she was now convinced, had just performed an act of courage. She went away silently, as one leaves a place where someone is dying, abandoned by the helpless science of men, so that his last moments may be peaceful.

Akhenaten sat down at the table on which the meats still lay, grown cold. He stared for a long time at the place where, so recently, his happy, loving wife had been . . . she would never come back now. He was alone for ever, face to face with the terrifying mystery of death.

But, though his heart was sad, it wasn't bitter. He had just carried out a deliberate act of love, the first in his life perhaps, the first which might be useful and which could mark his existence with the seal: 'Not born in vain'. He had saved Nefertiti; he had protected her against herself. To do this he had killed in her the love which had destroyed her equilibrium and which would have paralysed her beside her husband's corpse. Now he could disappear into the black abyss of his tomb: Nefertiti would not be prostrated by a grief which would set her against God and make her forget the need to fight and the target in view . . . because the loss of a loved one is harder to bear than the pain of not being loved, for the former withers the mind and dries up the soul for ever.

Because she scorned her husband's cowardice, Nefertiti would do all she could to keep her faith in Aten. She would harden herself against those who were responsible for the fall of the man she had mistakenly respected for so many years. She would become more zealous in her worship and would have the individual enthusiasm of a heart ruled by Absolute love. Then she, who was born energetic and active, would rise up in Egypt and impose the religion of the God of love. Akhenaten had been a voice crying in the wilderness, and in his pride he had believed he was the first-born of the Sun, as a slave will take up his master's stick and think himself fit to command. He had made decisions haphazardly, with the vanity, the arrogance and the inefficiency of a slave created only to serve. But he had been given a chance to redeem himself: he had been able to stand aside for her who must carry on the sacred flame.

CHAPTER THIRTEEN

In order to burn all bridges between himself and his wife, Akhenaten made a speech from the 'balcony of appearances'. To the astonished courtiers he announced: 'I acknowledge my error, and I recognize the truth of Amon. My brother Smenkh-ka-Rê will be crowned and will return to Thebes, the capital. However, Queen Nefertiti persists in her heretical beliefs, so I have sent her away. In future you will see me with Taduhepa at my side, and I expect you to treat her with the respect due to a Great Royal Wife. Let Amon have pity on those of us who have shown him ingratitude. Let him not order his innocent priests to take from us our riches, as we took theirs from them. Let our punishment not be unduly severe. Let us see Thebes again!'

These words had the effect Akhenaten had expected. Many of his subjects had continued to cling secretly to the comforting beliefs of their fathers, and should therefore have been grateful to their sovereign for his recantation; but he had been careful to sow a seed of fear with his words about punishment for those who had benefited from the riches confiscated from the priests of Amon.

Consequently, those who now felt that they might lose their titles and their lands, considered Akhenaten's public apology a betrayal, and they praised Nefertiti for her courage. They considered her the 'unfortunate victim of a coward who trembles to lose his possessions'. And since Akhenaten was no longer 'he who could terrorize the world' they were courageous enough to show their contempt of him; they left his palace empty to visit their sorrowing queen, so beautiful and dignified in her distress. Nevertheless they were careful to maintain a strict religious neutrality, so as not to be found too guilty in the eyes of their judges. If the latter were inclined to be merciful, but reproached them for their loyalty towards one who persisted in heretical beliefs, they would reply: 'We pitied her, for she loved her husband and didn't deserve her disgrace. We stayed with her to lessen her grief, for we have always despised Akhenaten, but put up with him because of our affection for his wife.'

On the other hand, if the religion of Aten triumphed, Nefertiti would be grateful to those who had supported her in her misfortune. There was in fact one last chance for the followers of Aten, for Maï and his wife had come up from On with a large body of troops. They had camped in the vicinity of the northern palace, to which the poor queen and her four daughters had withdrawn, and Maï waited for orders to attack . . . brave, loyal Maï, who would have been more at home on the throne of Egypt than the lazy, cowardly Amonhotep IV.

Akhenaten had few friends left and he was glad of it.

The unhappy queen thought that her bitterness had cured her of grief, but it was only sleeping. She drew strength from a heady wish to be revenged on Akhenaten, and felt she owed it to her friends to lead the worshippers of Aten to victory. With the obstinacy of someone ready to justify her sacrifice at any price in order to persuade herself that it was not in vain, she managed to convince herself that she had been chosen by Aten to impose his religion. And because her soul was empty of any other love, she gave herself entirely up to God.

Maï was a great comfort to his queen. There was no question of love between them, nothing except a clearly-defined and firm friendship, without undertones. Nefertiti would not have permitted it to be otherwise, for, with her new piety, her fastidious modesty had returned, and for herself she could conceive only the virginal existence of a priestess. She treated Maï like a dear brother and his wife Ourel like a sister, all the more beloved because for a long time she had shown her nothing but scorn and contempt. She repented this now, for hadn't Ourel and Maï voluntarily offered her their services?

292

What she didn't know was that Akhenaten had ordered Maï back from On. Upon his arrival in Akhet-Aten, Pharaoh had received him in private audience and had said to him:

'I am not asking you to approve my conduct, for I don't want to force you to spit in my face. I say only this: it is not sure that Amon's priests have all Egypt behind them, for the priests of On are powerful and have many followers. Perhaps Egypt will be split in two again as she was before the reign of the glorious Menes, "Uniter of the Two Kingdoms". The south could remain faithful to Amon and the north to the Only God. I want you to go to Queen Nefertiti, support her in her religious battle, and serve her in everything as you would serve myself. But first give me your word as a man of honour not to tell her it is I who have sent you. Don't try to understand my motives. It would take me too long to explain. I ask from you a blind obedience. Tell your queen you have joined her service of your own accord, and if she speaks scornfully of me in your presence, agree with all she says, for it is necessary that she be cured of me for ever. Do this, and you will earn all my gratitude and love . . . though my love can no longer do you any good. Above all, watch carefully over her life, for fanatics may try to put an end to her days. Post your troops well and trust no one, not even those at Hat-Aten who are considered friends. Go now, and may your loyalty be rewarded.'

This speech had astonished Maï, and at first it had hurt him to pretend contemptuousness for his king. However, by associating with those who professed the most complete disdain for the fallen Pharaoh and didn't hide the reasons for their just indignation, he finally consoled himself with the thought that one day he might win his queen's love, and with it a kingdom and a crown, even if it was only that of the Delta. He didn't admit it even to himself, but it was with this in mind that he sent his spies everywhere to sound out public opinion, and strengthened the alliances with the priests of On.

The storm clouds were gathering, even though for the moment the weather seemed once more set fair. The convocation of the priests of Amon seemed satisfied by Akhenaten's recantation.

They welcomed the young co-regents and the old Queen to Thebes. They were once more installed in the sacred precincts of Karnak and went about their duties as if nothing had ever happened. Not a word was said against the nobles who had stayed at Akhet-Aten. The priests of Amon were too satisfied at being able to surround Smenkh-ka-Rê with men in their pay, to worry about what the group of nobles at Akhet-Aten were plotting. In time the latter were even insulted by the way the Thebans ignored them, and seriously considered wholeheartedly supporting the cause of their unhappy queen . . . especially since Maï and his men seemed so strong.

Tiyi had accompanied her son Smenkh-ka-Rê at Akhenaten's request. He had said to her: 'Merit-Aten and her husband are young and inexperienced, they need your wisdom. I wish I had profited from it myself.'

And the old woman had gone back with them, leaving her two youngest children, Baket-Aten and the eight-and-a-half years-old Tut-ankh-Aten in the care of her first-born, for she feared to take them into the possible dangers of Thebes.

At the beginning of that winter, Tiyi died.

She breathed her last in the big bedroom of the royal apartments where she had lived for so many happy years, and though she had waited impatiently for death, her last moments were nonetheless filled with sorrow and anxiety. She was leaving behind her confusion and anarchy, as if she had always lived for idle pleasure; and because it seemed that all her efforts had been in vain, she regretted not having loved enough. Then she thought of the secret heart-break of her first-born and her daughter-in-law, and wished to warn them of the uselessness of unnecessary sacrifice; she sent for her scribe and dictated a letter to Nefertiti.

'I am dying alone because I have forced myself to live alone. No one can know the anguish of a solitary death. One is like a thirsty traveller in the middle of a desert, who sees in his delirium all the springs of water from which he once had the chance to drink. The traveller collapses onto the dunes, his mind filled with visions of floods, but his throat is dry and his heart is aching. Then with his finger he writes in the sand: "My brother, drink from the well, and when your thirst is quenched drink once again, so that you will not die regretting you did not drink enough." I, Tiyi, say to you, Nefertiti, my daughter whom I have loved, that if your thirst for your husband is slaked, drink again from the source before it is too late, for he will die soon. When you left the palace, he was old: his heart was withered, his eyes dull, his soul as weary as that of a man who has lived two thousand years. You must have been blinded by your grief not to have found his sudden treatment of you and of his God strange. There you were laughing and happy, seated together at the table; he looked at you affectionately . . . and suddenly, allowing no time for long death-throes of love, he became cold and distant, dry and arid. Why, if not because he killed himself of his own free will, so his life blood would enrich her whom he loved? I can only suppose he didn't want to drag you down in his fall, and that he took care to preserve your self-respect for you, for we both know the importance he gave to self-respect. Perhaps he intended more, who can say except himself? Swallow your pride, which never brings anything but heartache; don't believe what you hear about Taduhepa, for while I was still at Akhet-Aten I never saw him treat her with anything but exasperated patience. She is part of the game he is playing so carefully. Reflect, Nefertiti, my eldest daughter, and remember the words written by the traveller delirious with thirst.'

Nefertiti was deeply moved by this letter, and her first impulse was to hurry to her husband, for, despite her apparent self-reliance, she missed him unbearably. But in the end she didn't go; the foolish pride which Tiyi mentioned stopped her. She told herself that if her mother-in-law was wrong she might receive a public humiliation from which she would never recover. But her soul was no longer even outwardly at peace.

Then one morning there was a rumour that Akhenaten was on his deathbed. Nefertiti questioned Pentu anxiously: 'Has my husband asked for me?'

Pentu shook his head.

'Your husband asks for nothing; he won't let himself be nursed and refuses to see even his few friends. He said: "Medicines and tears are cruel when someone longs for the freedom of death; either the medicines cure him or the grief prevents him from dying in peace." I said to him: "Shall I tell the Great Royal Wife?" He replied: "Taduhepa is the Great Royal Wife and I don't want to see her." So I dared not speak your name.' Nefertiti bit her lip to stop herself from bursting into tears. Tiyi's letter had revived a secret hope, and had made her suffer in vain, since Akhenaten, on the very day of his death, had once more shown that his wife meant nothing to him. To think she had been on the point of running to the palace and shouting out her love! How he would have despised her!

She made a great effort and replied coldly: 'Well then, Pentu, let's leave him in peace, since that is all he asks from life. Let us grant him this last favour.'

The third day of the first month of summer, in the seventeenth year of his reign, Akhenaten, the vanquished king, slipped into the kindly sleep of death. His last glance was a look of love towards the north, where lived the woman he loved more than his God. His last thought brought him joy and peace: on the closed door of his tomb, Aten could put a seal of satisfaction: 'Not born in vain.'

The same day, his face worn and sorrowful, Ti's husband Ay came to announce the news at the palace of Hat-Aten, accompanied by Baket-Aten and the little Tut-ankh-Aten. He said to Nefertiti, who forced herself to stand straight-backed and proud before him: 'My master and my friend charged me to waste no time in confiding to your care his brother and sister; he said to me: "My mother Tiyi would have wished it thus, for she thought highly of Nefertiti".'

Because Akhenaten had spoken no phrase which expressed his feelings clearly at the moment of his last requests, Nefertiti refused to understand how much love and faith in her this gesture signified. She replied shortly: 'His sister and his brother will be brought up as though they were my own children. May his soul rest in peace.'

Nefertiti could have returned to the royal palace now, since it was empty, but she preferred to stay at Hat-Aten, which seemed to symbolize her secret fight against Amon and all the ugliness and the unworthy cowardice of which he was the cause.

She followed her husband's body to its last resting place, walking at the head of the harem women, among whom was Taduhepa; Taduhepa who had destroyed Nefertiti's happiness and who was mourning now with shameless affectation. Nefertiti shed no tears, but held herself straight and proud, her mouth hard and her eyes unmoving. She saw that two engravings of herself kept watch at the head and feet of the sarcophagus, but she told herself bitterly that they must have been made before the time of her disgrace and the engravers in the Necropolis hadn't had time to carve Taduhepa in her place.

She sent for the High Priest Marire and said to him: 'Pharaoh renounced his God, yet it seems that despite his criminal repudiation he has forbidden them to embalm his body according to the rites of Osiris. We could consider this evidence of secret repentance, so, since this doubt exists, we will conduct a funeral ceremony in the temple of Aten. We will lift up our voices and beg the radiant goodness of the Sun to pardon his renegade son.'

Marire looked unhappy.

'How can Aten ever forgive him,' he replied in a sincerely regretful voice, 'when his son has tried to insult him even in death? The embalmers tell me that he sent them a heathen text with orders to engrave it on gold leaf and place it under the bandages against his heart. The embalmers took pity on his soul and placed the shameless text beneath his feet. Just listen to it: "I drink the delicate breath from your mouth. I admire your beauty day by day. I long for the sound of your voice, even when it comes like the north wind, for I grow younger through your love. . . ." '

Nefertiti went white and continued expressionlessly:

' "Give me your hand and your soul so I may live. Call me eternally, so my name will never disappear".'

She knew and loved this prayer more than any of the hymns

to Aten. Her husband had written it for her. One morning—she would remember it all her life—he had woken her with a kiss and said: 'When the pink light of dawn fell on your sleeping face, I gazed long upon you and I have written you this prayer to speak my love. . . .'

'The north wind?' she had objected, after listening to the poem.

Akhenaten had started to laugh: 'The north wind is your anger, which doesn't dry things up but is refreshing in the dog days.'

She would never forget it, for it was the song of their love. She had set the words to music, and often sang them.

Akhenaten hadn't carried a hymn to his God into the dark night of death. He had instead proclaimed eternally his love for his wife. Tiyi had been right.

Tears sprang to Nefertiti's eyes and she didn't even try to hold them back.

'Yes,' she murmured, 'the embalmers did well to put this prayer beneath my husband's feet and I don't want his sarcophagus opened up to place it as he wanted on his heart. For I am happy at his feet and wouldn't dare to place myself any higher. I. . . .'

She couldn't continue, but ran from the room weeping, leaving behind her poor Marire, astonished at his queen's mental state.

Nefertiti wept long and bitterly in her room. Sometimes she hit the bed with her fist, sobbing: 'Why? Why?'

Why had he acted thus? Why hadn't she realized he had never stopped loving her? Why hadn't she run to the palace as soon as she read Tiyi's letter? Why hadn't she hurried to the bedside of her love, who had died alone with the despairing thought that his wife loved him no longer, despised him, refused to help him? Why?

It was only much later, when her body was exhausted, that she became calm again.

Then she remembered all the little details which in her despair she had ignored, and she came to the conclusion that her husband wished her to continue in the role of Aten's priestess. With the energy of those who want to make amends, she threw herself

298

more enthusiastically than ever into the worship of her husband's God, but only Aten and herself could know that when she sang the great hymn to the Sun, it was intended for the soul of the man she loved. For her, he was now a part of the radiant star which lit up the sad human world of ugliness and sorrow.

When Smenkh-ka-Rê died in Thebes, three months later, Nefertiti went back to her husband's palace and proclaimed Tut-ankh-Aten Pharaoh of all Egypt and husband of her third daughter, Ankhes-en-Pa-Aten. The priests of Amon realized bitterly that heresy had not been stamped out. They spread their propaganda everywhere and the priests of On, for their part, were not idle. Horem-Heb paraded his troops menacingly in Upper Egypt, and Maï did the same in the Delta. In short, public opinion wavered for two years, until the rebel general decided to put a stop to a state of things which could easily leave Egypt defenceless, to the greater joy of the enemies of the Empire.

Horem-Heb was not an evil man and it was with reluctance that he stooped to assassination. But he considered that his country's greatness was threatened, and this tipped the balance. He sent a man to Akhet-Aten, entrusted with the task of poisoning Nefertiti, who stood like a fortress between the Two Kingdoms, and prevented them from joining together in desirable unity.

One morning, as dawn reddened the eastern sky, the queen's sad eyes failed to open on the melancholy of another day.

She had waited long for this deliverance and the last song of her heart had been:

> Death is as near
> As the perfume of myrrh.
> Death is as real
> As a path in the rain;
> Death has drawn nearer today
> Like a man sailing home from war,
> Like a slave freed after many years,
> Eager to find his family again.

Mischere found her lying on her bed, pale, calm, at peace for ever.

Then the Syrian crouched down on the flagstones by the bed-side of the one who had been her goddess and all the world to her, and whimpered like an injured animal.

She continued to whimper during the seventy days needed for the bath of natron, and all the way along the road which led to the royal tomb, dug in the side of the southern *wadi*: she continued to whimper for weeks, her back against the white chalk cliff, while children came and threw stones at her, calling her: 'Daughter of a Syrian dog.'

One day she disappeared, and none could say where she had gone to hide her suffering, like a dying animal.

But who worried about a little slave whose only riches were the treasures in her heart?

CHAPTER FOURTEEN

As General Horem-Heb had calculated, Nefertiti's death brought about the necessary change. With her disappeared the enthusiasm of the supporters of the heresy. Like children whose father dies, they behaved with an anxious hesitancy and a timid irresolution from which the rebel chief well knew how to profit. He re-opened negotiations between the priests of Amon and the royal dynasty, represented by the eleven-year old king. He persuaded Tut-ankh-Aten to return to Thebes.

Tut-ankh-Aten was young, and he had inherited his father's character, with leanings towards laziness, luxury and vanity. When his respectful subjects bowed before him and waited for his orders, the little boy, who up to then had had to obey his mother-in-law or risk a beating, felt twenty cubits high, and realized that his time of happiness had come. Pharaoh only had to express a wish and it was fulfilled. With delighted surprise he played at being king, without realizing that he himself was only a toy in clever hands. *He* decided to return to Thebes, accompanied by the Great Royal Wife Taduhepa and the other harem women he had inherited from his brother. *He* decided to make peace with the priests of Amon and to change his name to Tut-ankh-Amon. *He* decided to banish the few remaining impenitent heretics from the court of the capital. *He* decided that Horem-Heb should be his Inspector of Troops and that Maï should be exiled, his tomb at Akhet-Aten destroyed, his goods confiscated.

Then, seeing they could hope for nothing more from Aten, the nobles returned repentantly to Thebes, swearing loudly that their good faith had been taken advantage of for too long. They left behind them their wonderful houses, carefully shut up and guarded by a few servants. They thought that one day it might become fashionable to spend the hottest summer months at Akhet-Aten.

Tut-ankh-Amon decided to pardon them, for he approved his Vizier's wise remark: 'A man who is pardoned after having felt the hot wind of blame about his head, generally makes an excellent follower, working with zeal for fear he will be thought indifferent.'

It was thus that Ti's husband Ay, the 'Divine Father', soon rose to favour again, as a prince of royal blood and an energetic convert. Ay had sincerely loved Akhenaten; he had believed in him and in his God, but he was still young for his age and feared retirement more than anything. His passion for work lifted him above the taking of sides in human quarrels, which was why he didn't consider it beneath his dignity to serve Amon with enthusiasm, as he had once once served Aten, and indeed Amon before that again.

When Tut-ankh-Amon died in his eighteenth year, worn out by his affectionate women, Ay saw no reason why he should not marry the young widow and mount the throne himself. He was more of an age to be her grandfather than her husband, but the good Ti, whom he had piously buried a few months earlier, could have confirmed that he still had some excellent moments.

Alas, man cannot avoid the hour which has been fixed for him to die. After ruling for four years Ay joined Ti in the family tomb in the western cliffs.

Then, because the dynasty ended with the old man's death, Horem-Heb thought it was time new blood ran in the veins of the Pharaohs, the old having become thin and weak. There was no need to look far for what he wanted: an excellent soldier, conscious of Egypt's power and superiority over the rest of the world; a loyal, brave, energetic champion of Amon: in a word, himself.

There was no opposition to his claim. The people rejoiced at the thought of regaining possession of the Asiatic provinces, from which gold and slaves could be drained, and it was a good guess

302

that a warrior Pharaoh would hardly fail to busy himself actively in this direction. Which was just what Horem-Heb did.

But he did something else.

He rooted up from the purified land of Egypt all the evil heresy which Akhenaten had sown there. He began by razing to the ground the great temple of Aten in the city of the Horizon. All the foundation stones were pulled up and a thick layer of cement levelled off the cursed place. The palaces were destroyed, the tombs of the nobility mutilated, and the 'criminal', the 'vanquished', the 'detestable heretic's' name was erased. The royal tomb was opened and Akhenaten's mummified body carried to Thebes, where it was placed in his mother's tomb, for Horem-Heb had always admired Tiyi and he hadn't the heart to burn the corpse of the son she had loved, despite his madness. But his anger was great against the unhappy queen Nefertiti, who had died rather than give in to him; he set fire to her shrivelled corpse and scattered the ashes to the four winds.

The nobles were worried about the houses they had left at Akhet-Aten, in the hope that it would become a fashionable holiday resort. Convinced that this particular form of snobbery was unlikely in the court of a Pharaoh so little addicted to pleasure as Horem-Heb, they hurriedly dismantled their rich but now useless homes, in order to recover the graceful, artistically decorated wooden columns, and anything else of value they could save from the mud.

Soon Akhet-Aten was a devastated city, littered with ruined walls which stood without reason, and porticos which opened onto emptiness and desolation.

As always, hyenas and jackals came down to rob the corpse. The poorest people, those who hadn't been able to afford the long journey back to Thebes, moved into what remained of the splendid houses, defiling the magnificent wall paintings with their sweaty hands and the simple habits of people who, possessing little, will willingly sacrifice a beauty they don't understand to their careless way of life.

Little by little, however, the rich habitations, layered with successive deposits of mud, were left to the vipers and scorpions . . .

the shadow of despair seemed to lie so heavily over the dead town that it frightened the superstitious hearts of men.

Regularly every year the *khamsin* blew in from the south-east. Patiently it wore down the walls, swept across the hillocks, blew sand onto the roads and into the rooms which gaped open like wounds. It flattened the sacred mount from which, for fourteen years, hymns of glory had risen to the Sun. It wiped out the memory of footsteps on the great alabaster paving stones. It poured golden sand dunes into the gutted royal treasure chambers, and covered the clay tablets which related the glory and the fall of the city of the Horizon of the Sun.

For more than three thousand years the wind wove a great winding sheet around this transitory capital which had been a shameful evil in the land of Egypt; and the winding sheet was called 'Forgetfulness', 'Abandon', 'Nothingness', 'Solitude'.

May the sacred Disc, whose burning gaze looks down upon his desolate kingdom, take pity on the blindness of men. May he grant to his first-born son and to his wife, the very beautiful, the very loving Nefertiti, a blue eternity of everlasting love.